The
Julie
Andrews
Edwards
❧ Treasury ❧
Two Magical Novels

written by Julie Andrews Edwards

HarperCollins*Publishers*

The Julie Andrews Edwards Treasury
Two Magical Novels

Mandy
Text copyright © 1971 by Julie Edwards
Pictures copyright © 1971 Judith Gwyn Brown

The Last of the Really Great Whangdoodles
Copyright © 1974 by Julie Edwards

ISBN 0-06-027392-5

❧ *Contents* ❧

MANDY

by

Julie Edwards

Illustrated by Judith Gwyn Brown

HARPER & ROW, PUBLISHERS

Spring

The Discovery

for jenny
because i promised

1

ON THE OUTSKIRTS of a pretty country village called St. Martin's Green, there stands a large, white house called St. Martin's Orphanage. It has been there for many years. An imposing residence, the house has obviously known better days. It has generous, tall windows and large, high-ceilinged rooms. A black wrought-iron railing runs around the front and two sides of the property and the fourth side has a high stone wall to mark the boundary. The grounds, although not extensive, provide enough room at the back for a substantial play area for the children, a kitchen garden, and a modest orchard close to the high stone wall. The front garden is simply an expanse of green lawn and a drive extending from the gate at the road to the main entrance of the house.

The orphanage is managed by a board of trustees, but the principal figure, around which the institution revolves, is its matron, Mrs. Hannah Bridie. A graying, elderly woman, she is a widow who has been in charge of St. Martin's ever since the death of her husband some twenty years ago.

In her care she has, on the average, thirty children. Apart from ensuring that they receive as good an education as possible, she oversees the laundry, the food, and the cleaning of the home. She maintains discipline and tries to observe and help each child in a personal way. Her day begins at the first light of dawn, and she is never finished until late in the evening.

Most people would buckle under the strain of so much hard work, but this plain, good-natured woman seems unflagging in her energies, and although the home is constantly understaffed and she is underpaid, it is thanks to her devotion that the orphanage has a higher reputation than most other institutions of its kind.

Mandy had been there for as long as she could remember. She was a bright ten-year-old, with dark hair that fell boyishly straight and short, around her sweet face. Since she had no known relatives, the orphanage was her home, her whole world.

She had many friends and she was much loved. Because she had been at St. Martin's most of her young life, the staff favored her somewhat, and she was given certain privileges and more freedom than the other children. She could be trusted and relied upon. Apart from schooling and a few special duties, Mandy had plenty of time to herself.

Basically, she preferred to be alone. She was inventive and quick-witted, but, above all, she was a dreamer. Most of the time she lived in a make-believe world of her own. She loved to read. She exchanged books at the local library at least once a week. The wonders of *Robinson Crusoe* and *Alice in Wonderland* and *Gulliver's Travels* were very real to her and offered far more excitement than the reality of her life could ever provide.

On Saturday mornings she helped out at the local grocery store. She was given a small sum of money for her work, and she used it as she pleased. Most of her money was spent on her precious books and sometimes on paints, crayons, and paper for painting and drawing.

Only the younger children at the orphanage attended school

on the premises. Mandy, with the other older children, was sent out each day to attend the local school, which was on the other side of the village green.

Sometimes, after her classes were finished for the day, she wandered slowly home enjoying the pleasures of the soft countryside around her. She loved the outdoors and everything to do with nature. More often than not, having first obtained permission from the staff, she would go for a walk by herself.

She was rarely lonely at such times. The trees and flowers were very special to her and she knew the names of most of them by heart.

Living in her own dream world, as she did, it was never long before she had invented some situation to match her mood, and she was able to occupy herself for hours.

But it did not follow that Mandy was completely happy. How could she be? She had neither mother nor father and not even memories of them to sustain her.

She occasionally experienced very disturbing feelings. Sometimes she felt an ache inside that would not go away. It seemed then as though her life were very empty.

She would cry for no reason at all, seemingly, and it frightened her when she did. She tried to be brave and put away her feelings.

"I'm having one of my attacks again," she would think, trying hard not to let people see her tears.

Her attempts to keep busy were mostly an effort to fill her life so that she had no time to feel disconsolate. But the nagging sadness was persistent, and it would envelop her when she least expected it.

As Mandy grew, her longings grew stronger and sometimes she felt as though she must surely break apart with so much going on inside her. It was as though she were searching for something, though what or where it was she could not say.

2

THE HIGH stone wall at the back of the orphanage held a great fascination for Mandy. It was behind the orchard and stretched for miles to either side of it. None of the other children seemed to know or care what lay beyond. But Mandy was immensely curious. She speculated for hours, wondering what lay on the other side. By standing on tiptoe she could glimpse many trees growing thick and strong.

"There's got to be something splendid over there," she told herself. "I just know there's a castle hidden among the trees. And I'll bet a handsome prince lives in it. He's probably very lonely."

Sometimes she imagined a forest full of animals that could actually speak to her. Her favorite dream was of a white unicorn that would follow her everywhere, who would lie beside her and put his head on her lap.

"I would call him Snow," she thought.

Her desire to see over the wall became an obsession. She felt that just a glimpse of the other side might reveal what she always seemed to be searching for.

She tentatively broached the subject to her friend, Ellie, a maid at the orphanage.

"Ellie, you know the big wall?"

"Mm-mm."

"What's on the other side?"

"Ooh, heavens, I don't rightly know. Just more country, I suppose."

"Has anyone from here ever seen it?"

"Not that I know."

One afternoon after school Mandy went to the wall and studied it carefully. At one end, a large apple tree growing on the other side thrust long, pink-and-white-blossomed branches over into the orchard.

Intrigued, Mandy went closer, and upon further examina- tion, she found that a number of the big yellow stones in the wall protruded just far enough for her to gain a precarious foothold.

"I might just make it to the top," she thought. "With luck I could reach that big branch of the apple tree, and, once on it, I could really see for miles and miles."

The prospect of such a view was a challenge to Mandy's adventurous nature, and on an impulse she decided to try it that very second. She took a deep breath and began to climb. She hoped no one would see her.

Carefully, testing every stone before she put her weight on it, Mandy pulled herself up inch by inch.

At one point her fingers fumbled, and she clung for a moment, breathing hard. Then, with a last careful effort, she pulled herself to the top of the wall and threw her arms around the branch of the apple tree. Now, looking down, she found the effect quite frightening. The ground seemed a long way away.

7

"Wow, I didn't realize this was so high!" she thought. The orchard was awash with soft frothy blossoms. She turned and peered excitedly through the apple branches. An incredible vista was spread out before her, and Mandy drew in her breath with excitement.

She was looking at a whole new world: hundreds of trees stretching as far as the eye could see—most of them with that soft, silvery-green trunk and fine-textured bark that make the beech tree so easily recognizable. Sunlight filtered through the leaves in bright patches. The woods were open and clear— not dense at all. It looked wonderfully inviting and explorable. Mandy saw a small footpath leading through the trees and longed to see where it led.

"I've come this far; now if I could just get down the other side," she thought.

She saw that the apple tree forked near its base, and it continued to subdivide, giving her numerous climbable branches. The bark felt smooth and soft beneath her hands as she eased herself to the ground.

"Now to look for my unicorn."

She set off along the path, which led into the heart of the woods. She was acutely aware of the blue sky, the heat from the sun, and the wonderful warm smell of earth and moss and flowers.

"Surely I'll find the prince's castle in a little while," she thought.

But each new dip and bend in the path revealed only more trees. She was just beginning to feel a keen sense of disappointment when the path suddenly widened, and, almost immediately, she found herself in an open and sunny clearing. It was quite wide, almost a grassy meadow, and dotted with evergreens.

Mandy could hear the sound of running water, but her immediate attention was attracted to the far end of the clearing where stood a very old and very small cottage. Most of its windows were broken, and there was no door. Tiles had slipped off the roof, and the little chimney had a ridiculous tilt to it. It was in a very bad state of repair.

"Gosh, I wonder if someone lives here," thought Mandy. "Should I go and see? Ooh! — perhaps I'd better not." But her curiosity was stimulated. "It certainly looks empty. But there might be someone in there. An old tramp, or a witch, or an animal."

Matron Bridie was always reminding the children never to talk to strangers and to watch out for the unexpected, so Mandy quietly crept closer, keeping well out of sight behind the trees so that she wouldn't be detected.

She could tell that someone once must have cultivated a garden. There was a low fence, broken in several places, with a little gate. Underneath the weeds she could see the remains of a paved pathway leading to the space where the front door had been.

Mandy kept perfectly still, straining her ears for the slightest noise. The gurgling sound of running water was nearer now, and birds sang in the trees. It was a perfectly lovely afternoon.

She moved closer and lifted the gate, which was hanging by a single hinge.

She tiptoed up the path, being careful to avoid a large patch

of stinging nettles, and tentatively peeked through the door-way. She was looking into a small room. And it was empty. Mandy gave a big sigh of relief.

A staircase, seemingly, led to another room upstairs. In the back wall were two small doors. The house had no furniture. An old garden rake lay across the floor. Mandy moved to the stairs, treading carefully on the loose boards. Each step that she took caused little puffs of dust to rise and swirl in the shafts of sunshine that came through the windows. She climbed up into a tiny bedroom. There was no one about and no furniture here either. The windows were intact, but extremely dirty. Mandy wiped at the glass with her hand and had a splendid view of the meadow and the woods through which she had just traveled. A little brook was visible, too. It splashed and danced along the base of a hillock and was enchantingly pretty.

Downstairs again and gaining courage with every step, she pushed gently at the first of the two small doors. It swung open, creaking on old hinges. She was in a tiny kitchen. There was a sink in one corner with a single, iron water tap attached to the wall above it. When she turned the tap, drops of rusty liquid dripped out and a spider scuttled from the drain.

There was a cupboard which contained nothing but a few broken bottles and an old tin basin. And there was a back door. Mandy pulled it open. She saw the remains of an old bonfire in the tall grass and a path leading around to the front of the house. Re-entering through the doorway, she went back to the main room and tried the second small door.

This one opened easily at her touch, and, as it swung wide, Mandy was totally unprepared for what she saw. To her amazement, she found herself staring at a room which was entirely decorated with seashells.

It was absolutely incredible. Lovely shells of every shape and size and all colors of white and pink and iridescent mother-of-pearl lined every wall and the ceiling, too.

The effect was one of the most beautiful sights Mandy had ever seen.

The afternoon light shone softly through a big bay window at the end of the room. Cobwebs hung in silken strands. A pair of old curtains made of some soft material moved gently in the breeze coming through the open door. The woodwork and the window and door trimmings were painted gold, and the flooring was of tile or marble. A large fireplace was set into the left wall, and the mantelpiece seemed to be of marble, too.

How this extraordinary room came to be in this small cottage, so many miles from anywhere, Mandy couldn't begin to imagine, and it was a full minute before she recovered from the surprise of finding it there at all.

She moved around touching the shells and the curtains, and looking into the fireplace. Everything was coated with dust.

She wandered outside to the clearing and sat down on the grass, drawing her knees up under her chin. She stared at the little house and garden for a very long time.

"Who could have lived here?" she wondered. "It can't have been a family, for there's just the one bedroom and the whole house is hardly big enough. Maybe somebody lived here alone. But what kind of person would do that? And did he make the shell room?"

The discovery of this wonderful place was almost more exciting than finding a castle. The cottage was so charming and quaint. There was a quality about it — an entrancing air.

An idea began to take shape in her mind, and the more she thought about it, the more it appealed to her.

"What if . . ." said Mandy to herself, "what if I pretended this cottage were mine? I could sort of adopt it. Who would know? Who would care? Nobody lives here. I'm sure of that, now. And somebody needs to take care of it. And, oh, I *could* take care of it." She sprang to her feet. "I could. This place could really be mine, a house of my very own." She ran back into the little garden. "I could pull all the weeds out of here, and plant flowers and mend the fence and make the path tidy.

"I could sweep and dust inside and clean the shell room and wash the curtains and the windows. Oh — little house," and she turned to it. "I could take such *good* care of you."

Mandy went all through the cottage once more, seeing the rooms in a new perspective. A thousand thoughts ran through her head. She would have to make a list of all the things she would need. How was she to get them? And from where? She would have to be careful not to let anyone know of this secret place. It would be difficult to come here every day without being seen.

She had no idea how late it was getting until, suddenly, she realized the sky was darkening with the oncoming night.

"Heavens, I must get back. Matron will be worried about me."

Running across the meadow, Mandy paused briefly for a final look at her new-found delight. The little house was soft white in the gray dusk.

"I'll be back tomorrow," Mandy whispered to it, and, turning, she sped through the woods along the path she had followed earlier that afternoon.

She reached the high stone wall and swiftly climbed the old apple tree. Once onto the branch that extended over into the orchard, she eased herself down until she was hanging by her hands and then lightly dropped to the ground.

In a matter of moments she was inside the orphanage and racing up the stairs to her room to wash her face and hands before dinner.

3

MANDY SHARED a bedroom with one other girl. Her name was Sue. She and Mandy were close friends. The girls were almost the same age, Sue being the younger of the two by three months. She was not as strong a personality as Mandy and preferred to have Mandy take the initiative in all things. This suited Mandy very well and she happily allowed Sue to share most of her activities. There were times, of course, when this was not convenient, and Sue would sulk and feel out of sorts whenever Mandy expressed her desire to be alone. This was difficult for Mandy, for then she felt as if she were responsible for the other girl's happiness and well-being, and it lay very heavily on her.

But, luckily, these times were few and far between and generally the girls got on very well. They shared confidences and exchanged ideas. They even borrowed items of clothing and behaved much like two sisters would who were very close.

Being seniors, the girls were privileged to have a room to themselves. It was an attic bedroom, and Mandy loved it. She enjoyed being high up in the house, away from the other children. There was a small skylight in the roof just over her bed. Many nights she lay awake thinking and gazing at the distant stars in the sky above her. She found them very comforting, especially during the difficult nights when she felt troubled and disturbed.

But on the evening of the day she discovered the cottage, she was happily preoccupied with thoughts of the pretty little house and the wonderful afternoon she had had.

As Mandy and Sue were preparing for bed, Ellie, the maid, appeared around the door.

"Hey, Mandy, I found out something for you. You know you asked what was on the other side of the big wall?"

Mandy's heart skipped a beat. She busied herself and managed to appear nonchalant.

"Yes?"

"Well, Matron says it's a big estate in there. A really big one. Only nobody lives there any more."

"Oh, thank you, Ellie."

What a marvelous piece of luck. If nobody lived there, then she wouldn't be bothering a soul if she visited the cottage. It really could be hers. As she snuggled into bed and turned out the light, Mandy felt wonderfully content.

"Sue?" she whispered into the darkness.

"Mm-hmm?"

"Oh — nothing. Good night."

She decided that she would say nothing about the cottage just yet.

Mandy lay on her back, arms behind her head, staring at the night sky winking above her. She pictured the little house, alone and silent, under the same stars. Her mind was filled with plans and ideas and lists of things to get for it. It was midnight before she fell asleep.

4

THE NEXT DAY was bright and sunny. Mandy could hardly wait for school to be over. It was Friday, so she had only a half-day of studies, and all of the weekend before her.

Immediately after lunch, Mandy sped to her room and put on her oldest clothes. She ran into the garden and began looking for old Jake, the handyman and gardener at the orphanage. Mandy wanted to ask his advice and, possibly, borrow a few tools. She found him in the potting shed at the end of the kitchen garden. He was an old man, and very stooped. He wore exactly the same clothes day in and day out — black shiny pants, a collarless shirt with the sleeves rolled up to the elbow, and a dark-blue striped waistcoat. He brought his own lunch to the orphanage in a little tin box. His lunchtime drink was always two bottles of beer, and, predictably, he would snooze for a while in the early afternoon — propped up against the potting shed among the rakes and spades and brooms and

17

buckets and pots of every shape and size. He knew just about all there was to know about nature. It was his religion and he spent most of his life outdoors, rain or shine.

He was just finishing his lunch when Mandy found him.

"Now, Mandy, don't you come bothering me. I'm going to take my snooze in a while."

"Oh, Jake, I won't stay long. I just wanted to ask you a few questions."

"Mm — Well?"

"Is it very difficult to weed a garden?" asked Mandy. "Do I have to know anything special?"

"Bless my soul," Jake looked surprised. "Whose garden are you going to weed?"

"Nobody's," said Mandy, "but is it very difficult?"

"Well, it depends on your soil." Jake took a long drink from his beer bottle and wiped his lips with the back of his hand.

"You see, if it's good and rich and soft, then really most of your weeding can be done by just pulling at the roots, very gently, mind you, until they sort of ease out, and then you can shake 'em off and throw 'em away. But if the earth is packed and hard, then you need a small fork or trowel, and you sort of dig it in under the weeds, lift 'em up gently, and kind of shake the earth loose before pulling the plant out. But anyone can do it," he added, almost as an afterthought.

"I see," said Mandy. "Do you have a small fork I could borrow?"

"Thought you weren't going to be doing any of that," said Jake, squinting up at Mandy in a teasing way.

"I *sort* of am." Mandy didn't want to tell Jake about her secret plans. "It's . . . it's a project," she added hurriedly.

18

"Well, I can't let you take my things. . ." Jake began.

"Oh, I'll return it by tonight," Mandy broke in. "I promise, Jake — just try me this once and see if I don't. By the time you get here tomorrow, it'll be back in the shed."

Jake wanted his afternoon sleep, and Mandy was in a persistent mood.

"All right, Mandy, but you're on your honor now. I hope you can be trusted." He slowly got up and found her a small fork. It was old and had a smooth, worn handle.

"Oh, Jake, thank you." Mandy beamed with delight.

"You just bring it back." He seemed rather pleased with himself. "Now, since you're borrowing that, what about a rake to smooth your garden over when the weeds are out?" he added.

Mandy could have hugged him.

Gathering up the tools, she hurried around to the back door of the orphanage. Leaving the rake and the fork on the doorstep, she burst into the big kitchen and found Alice, the cook, just sitting down at the large wooden table to eat her own belated lunch.

"Alice, could I please have some bread and butter and water to take out for the afternoon?" She moved quickly behind the lady and threw her arms around her shoulders in a hug. "I'm going for a long walk, and I won't be back 'til dinner."

Alice had her mouth full, but she pointed at the pantry. "Bread's in there and a couple of scones, too. Help yourself. You can use one of those old ginger-beer bottles for water."

Mandy buttered the bread and the scones and rinsed out the bottle and filled it with fresh, cold water.

"You don't have any old dusters you don't want, do you?"

19

she suddenly asked, and then, seeing the surprised look on the cook's face, she added, rather lamely, "I thought I might do my room later."

Alice smiled. She heaved her big frame up from the table and went to a cupboard under the sink. "Will this do?" She held up a torn piece of muslin about the size of a kitchen towel.

"O-o-o-h, yes," Mandy sighed happily. "Thank you, Alice."

She gathered up her food and her water and her duster and slammed out of the kitchen door. Well-laden, she staggered into the orchard a few moments later.

The problem for Mandy was how to get all her things over the wall. She finally decided to tie everything up in the muslin cloth and attach that to the big rake. Then she placed it in an upright position against the wall. Finding the same footholds she had used the previous day, she scrambled to the top.

Leaning down carefully, she took hold of the rake and eased it safely up beside her. Then she let it down on the other side of the wall and swung herself into the apple tree. Within seconds she was racing along the pathway, clutching her possessions, her whole being filled with anticipation and excitement at the thought of seeing the cottage once again. She burst through the trees into the clearing and stopped short. A fat rabbit disappeared quickly into the bank by the stream. A blackbird "tick-ticked" and flew into the trees. She was afraid she had dreamed it all yesterday, but there it was — solid and welcoming.

It was a glorious afternoon. The sun beat down and the scent of the earth mingled with grass and clover. Mandy noticed a May tree that she hadn't seen the day before. It was in full bloom. Behind the house there was a bank of rhododendrons, their fat buds due to open almost any day now.

There was so much she wanted to do and to see. It would obviously be impossible to do all that needed to be done this afternoon. Since Jake had lent her the rake and the fork, and she had promised to return them by the evening, and since the weather was so fine, she decided to attend to the garden first. The cottage could always be cleaned on a rainy day.

So she set her things down by the door and surveyed the garden. *Her* garden. The little path was obviously the first thing to be cleared. She decided to begin by the front doorstep.

Kneeling down, she pulled at the long weeds. To her delight they came out of the ground very easily. Carefully and methodi-cally, she worked her way toward the little gate, avoiding the patch of stinging nettles. She made a mental note to try to get a pair of gardening gloves. They would really help to protect her hands on some of the rougher jobs.

She discovered pale gray flagstones beneath the weeds; so she cleared out all the grass around them and in between them.

It was a big improvement the minute the path was cleared. It gave her a real sense of what needed to be done next. The clean line of the flagstones directed her attention to a very pretty wild-rose tree that was growing around the door. It needed tying back. Mandy made another note to try to get some twine the following day.

Next to the door there were Michaelmas daisies—dry and dusty looking stalks, closely growing. They were not yet in bloom, but would be a fine splash of color by late summer.

There were many shrubs and flowers that Mandy didn't

recognize, but she knew some of the wild flowers and left them in the ground. She wasn't sure what to do about the weed called convolvulus. It was growing over everything and although Mandy knew that it produced a pretty, white trumpetlike flower, she decided to pull it all out, feeling that its many tendrils might choke some of the better things.

She worked hard all afternoon. Her back began to ache and her knees were scraped and dirty. She became so warm in the full sun that she removed her cardigan. She was totally engrossed in her work. Every foot of earth that she cleared seemed to reveal some new treasure. She was fascinated by the beauty of the snails and the long worms that came to light. At one point she discovered an anthill and watched it with wonder. The little insects were so busy and seemed to have such a sense of purpose. Mandy wished she could be part of their world for just a little while. A sparrow came and perched on the low fence and watched her with a beady eye. Wood pigeons cooed softly in the trees, where they probably had a nest.

By late afternoon Mandy had cleared the path and one whole side of the garden. Near the fence she discovered quite a large clump of nasturtiums. They would soon be glorious colors of red, orange, yellow, and gold.

Mandy wiped her brow. She was hot and thirsty.

She decided to rest for a moment. Fetching her bread and scones and water, she sat on the front doorstep and contemplated her work. Now that the garden was partially cleared, it was easier to guess at its original shape and form. There must once have been a tiny lawn, and flower beds under the windows and along the fence. There was a box hedge running around the back of the house and a lot of privet hedges, too. They would need trimming and the grass would need cutting. She would have to be nice to Jake and, perhaps, he would lend her some more tools.

She munched on her bread and drank from the ginger-beer bottle. She was feeling pleased with herself. The little stream gurgled nearby, and the afternoon was lazy and quiet.

"This is all too wonderful. I could stay here forever," she thought. She leaned against the doorframe. "I wonder what I should tackle next? The other flower beds, I suppose, especially if I buy some seeds tomorrow. I'll want to plant them."

She thought of the shopping she should do. Money was going to be a problem. She had pocket money saved, and she received a little every Saturday for her work in the grocery store.

So, tomorrow she'd have enough money to make a start on flowers and things. She'd also need a pair of gloves and some twine for the roses. Jake could help her with that. She would need a lot of things for the inside of the cottage, too.

Mandy got up and wandered indoors. She immediately noticed the old rake lying on the floor, and her breath caught with pleasure.

Well, at least she had her own rake and didn't have to borrow that from Jake. But how was she to clean the windows? Where would she find a broom and enough dusters?

She went into the little kitchen and looked in the cupboard. She examined the old tin basin. As far as she could tell, it was intact.

"I can get water from the stream for washing up. I wish I had a little stove. It would be fun to make tea and things. I must make a grocery list. Phew! Housekeeping isn't easy. There's so much to remember."

In the shell room she crossed to the fireplace and looked at it carefully. On the side, there was a little trivet held by a bracket. When Mandy touched it, it swung over the fireplace.

It must have been used for cooking. So, she wouldn't need a stove. Now, if only the fireplace would work. She would collect some wood later and try it. She decided to add pencil and paper to her list so that she could write down all the things to do and not forget them.

It was getting late and time to leave for this day. Mandy wandered through the cottage feeling the pride of ownership. She stood at her front door looking down the newly weeded garden path. The freshly turned earth smelled wonderful. She wandered slowly to the little stream and bathed her face and hands in the clear water. It was pretty and shaded there with green ferns growing on the banks. The water was no more than a foot or so deep. The hill beyond was solid with trees. It would be fun to follow along the stream one day to see where it went.

She put the muslin duster in the kitchen cupboard along with the ginger-beer bottle. The tin basin went into the sink. She took the weeds she had pulled around to the back of the house and put them with the remains of the old bonfire. She would be making her own bonfire there soon if the rubbish kept building up at this rate.

It was time to go. Gathering up Jake's tools she headed toward the meadow and home, pausing just long enough to adjust the little white gate. Pulling it straight and setting it up neatly alongside the fence, she noted with pride that the little garden was already beginning to have a trim, cared-for look.

5

On Saturday morning, Mandy emptied her money box and counted her savings. She planned to spend them when she had finished work at the store.

Sue wanted to know what she was going to do.

"Oh, buy a few things."

"Can I come with you?"

"Well . . ." Mandy didn't know what to say. "I'll be shopping right after work. It would be difficult for us to meet. Besides, I don't quite know what I'll buy."

It was true. Until she found out the price of some of the things she needed, she couldn't be sure just what she would purchase.

Sue looked hurt. Mandy felt bad.

"Tell you what," she said. "If I do buy something, I'll show it to you later. I probably won't get much though."

She ran off down the hallway, yelling at the top of her lungs as she went.

" 'Bye, Ellie, I'm just on my way to the store."

Mandy rounded a corner and ran full tilt into Matron Bridie.

"Gracious, Mandy, will you look where you're going!"

"Oops, sorry, Mrs. Bridie. I'm terribly sorry."

"My, you're in a hurry this morning," Matron smiled, "and could you, please, be a little more quiet. I think the entire household now knows that you're going to the store."

"Yes, Mrs. Bridie. Thank you, Mrs. Bridie." Mandy scurried away.

Walking into the village, she passed Jake riding to work on his bicycle. She waved to him and was glad that she had replaced his tools safely in the potting shed last night. Hopefully, he would let her borrow them again. She would really have to keep on the right side of Jake and show him that she could be responsible and conscientious. Her garden would never be right if she were not able to borrow from him some of the things she needed.

Mandy worked hard in the shop all morning. She was there from nine until one o'clock every Saturday, and she always

enjoyed herself. She loved the smell of fresh bread and bacon and coffee and fruit and vegetables. Mr. and Mrs. Jennings, who owned the store, were very good to her. She was too young to serve at the counter and to handle the money, but she did a lot of fetching and carrying. She unpacked the new goods and stored them on the shelves and made herself generally useful. Sometimes in the middle of the morning, she was given a hot cup of tea and a biscuit. She was usually so busy that the time passed quickly.

Today, Mandy was particularly anxious for her work to be finished. She looked at some of the items on the shelves. Soups, chocolate drinks, canned milk, cookies. Wouldn't it be wonderful if she had enough money to buy them all!

She decided that she would see how much she had left over after she had purchased her seeds, and then perhaps she would splurge a little.

At one o'clock she raced out of the store and down the street to the garden supply shop, with her wages clutched in her hand and her savings jingling in her pocket.

To her dismay she discovered that the garden store had just closed for the lunch hour. She peered through the window and saw the proprietor, Mr. Simple, clearing away some things at the back. She tapped urgently on the glass, trying to attract his attention, but he seemed not to hear her. She moved to the door and shook it hard. He looked up and she waved, making frantic signs for him to let her in.

He hesitated and consulted his watch.

"Oh, please, Mr. Simple — *dear* Mr. Simple — do let me come in," breathed Mandy, and she pressed her face urgently

27

against the glass. Wilfred Simple ambled slowly across the floor and unlocked the door.

"Well, Mandy?"

"Oh, thank you, Mr. Simple. I'm terribly sorry to bother you at your lunch hour, but I need to buy some things — some seeds and things for a garden, and I wondered if you could possibly help me choose some. It's terribly important. I — I only have the rest of this weekend to do it in. It's a special project, and, well, could I please buy some now? I have my money."

He smiled at her.

"Come in. What sort of things do you need?"

"Oh, gosh, flowers, mostly. You know, packages of seeds that I can grow. Ooooh, what are these?" She crossed to a box packed with earth that was sprouting green leaf-clusters.

"They're pansies, ready for planting out."

"How much are they?"

"About four pence or five pence a plant."

"Five pence a *plant*? A single plant?" Mandy was aghast. "But I'll need so many. What about seeds? How much would they cost?"

"Well, it's a bit late for seeds, Mandy. You should have planted most of them in February if you wanted to have them ready for transplanting now."

"Oh, dear, what shall I do?" Mandy was in despair. With everything so terribly expensive, she didn't see how it would be possible to fill her garden with all the lovely things she had in mind.

Mr. Simple put his hand on her shoulder.

28

"Now, it's not so bad. You don't have to buy just pansies, you know. Come and see what else I have.

"Here, for instance. These are marigold seedlings and these are what you would call snapdragons, but they're really named antirrhinums. Now, they're not expensive. And these salvias would be lovely for your garden. They come up a gorgeous red, flamelike color and have a leaf that looks a bit like mint. They last a long time, too."

Mandy brightened. "Could you tell me how to plant them?"

"Yes, but first things first. Do you have things like a spade and a trowel and a fork?"

"Oh, I think Jake would lend me most of those things."

"That's good. Would he lend you a watering can?"

Mandy thought about it. "I don't think he'd let me have it for that long. And I'd need to water almost every day, wouldn't I?"

Mr. Simple nodded. "Well then, let's see. What kind of a garden plot do you have?"

Mandy described it as best she could without saying too much for fear that Mr. Simple would discover what she was up to. He seemed satisfied, however, with the details that she gave him.

"All right now, here's what I suggest and you tell me if you like the idea. I think you need about thirty mixed plants. First of all, you should have some of these wallflowers." He got an empty flat-box and packed some wallflower seedlings into it.

"And marigolds would be a nice splash of color," he added them to the box, "and some of these salvias. Like I just said, they'd look lovely. This little plant here is called sweet alyssum.

It smells marvelous in the summer. It's a little white flower, and it lasts and spreads all the time. It should go around the borders of your garden." As he was talking, he was packing more and more plants into the box. ". . . And I think maybe just a few big pansies would finish your garden off a real treat.

"Planting these out will be easy, Mandy. Just make a hole in the ground with your finger or a stick, place the seedling in gently, and make the earth around it firm. Put the plants a few inches apart. Then take this little watering can," and he took down a small plastic watering can from the shelf. "Now, see, it has a very good head on it, with the smallest holes, so that the water doesn't rush through and drown your plants. It lets out nice and easy, just like the soft rain. Water your flowers after planting, and they'll come up strong and healthy."

Mandy was thrilled. "Here," she said, putting all her money on the counter.

"Well now, the plants are a gift from me. The watering can doesn't cost very much." Mr. Simple picked up a few coins from the counter. "You keep the rest of the money, Mandy." He rang up the amount. "Is that all right?"

"Oh, Mr. Simple —" Mandy hardly knew what to say. "That's just marvelous," she beamed. "Oh, one more thing. How much do gardening gloves cost?" She had noticed some hanging on display.

"They're expensive. Why don't you ask Jake if he has an old pair he wouldn't need anymore?"

"I will," said Mandy.

She gathered up her box of seedlings and her watering can very carefully.

"Sure you can manage, now?" said Mr. Simple, letting her out.

"Oh, yes, and thank you very much."

"Let me know how they all turn out," Mr. Simple said. He smiled and watched Mandy walk down the road. Then he went back into his shop to his belated lunch.

6

MANDY HID her purchases in the orchard. The staff and children at the orphanage were at lunch, so she was unobserved. She took one look at the wall and her heart sank at the thought of getting the plants over to the other side. How was she going to manage it?

She was too late to eat in the dining room. So she went to the kitchen and ate a sandwich and watched Alice go through the piles of dishes.

She noted that Alice got a new package of soap flakes from the store cupboard. She wondered if she could persuade her to give her a package for the cottage. But — one thing at a time.

"Alice, I need a broom."

"Oh you do, do you? Since when did you decide to be such a housewife? Yesterday it was dusters; today it's a broom."

"I'd like some more dusters, too."

Alice laughed. "Now, what are you up to, Mandy?"

"Oh, just a game."

"Ellie might have a broom. I can give you some more muslin."

"Super." Mandy smiled.

Tomorrow, she would talk to Ellie. Meanwhile, Alice seemed in a good mood. She decided to see just how far she could go.

"Do you have an old saucepan or jug you won't be using?"

Alice stopped her washing up. She gave Mandy a long, hard look. "I might have. I'm busy right now. Ask me later."

"And could I take a box of soap flakes, please?"

Alice shook her head. "No, Mandy, I'm sorry, but these things cost money, and Matron wouldn't want me to be giving things like that away. Now, I've already said I'll see if I can find a pan or something, and you'll get your dusters, but that's enough."

"All right." Mandy decided to change the subject. "I'd like to take some bread and butter again today. I'm going to be out most of the afternoon."

Alice laughed. "You're a fine one. All this talk about cleaning up and the next thing you're going out. I don't know what you're up to, Mandy. You take care and be sure to be in by dinner time."

Mandy promised that she would. She fetched her tea and ran into the garden looking for Jake. She found him about to cut the edges of the front lawn.

"Hello, Mandy. You brought the rake back. I'm very pleased."

"I was wondering, Jake, could I please borrow the fork again — just today? I don't need the rake, just the fork. I didn't quite finish yesterday."

"I don't see why not. How's the project coming along?"

32

"Fine." Mandy smiled at him. "But, Jake, I need a few extra things."

"Oh. Like what?"

"Well, I need twine, and I really need some gloves so that the stinging nettles don't get my hands."

Jake stood up and looked at her thoughtfully. "This seems a very big thing you're doing. What is it, Mandy? Where is it?"

Mandy felt a rush of impatience. It was so maddening to have everybody asking her questions. She wished she didn't need to let anyone know that she was doing anything.

"I don't want to talk about it yet," she murmured.

"Wherever it is, it is not around here," Jake said emphatically. "We don't have a stinging nettle on the property. You'd better take care, my girl. Come on, I'll find you some twine."

Mandy trotted along beside him. He went into the potting shed and took down a ball of twine from a shelf.

"About this much?" He held out a long piece.

Mandy nodded.

"I'll cut it up into different lengths for you. And gloves — gloves. Let me see now." Jake scratched his head and looked around.

Mandy's attention was caught by a large coil of rope hanging on a nail. If she could borrow it she could use it to tie around her box of seedlings and pull them over the wall.

"Try these on," Jake was saying. "They'll be big, but I think they'll do."

Mandy held out her hand, and Jake slipped on a glove which was at least two sizes too large.

"For what you need 'em for, they'll do just fine. Here's your

33

fork and the twine. Now off you go. And be sure to bring it back by tonight."

Mandy dared not ask for another thing. She ran to the orchard and hid her things along with the seedlings and the watering can she had placed there earlier. But, making sure that she was unobserved, she made her way back to the potting shed in time to see Jake going toward the front lawn. He did not see her.

She slipped into the shed and took down the rope. After making sure the coast was still clear, she raced as quickly as she could back to the orchard.

She would have to be quick. Jake could return at any moment, and some of the orphanage children might come along. She could hear their voices as they played by the kitchen garden.

She took hold of the fork, stood back, and hurled it as hard as she could over the wall. She heard it land with a clatter.

Next she took up the watering can and threw that, too. Because it was plastic, she didn't think it would be damaged, just this once.

She tucked the twine and the gloves in her blouse. Unfolding the long piece of rope, she tied one end of it twice around the box of seedlings, trying to tie the knot in the very center. Then, taking careful aim, she threw the other end at the overhanging branch of the apple tree. After a couple of attempts, it went over and swung loosely.

There was no one in sight. Mandy scrambled as quickly as she could to the top of the wall. She was in such a hurry and so anxious not to be seen that she scraped her knees and her hands.

34

Very gently, she took hold of the rope and drew the box up toward her. It swayed and bumped against the wall and, for one heart-stopping moment, Mandy felt she would lose all her plants. Some of the packed earth spilled to the ground.

She held the rope steady and gradually the swaying stopped. Beads of perspiration stood out on her forehead. She hoped no one would see her. There was nowhere she could hide herself and she was absolutely committed now to getting the box over the wall.

It was within reach. Holding the apple-tree branch with one hand, Mandy reached down and grabbed the rope firmly where it knotted at the center. She pulled it to the top of the wall and slowly let it down the other side, playing out the rope inch by inch. She felt the box touch the ground gently, and she heaved a sigh of relief. She was down the apple tree and untying the knots in a second. Her precious plants were safe.

Now, all she had to do was return the rope and gather up her food which she had left in the orchard. She found the fork and the watering can and put them beside the seedlings. She coiled the rope and slung it over her shoulder and climbed the apple tree once more. She was just about to put her leg over the top of the wall when she heard someone calling her name.

"Mandy!"

She hunched down and prayed that she hadn't been seen.

"M-a-n-d-y-y!"

The voice was nearer. Lifting her head carefully, she looked over the wall. It was Sue, wandering disconsolately through the orchard.

Mandy bit her lip in annoyance. Why did Sue have to come along right now? Why did she have to call at the very moment when time was so precious and she had so much to get done? She huddled into the tree and kept very quiet.

Sue came to a stop almost underneath the overhanging branch, and Mandy held her breath, feeling her head would burst. It would be so easy to respond to Sue's call. So simple to tell her about everything. But the cottage was her secret. She had found it. It *belonged* to her. She didn't want to share. Not just yet.

Sue gave a big sigh. Then she wandered off, disappearing through the orchard trees.

Mandy was over the wall in a second. Her legs were aching from crouching. She raced to the potting shed and hung the coil of rope back on the nail. Then sprinting back into the orchard, she took the little package containing her tea from its hiding place under a bush. She tucked it inside her blouse and climbed the big wall for the third time that day. She was absolutely exhausted by the time she reached the cottage, but she still had a full afternoon's work to do.

7

MANDY KNEW that she must get her plants bedded out by the end of the day or they would suffer. She looked upon them as her children. They were her responsibility. Only she could give them care and nourishment. Without her they would die.

She cleared the weeds from the other flower bed under the

windows. She picked up the old rake from the floor inside the house and smoothed over the earth. With the work that she had done yesterday, she now had two completely cleared beds, and she decided that she had just enough plants to fill them.

It was with mixed feelings of anticipation and pride that she laid out her seedlings. First came the wallflowers, right under the windows against the wall. Next, she planted the salvias, and then the marigolds. She spaced the pansies in front, and last of all, as a border, she planted the sweet alyssum. She made many trips to the little stream to fill her watering can. After each trip, she gently emptied the contents in a fine spray over her beloved plants.

When she had finished she stood back to admire the total effect. It was a trifle disappointing. For all her hard work and careful spacing, the flower beds still looked bare. The plants themselves looked bedraggled and skimpy.

She hoped they would brighten up by tomorrow.

She put on Jake's big gardening gloves and turned her attention to the stinging nettles in the pathway. After she pulled them out, the little paved area really looked neat and clean. She tied back the rose tree over the door. Every small thing she did made the garden look just that little bit better, which was very rewarding.

Mandy knew that she would have to return Jake's fork that evening. She was extremely weary and longed to sit and have her tea, but she decided to forego it and concentrate on the remaining two flower beds by the fence. If she could just get them cleared by tonight, she wouldn't need the fork anymore—not for a while anyway.

The sun was setting as she finished, and her aching knees and back told her that she would be stiff and sore in an hour or so. But it had been worth it. She was over the worst of the weeding.

She was so weary that it was all she could do to climb over the wall back to the orphanage. She was not only trembling from fatigue, but working in the hot sunlight had given her a slightly dizzy feeling.

She couldn't wait to get to bed. At dinner she ate very little, and afterward she headed straight for her room.

Sue was quiet as both girls prepared for bed. Then she suddenly said, "I looked for you today, but I couldn't find you."

Mandy was brushing her teeth and was glad that she could use that as an excuse not to talk.

"U-m-m-m," she mumbled.

"I wanted to know if you bought anything today. I thought you might be by the big wall where you usually go, so I went there to look for you."

Mandy felt a kind of pain inside. She knew she would have to lie. And it was unpleasant. She hated fibbing to anybody.

"No, I went for a walk this afternoon."

"Did you buy anything?"

Mandy decided on a half-truth. "I bought some flowers from Mr. Simple."

She saw the surprised look on Sue's face.

"I just felt like it," she added and then, "but I gave them to Mrs. Rose. You know, the old lady who lives in the cottage just before the shops."

Sue accepted this explanation. Both girls climbed into bed

and turned out the lights. They lay in the darkness, listening to the sounds of bedtime all over the big house—slamming doors, children arguing or playing, the voices of the adults, firm and strong, establishing order, then quiet.

Sue spoke in a soft voice. "Mandy, shall we go to the old quarry tomorrow and play? It's Sunday and it would be fun."

But she got no reply. Mandy had already fallen fast asleep.

8

MANDY WOKE late the following morning. The children were clattering downstairs to breakfast when she finally opened her eyes.

"My gosh, it's late." Mandy sprang out of bed and then winced. Her back was stiff and sore from all the hard work yesterday. She ran to the window and looked at the sky. It was a little gray and overcast, but she didn't think it would rain. She hurriedly brushed her teeth and washed her face and raced downstairs to the dining room.

"You're late, Mandy."

"Mandy over-sle-ept," chanted someone. "You'll be late for church, Mandy."

Mandy grinned good-naturedly.

Sue had saved a place for her at one of the long tables. She sat down and ate her porridge and toast hungrily.

"What do you want to do today?" Sue asked.

Mandy felt again that flash of annoyance that she had experienced yesterday. If only Sue wouldn't rely on her so much.

"I'm going to be busy," she replied.

"Doing what?"

"Oh . . . things."

Mandy looked at the spoons and the knives on the table. She wondered if she dared take one for her cottage. Perhaps she could get a cup and a plate, too. If she were careful she might be able to take something each day.

The children were made to clear away their plates after each meal. They carried their dishes and cutlery to the end of the room where they were stacked, ready for the kitchen.

"Here, I'll take these today." Mandy leaned across and picked up Sue's dishes. Before the other girl could protest, Mandy had put them with her own and carried them to the sideboard.

She made a great pretense of stacking the plates neatly. At the same time she slid a knife into the sleeve of her blouse. By cupping her hand and bending her wrist, she prevented it from sliding out.

"You'll be late for church if you don't hurry," Sue said, as the children left the dining room.

Mandy nodded. She raced up the stairs to her bedroom and hid the knife in a drawer. Throwing a sweater around her shoulders, she rejoined Sue just as the children were forming a double line for the walk into the village.

Most Sundays, Mandy enjoyed going to church. The little chapel was on St. Martin's Green, the wide grassed area in the center of the village, and from which the village took its name.

Church was the one big social event of the week.

Mandy watched Matron Bridie, dressed in the starched clothes that she reserved especially for Sunday, saying good morning to all the local people. Jake was there. And old Mrs. Rose. She hoped she wouldn't have to stop and talk to her for fear Sue would question Mrs. Rose about the flowers Mandy had said she had given her.

Suddenly, Mandy saw Wilfred Simple and his wife walking directly toward her. She knew exactly what Mr. Simple was going to say. It would be a disaster if Sue or any of the orphanage children heard the conversation. Without pausing to think, Mandy broke from the line and ran to the couple, forcing them to stop a good twenty yards or so from Matron Bridie.

"Good morning, Mandy. How did you get on with the plants?"

"Oh, fine, just fine." Mandy smiled nervously. "Good morning, Mrs. Simple. But, Mr. Simple, er — please don't mention the plants at all, it's — uum — well, they're going to be a surprise, you see."

"A-a-ah," Mr. Simple nodded knowingly. "A surprise for Matron, is it?"

"Mandy." It was Matron's voice, stern and reproving. "Will you please get back into line, at *once*."

"Yes, Mrs. Bridie. Sorry." Mandy scurried to rejoin the children. She threw an imploring glance at Mr. Simple as they walked into the church. He winked at her and tapped the side of his nose in a conspiratorial way.

Sue was inquisitive. "What was that all about?" she whispered.

"Oh, nothing much. I just wanted to say hello."

Matron Bridie turned to the girls. "*Will* you two be *quiet?*"

Mandy sat in the church pew feeling nervous and uncomfortable. She wished that the service would be over quickly so that she could get away. During prayers she asked especially that her garden would flourish and her plants grow strong and healthy.

The light shone through the stained-glass windows and Mandy looked at the saints and apostles and hoped that Father Mulligan would hurry and finish his sermon. Today he seemed to be droning on forever. She thought of her cottage and felt a surge of excitement within her.

"Do not collect for yourselves treasures on this earth." Father Mulligan's voice penetrated Mandy's thoughts.

Her eyes flew open wide.

Had Father Mulligan been speaking directly to her? Was he referring to the cottage? Or did he know that she had taken the knife at breakfast this morning? Another glance in his direction showed him to be gazing at the chapel ceiling, fingers intertwined, pondering the value of his own words.

"—And besides, I didn't exactly *steal* the knife," Mandy told herself. "I really only borrowed it for a while. When I earn enough money I can buy one of my own." And so she justified her actions and felt better.

She sang the hymns in a loud, clear voice. When the service came to an end, Mandy was first in line for the walk back to the orphanage. Once there she managed to evade Sue and the other children. Collecting the knife from the drawer, she raced through the garden and was over the wall in an instant.

9

MANDY FELT free at last and exhilarated. Sunday! A whole day to herself! No troubles. No worries for the time being. And her cottage was waiting. She stood on the edge of the clearing, quietly enjoying the pleasure of seeing it again. It was the first time she had seen it in the early morning.

The day smelled fresh and clean. The grass was wet underfoot as she crossed the clearing. A family of rabbits scuttled away into the bank by the stream. Mandy wished that they would get used to her presence.

She noted, happily, that her plants had taken hold well. They looked stronger this morning.

She began a few chores. She put the borrowed knife in the pantry. She picked up the weeds from the previous day and carried them to the bonfire.

Mandy would have liked to cut the grass somehow and trim the hedges. She noted again the nasturtiums growing wild, and, suddenly, she had an idea.

"I'll transplant them into the other flower beds by the fence. I know that they grow very rapidly and keep on spreading. With any luck, they'll be quite a show once summer is really here. And I won't need to buy extra plants."

Carefully, she prepared and raked the ground, and then gently lifted a few of the trailing leaves. She made sure to leave a lot of earth around the roots.

Mandy scooped a hole with her hands and pressed the nasturtiums into it. She then proceeded to do the same thing with the remaining plants until they were spread out all along the fence. She fetched her watering can and sprinkled the plants gently as Mr. Simple had told her to do.

She tidied the area where the nasturtiums had been and stood back to look at the whole garden. "Now, I suppose I'll have to wait for a few weeks until they all come into bloom," thought Mandy. "I do hope they'll be all right."

She went indoors to the shell room and gazed at it for a long time. It was such a beautiful room. A peaceful room. Mandy felt calm and untroubled as she lovingly fingered the pretty shells. They were very dusty. She decided she would begin cleaning her house that very afternoon after lunch.

Ellie was cooperative, at lunchtime, when Mandy tackled her about the broom.

"Of course you can borrow it," she said. "Just put it back when you're done."

Alice called to Mandy just as lunch was finished. "I have something for you." She produced a roll of muslin and a small, rather old saucepan. "Will these do?"

Mandy reached up and hugged her. "Oh, Alice, that's super. Thank you."

She raced back to the cottage, almost tripping over the broom in her haste and excitement.

It was a perfect afternoon for being indoors. The gray skies had become even grayer and soon it started to rain.

Mandy swept the shell room out thoroughly. She lifted the brush and pulled down all the cobwebs and went over the

window frames. She brushed the shells as best she could and then used one of her dusters to clean them a little more thoroughly.

She brushed through into the main room, up the staircase and down again, and into the kitchen. All the debris went out the back door.

A lot of dust had arisen and settled back onto the stair rail and the window ledges. Mandy ran to the stream and dipped a fresh piece of muslin into the water and wrung it out. She wiped the dusty areas once again. She cleaned the pantry shelves and then washed out her dusters and hung them over the edge of the sink to dry.

She was filthy by the time she had finished, but very well-pleased with herself.

It was getting dark and Mandy was amazed how the time had flown. She decided to wait for the rain to ease off a little, so she stood at the window looking out at the dripping black trees.

It was nice to be snug and cozy inside with a roof over her head to protect her. It would be even nicer when she could collect some wood to get a fire going.

A little sparrow was trying to take a bath in a puddle that had formed in the center of one of the flagstones in the pathway. Mandy watched with delight as the tiny creature fluffed himself out and hunched himself down with much ruffling and shaking of his feathers.

"He's like a small engine when he gets going," she marveled. "I shall bring some bread tomorrow after school so that I can feed him. Maybe I'll even build a birdbath one day."

10

THE FOLLOWING week was a busy one. On Monday immediately after school, Mandy went to the shops, and, with some of the money she had left, she purchased a small dustpan and brush, a scrubbing brush, a box of matches, and some scouring powder. She delightedly stored them in the pantry at the cottage.

She wiped all the windows and scrubbed out her sink and her washing bowl. The curtains came down in the shell room and she folded them away until she would have time to wash them. She tried to trim the edges of the pocket-handkerchief lawn with the kitchen knife and did a fairly good job of it. She even pulled up great handfuls of the longer grass and got it looking a little shorter, though it really did need a good clipping.

It was difficult finding enough time to spend at the cottage. School occupied nearly all of the day, and there was homework to do in the evenings. Mandy found it hard to concentrate on either. She longed for the summer holidays to come, when she would have more freedom to do the many things she planned.

Every evening at the dinner table she hid away a spoon, or a fork, and even managed a cup and a plate one night. They were all duly taken and stored in the cottage.

By now, she was quick and adept at getting over the big wall. There was always the worrying possibility that somebody might catch her, but she developed a keen ear and a sure instinct as to when it was safe to try. Nevertheless, it was always a bother to climb it, especially when she was carrying things.

She wished she could find a better way to get to the cottage.

Mandy collected firewood every chance that she had. Walking to the cottage each day, she picked up any log or small twig that might eventually help keep a fire going. She made a woodpile against the wall just outside the kitchen door.

Toward the end of the week she put a few twigs into the fireplace and lit them. It was a disaster. Clouds of smoke filled the room, covering the newly cleaned shells and windows with a fine layer of dust. Mandy coughed and spluttered and ran outside the cottage to catch her breath. Her eyes were streaming with tears. She waited until the smoke subsided, praying that the chimney wouldn't catch fire. Finally, she went back indoors and tentatively examined the fireplace. Perhaps there was a flue or something that she should have opened.

Getting on her hands and knees she peered up the chimney and groped about for a possible handle. She was instantly doused with a liberal amount of soot.

"Oh, gosh." Mandy brushed her clothes in disgust. "Matron's going to be *furious*." She would have to bathe and change as quickly as possible. But for the moment she was more determined than ever to find out why the chimney smoked so badly.

There was no flue of any kind, so obviously the trouble came from another source.

Mandy went outside once more. One side of the cottage roof sloped down to the hill by the stream. It was an easy matter to climb the hill and make a small jump onto the roof. Unsteadily, Mandy made her way up toward the chimney, dislodging the loose tiles and sending them skittering down to crash on the grass below. She made it safely to the rooftop and immediately saw the cause of her smoking fireplace.

It was a bird's nest, perfectly formed and completely blocking the top of the chimney. It seemed like an old nest, and Mandy was glad. She wouldn't have had the heart to remove it if there were eggs in it. She lifted up the mass of twigs and straw and looked down into the chimney to make sure there was no other obstruction. There was none, and so now Mandy had a fireplace that finally worked and a room so covered with smoke that it needed cleaning all over again. But it didn't matter. It was part of the fun of putting her house in order.

That night Mandy bathed and put her dirty clothes in the linen basket. She congratulated herself on being smart enough to avoid any comment on her disheveled appearance.

It was a surprise, therefore, when Sue turned to her at bedtime and said in a shocked voice, "Pooh, Mandy, you smell like you've been in a bonfire."

"What do you mean?" Mandy was startled.

She sniffed the air and then pointed. "It's your hair. It's covered with bits of soot. Where have you been?" Mandy thought wildly for a moment, then realized that Sue had unwittingly supplied an answer.

"It was a bonfire," she said. "I was helping Jake today." Sue accepted the explanation.

"Well, you sure do smell," was all she said in reply.

Mandy suddenly saw the funny side of the situation. Long after the lights were out, she lay in bed giggling helplessly, stuffing the pillow into her mouth for fear she would give herself away.

11

AT THE END of the week, Matron Bridie sent for Mandy to come to her study. Mandy was nervous. What could Matron possibly want? She went with great trepidation and an instinct that something bad was about to happen.

Matron Bridie wasted no words.

"Mandy, I gather that you've been spending a great deal of time away from the orphanage. I'm told that you have a project that you're working on. Would you care to tell me about it?"

Mandy experienced a moment's sheer panic. The palms of her hands were wet and she began to tremble. How much did Matron know? Who could have told her? Jake or Ellie? Possibly Mr. Simple? Or Alice? She wished she had been more careful.

"You must understand that it is very worrying to have you going off for hours at a time without our knowledge," Matron was saying. "The orphanage is responsible for you, and anything could happen when you're away from us like that."

"Yes, ma'am," Mandy whispered.

"Would you like to tell me about it? Could I help in some way?" Matron obviously knew very little.

Mandy hesitated, wondering what to say. Her mind was in turmoil. She was sure to be stopped from visiting the cottage if she told the truth. Yet she hated to lie. And what if she did lie and then Matron found out about it? But better to lie than to be forbidden to go to her beloved cottage again. She heard herself saying, "Well, I—I *did* have a project going, but I've given it up now."

"Oh?" Matron seemed surprised.

"Yes, I found a spot when I was out walking one day and thought it would be fun to try to make it into a sort of place of my own. You know, a little garden and things. But it was just too much to do, so I stopped."

She felt simply awful standing there. Everything seemed rather fuzzy. She was afraid that she would faint.

"I see." Matron looked somewhat puzzled. "Well, please know that I don't like your going out alone. I'd rather you didn't."

"I always told Ellie when I'd be back."

"Yes, I know, Mandy. You're a very sensible girl, and I trust you completely. But you must understand my position."

"Oh, I do." Mandy's voice was high and overly sincere. "That's why I stopped, Matron. I knew you wouldn't like my being out like that."

"Good." Matron seemed relieved. There was a moment's silence. Mandy was sure her heart could be heard, it was beating so loud.

"I think you were wise to stop your project," said Matron thoughtfully. "But I'm a little sorry, too. You see, I do understand your wanting to make a place that you could call your own. You must long for it very much sometimes." She smiled kindly.

Mandy suddenly realized that she was about to cry, and she swallowed hard.

"Oh," she said in a small voice, "well — it doesn't matter."

"I was wondering," continued Matron in a bright voice, "if you would like me to ask Jake to put aside a small plot in the garden that you could work on. It could be your special place. It might be fun."

Mandy forced her eyes to stay open wide. "No, thank you, ma'am. I've sort of lost interest now."

Matron gave Mandy a long and penetrating look. Then she said quietly, "Very well, but let me know if you change your mind. Now, Mandy, that will be all."

Mandy went out of the room slowly. Her eyes were brimming with tears.

12

ONCE OUTSIDE, Mandy leaned against the wall and let the tears flow. She couldn't understand why she was crying. Perhaps she hadn't realized how much the little cottage meant to her. The thought of having to give it up was unbearable.

She would have to be terribly careful from now on. She was sure that Matron was only half-convinced that she had told the truth. And Mandy felt so bad about lying that she really ached inside.

She decided that she would try to make a reasonable-sounding excuse for every trip that she made to the cottage.

She could say that she was going to stay late at school one day, or that she was going into town to visit the grocery store. A visit to old Mrs. Rose would always be acceptable. The weekends were going to be the main problem. There was always the excuse of going for a short walk, but she didn't think she could use it too often.

The next Saturday she told everyone she would be working a little late at the Jennings' store. Actually, she finished at lunch-time as usual and set out almost immediately for the cottage.

With her morning's earnings, she had purchased a bottle of concentrated beef broth, some biscuits, raisins, a small package of tea, and a tiny box of soap flakes. Also, she had saved a doughnut from her mid-morning coffee break.

Once at the cottage, she discovered she was famished. She skillfully got a fire burning in the shell room. Then, fetching her saucepan, Mandy filled it with cool, clear water from the stream and set it to boil on the trivet. To her delight it didn't take very long, and soon she was sitting happily on her front doorstep, drinking hot beef broth out of a cup and munching on raisins and biscuits and her doughnut. Never had anything tasted so delicious.

It was a brisk, sunny day, and Mandy looked at her garden and her plants, which were almost full-grown. They would be blooming in a week or so and she could hardly wait.

"I wish I could live here always," she thought wistfully. A blue jay winged back and forth across the clearing. He was finding food for his family. The same sparrow that had been bathing in the puddle the other day flew onto the garden fence.

"Hello, my friend," said Mandy and she smiled as the little bird cocked his head onto one side looking at her with a beady eye. "Would you like some crumbs?" Very gently, she tossed some onto the pathway, and, although he flew away for a second, the bird immediately returned and cautiously looked at the food.

"It won't hurt you," Mandy spoke in a soft voice. "Come on now." She sat perfectly still and suddenly the cheeky sparrow darted down and picked up the morsels.

Mandy threw him the last piece of her doughnut and he took that, too.

"I think you'll soon get used to me," Mandy said. "Now what shall I call you? Chip would be a good name, I think. That's the sound you make sometimes. Yes, Chip is a nice name."

She went into her little kitchen. She took the tin basin out of the sink and the box of soap out of the cupboard and carried them down to the stream. She filled the basin with water and poured the soap flakes in and stirred them around. Then she fetched the shell-room curtains and put them into the suds and washed them thoroughly. She rinsed them in the stream and wrung them and flapped them in the air to get the main creases out.

Mandy looked about her for a place to put them to dry. There was no clothesline and nothing to make one with. She thought of using the remainder of the twine that Jake had given her, but she feared it wouldn't be strong enough. Finally, she laid them out on top of the box hedge and weighted them down with stones so that they wouldn't blow away. She washed out her dirty dusters and laid them out to dry, too.

She tipped away her washing water and watched the remaining suds move slowly downstream.

The water rushed and tumbled along, making a soft, soothing sound. Mandy lay back on the grass and gazed at the clouds.

"What a super afternoon,' she breathed and gave a big, satisfied sigh.

Turning her head, Mandy could see the rhododendrons, behind the house, in full and beautiful bloom. The colors were breathtaking, maroon and pink and white. The sun beat down and the trees made dappled shadows. Before she knew it, Mandy had fallen fast asleep.

She could not see the little baby rabbit, fat and soft, that came out of the bank to stare at her curiously. She would have been delighted to know that he hopped quite close, ears twitching, alert and cautious, to obtain a better view of the girl asleep on the ground.

Mandy awoke with a start.

She sat up and rubbed her eyes, then she squinted up at the sky and tried to gauge the hour. It was almost dusk and time to return to the orphanage. How lucky it was that she had awakened.

She gathered her things together and stored them away neatly.

As she started out across the clearing a very large brown, gray, and white bird flew low over the grass, right in front of her.

Mandy stopped in her tracks. She saw the big blunt head and an enormous wingspan which she guessed to be two feet at least.

It was a barn owl.

The beautiful creature soared onto the limb of a tree and Mandy kept absolutely still, hoping it wouldn't see her. The bird looked around with great majesty, turning its head from side to side. Mandy knew that an owl cannot swivel its eyes as a human being can, and so it has to turn its whole head in order to see to left and to right.

She must have stood quietly for five minutes or more. Suddenly the creature, without seeming to move a feather, tipped forward off the bough and plummeted to the earth. Now the great wings beat in the tall grass and for a moment the rounded head came up to stare bleakly in her direction. Then, lifting up once more, the bird flew away into the trees, a small mouse dangling from its beak.

Mandy felt mixed emotions. She was painfully sorry for the little mouse, but was delighted to see the beautiful bird. It was a thrill to see him hunting like that.

She began to walk on home. Perhaps the owl lived nearby. If he did, then there were probably some buildings in the vicinity, for Mandy knew that barn owls prefer to nest in an outhouse or a barn. It was strange though that she had never come across any other buildings in the area.

She reached the big wall and resignedly climbed over it, leaving her world of nature and all things lovely behind, and rejoined the usual existence of noise and turmoil and children. It had been a wonderful afternoon.

Summer

The Garden

1

IT BECAME obvious to Mandy after a while that Sue definitely had the sulks. She knew the cause of the trouble. She and Sue were usually very close, but since the discovery of the cottage, Mandy had seen less and less of her friend, and, at times, had been quite rude about wanting to be alone. It was a bad situation.

One evening Sue said bitterly, "You're *always* going out by yourself. We never do anything together anymore."

Mandy tried to placate her, but Sue mumbled, "I just know you're up to something. I'll find out one day. You'll see."

The trouble was that Mandy began to feel very impatient. At first she tried to tolerate the other girl's mood, but, as time went by, she felt herself getting angry and that didn't help matters at all. One day things really came to a head.

Mandy had planned to spend a quiet hour at the cottage. Her plants were budding now and showing spots of color. With summer approaching there was always something new in the garden, or the clearing.

Mandy thought she had been unobserved as she climbed the wall, but, just as she came down from the apple tree, she heard a scuffling noise from the other side. Before she could hide, to her absolute horror Sue appeared at the top of the wall and gazed down at her.

"Hello. What are you doing?" she asked. Sue was smiling triumphantly, and Mandy knew that she had been deliberately following her.

She felt sick with anger, and it was with a great effort that she managed to keep her voice light.

"Oh, nothing. I'm just looking around."

She wasn't going to give Sue the satisfaction of seeing that she was in any way disturbed by her presence. If she could just act as though nothing bothered her, then maybe Sue would get bored and leave her alone.

"You're not supposed to be over there."

"I know," said Mandy. "But you do things you're not supposed to do sometimes. I'll come back over though."

She started to climb the tree, but Sue said, "No, I'll come down, too. It'll be fun."

"But you're not *supposed* to. You just said." Mandy had an edge to her voice. "We'll get into awful trouble." She tried to sound concerned, and indeed she was concerned, but for a different reason. If Sue came into the woods, she didn't know how she could stop her from exploring and discovering the cottage, too.

"Oh, phooey," Sue was saying. "It'll be an adventure." She climbed down the apple tree. "Hey, isn't it super over here!"

Mandy wanted to hit out and push Sue away. Never had she felt so angry. She considered climbing back over the wall to the orphanage and just leaving Sue alone. Maybe without her, Sue would give up any ideas she had of looking around. But what if she went off by herself and discovered the cottage anyway? It was better to stay and try to avert disaster.

"Let's explore," said Sue.

"No," Mandy said in a loud voice. "It might be dangerous."

"Well, I'm going to anyway." Sue started out.

"Oh, all right." Mandy pretended to give in. "But I'm going

this way," she said firmly and turned to the left onto a small track instead of following the bigger path to the cottage. It was the only thing she could think of to do.

Sue stopped. "Why?" she asked.

"I don't know. It looks more exciting. And there could be people on the main path. This way we won't be discovered."

Mandy walked on, praying that Sue would follow her. After a moment's hesitation the other girl ran to catch up with her. Mandy found herself trembling with relief. She strode out briskly, tight-lipped and furious. She wanted to get as far away from the cottage as possible.

The track kept parallel with the big wall. Both girls were silent as they walked. Mandy knew that Sue sensed her mood. The other girl was sullen and had an almost defiant air. There was not much to say.

"Must you walk so fast?"

"I'm sorry. *You* wanted to explore," Mandy replied.

But she slowed down a little. Somehow she would have to check her anger. She didn't dare antagonize Sue too much.

The wood became less dense. It was obvious that the narrow path was getting wider. A few hundred yards farther on, it was joined by two other paths coming in at right angles to theirs.

The really interesting fact was that all the paths led to a large wrought-iron gate which was set into the wall. Mandy was immediately interested. She wandered over to look at it and noted that the main road passed by just a few yards beyond. She saw a padlock on the gate and then her heart missed a beat. It wasn't locked.

"Sue, come and look at this." Mandy pushed the gate tentatively. It didn't move. She applied her weight to it, and it slowly swung wide.

"Golly." Sue was almost as interested as Mandy. "Be careful, Mandy. Don't go out until you're sure no one can see us."

The girls peeked out. Not a soul was around. They emerged and carefully swung the gate to a close behind them.

"But this is the road that leads back to the orphanage." Sue seemed surprised.

"I know," said Mandy.

She was delightedly aware of the fact. If the gate could remain unlocked, and she could see no reason why it couldn't, then this was exactly the new way to the cottage she had been hoping for. This would mean no more sneaking into the orchard when people weren't looking. No more fear of discovery. Now she could really leave the orphanage in full view of everyone, as though indeed she were going off on some errand. She could then sneak through the gate and double back to the cottage. Mandy smiled. Things were going to be much easier from now on.

"I wonder where those other paths lead to," Sue was saying. "Oh, Mandy, let's go there again one day and explore. It was fun."

"Perhaps," Mandy said.

It was too late now to get to the cottage, and, since she felt almost thankful to Sue for having unwittingly helped her, she linked arms with her friend and they spent the rest of the day together. For the first time in ages, they enjoyed themselves and the hostility of the recent past faded away. For the time being, at least.

2

BY THE FIRST of July all of Mandy's plants were in full bloom. The garden was a mass of color and she was beside herself with delight. It was a small miracle. She was kept busy with a lot of weeding, for not only the flowers thrived, but everything else as well. But it was worth it. The roses were blooming around the door. The nasturtiums were bursting all over the front flower beds, seeming to have no sense of direction and growing in a wonderfully untidy way, the curling stems hiding and twisting beneath the big leaves. Their flowers were mostly a bright orange or yellow with an occasional mahogany red bloom. And they had a coarse, tangy fragrance — an unforgettable scent.

The wallflowers were tall and dark and strong and a sort of brick-red or yellow color. The salvias were bushy and sharp crimson in flower. And the beautiful marigolds! Mandy liked them best of all. They looked as if they had actually caught hold of the sun and it had burnished them to a golden orange hue. They stood so rigidly proud, a wondrous mass of tiny petals laid thickly one on top of another.

In front of them the lovely pansies with their sweet faces and beautiful blotched markings were in all colors of red, apricot, deep yellow, blue, and velvety black. Mandy couldn't believe that such generous blooms could grow on such fine stalks.

The sweet alyssum grew in clumps to begin with. But it spread and spread as the summer wore on. It gave off a sweet, delicate perfume that was particularly noticeable in the late afternoon and early evenings.

Mandy's garden received many visitors. Bees, snails, ants and worms, the beautiful butterflies, and all manner of tiny creatures that she'd never seen before. The birds came, too. Blackbirds, thrushes, chaffinches, blue jays, even a tiny wren. Chip was a constant visitor now and seemed to bring all his relatives, as well as his own babies, to visit.

Mandy loved it all. She worked in her garden every chance that she had. She purchased a large pair of garden scissors from Mr. Simple and painstakingly used them to cut her tiny lawn. They were the best thing she could think of in order to level the grass. It took her ages and her hands were blistered, but she found it all worthwhile.

She purchased other items, too: cornflakes, powdered milk, a small loaf of bread, sugar, and a pot of Marmite. Every afternoon immediately after school was over, she made herself tea at the cottage and sat on her doorstep, drinking and enjoying the peace and quiet before commencing her chores.

One afternoon she made a pleasant discovery. She had been trying to tidy up some of the weeds at the back of the house near the kitchen door. Mandy noticed a large object lying half-hidden in the long grass. She picked it up and discovered it was a garden broom. The head of the broom was made of fine twigs bound together, and it would be splendid for tidying the pathway and the doorstep and even inside the house. Mandy was delighted with her find.

July progressed and the good weather continued. Mandy used the new route to the cottage every day and found that going through the little iron gate made the traveling much simpler, especially when she had things to carry. Sue occasionally suggested taking a walk in that area, but Mandy always found a reason to dissuade her.

The summer holidays were approaching. Mandy planned to clean the inside of her house from top to bottom. She wanted to do it once the school term was over, so that she could really take her time. She began collecting a supply of cleaning things, so that she would have the items at hand when she needed them.

Funds were short, of course. But now that she had taken what she wanted in the way of cutlery and china from the orphanage, she began to hide away small things like a bar of soap, or a washcloth, and one day she stole a large box of soap from the store cupboard.

Mandy's conscience troubled her, but she told herself that as soon as she had saved up enough money she would replace the items and no one would ever know the difference.

Unfortunately, the difference was spotted almost immediately.

3

MATRON BRIDIE didn't wait to summon Mandy to her study. She bore down on her one day immediately after breakfast was over.

Mandy spun around as her name was called. Her stomach kicked in panic as Matron's ample figure approached, reminding the already guilty child of a ship advancing under full sail.

"Mandy."

"Yes, ma'am."

"Have you been taking things from the orphanage?"

A pause.

"What things, ma'am?"

"Cutlery, crockery, some dry goods. Have you?"

Another pause.

"No, ma'am."

"I want the truth, Mandy."

Mandy felt that she was suffocating. She tried to look at Matron, tried to smile, but a pulse was beating at the side of her mouth.

"Mandy, *something* is the matter with you these days. I don't know what it is, but I do wish that you would consider telling me about it." Matron swept past her, leaving Mandy in a frightful state of anxiety.

The following morning, Matron assembled the entire orphanage in the dining room. She spoke in a very stern voice.

"Somebody in this house, I don't know who, has been taking certain items, and I want it stopped. Immediately. I am giving her one week in which to return them. If they are put back by the end of this week, there will be no punishment and I will say no more about it. However . . ." Matron paused and looked at the children. Mandy wanted to yell at the top of her voice, "It was *me;* I took them." But she bit her lip and remained silent. ". . . if they are not returned, and I do find the culprit," Matron continued, "and I *assure* you that I will, then, I shall be very angry, indeed."

The children buzzed with excitement. Who could it be?

Who could have done such a silly thing? And for what reason?

Mandy went to her room and lay on the bed. She felt sick and very unhappy. Did Matron know that she had taken the things? Did she address the entire orphanage just to make her feel bad? Mandy couldn't be sure. But she was sure of one thing. This terrible feeling inside her had to be stopped. She couldn't live with her conscience much longer. She had been lying about her activities for so long now that each day the strain seemed harder to bear. Now, to have the extra burden of guilt about the stolen goods was just too much. Mandy decided there was at least one thing she could do to make herself feel better. She could return the items she had taken, and as quickly as possible. She resolved to try to work overtime at the Jennings' store on Saturdays in order to buy her own cups and plates and knives and spoons.

And that is exactly what she did. By the end of the week Mandy had returned everything except the soap flakes which had already been used.

That Saturday, and the next, Mandy worked a full day and was able to make enough money to purchase a plastic cup and saucer and a plate, then a knife and fork and spoon. She had enough money left over for a good strong kitchen knife and a can opener.

She felt much better about it and wondered that she hadn't thought to work overtime before. It took hours away from her precious weekends, but it was a good way to make the extra money she needed.

Matron made no more mention of the stolen goods, and things seemed to return to normal.

4

THE SUMMER holidays arrived at last. The days blended into one long impression of sun and hazy skies, sweet-smelling grass and summer showers staining the brown earth black. For Mandy it was the happiest time she had ever known and her every waking moment seemed filled with birdsong and the ripple of the stream and the colors of her flowers.

She cleaned her cottage from top to bottom. She swept and dusted and scrubbed the front porch and the stairs. She washed the windows again and hung the clean curtains up in the shell room. She put shelf paper in the kitchen cupboard.

Also, she found a large wooden crate at the orphanage and managed to get it to the cottage. She covered it with the remaining shelf paper and it made a good table. She wished she had a chair to sit on. Since that was impossible, Mandy looked around for a large log, and she soon found one that made a very good seat. Not that she used it much. She usually preferred to sit on the front doorstep.

The rabbit family became used to her comings and goings and eventually took no notice of her at all. Quite often, when she was working in her garden, Mandy would stop and quietly watch one of them hop into the shadow of the hedge to play.

Chip was present almost every morning and seemed quite put out on the few occasions when she didn't bring him bread from the breakfast table.

There were days when Mandy didn't bother to work on the house or the garden at all. She lay on her tummy in the grass and discovered that, even though her garden might appear to

be totally still, the more she waited and watched and immo-
bilized herself, the more she became aware that her garden was
alive and moving in a hundred different ways.

It was a wondrous thing to discover an ant carrying something twice as large as itself, or a beetle moving slowly over the
blades of green to an unknown destination. She watched the
bees gathering nectar from her flowers and the small spiders
scuttling in all directions. At such times she forgot about her
everyday world and was transported into the kingdom of all
things small where a butterfly seems like an overwhelmingly
beautiful giant creature; where the smallest twig is a tree, and a
pebble a mountain.

Mandy was lying on the lawn one quiet afternoon. She had
been daydreaming for so long that she was in a sleepy stupor.
Suddenly, she was aware of a movement off to her right by
the stream. There was the noise of a displaced stone falling into
the water. For one paralyzing moment she feared that she had
been discovered. A hundred thoughts raced through her mind.
Who could it be? What should she say? Should she get up and
run? Luckily, she had the good sense to remain where she was,
and it was as well she did.

When she carefully raised her head a few seconds later, she
was rewarded with a most wonderful and surprising sight. A
young fallow deer had come down to the stream to drink. It
was standing so near to Mandy that she could clearly see the
brown spots on the fawn coloring and the small lump of a
tail with the white patch around it.

She drew in her breath with excitement and the lovely creature raised its head and gazed at her, seeming not at all afraid.
For the longest moment it stood there, the prominent ears

twitching. Mandy marveled at the creature's exquisite beauty — the delicate face with the almond-shaped eyes and the soft wet muzzle.

"Oooh," Mandy breathed. "You are lovely. Where do you come from? What shall I call you? Oh, please don't leave," she whispered. But the deer began to pick its way back into the woods, carefully placing one shiny black hoof precisely after another on the long grass.

Mandy watched until it disappeared almost magically through a shaft of sunlight in the trees.

"I hope he comes to visit again. I *hope* he does," she murmured fervently. "I shall call him Snow."

That night she dreamed of the deer. Strangely, the animal was holding her. She cuddled close into the soft fur and touched and kissed it gently. In the morning her pillow was wet with tears.

5

MANDY WANTED to borrow some garden shears from Jake. She needed them to cut her box hedges and trim her lawn properly. But she couldn't think how to get the shears without letting Jake know what she really wanted them for. She couldn't tell even a half-truth because he would know immediately that she still had a "project," and she was sure that he would mention it to Matron. Then she'd be in trouble again.

She still had problems getting away to the cottage each day. Her excuses were getting more and more difficult to find. She longed for just one complete day to herself, a day that could be free from worries and guilt and conscience. It seemed unlikely that she'd ever get it.

Meanwhile, there was the problem of the shears. She chatted with Jake one day about the garden and his plants, and in a nonchalant way she got around to mentioning the tools he used.

"Jake, your hedges are so nice — all neat and tidy. How do you keep them like that?"

"I use my big shears. Now, Mandy, you've seen me use them."

"Oh, yes," Mandy feigned surprise. "Aren't they heavy?"

"Yup." Jake was not in a talkative mood.

"Could I manage them?" Mandy asked innocently.

"I wouldn't let you."

"Why not?" She was startled.

"Because they're sharp, and they're my best, and they're not for the likes of little girls like you."

"But I could hold them, couldn't I? I mean, if you wanted to let me try them I could manage them? Couldn't I?"

"You could. . . ."

Mandy smiled.

"But I wouldn't," added Jake, after a pause. "So keep your thieving eyes off, young lady." He grinned at her.

And that was that!

Mandy wished very much that she hadn't brought up the subject. Now she was really stumped. She couldn't think of a single way to get around the problem. She let it go for a while, and just sulked every time she looked at her untidy hedges and her ragged lawn. She couldn't face the agony of using the scissors again — too many blisters that way and too much time spent on the job. And, anyway, scissors would be no good on the box hedges. She was determined to get those shears somehow.

And very suddenly a way presented itself.

Every August, during the Bank Holiday weekend, Matron Bridie took all the orphanage children on a day-trip to the sea. It was always a wonderfully exciting time and tremendous fun. The children looked forward to it each year. A charabanc was hired especially for the event!

This year, however, for the first time in her young life, Mandy had absolutely no desire to go on the excursion. She was far too preoccupied and involved with the cottage. She suddenly realized that, if she could avoid the annual outing, she would have one entire day to herself, which was exactly what she had been yearning for. And perhaps she could "borrow" Jake's shears without his ever knowing that she had touched them.

6

ON THE MORNING of the excursion, Mandy went down to breakfast with a serious face. She pretended she wasn't hungry and hardly ate a thing.

Afterward she approached Matron Bridie timidly. "Matron, I'm afraid I don't feel too well."

"What?" Matron seemed distracted. She was trying to gather all the children together for the outing. They were very excited and the noise was deafening.

"I said I feel rather queasy. I'm a bit trembly. I'm afraid I might be sick."

"Oh, Mandy." It was a sound of exasperation. Matron gave Mandy a long, hard look. "Do you have a fever?"

"I don't think so. I'm not sure."

Matron put her hand on Mandy's brow.

"No, you're as cool as can be. You'll be all right. A day at the sea is just what you need. The fresh air will do you good."

Mandy began to feel desperate.

"Oh, but . . . I honestly don't feel like a whole big day. Couldn't I just stay here and rest? I really do feel very odd."

She was by now so nervous and tense that she did indeed feel odd. It was easy to be convincing. Beads of perspiration stood out on her brow, and she swayed a little.

Matron hesitated.

"If I could just lie down for a while, I think I'd feel better. I could sunbathe in the garden later."

"Oh well, you'll have to stay here with Ellie. There's no one else around. It's really maddening that this should happen today."

The distracted woman moved off to find Ellie, and Mandy ran up to her room. She wanted to get away in case Matron suddenly changed her mind.

Though she felt guilty, Mandy was filled with a tremendous sense of relief. She so desperately needed a little peace and time to herself and she quite contentedly lay on the bed in no hurry to make a move. Today was a day to be savored. She listened to the children noisily departing below. She heard the big bus start up and accelerate away down the road. Suddenly everything was quiet.

Mandy felt that even if she didn't go to the cottage today she

73

was still justified in wanting to stay home. The quiet alone was worth it.

Ellie came in to see how she was.

"Are you feeling a little better?"

"Oh, yes," Mandy smiled. "Really, I just was feeling a bit wobbly and sick. I'm much stronger already."

"Did you eat any breakfast?"

"No."

"Well, you know it could be that you're hungry. Would you like me to get something for you?"

"Oh, Ellie." Mandy was starving. "I think it would be lovely. Shall I come down and help?"

"No, you stay there. I'll bring it up. How about bacon and eggs?"

"Mmm." Mandy beamed and felt warm all over. She snuggled back in the covers and relaxed. Already this was the most wonderful day. Never had she been so spoiled. She actually fell asleep for a half-hour and was surprised when Ellie came back with the tray.

She ate steaming hot scrambled eggs and bacon and drank a cup of warm, sugary tea.

Ellie sat on the bed and watched her.

"That's what you needed. You'll be all right now."

"Oh, yes. Thank you. I really feel fine. I think I could get up, actually."

"Good. What would you like to do?"

"Well, I think I'll play in the garden for a while. What about you?"

Mandy looked at Ellie and then smiled, because Ellie was blushing.

"Oh, I know. I bet Ron's coming over."

Ellie nodded. Ron was her boyfriend. He was apprenticed to Hutchins and Company, the local cabinetmakers, and he planned to marry Ellie as soon as he had saved enough money.

"Well, don't worry about me," Mandy said generously. "There's plenty for me to do. I feel just marvelous now, so you have a nice day with Ron."

She helped Ellie carry the tray downstairs, and she dried the dishes while Ellie washed them. It was glorious outdoors. It would be lovely at the seaside. Mandy hoped that all the children were having a good time.

She went into the garden and ran to Jake's potting shed. He, too, had the day off. She went inside and carefully took down the big clipping shears. They made a sharp, slippery sound as she scissored the air.

"Oooh, I'll have to be careful with these."

Mandy hid them in the orchard and ran back to find Ellie, who was sitting in the big kitchen with Ron.

"It's so lovely. I think I'll go for a walk. Hi, Ron. Okay, Ellie?"

"Don't be too long, Mandy."

"I won't. I'll be back to check with you."

7

SHE CLIMBED over the big wall because it was quicker and there was no risk of being caught today. Clutching the big shears, she ran all the way to the cottage.

The rabbits were out playing.

"Hello, family," Mandy called out to them gently. They sat up on their hind legs, looking alert and inquisitive, resting their front paws on white furry tummies.

"Good morning, birds. Good morning, Chip."

She threw the little sparrows some crumbs of bread and put some in the palm of her hand and held it out to Chip. But he wouldn't come that close.

"All right. I can wait," Mandy smiled. She chatted as she began to work.

"Now see, I'm going to cut the lawn today, so look out for worms, Chip. There'll probably be some."

She snipped at the tall grass with the shears and the sliced green blades fell easily and quickly.

"This is super!"

She worked diligently and within an hour had it completely finished. She brushed away the loose grass and carried it to the bonfire patch. Then she began to work on the hedges. They were overgrown and thick.

Mandy hacked away at a particularly stubborn branch and the shears went slithering all over the place.

"Oh, dash it." She sliced at the branch even harder. But the shears would not cut. The fact was that the branch was too thick and cutting with the shears was as ridiculous as trying to cut a telephone book with scissors.

Mandy threw them to the ground in disgust. "All that trouble to get the wretched things and now they don't work."

She stomped down to the stream and bathed her face in the cool, clear water. Something was disturbing her and she felt vaguely depressed. She stretched out on the mossy bank and took in deep breaths of fresh air. She stared up at the sky and noticed a beautiful hawk wheeling in slow circles overhead. He coasted on the warm air currents. She could even see the feathering on the tip of his wings. She wished she could fly, too, and be as free.

She thought about the hedge. "Now, obviously the thing to do is to cut all the easy stuff first. Then, maybe I can break the bigger branches off." She decided to try again.

Mandy snipped and cut. The thick branches stuck out and made the hedge look worse than ever.

She grabbed one with her hands and tried to twist it off but it was sharp and rough. Before she knew what was happening, she had skinned herself badly.

She began to cry. She really wasn't sure why. The hand didn't hurt that much. It was just so frustrating to have this lovely day go all wrong. It had started out so well and she had just this one chance to use the shears without Jake knowing. Now they were proving too difficult to handle. It was so frustrating.

Mandy blinked away her tears and picked up the shears once more. She was determined to make one last effort.

Angrily, she flailed at the offending branches, hacking and chopping and bending them in all directions. She got a firm grip on one branch, the shears bit into it well and she applied all her strength. Very quickly a disastrous thing happened. The shears twisted in her hands, widening the gap between the blades. The two halves were split apart by the thickness of the branch, and with a snap they broke altogether.

Mandy was aghast. She stared at the two blades in her hand, wishing that they would somehow magically come together again. The screw that held the blades had fallen into the grass.

She sank to her knees to search for it. It was nowhere to be seen. Even were she able to mend the shears, they would be so out of alignment and so terribly blunt that it would be impossible to use them again.

What should she do? Should she tell Jake? Or Matron? Or just wait until the damage was discovered?

She was very anxious. If Matron found out about the shears, she must surely then find out about the cottage. At the very least, she would know that Mandy still had some secret project going. Maybe she should throw herself on Jake's mercy. She could offer to buy a new pair of shears, but that still didn't solve the problem of explaining away the accident. Telling the truth to Matron might make punishment a little less severe. But then, for sure, her visits to the cottage would be forbidden.

On an impulse Mandy turned and threw the broken parts as far as she could into the bushes. The best thing was to say and do nothing at all. She would wait to see what happened.

Miserably, Mandy returned to the orphanage. She had no desire to stay at the cottage. Ron and Ellie were nowhere about. They had left a note for Mandy on the kitchen table saying that they, too, had gone for a walk and would be back soon. Mandy went to her room and pulled the curtains to shut out the light. Her hand throbbed from the skinning she had given it. She put on her pajamas and climbed into bed.

How she wished now that she had gone to the seaside. None of this awful, depressing day would have happened. By the time the children returned home, in the late evening, she had fallen into an uneasy sleep.

FOR TWO DAYS life went on much as usual, except that Mandy lived in a constant state of anxiety the whole time. It was almost a relief when the inevitable summons came to visit Matron in her study.

"Mandy, Jake tells me he's missing the new garden shears, and that you were the last person he talked to about them. Do you know anything about this?"

Silence.

"Mandy?"

The bile rose in Mandy's nervous stomach. Her heart beat a loud thump-thump.

"Come along, Mandy. Let's not have any of this nonsense."

The tears came. They coursed down Mandy's cheeks. She couldn't think what to say.

"Mmm. I see you *do* know something about this." Matron looked at her and then said almost sadly, "Oh, Mandy. I just don't understand it. You've always been such a reliable girl. And now this willful stealing. It was you who took the other things, wasn't it?"

Mandy nodded.

"I thought so. Of course, you'll return the shears to Jake immediately."

Mandy shook her head. "I can't," she gulped.

"Why not?"

79

"They're broken," she whispered.

Another pause.

Matron seemed at a loss for words. She finally said, "I think I'm entitled to an explanation of all this, Mandy."

"I can't."

"Is that all you can say, 'I can't?' Really now, tell me what all these silly tears are for. It's so unlike you."

Mandy remained silent.

"Mandy, I must tell you that if you don't tell me what all this is about, I shall have to give you some sort of punishment. I don't want to, but I can see no alternative. Now I'm asking you just once more. Won't you please tell me what is the matter?"

Mandy was almost at a bursting point. She longed for fresh air. She was determined to say nothing. Better to take her punishment than to have her beloved cottage taken away.

"Very well," Matron spoke quietly. "First of all, you will buy another pair of shears for Jake. I don't care how long it takes to save up for them. You will turn in your pocket money to me every week, and I will tell you when you have saved enough. Second, I am going to insist that you stay within the boundaries of the orphanage for the next week. No treats, no excursions, and early to bed."

"Oh, Matron . . ."

"Mandy! If you can't bring yourself to tell me the truth, then you'll have to suffer the consequences. Now I suggest that you go to your room and think about it. Should you change your mind and decide to tell me, you'll know where to find me. I'll be only too delighted to reduce your punishment."

Autumn

Foreboding and Punishment

1

IT RAINED on four of the following seven days. It was the longest, most miserable week of Mandy's young life.

She had never felt so desperate or depressed. Not to see her beloved cottage. To wonder how it looked and how her precious flowers were doing. Would they survive without her care? She felt claustrophobic and imprisoned. It was terrible.

Mandy wept copiously at first. Then, as the week slowly passed, her distress became resentment, then it grew into deep anger at everyone and everything around her. Many times she contemplated leaving the orphanage and running away to the cottage. Matron Bridie would be sick with worry about her. But no one would ever find her. She would live at the cottage forever. And it would serve Matron right!

Eventually, common sense prevailed, and she resigned herself to waiting out the week. The bad weather helped a little. At least there wouldn't be much to do in the garden, and the rain would certainly help her flowers.

She spent long hours in her attic bedroom, her face pressed to the window, not caring to do much of anything except sit and stare at the gloomy, gray skies.

The worst problem was that the children knew of her punishment. They saw her anguish and sensed that something was very wrong. Solicitous and curious, they fussed and crowded around Mandy. But she gave them no explanation. Sue seemed very concerned and really tried to be helpful. That was almost the worst part of all, for then Mandy longed to break down and tell her friend everything. She ached for sympathy and understanding. But she remained silent, and that was the very thing guaranteed to change Sue's mood and make her almost antagonistic toward Mandy.

She talked *at* Mandy, rather than *to* her.

"I just felt something was going on, Mandy. I knew you'd get into trouble sooner or later."

"Let's not talk about it, Sue."

"Besides, it's not right for you to be off by yourself all the time. Everybody's noticed it."

"Oh, shut up! Just *shut up!*"

The girls avoided each other the rest of the week.

2

MANDY NEARLY wept all over again when she finally saw her beloved cottage. She was so overjoyed at being there once more. The rain had played havoc with her garden, leveling a lot of the flowers and bringing the weeds up in profusion. It was amazing that in a single week they could grow so fast.

The stream was running higher than usual because of the rain. The current was strong and the water turbulent, carrying leaves and twigs that had fallen from the trees. Autumn was beginning. The big horse-chestnut tree was bearing its fruit —

rounded spiky capsules that carried the deep brown conkers that Mandy loved to collect. A pheasant picked its way slowly through the tall grass. Everything was still and gray and dripping wet. Mandy's feet got soaked.

She lit a fire in the shell room and put her shoes by the fire to dry. She was glad she had thought to store all of the wood. She made a trip to the woodpile for some extra logs.

When she opened the kitchen door, she received the most awful shock. There in the muddy earth just outside were two distinct, large footprints. Mandy couldn't believe her eyes. The footprints must have been made recently, otherwise the rain would have washed them away. They were big — probably made by a tall man's shoes or boots. It was alarming. For six months or more, she had not seen evidence of another soul. And now this.

Mandy felt scared for the very first time since she had discovered the cottage. Who could possibly have been wandering around the place? Was he a tramp? Or a burglar? Maybe he was still hiding in the woods. It was chilling to think that someone might be lurking around at this very moment.

Mandy found herself looking over her shoulder many times, as she sat before the fire. She wished she could lock the doors and close the curtains. The gray, bleak day didn't help matters either. It heightened her apprehension.

She tried to tell herself that it was silly to be frightened. Perhaps it wasn't someone bad. Perhaps it was the prince, the one she imagined lived in his castle somewhere in these same woods. Mandy brightened at this possibility.

She resolved to be more watchful and careful going to and

from the cottage from now on. She would notice someone before he noticed her, that was for sure.

On her way back to the orphanage she traced the ground carefully, looking for other footprints or clues. She almost jumped out of her skin when, as if put there purposely for her to discover, she stumbled upon the clear print of a horseshoe.

So, someone had been riding to the cottage. Mandy was excited. It couldn't have been a tramp. A tramp wouldn't ride a horse. But a prince would. So her guess was probably right. She tried to picture him. What would a prince look like? Did he ride a white horse? Maybe a shiny black one?

For many days she looked for other signs but found none. The beautiful deer, Snow, came to visit again though. He usually went to the stream, late in the day. Mandy always stopped whatever she was doing to watch him. She was convinced he saw her. Certainly he must have known she was near, must have scented one who visited the cottage so regularly. He seemed not to mind, and Mandy loved his company.

She idly wondered if the deer belonged to the prince. Did the prince feed him and stroke him and have him near always? It was comforting to feel that the animal was a presence they shared.

The autumn school term began. The weather was brisk and clear. The days grew shorter and it became dark earlier in the evenings. There wasn't much time for gardening except on the weekends.

Mandy tidied the weeds and pulled out some of the dead

summer flowers. It saddened her to do so. She was parting with beloved friends.

Somehow with the coming of autumn, her previous longings and depressions seemed to return.

She was a little cheered to note the Michaelmas daisies come into bloom. Pale mauve flowers, with slender, green, upward-growing leaves. She discovered a few straggly chrysanthemums. The holly trees were showing a lot of red berries. The more berries, the harder the winter, people said.

Matron informed Mandy that she would deduct six weeks of her pocket money in order to pay for a new pair of shears. When all was said and done, Mandy felt that she had been let off lightly, considering what might have happened as a result of the incident. Though she would never forget the misery or the anxiety she felt during her week's detention, nevertheless she had still managed to keep her secret. And that was worth almost anything.

3

SUE INFORMED Mandy one day that she was going to take a walk by the gate in the stone wall. She said it somewhat defiantly. Then she looked directly at Mandy and added nonchalantly, "You can come, too, if you like."

Mandy felt she had no choice. She had been avoiding this for so long. Sue had once intimated that she thought Mandy used the gate all the time. She was sure Sue was only going there because she knew Mandy didn't want her to. Mandy anxiously wondered just how long it would be before someone inevitably discovered the cottage, as she had done. It was a depressing thought. Reluctantly, she trudged along the road, silent and angry, beside Sue.

It was a total surprise to both girls when they reached the gate to discover that it was locked. There was a brand-new chain and padlock attached to the iron bars.

Sue asked, "Did you put this on, Mandy?"

"No, I was just about to ask you." Mandy stared at it, somewhat dazed.

"Not me. I wonder who did."

Mandy was thinking of all the people who might want the gate locked. Matron? Possibly. Jake? That was more probable. He could have discovered the open gate and locked it to prevent any orphanage children from going through. It was very puzzling though. The only other thought that occurred to her was that it was somehow all connected with the footprints she had found. Perhaps that unknown someone was responsible for the padlock and chain. Her heart skipped a beat.

"Well, it looks like you won't be walking this way any more." Sue looked slyly at Mandy.

Mandy shrugged with a couldn't-care-less attitude. "Let's go look for blackberries," she said, proud of herself for not rising to the bait.

She was glad that the gate had been locked. Maybe it would stop Sue from being so suspicious of her. But now she would have to climb the orchard wall again. And that was a problem. It was always risky.

4

NOVEMBER CAME roaring in with gusty winds and more wet weather. Mandy's depression would not go away. Her garden seemed sad, too. It was virtually empty now, and the few brave flowers that remained were flattened by the rain, their yellow stalks sprawling in all directions. Most of the trees were bare, and the woods had a wet carpet of leaves.

The cottage was damp and cold. Drafts came sharply through every crack in the walls and even into the shell room. Mandy kept a fire going as often as possible. Her supply of wood was not large and would soon be finished. It was impossible to collect more because of the rain.

She longed for the spring to come again, for sunny days and a time when she could plant her garden once more and watch it grow. The prospect of the long, cold winter made her despondent.

Matron informed her that she could keep her earnings again from the Jennings' store. The shears were finally paid for.

Mandy immediately purchased more matches and a lot of candles. She often did her homework by their flickering light. In the cottage in the late afternoon, Mandy sat in an empty room, with only her books and a fire for company.

The weather remained cold. Mandy woke one Sunday morning to discover frost on the ground. She ate a hurried breakfast and slipped away to the cottage. It was becoming increasingly difficult to climb the big wall. In wet weather the bricks were slippery. She suffered scraped shins, and once she had fallen and banged her knee badly. Today her fingers ached from the cold. She paused to blow on them to warm them, but seconds later they only felt colder. Her breath hung mistily in the air. She ran to keep herself warm, but running made her chest hurt, so she slowed to a walk. She wished she had put on warmer clothes and some gloves.

When she reached the clearing she paused. The cottage looked pretty in the pale morning light. For a moment she felt the old thrill of excitement at seeing it.

For the best part of a year she had cherished and loved this special place. It was her very own and still no one knew her secret.

There were patches of sparkling frost on the grass. It had outlined the spider webs in the garden. They shimmered and swung gently like beaded, gossamer curtains.

A sound over her head made her look up. A heron was moving in slow majesty low over the trees, its wings beating heavily at the air, its long neck extended in purposeful flight.

Mandy wondered what the heron was doing in this neighborhood. Perhaps the stream led to a river or a weir. But if it lived nearby it was strange that she had not seen it before now.

She crossed the wet clearing, opened the garden gate, and walked up the path. Suddenly she spun around in her tracks. She had never opened the gate before.

Usually it was leaning neatly alongside the fence where she had once placed it. It had been broken. Now it was mended and had a shiny new black latch.

Her heart turning somersaults, Mandy tried to remember if it had been like this the day before. She couldn't remember.

She thought of the other gate, the big iron one that had the new padlock. Strange that these two things should happen in such quick succession. Who could have mended this gate? And why?

She fetched a saucepan and filled it with clear, icy water. Then she boiled it on the trivet, and made herself tea. The hot liquid tasted good, but it hurt when she drank it down. She realized, with a small shock, that she had been experiencing a sore throat for the past two days. She really hadn't been conscious of it until now.

Holding the cup in both hands and trying to warm her fingers, she shivered slightly. She wasn't sure if it was because she was cold or if she was just frightened.

It was disturbing to feel that someone had been around the cottage again. Although mending the gate was actually a harmless thing to do, nevertheless, *someone else knew of the place* and surely knew of Mandy, too. Until Mandy found out who he was, she couldn't feel safe. She didn't like the uneasy feeling she experienced.

She didn't stay long at the cottage. Today she had a desire to return to the security of the orphanage. She couldn't get rid of the premonition that something was about to happen.

5

STRANGELY ENOUGH, something *did* happen, and almost immediately. First of all, Mandy came down with a cold. It didn't seem anything to worry about though, so she said nothing to Matron or Ellie. The last thing she wanted was to be kept indoors on account of a common cold.

The other something that happened was far more important. On her next visit to the cottage, she received the most incredible surprise. Her garden had magically been cleared of all the weeds and dead flowers. The box hedges had been trimmed and the lawn clipped. A considerable area of the clearing had been tidied, too. The Michaelmas daisies were untouched and so was the rose tree over the doorway.

Feeling already somewhat fuzzy from the cold, Mandy had the distinct impression that she was in the middle of a strange and wonderful dream. Who could possibly have done this marvelous work? Was it the same someone who had fixed the gate?

Then Mandy received the biggest surprise of all. Nailed to the doorjamb was a note — a plain piece of white paper with capital letters printed on it.

Her heart thumping, Mandy removed the paper carefully and read.

FOR THE LITTLE GIRL WHO COMES HERE. HOPE YOU LIKE THE GARDEN.

And it was signed: AN ADMIRER.

"Oh, golly," Mandy spoke out loud. Hardly knowing what she was doing, she wandered around the garden in a dazed state, touching the gate and its new latch and smoothing her hand over the short, clipped grass. She fingered the note lovingly and read it over and over again. Her excitement was so great that she wanted to shout out loud, *everything is all right now*. Whoever had written the note *must* be kind and generous and good. Not someone to frighten and hurt her. It was a tremendous relief.

But where, oh where, was the friend who had done this lovely thing? Who was he? Mandy was almost convinced now that he was her prince. Who else could have managed surprises of such magnitude?

It seemed that all her dreams were coming true. Would the prince appear one day? She prayed that she would meet him. She stayed at the cottage as late as she dared just in case he returned. When nothing happened, she slowly wandered home toward the orphanage with many a backward glance at the cottage, still hoping he would come.

What a lovely world it was. Mandy wished that there was someone with whom she could share her secret.

All night long she lay awake wondering whether she should confide in Sue, or maybe Ellie.

As the hours lengthened, she tossed and turned and longed for sleep. But it would not come. This intense excitement was worse than any Christmas Eve, wondering what the next day would bring. Mandy wanted more than anything else in the world to solve this mystery, to meet her prince, to know him, to thank him. Perhaps tomorrow.

As the dawn crept into the sky, Mandy wearily decided, once again, that she would keep her secret to herself. When all was said and done, it was still too risky. If Matron found out, or if Sue couldn't keep the secret, the whole orphanage would know in no time.

Mandy need not have worried. By the following afternoon the issue had resolved itself.

6

MANDY WISHED that she didn't have to go to school the next morning. Her cold was worse. Her head was so stuffy and she was so tired from not sleeping that she couldn't think clearly. And, of course, she wanted very much to see if there was another surprise at the cottage.

But there was a problem. If she didn't go to school, she would have to think of a reasonable excuse. If she admitted to fatigue or a cold, she would be kept at home. That would mean no trip to the cottage at all. So avoiding Matron and Ellie, she forced herself to dress, eat breakfast, and go to school. She tried to behave as though nothing were wrong.

She wondered what she would find at the cottage later that day; hopefully, an explanation of all the wonderful happenings there. Would AN ADMIRER make himself known? If he didn't, perhaps she should leave him some kind of a thank-you note for his generosity? That would be the polite thing to do.

It was all so exciting. Mandy felt fevered and flushed. There was a strange throbbing in her head. It seemed that school would never come to an end. She was not interested in writing and mathematics and basic grammar today. It was impossible to concentrate.

94

Mandy felt tremendous relief when the school bell finally rang. At least the rest of the afternoon was her own.

She would have run to the cottage had she not been so tired. All was serenely quiet when she arrived — such a contrast from school.

Mandy looked across the clearing. Everything was as usual. Nothing changed. Nothing stirred. She experienced a feeling of disappointment. She had been so keyed-up all day, looking forward to this one moment.

She told herself that it was early yet, that she really mustn't expect too much. Perhaps AN ADMIRER was not able to come here every day.

Then, as she walked through the doorway into the cottage, she gave a cry of joy. In the middle of the living-room floor was an object wrapped in cellophane. It was a huge chrysanthemum plant, all russet and golden blooms, bursting with life. Nestled among the suede-soft leaves there was *another note*. So he had been here today. She hadn't been just daydreaming or letting her imagination run wild.

Mandy snatched up the note with trembling fingers and read:

FLOWERS FOR MY DARK-HAIRED FRIEND
TO PUT IN THE GARDEN BECAUSE I TOOK
SO MANY AWAY.

AN ADMIRER

Mandy touched her hand to her forehead. It was all so incredible. Why would anyone be so wonderfully kind? Why should this be happening to her?

She was just about to remove the cellophane from the flowers when she sensed a movement behind her. For one paralyzing moment she knew there was another presence in the room besides her own. She spun around quickly and saw a dark shape silhouetted against the light. She screamed.

Sue was standing in the doorway.

"Hey, I'm sorry. Did I frighten you?"

Mandy was speechless. For a full second she was unable to move, but then she instinctively drew her hands behind her back to hide the note. Had Sue seen her reading it?

"I followed you from school," Sue said by way of explanation. "I could just tell you had something to do today. You couldn't concentrate for anything." She stepped into the room. "Gosh, this is really neat."

Mandy found her voice. "It's mine," she said.

"So?" Sue shrugged her shoulders. "How did you find it?"

"Oh, I — just did." Mandy felt a wave of anger. What a horrible thing for Sue to have done! How could she have followed her? What on earth was she going to say to her? How could she explain this cottage? How could she get Sue away from here?

"Is this where you've been coming every day?" Sue excitedly moved toward the shell-room door and gasped as she opened it. "Wow — look at this."

"Get out of there," Mandy said with such vehemence that Sue looked startled.

96

"What's the matter with you?"

"You shouldn't have followed me. You had no right to just come barging in here. That's a mean and sneaky thing . . . "

Sue interrupted, "Well, you're not supposed to be here either."

"That doesn't matter." Mandy was becoming confused. "This is my place. It's been mine for ages. Now go away, and leave me alone. Go and find some other place of your own."

She was so angry she began to cry. Then she started to cough. She felt simply awful. The worst thing was that, even should she be able to make Sue go away, she knew about the cottage now. Nothing could change that. It spoiled everything. No more secret days to herself. No longer could she pretend that this cottage was her very own place.

"There's no need to get so upset," Sue was saying. "You look awful. Are you all right?"

"Of course I am. It's just that you make me so angry. It's all your fault."

"Well, how was I to know?" Sue was getting angry, too. "Where'd you get these?" She pointed to the chrysanthemums.

"I bought them."

"How'd you get the money?"

"I saved it."

Mandy desperately cast about in her mind for something to distract the other girl. What if she found out about AN ADMIRER? It seemed that the whole world was beginning to collapse today. And she felt so sick! She began to cry again.

Sue looked at Mandy and then said, in a more subdued voice, "I think we should get out of here. We ought to go home. Matron doesn't know where we are. We could get into trouble."

"Don't you tell her." Mandy became almost hysterical. "You're *not* to tell her."

"All right, all right. I won't." Sue seemed anxious now and began to pull Mandy outside. "I think you're getting sick. You really look sort of queer. Let's go, Mandy. Please."

Mandy felt tremendous relief. Unwittingly, her tears had been the answer. Sue was so concerned about Mandy that her interest in the cottage was temporarily put aside. Mandy willingly let herself be led away.

"If you don't say anything," she babbled, "I'll show you the cottage another time. But you must let me do it, because I found it. Maybe I'll let you share it, too. Only you mustn't say a word."

Mandy would have promised Sue anything at this point. Better to try to make her an ally than to have her hostile and telling tales. If only she could keep Sue out of the cottage until she felt just a little better. Then she'd think of something. She wished she could get rid of the fuzzy feeling in her head.

The girls climbed the big stone wall. Mandy was trembling. She was still terribly upset and supposed it was some sort of reaction to that.

Matron worriedly accosted them the minute the girls entered the house. "Where have you two been?"

They hesitated and she looked sharply at Mandy's tear-stained face. "What's the matter, Mandy? What happened?"

Mandy opened her mouth to speak, but Sue broke in first. "She's not feeling very well, Matron. We — uh — stayed at school for a while — and then I brought her home."

Matron placed a hand on Mandy's brow.

"You're running a fever, child. Go and get into bed immediately," she said. "Sue, run and tell the cook to make a hot drink. I'll bring you some aspirin in a moment, Mandy."

7   🙢🙠🙢🙠🙢🙠🙢🙠🙢🙠🙢🙠🙢🙠🙢

IT WAS THE most exquisite relief to lie down in bed between the cool sheets. Mandy buried her face in the pillow and tried to sort out her chaotic emotions. Was she getting really sick? What would happen if she were? She realized that she was still clutching the note from AN ADMIRER in her hand.

She read it again. It was a great comfort. At least this was one thing Sue didn't know about.

Matron came in with a hot drink and some aspirin.

She took Mandy's temperature. "Hmmm — not too bad, but that's a nasty cough, Mandy. You'll have to stay in bed until I say you can get up."

"Oh, but, Matron," Mandy sat up, suddenly concerned, "I can't stay in bed."

Matron feigned surprise.

"You can't?" She smiled.

"No — I — oh, please don't make me. I hate it so." Mandy couldn't find the right words. "I really don't feel too bad at all."

Matron sat down on the edge of the bed. "Well, we'll see how you go. It won't be for so very long. I've asked Dr. Matthews to stop by in the morning. He'll take a look at you." She folded her hands. "But, Mandy, I'm afraid I must ask you not to stay outdoors as much as you have been doing."

She mistook Mandy's horrified look for one of guilty surprise.

"Yes, I've been meaning to mention this. You're out all day long. We never see you. I spoke to you about it once before, if you remember. I'll say nothing more now. But I don't want it to continue."

"But why?" Mandy blurted out.

"Because it's late in the year. And too cold. I'm sure that's why you've caught this chill. Also, it gets dark so very early. I don't think it's safe."

Mandy was beside herself with grief. "No, no." She was

shaking her head. "That's not fair. You don't understand. You mustn't stop me."

"Mandy," Matron's voice was firm, "I don't want any more talk about it."

"But —"

"No 'buts' — when the warmer weather comes again, we'll discuss this matter. Until then, I do *not* want you staying out until all hours. You are to return home immediately after school. And you are to stay in the orphanage vicinity on weekends. Is that understood?"

Matron's words left Mandy feeling utterly desolate. How could she explain that taking away her freedom was like taking half her life as well? Her whole being was centered around the cottage, and now that such exciting things were happening, she shouldn't be prevented from going there. But what could she say to Matron? Mandy had no desire to tell anyone about AN ADMIRER. She was terrified that he would disappear if she so much as breathed a word.

And what of Sue? Would she say something to Matron? Or would she just investigate the cottage by herself? Matron hadn't said anything to *her* about not going out.

At bedtime Sue was quiet and concerned. She made no mention of the afternoon, and Mandy was feeling too ill and miserable to bring the subject up.

She was in a dreadfully anxious state. She tossed and turned most of the night. A wind had sprung up, and it buffeted around the big house. Mandy, restlessly, thought it a bad omen.

She eventually fell into an exhausted and fitful sleep.

She never heard Sue get up and leave for school the following day. It was late when Matron Bridie bustled in to wake her up.

"Good morning, good morning." She flung wide the curtains. "Dr. Matthews is here to see you, Mandy. Do you think you can wake up?"

Mandy groggily raised herself up and blinked in the daylight. She had had bad dreams and she felt heavy-headed.

Dr. Matthews' big frame filled the doorway. "Well now, what have we here? Someone not feeling too well?"

Mandy managed a weak smile. She liked Dr. Matthews. He exuded warmth and cheerfulness wherever he went. It was always good to see him. He wore a dark jacket and faintly striped trousers. She noted that he had a diamond tiepin. He always looked as if he had just come from a wedding. He sat down beside her on the bed.

"Anything to tell me?" he asked. "What's been happening in your young life lately?" He watched her closely.

"Oh, nothing much."

Mandy wondered what he would think if she told him about the cottage. She wished she could tell him.

Dr. Matthews examined her chest and back. He looked into her throat and her

102

nose and her ears. He smelled of antiseptic and expensive toilet water. She liked the feeling of comfort he gave her.

"Now, my dear, you're really not too bad at all. But do as Matron says and stay in bed. You'll be right as rain soon." He looked down into her troubled face. Bending slightly he cupped his hand under her chin.

"You're *sure* there's nothing you'd like to tell me? Nothing on your mind?"

For an aching moment Mandy's eyes brimmed with tears. If she could just unburden herself to someone. She shook her head and said simply, "I don't like you to go so soon."

"Oh, Mandy, neither do I. But I have to get to the hospital. I'll look in on you this evening though. Maybe we can spend a little more time together then."

She watched him gather up his instruments and stride briskly to the door. He winked at her and went out of the room. She listened as he walked quickly down the hall and then she heard him talking quietly to Matron. She couldn't hear what they were saying.

"How is she, Doctor?"

"Well, I want her kept in bed for a few days. She does have a fever and also some faint sounds in her chest that bother me. But I'll keep a close watch on that. I'll drop by this evening."

"Anything special that we should do?"

"No. Keep her on plenty of liquids, and rest, of course. Have this prescription made up for her." He scribbled rapidly on a pad. "If she's not improved in a day or two, I'll have her brought into the hospital for some X rays." He lowered his voice. "She seems a bit sad — a little sorry for herself, perhaps?"

"Yes. I've been terribly concerned about her for some time. She has been so evasive, and I can't seem to reach her. Something is troubling her. She looks as if she didn't sleep a wink last night."

"Hm. I wonder what goes on in that head of hers! She's a sweet child." Dr. Matthews looked at his watch. "Hannah, I must dash. I'm late already."

"Thanks for stopping by, Brian."

"No trouble. See you tonight."

Mandy lay in bed staring through the skylight at the gray clouds scudding by outside. It seemed so quiet and lonely in her room now that the doctor had gone. The day stretched ahead of her interminably long.

The miserable, lonely ache was with her again. What was she to do? Dr. Matthews had said to stay in bed until she was better. But what if that were two or three days from now? Or even a whole week?

She thought of the cottage, alone and unattended for all that time. She remembered that other agonizing week when she had been unable to visit it. Her anxieties came flooding back. She sat up in bed, her chin on her knees.

What if AN ADMIRER left another note for her today? What if he returned later to discover that it hadn't been received? Supposing he gave up trying to communicate with her after a while. What would he feel when he saw that she had neglected to take care of the beautiful plant he had given her? For the rest of the morning Mandy worried the problems around in her head.

Ellie brought her in some lunch and she picked at it listlessly, not hungry at all.

If only she could somehow leave a note for AN ADMIRER. Tell him that she was not feeling well and was confined to bed. That she was forbidden to visit the cottage anymore. He would surely understand. She would leave the orphanage address on the note, too. Then one day they could arrange to meet. Perhaps in the spring.

But how was she to get the note to him? If only she could visit the cottage just once more.

She considered taking Sue into her confidence after all. But she wouldn't be back from school until the late afternoon. What if Sue didn't return from school, but went straight to the cottage to see it again for herself? It was possible that AN ADMIRER would leave a note for Mandy as he had before, and Sue would discover it.

It was these last thoughts that drove Mandy to a foolish decision. No matter how dangerous and risky the undertaking, and even should Matron find out and give her the worst possible punishment, she had to get to the cottage herself. Today!

8

MANDY PRETENDED great fatigue. She told Ellie that she thought she would sleep all afternoon and asked if she would mind leaving her alone until she woke up and called for her.

Ellie was only too delighted. She pulled up the curtains in Mandy's room and made a big fuss about tucking her in and getting her comfortably settled.

"Please close the door, Ellie, so I don't hear any noise."

"Right-ho. Sleep well, Mandy."

"Mm. Thank you."

Mandy waited a good five minutes. Her heart was thumping loudly. The big house seemed very quiet. None of the older children were home from school yet. The younger ones were either resting or attending classes.

She got out of bed as quietly as possible and pulled on some slacks and a sweater. She was nervous and her legs felt wobbly.

She stuffed a pillow into her bed and rearranged the covers over it in such a way that anyone looking from the door would think she was still huddled under the blankets, fast asleep.

She hoped no one would bother to check on her. With any luck, she would easily be back within the hour.

Pulling open her bedroom door, she looked down the corridor. Not a soul in sight. She stealthily made her way down the stairs. It was quite terrifying to imagine being caught and she had no ready explanation for her disobedience. She didn't dare think of the consequences if someone should see her. She paused at the bottom of the stairwell and tried to gauge where the sounds in the house were coming from. She could hear Alice in the kitchen talking to Ellie. A typewriter clacked in Matron's study. Quietly running to a side door, Mandy tentatively opened it and was greeted by a blast of cold air. It was blowing hard outside.

The wind was whipping around the corners of the big house.

Ominous clouds chased each other across the gray sky.

Mandy hesitated. The cold air penetrated her clothing and seemed to reach to her very marrow, making her aware how feverish and vulnerable she was. But she had come this far and, having made the effort, it seemed silly to turn back now. It was imperative that she leave some word for AN ADMIRER. If she kept moving, she would stay warm.

She hurried through the orchard, keeping low in case someone spotted her. She came to the foot of the big wall and looked up. It towered above her head. She had not noticed how really high it was until today.

If only the big gate could have remained unlocked, she wouldn't have to make this terrible climb. Shivering, Mandy grasped for the familiar footholds and slowly pulled herself to the top. The wind sighed through the orchard. The branches of the apple tree whipped across her face.

She had just lowered herself to the ground on the other side when the deluge began. It seemed as though the heavens opened up and descended in one massive torrent. The rain poured down.

Mandy was at her wit's end. Fearful and already soaking wet, she wondered what she ought to do. She didn't have the energy to climb back over the wall. Taking refuge under a tree seemed foolish. That way she would only get colder and wetter. It was better to push on toward the cottage.

Though she had traveled the path so many hundreds of times before, the driving rain obscured everything and for a moment she was even unsure that she was going in the right direction. But then a flash of lightning split open the sky and she saw for an instant the clearing and her little cottage brilliantly il-luminated in the furious downpour. She ran the last hundred yards or so and stumbled through the doorway just as the rumbling thunder crashed out directly overhead.

9

MANDY WAS soaked to the skin. Her teeth were chattering. She felt horribly dizzy, and she had a sharp pain in her chest from running so hard.

Inside the cottage it seemed unusually dark. The stormy sky made it seem like night instead of midafternoon. She went to the kitchen cupboard and fumbled for the matches. She found candles and lit them. They flickered fitfully in the draft.

Was there another note from AN ADMIRER? Mandy wandered through the house looking for some sign that he had returned. She found none. Possibly he hadn't come because of the bad weather.

She was concerned about being so wet. Instinct told her that her fever was higher. The first thing to do was to get dry some-how.

She gathered the last of her firewood and managed to get it burning in the grate. She huddled close to it, her clothes steaming. But the warmth made her feel sick and she moved away. She wished there were somewhere she could lie down.

It was so cold that she tugged one of the curtains down from the window and wrapped it about her. Lightning flashed and she recoiled in fright.

She began to talk aloud in order to comfort herself. "I mustn't forget what I came here to do. I shall write my letter. That's the most important thing. Then I shall try to get home." Again the thunder rumbled overhead.

For the first time, the orphanage seemed an awfully long way away. Mandy began to worry that she would not make it back through the woods. She felt so weak.

"What I'll do is just rest here a while, 'til I feel a little better. And the storm will go away. And then it will be easy."

She found a pencil and some paper and wondered what she should say to AN ADMIRER. It was difficult to concentrate. Her hand was shaking. She printed as best she could, DEAR SIR.

It didn't look right on the paper and she crumpled it up and tossed it on the fire. On a fresh piece she wrote:

DEAR ADMIRER

I AM NOT FEELING WELL AND CANNOT COME TO THE COTTAGE ANYMORE.

She hesitated, then crumpled that piece of paper up, too. What a silly thing to write! What would AN ADMIRER think of her? Just because she was sick didn't mean that she couldn't come to the cottage *ever again*. Though, in fact, that was what she was trying to say, wasn't it? Mandy wished she didn't feel so muddled.

She began again, laboriously:

DEAR FRIEND

The words seemed to blur in front of her. Mandy put a hand to her brow and was amazed to feel how burningly hot her forehead had become.

"Oh dear." She looked up and saw the flickering candlelight playing over the luminous shell walls. They seemed to be undulating waves of mother-of-pearl. The lightning flashed again, and through the window the bare trees were silhouetted against the turbulent sky. Mandy held her breath in very real panic.

If only somebody could be with her. She wished now that she had waited for Sue before coming to the cottage. She would never have come at all if she had known there was going to be a storm like this. If only there were someone here to talk to. Even Chip, the sparrow, would have been company. The little bird was probably tucked away somewhere, safe and dry. Mandy wondered about the beautiful deer Snow. Was he alone out there trembling and frightened by the noise and the lightning? Perhaps the prince had taken Snow into the castle for warmth and shelter. She hoped so.

Mandy remembered her letter and absently picked up the pencil to write once more. Her brain seemed to be turning around and around. Why had she come? To write the letter, of course. But how silly! The prince couldn't possibly come here today. Not in this weather. What was so important about a letter? Something to do with Sue. And Matron would be so angry.

DEAR FRIEND,

I AM VERY SICK. AND I AM WORRIED THAT

A stabbing pain went through her chest, and Mandy was suddenly very short of breath. There was a loud crash against the window, and she screamed and stumbled to her feet. She had a glimpse of some wild, storm-frightened bird careening off into the darkness. She stepped back and fell against the stool that she had been sitting on. The room spun about her. Mandy whimpered in fear and pain, rocking herself backward and forward.

If only the fire hadn't burnt out. The candles were dripping, crying like the black skies outside. There were more flashes of light and the walls seemed to be coming in close to fall on top of her. *Go away.* There were dark shadows all around her. And a shape in the corner, like a man. Arms raised high.

But this is *my* house, she thought. *Get out.* Oh, please, don't frighten me so. Stop this spinning in my head. This pain in my chest. This noise. Will someone come from the orphanage? Will they know that I've gone out into the storm? But no one will know where to look for me.

Mandy's panic was suddenly so great that she managed to stumble to her feet. She had to get away from the cottage. She must somehow get home.

She flung the shell-room door wide and was greeted by a blast of icy air and sheets of rain driving in through the open front door.

The lightning split the sky once more, and it was too much for Mandy. Too frightened now and too ill to go anywhere, she sank to the floor, her hands over her ears to shut out the fury and the noise all around her.

"Mummy," she heard herself crying. "Oh, Mummy."

And then black spinning darkness engulfed her.

10

MATRON BRIDIE stared at Ellie in some consternation.

"What do you mean, she's not there?" she asked.

"Just that, ma'am. I went up to wake her like you said. But she's not in her bed."

"Well, she's probably in the bathroom. Did you look?"

"Yes, I . . . ma'am, her bed had the pillow all stuffed down, like it was meant to be her, still lying there."

There was a pause. Hannah Bridie felt a growing sense of apprehension. She had felt the same the previous evening, but she had not really examined her feelings at the time. Now, it seemed she should have been more aware. She should have watched Mandy more closely.

"What on earth is that child up to!"

She swept past Ellie and climbed the stairs to the attic bedroom. She wanted to see for herself. Mandy was obviously not there, and the bed did have a deliberately "made-up" look. The pillow lay neatly beneath the covers, looking very much like a body asleep.

"Mandy," Matron called the name once in the darkened room. She knew there would be no answer. There was just the sound of the rain pounding down on the attic roof. Slowly she made her way down the stairs again. She was very concerned.

Ellie was waiting at the foot of the stairway.

"Dr. Matthews is here," she said quietly.

Matron paused a moment and then said, "Come with me,

Ellie." She walked into her study.

Dr. Matthews was standing by the fire. He was shaking drops of rain from his hair and wiping his forehead with a handkerchief.

"My God, it's a dreadful evening out there. I got soaked just coming in from the car."

"Brian, a very worrying thing has happened. It's unbelievable, but Mandy is missing. We can't find her. Ellie went to her room to wake her up just now and she wasn't there."

"What!" The doctor looked startled. "What do you mean?"

"A pillow has been left deliberately between the sheets of the bed. It looks as though she meant us to think that she is still there."

"But why would she do that? Surely she didn't go outside?"

"I've no idea. I can't see why she would on such a terrible day. Unless she was delirious or sleepwalking or something!"

"She seemed fine, Matron, when I put her down to rest," Ellie spoke up.

"But, good God, if she is out in this weather she'll catch her death." The doctor spoke on a rising note of anxiety. "She could come down with pneumonia in two seconds flat. That child shouldn't be out of bed at all."

Matron turned to Ellie.

"Ellie, I want you to look all over the building. Don't say a word to anyone. Maybe she went to the kitchen to see Alice. Try there first. We musn't panic about this until we're quite sure she's not in the house. Oh, and, Ellie, find Sue and send her to me." Ellie nodded and hurried out.

"Why Sue?" The doctor was surprised.

"Oh, just a thought. She and Mandy are very close. And something about the way they came home from school yesterday — it was when I first noticed Mandy was sick."

Matron thought back to the moment when she had seen Sue and Mandy entering the big house. Mandy had not only looked sick, but she had seemed upset and distraught as well. But the events that followed had taken Matron's mind away from that fact. She recalled it was then that she had first felt some vague apprehension.

"What if she's not in the house?" Dr. Matthews was asking.

"Then I suppose I should call the police or something. Oh, dear."

"Mmm." The doctor drew a pipe out of his pocket and lit it. "Don't worry, Hannah; she can't have gone far. There's probably some very simple explanation for all of this."

There was a knock on the door and Sue came in.

Matron tried to hide her anxiety as she spoke. "Sue, here's a fine thing. The doctor is here to see Mandy, but we can't seem to find her."

Sue looked from the doctor to Matron and back again. She hesitated.

"Have you seen her at all? Did you see her go anywhere?"

"No, I . . . Ellie told me not to disturb Mandy because she was sleeping. So I stayed downstairs when I got home."

"Then we have no idea how long she's been gone." Dr. Matthews looked significantly at Matron.

"Sue, this is very serious." Matron spoke slowly and clearly. "We think Mandy has run away. Or perhaps she's hiding. I don't know. But she must be found. Otherwise she could become very ill. Do you have any idea where she might be?"

"Well . . ." The young girl paused, frowning. Then she came to a decision. "She may have gone back to the little cottage in the woods."

Matron was aware that she must have had an incredulous look on her face. "What cottage in what woods?"

"The one over the wall, ma'am."

"You mean over the big orchard wall? But why would Mandy go there?"

Dr. Matthews cut in. "Isn't that part of the big estate? A man called Bill Fitzgerald just bought it."

"I think so." Matron Bridie tried to gather together her thoughts. "But, Sue, that's ridiculous. How could she get over the wall? What did she do, climb it?" Even as she asked the question, she knew the answer. Her heart sank as Sue nodded her head in affirmation.

Matron sat down in the chair by her desk. "I think you'd better tell us all you know," she said in a weak voice.

Sue recounted the events of the previous day. She told of following Mandy to the cottage and of how Mandy had been so upset and had begged her not to say a word to anyone about the place.

Dr. Matthews was plainly puzzled as to why it was all so important. But Matron Bridie understood.

She realized now why Mandy's behavior had been so strange the past few months, why she would need to steal the cups and saucers and knives and forks. She remembered how Alice had mentioned Mandy's requests for dusters and a broom. And Jake had spoken of Mandy's onetime interest in a garden project.

She had wondered if it had anything to do with the incident concerning the shears. Now, she knew that it all fitted together.

She pictured Mandy, flushed and anxious, saying, "You mustn't stop me from going. You don't understand," when she had forbidden her yesterday to take any more long walks.

Those "long walks" no doubt had been to the cottage, a place that she had tried to make her very own. Matron Bridie reflected that in all her years at the orphanage she had never seen a child express her desire for a home and a family more vividly. Her heart went out to Mandy.

When Sue finished her story there was a moment's pause. Then Matron spoke quietly. "Thank you, Sue. You've been a tremendous help. And I think I understand. Now, I want you to be very grown-up and not say a word about this, about the cottage, or Mandy, or that she's missing, to anyone. Do you think you could do that? You know how upsetting it would be to the rest of the children."

Sue nodded. "Will Mandy be all right? Will you be able to find her?" she asked in a small, worried voice.

"Yes, I think so. And we'll tell you the minute we do."

Ellie knocked on the door and came in hurriedly.

"Matron, she's positively not in the house. I really looked everywhere." She was breathless.

"Yes, Ellie. I think we know where she is now, thanks to Sue. You'd better run along. Both of you. It's almost dinner time."

When they had gone, Matron looked across at Dr. Matthews. She sighed. "Oh, Brian, what a worry. I'll have to explain all of this later. Right now I'm very much afraid that I have to make a phone call to the police station." She reached for the phone.

"No, wait a minute." The doctor spoke quickly. "You're going about this the wrong way, Hannah. If Mandy is on the Fitzgerald property, then the person to call is Bill Fitzgerald himself. He can reach Mandy far more quickly than the police can. They'd have to get his permission to go to the cottage anyway. It would waste a lot of time. We need to reach the child as fast as we can."

Matron hesitated. "Yes. You're right. Well, at least I can try. Do you have the new number?"

"Yes, I do." The doctor took a small diary from the inner pocket of his coat. "Here we are: Fitzgerald, Cranton House. It's 42731."

As she dialed the number, Matron Bridie prayed that Mr. Fitzgerald would be able to help, and that they would find Mandy soon.

11 ♬♫♪♬♫♪♬♫♪♬♫♪♬♫♪

BILL FITZGERALD looked at his pretty wife Ann, sitting across from him at the dining table. He thought how nice it was to be having dinner with her in this cozy room. A fire was blazing in the grate. The silver shone in the candlelight. Samson, the butler, puttered at the sideboard, handling the warm plates and covered tureens with accustomed assurance. He was the complete opposite of his Biblical namesake. Old and tall and thin as a reed, he had been with the family for many years.

Bill looked out at the rain beating against the sash windows. It was driving so hard that the park at the back of the house was completely obscured. It was dark early tonight. Good to be indoors at such a time. He was glad of the break for dinner. All through the late afternoon he had been working in his study, poring over the financial ledgers concerning the big estate, trying to plan and shape the future and draw up a suitable budget that would keep them within their means through the difficult months ahead.

He turned to Ann. "What date does Jonathan finish school?"

"Mm, the sixteenth, I think."

"I can't wait to see his face when he sees this house."

"Ohh, he'll *love* it. As I do. It's so beautiful here." She smiled across at him.

"Happy?"

"Yes." Her eyes were warm and affectionate.

Samson came across the room carrying a silver platter. He bent and offered it to Ann. As she helped herself to the thinly sliced meat, a telephone in the hallway began to ring.

"Dash it." Bill drew a weary hand across his eyes. "Why does everyone choose the dinner hour to phone? Sam, take it, will you? Tell whoever it is that I'll have to call back."

"Yes, sir." The old man placed the meat platter carefully on the sideboard and went quietly out of the room.

Ann got to her feet. "Here, darling, I'll serve. No sense in all this getting cold." She placed the steaming food in front of her husband, then busied herself with her own plate.

118

She looked across at him. "How did you manage this afternoon? Are we going to be able to cope financially?"

Bill grimaced. "Just. It'll mean really pulling in our belts — using as much stuff as we can get from the home farm, that sort of thing. Think you can manage on a reduced allowance for a while?"

She nodded. "It's worth it."

Samson came back into the room. "Sorry, sir. It's the Matron from the orphanage on the phone. I told her you were at dinner. She apologized and said it's very important. She must speak with you, right away."

Bill made a sound of exasperation. "Wouldn't you know it. I'm sure the old dear just wants to introduce herself or make an appointment to visit or something." He got up reluctantly. "All right. I'll take it."

He strode quickly into the hall and picked up the telephone. He made his voice deliberately brisk. "This is Mr. Fitzgerald. What can I do for you, Matron?"

"Oh, I'm sorry to bother you, Mr. Fitzgerald. But something quite dreadful has happened here. I hope you can help me."

Bill noted the anxiety in the woman's voice.

"We've just discovered that one of my girls is missing. It's hard to tell how long she's been gone. The worst part is that she is quite sick. She had a fever this morning, and I can't imagine what made her get up and leave the orphanage."

"Good Lord!"

"I think she may be on your property. That's why I'm calling. I was going to call the police, but I wanted to ask you first if you could possibly help us find her."

119

"Is she dark-haired — about ten years old?"

"Yes." Matron sounded surprised. "One of her friends thinks she may be in an old building in the woods. You know, near the wall that divides your property from ours?"

"The Shell Cottage," Bill murmured.

"Yes — yes, that's it. Oh, do you think you could check for me? I'm really quite worried. She could be seriously ill by now."

"I'll certainly do my best. I'm glad you called. Look, I'll get onto it right away. And I'll call you back."

"Oh, thank you." There was relief in the woman's voice.

"Give me your number." Bill scribbled hastily on a pad as she gave it to him. "Right. Now if I find her, I'll bring her here. Could you call a doctor?"

"Well, Dr. Matthews is with me now. He can go immediately."

"Good. I'll get back to you as soon as I can."

Bill hung up the phone and went back into the dining room.

"Ann, a terrible thing! You know that girl I told you about, from the orphanage? Well, apparently she's at the Shell Cottage or they think she is, and she's sick and running a fever."

"You mean she's out there *now*?" Ann was instantly concerned.

"Yes, the Matron's frightfully worried. Darling, I'll need my raincoat. Quickly. I'll have to go and see if I can find her."

"Should I come with you?"

"No, I'll have to take the mare. The car would never get through."

Bill ran across the hall and down a passageway leading to the stable yard. "Brendan!" he shouted from the porch.

120

"Sir!" The groom appeared at the door of the tack room, looking out through the rain.

"Saddle up the mare. I've got to go to the cottage in the beech woods."

"Tonight, sir?"

" 'Fraid so. We think a child from the orphanage may be out there."

"Oh, sir. Right away, sir."

Ann hurried out on the porch with Bill's raincoat over her arm.

"I brought your hat, too, darling. You'll need it. Heavens, that poor child. I hope you find her."

Bill hunched into his coat. "So do I. I wonder if this is ever going to stop." He looked up at the rain.

"Take care, darling." Ann's face was clouded with anxiety. "I'll turn down a bed and put some water on to boil. The child may need a hot drink or something. I'll keep your dinner warm."

"Yes. Oh, the doctor is coming on over here. He was at the orphanage when the Matron rang. *Brendan!*"

"Coming, sir."

Bill jammed his hat on his head. There was a clatter of iron hooves on the cobblestones. Brendan ran out pulling the big mare behind him. She was reluctant and nervous in the driv-ing rain.

Bill swung up into the saddle. "Whoa there, easy, girl."

The animal skittered and slid on the wet cobbles.

"Open the gate to the back, Brendan, and get me a lantern."

"Yes, sir."

The big gates swung wide slowly. Bill eased the dancing mare

121

toward the opening. The wind was howling around the corners of the yard. Glancing back to the house, he saw Ann standing on the porch, her face white against the darkness. She waved anxiously. He raised an arm in farewell.

The cold rain was already beginning to trickle down his neck. He turned up the collar of his coat and pulled it more tightly about him.

Brendan hurried out with a lantern. Bill leaned down to take it.

"Be careful, sir!" the groom yelled.

"Yes. Tell Mrs. Fitzgerald to turn on as many lights on the park side of the house as she can. It'll help me coming back."

"Yes, sir."

"God, what a night."

Bill bent his head to screen his eyes from the rain and urged the big mare into a canter. They went streaking out through the tall white gates and disappeared into the pitch blackness.

12 ❧❧❧❧❧❧❧❧❧❧❧❧❧❧❧

SOMETHING WAS making a terrible noise. It was banging loudly and insistently, penetrating the thick fog in Mandy's head. "Get up, get up, get up, get up," it seemed to be saying. She tried to move, but, the moment she did, a wave of nausea passed over her. She lay on the floor of the cottage, retching and coughing, reaching out for something to hold on to until the world stopped spinning. She could not lift her head. It seemed the heaviest part of her body. She must be in the middle of some terrible nightmare. She would wake up soon and everything would be all right again.

"Get up, get up, get up, get up." Oh, stop the noise. Please, stop! Mandy drew her knees up close to her chest and slowly rolled over on to them. She lay in a crouching, kneeling position. Opening her eyes, she saw her hands on the floor in front of her. They looked strangely large and thick. The banging noise was coming from directly above her head. She managed to look up. A strand of the rose tree was whipping in the wind against the frame of the doorway. Sharp, cruel lashes. "Get up. Get up."

The sky outside was vividly bright for a moment and Mandy moaned and shivered as the inevitable thunder followed. Wind and rain and noise and chills and dampness. And such a spinning in her head. Round and round went the room, then up and down, like a roller coaster, first one way, then another. And more flashing lights. One like a beacon in the dark. She shielded her eyes from the glare and saw for an instant the dashing rain and the tall trees, and the white garden gate, like a skeleton in the night.

And something else. Tall and straight — silhouetted, standing still out there. It seemed to be reaching for the sky. She closed her eyes and when she opened them again, the vision came sharply into focus. It was a knight on horseback. Mandy thought it was her prince. Had he worried about her in the storm and come to rescue her? He held a lamp high above his head and looked around in the rain as though he were lost and needed to find his way. Mandy cried out. The light swung around in her direction, and she knew that he had seen her.

The tall shape moved. Mandy could not see a face in the darkness, but as the silhouette came closer, she saw that it wasn't a knight or her prince, but a giant, with long legs and feet so large that they swallowed up her garden in three strides. Wild-eyed and terrified, Mandy backed away. Arms reached out for her and she screamed and couldn't stop screaming. Incoherent words came tumbling out, too.

She struggled weakly, but the arms were strong and lifted her high into the air.

"It's all right, little girl. It's all right. No one's going to hurt you." But still Mandy cried out and fought against the softness that was being wrapped around her shoulders. She moaned and the world was spinning again. There was movement and motion and the voice kept on talking, softly.

Mandy was so weak and exhausted that she couldn't fight for long. Little by little she quieted and lay still, her senses spinning down, down into unconsciousness again. She whimpered and turned her face away from the driving rain. She felt rough cloth against her cheek. To her surprise it smelled good and felt warm. The arms about her were firm, holding her tight. She burrowed closer. Rocking gently in the dark night, she sensed the strong body moving with her. And still the voice spoke soothingly and continuously.

"There we are, little girl. Nearly home now. You'll be all right soon. Everything is over now. There, there, don't cry."

And though the pain in her chest and head was still terrible and she had never been as ill in her life, Mandy heard the words, and instinct told her that the nightmare was passing. The worst was behind her.

124

Winter

A Christmas Wish

1

THE DAYS THAT followed were distorted and terrifying for Mandy. Afterward she couldn't recall whether they had been reality or whether they were still part of her dream. She was delirious most of the time; her fever was dangerously high.

Whenever she opened her eyes she discovered she couldn't focus on anything. There was a vibrating sensation in her body. A constant buzzing in her head.

She was conscious of voices from time to time. She recognized Dr. Matthews' and thought she heard Matron Bridie's, too. But other voices were unfamiliar. She couldn't place them. And just as she tried to grasp what they might be saying to her, they would fade away or roar so loudly she thought her head would explode with the noise.

At times she felt a soft, cool hand on her brow, and saw a woman's face, sweet and concerned. And often an arm was about her shoulders and a cup of liquid held to her lips. Mandy was aware of tender and loving care, but sometimes it threatened to become the nightmare again and she cried out in fear.

When she drank to ease her parched throat, the cup in front of her often seemed as small as a thimble and her lips would feel so thick and swollen it was impossible to encompass it. Then, again, the cup would appear as large as a bowl and she would have to adjust to that.

She was incredibly weak and couldn't move without someone helping her. The effort of breathing required all the strength she posessed. As she fought for air she heard the sounds that her breathing made and felt the painful thickness in her chest.

Once, she vaguely heard Dr. Matthews' voice, serious and far away. "She mustn't be moved. She should stay here." And there was the sharp prick of a needle and always the burning skin and limbs aching from fever.

But gradually the pain lessened and her temperature subsided a little. She no longer cried out and spoke deliriously. Sleep claimed her for long, restoring periods. If she did wake in the dark and lonely nights, then the woman with the soft voice was miraculously there to soothe and comfort her.

Finally, the day came when Mandy awoke to discover that the world was no longer out of focus. She opened her eyes slowly and became aware of a soft pink room and watery sunlight shining gently through transparent curtains at a high window. Mandy slowly turned her head and saw a chair, a fireplace, a table in one corner of the room with bottles and glasses and a thermometer on it. A pretty coverlet was on her bed.

She looked up and noticed every detail of the ceiling — molded plaster flowers and garlands standing out in sharp, clear relief.

She stirred and immediately there was a movement beside her. The lady with the sweet face had been sitting in a chair near her bed. Now she came to her and smiled.

"Hello, Mandy. It's good to see you awake at last." The gentle voice was warm and friendly. "How are you feeling?"

"A bit thirsty," Mandy spoke shyly.

"Well, that's easily remedied — here." She filled a glass with water and helped Mandy sit up to drink it.

"I've been wondering when you would finally open your eyes. You know, this is the first time you've been really awake in three whole days."

"Oh." Mandy wondered where she was. And why she wasn't at the orphanage.

"You've been a very sick little girl."

"Yes." She lay back against the pillow.

Everything seemed too bright. The light from the window made her head ache. She couldn't understand why it was all so clear and sharp. Why the room and even the woman — her face, dress, the ring on her finger — stood out in such detail.

This clarity of vision was such a contrast to the confusing period she had just been through that it was almost painful. Mandy closed her eyes again. Better to shut it all out.

She heard a door open quietly. The lady spoke softly. "Oh, Bill, she's awake. She just came to and seemed quite lucid."

"Good." Mandy heard someone move toward the bed, and she felt a hand on her brow. "Fever's gone down, too, I should say."

Mandy would like to have seen who it was who spoke. There were so many questions she wanted to ask.

But, somehow, the thought of facing the world so soon was too much. Too real, too immediate. If she could keep her eyes closed just a little longer, it was so comfortable in the bed, and everything would wait until another day. She turned away and let herself slip down into sleep again. The voices beside her faded away.

"It'll be a while yet before she's able to sit up and take notice. This was an emotional illness, too."

"Yes. Poor child. She'll need a lot of rest. And love."

2

MUCH LATER Mandy awoke to find Dr. Matthews standing beside her. It was dark outside the window, and a soft light was burning in one corner of the room.

"Hello." She managed a weak smile.

"Well, it's about time you woke up, young lady. How are you feeling?"

"Much better."

"You look better, too. You've been quite a sorry sight these past few days."

"What happened?"

"Ho — what didn't happen!" Dr. Matthews sat down beside her on the bed and took her hand. "Do you remember anything at all?"

Mandy tried to recall the pattern of events leading to her illness. It was too much of an effort to concentrate. She shook her head.

"Well, briefly, you were found in a cottage in the woods. You remember leaving the orphanage?"

"Yes." Memory came flooding back. Mandy's heart sank.

"A man named Mr. Fitzgerald brought you to his house, which is where you are now." The doctor spoke slowly and quietly. "You've had a nasty bout with pneumonia. We decided to keep you here because I didn't want you moved at all."

"Oh. Where's Matron?"

"At the orphanage. She'll be by tomorrow."

"Is she angry with me?"

"No, I don't think so. She's very worried about you, though. You gave her a bad time there for a while."

"Oh, dear." Mandy's fingers clutched anxiously at the coverlet.

"But it's over and done with now." The doctor's voice was firm. "The main thing is for you not to worry about anything. I want you to concentrate on getting well. Are you hungry? Could you eat something?"

Mandy was surprised to discover that she was hungry. Dr. Matthews went off to arrange for some food for her, and she lay back in her bed, looking at the pretty room and wondering how it was that she came to be here.

Compared with her room at the orphanage, this room was very large. She wondered if the rest of the house was big, too. What did it look like? Was there a garden? She tried to see out of the window, but it was too dark.

What would Matron say when she came to see her, tomorrow? Would she be annoyed? Would she insist that Mandy be returned to the orphanage? She hoped not.

There was the sound of footsteps coming toward her room, and the doctor came in again. Mandy recognized the woman with him. She carried a tray of food.

"Mandy, this is Ann Fitzgerald. This good woman has been

134

with you night and day since you got here."

"Hello, Mandy. We spoke earlier, didn't we?"

Ann helped Mandy to sit up and she arranged the pillows behind her back. "There, how does that look to you?" She placed the tray on Mandy's knees.

"Mmmm — fine, thank you." But she was suddenly too weak to pick up the spoon for the broth, and she lay back listlessly.

"Let me help." Ann took the bowl and gently fed Mandy spoonfuls of the warm liquid. Dr. Matthews sat close by and nodded approvingly. He kept up a stream of cheery conversation, watching her closely all the while. Mandy was glad to have him near.

"May I say hello, too?" A tall man entered the room and crossed quietly to the bedside. Mandy recognized the voice. It had been part of her dream — part of the nightmare, too.

"Mandy, this is my husband Bill," Ann said. Mandy looked up and knew this was the knight she had seen on horseback in the rain. This was the man who had brought her to safety here. She faintly remembered the horror of that time. She shuddered and managed to say, "Thank you very much for all you've done. You've been very kind."

"Oh, my dear, it's been a pleasure." He had a nice smile and laughing gray eyes. "Are you feeling better?"

Mandy nodded. For some reason she felt a little tearful. Why were they all being so good to her? She blinked and looked away.

Everyone started to speak at once.

Dr. Matthews got up and announced that it was time for her

to rest again. Ann whisked away the tray and helped her lie down once more. She and her husband prepared to leave the room.

"Wait." Mandy found her voice. "Could you — could you please just tell me what happened. I mean how it happened, and why I'm here."

"Well," Bill looked quickly across to Dr. Matthews as if seeking permission to speak, "let's see now. As far as I can gather, it was like this. Matron discovered you were missing. But she had no idea where you were. Then someone called Sue, I think — is that your friend? — told her that you might be at the cottage which is on my property, you see. So Matron called me to help, and I went out on a frightful, rainy night and found you and brought you home. Does that make sense?" He smiled.

Mandy nodded. It suddenly all made sense. It was Sue who had really saved her. She alone knew that Mandy might have gone to the cottage. How fortunate it was, after all, that Sue had followed her that day and discovered the cottage for herself. But for that, Mandy might never have been found. It was a chilling thought. Her rescue seemed like a miracle.

Dr. Matthews spoke up. "Now, young lady. You may look better, but you've got a lot of convalescing to do. That's enough excitement for one night." He tucked Mandy down in bed. She was exhausted and only too glad to be lying flat on her back again.

Bill and Ann said goodnight and presently the good doctor departed also, promising to return the following morning.

Mandy drifted into sleep and wasn't sure if it were minutes

or hours later that she felt the familiar, cool hand on her brow. The woman's soft voice whispered, "Good night, Mandy. Sleep well. I'll be here if you need me."

3

THE DAYS passed and Mandy improved rapidly. She looked better and felt much better. But she still had a cough that threatened to tear her insides apart.

It wasn't long before she was able to feed herself and take notice of much that was going on around her.

She met Mary, the middle-aged cleaning woman, who came every day except Sundays to help Ann with the house. And she also met Sally, the cook.

One cold, clear morning there was a knock on her bedroom door. An old, thin man entered, his arms full of wood.

"Good morning, Miss. Is it all right if I light the fire for you?"

"Oh, yes." Mandy watched him as he laboriously applied the small sticks and logs to the already crumpled newspaper in the grate.

"What is your name?"

"I'm called Samson, Miss. I'm the butler." He paused to grin at her.

Mandy laughed aloud for the first time since her illness. Such a ludicrous name for such a dear, old man. She liked him instantly.

She became enormously fond of Ann, too, and was anxious when she wasn't close by. Bill came to visit her often and she listened for and learned to distinguish their footsteps about the house.

She was aware of the house itself now. Voices echoed up from the downstairs rooms, suggesting high ceilings. When a door banged, it had a hollow, heavy sound, and Mandy counted the many steps it took for someone to climb the stairs.

These small details gave her the impression that the house was quite large. The impression was confirmed when she got her first glimpse of the view from her window.

A beautiful garden was immediately beneath her room, consisting mostly of low, box-hedged areas containing several hundred rose trees. Beyond the formal planting was a large green lawn leading to a wide stream which separated the lawn from several acres of pastureland. Beyond the fields were miles of woodland stretching as far as Mandy could see. It was a beautiful sight.

Mandy's bedroom was obviously in the center portion of the house, for from where she sat in bed she could see two wings of the building, one extending to her left and the other to her right. Though much larger and grander, it looked a little like the orphanage. The windows were similarly proportioned and the house was built of the same indigenous stone.

Mandy spoke to Ann about it one day. "How long have you lived here, Ann?"

"Not long at all. We moved in late this summer."

"Where did you live before that?"

"Oh, a long way away. But, you know, hundreds of years ago, Bill's ancestors built this place. Unfortunately, the whole house was destroyed by a huge fire and the family lost all of their money and had to sell the estate. Other owners restored the house over the years. It's been Bill's dream to buy it back. All his life he's wanted to live here. Just this year it became possible."

"How marvelous." Mandy was enthralled.

"Yes, it is, isn't it? I just hope and pray we can afford to keep it all going. The forestry and farming can be very productive one day, but it's a terrible expense at the moment." Ann looked out across the park. "It means such a lot to us both. And it's such a beautiful place." Her voice was low and loving.

Mandy watched her as she spoke and knew instinctively what she must be feeling. To have waited so long to regain the house only to have the threat of losing it hanging over their heads must be enormously worrying.

Ann changed the subject. "You know, it's so cold out there today, it's just possible we'll have some snow. Before Christmas, too."

"What date is it?" Mandy had no idea.

"December, the tenth. Jonathan'll be home from school soon."

"Jonathan?"

"Our son. You'll like him a lot, Mandy. He's fourteen years old and very handsome." Ann smiled in a teasing way.

Mandy was taken aback. She hadn't realized that Bill and Ann had a child. She hadn't given it a thought, in fact. She had been so content with the spoiling and the love she had received from these two people. Now the thought of sharing it with someone else, someone much closer to them than she was, was disturbing.

She wondered what Jonathan was really like, and if he would like her.

She had the vague feeling that she wouldn't like *him* at all!

4 ❧❧❧❧❧❧❧❧❧❧❧

AS MANDY's health improved, she received a stream of visitors. Dr. Matthews came to see her daily, of course, and Matron Bridie visited as often as her busy schedule permitted. Mandy was always a little anxious when she came. She was afraid that Matron would suggest it was time for her to return to the orphanage, and she wasn't ready to do any such thing. But Matron made no mention of it. She didn't mention the cottage or Mandy's behavior the day of the storm either. Far from being angry, she showed nothing but concern. Mandy was greatly relieved.

Alice and Ellie visited one day. Alice had baked a cake for her as a surprise. Ellie brought messages and letters from some of the children. Mandy was touched that they thought of her. But this, too, made her anxious. Any reminder of the orphanage was unpleasant at the moment. Thoughts of the past were very painful. She herself never once mentioned the cottage. It was as if it had never existed.

Sue was the most important visitor. Matron said that she had asked if she might come. Mandy, somewhat hesitantly, agreed.

Sue arrived one cold, cloudy afternoon holding a small bunch of brightly colored anemones which she shyly handed to Mandy.

"Hello, Mandy. Are you feeling better?"

"Yes, thank you."

"Jake sent these flowers to you. They come from Mr. Simple's shop. He thought they would cheer you up and look nice in your room." Sue looked around. "It's a lovely room, isn't it? And a super house."

"I haven't really seen it yet."

"Oh, it's huge, Mandy. It takes ages to get up here. You come along this long drive. And you know that gate in the wall we found? When we went exploring? Well, it's all part of this place."

"Yes, I know."

"I suppose it was the owners who put the padlock on it."

"Yes."

"What are they like?" Sue was asking questions again. Mandy wished she wouldn't.

"Oh, they're very kind." She tried not to make her voice too abrupt.

"I met the lady. She seems nice." There was a pause. Sue looked down at the floor and then said, almost fiercely, "You are *lucky*."

Mandy was startled. "Why?"

"Oh, I don't know. Everything seems to happen to you. You're always the one who goes and does something. I never seem to have any good ideas like you do. You know, you found the cottage. And now, all of this." She indicated the house and the beautiful garden. It was a sad gesture. A little hopeless.

Mandy's heart softened. She wished she could explain to Sue how often it was that she felt lost and lonely. She opened her mouth to speak. But Sue interrupted.

"Mandy, I hope you didn't mind my telling Matron about the cottage. I didn't want to. I wasn't going to tell on you or anything. But I got sort of frightened."

"Oh, Sue." Mandy spoke with all the sincerity she felt. "I'm so glad you did."

"Yes, but I know you wanted it kept a secret."

"If you hadn't told about it, I might never have been found, might I?"

"No — oh gosh." Sue looked at Mandy, her face solemn, her eyes filling with tears.

"So you see, it's really you who saved me. And I have to thank you."

Mandy felt tearful, too, and suddenly the girls were embracing each other and crying and laughing at the same time. It cleared away the awkwardness between them. They both felt better afterward. Sue sniffed and blew her nose and Mandy was so full of emotion that she coughed her hollow cough and it sounded so terrible that both girls burst out laughing again.

They had tea and some of Alice's cake and spent a pleasant afternoon together.

When it was time to go, Sue paused at the doorway. "Can I come to see you again?"

"Yes."

"When are you coming back?"

"I don't know."

"It's awfully quiet there without you. The attic seems ever so empty."

"I expect it will be soon." Mandy spoke the words bravely, trying to be cheerful for Sue's sake. But she wished with all her heart that she need never think about going back to the orphanage again.

5

"MANDY, I WANT you to meet Jonathan." Ann spoke happily as she came into the bedroom. "Jonathan, this is Mandy."

Mandy put aside the book she had been reading. Her heart beat a little faster. "How do you do, Jonathan."

"Hi." His voice cracked with enthusiasm and ended up somewhere in his boots. Jonathan cleared his throat and took her extended hand in his somewhat moist one.

Mandy had the impression of a tall, gangling boy, his dark hair falling loosely across his forehead, with ruddy cheeks and his mother's very clear, blue eyes. He was dressed in his school uniform but was obviously restless and aching to put on more comfortable clothes.

His mother anticipated this. "You'll probably want to change, darling. But will you have some lemonade or something first?"

"I'd love it." He moved to the window and looked eagerly out across the park. His hands thrust deep in his pockets.

"Oh, Mum, this is super." He whirled on Mandy. "Don't you like it?"

Mandy had a hard time finding her voice. Never had she met anyone who exuded so much energy. He dominated the entire room. If only he weren't so tall. She was a little fright-ened.

"I — oh, yes — I mean — what I've *seen* of it I like." She stammered and wished she could appear calm and not so shy.

"Perhaps later on, when Mandy's able to get up, you'll show her around the house, Jon. She might enjoy it." Ann watched both children closely.

"Yes, all right." He stood nonchalantly looking at her. A couldn't-care-less attitude. "When would you like to do that?" he asked.

"Oh — I . . ."

"It won't be possible for a day or two, Jon," Ann spoke quickly. "Maybe, tomorrow, at the earliest."

"Okay . . ." A pause, then: "Well, see you later." A remote casual wave, and he was gone, although Mandy felt his pres-ence still lingering in the room.

Ann smiled a secret sort of smile. She winked at Mandy and said, "I'll be back soon, darling." Then she hurried out after the boy.

Mandy was left with a distinctly stunned feeling. She wasn't sure what she had expected. But this boy, this mixture of grace and awkwardness, self-contained, yet so full of life, was cer-tainly not what she had anticipated at all.

For the rest of the day she lay in bed, listening to every foot-step that passed her door and praying that Jonathan wouldn't come back into her room. He didn't. But she could hear him about the house. The place seemed to come alive now that he was home.

She could hear Bill laughing in a downstairs room and the

boy explaining something in detail and laughing about it, too. It sounded as if he were telling about some escapade at school.

At dinner time she heard the bright chatter and the clink of silver and plates coming from the dining room. It made her feel lonely and sad and left out. Later, when Ann came to sit with her for a while, she lay listlessly against the pillows, quieter than usual. Ann curled up in a chair by the fire and tucked her legs underneath her.

"It's fun having Jonathan home."

"Yes." Mandy hesitated, then bravely lied. "He seems — very nice."

"Well, you hardly got a chance to say hello to him at all." Ann smiled at Mandy, then leaned on the arm of the chair and said in a quieter voice, "He's rather bouncy, isn't he, though?"

"Oh — well — "

"I think if I were your age I'd be rather overwhelmed by him."

Mandy was surprised. Ann had touched on the very thing that she was feeling. Suddenly it became easy to talk.

"It's just that — well, I got sort of frightened. I don't know why." She laughed nervously.

"Oh, I do, Mandy. You've been waiting to see our son whom you know I adore. And you must wonder if he'll like you. Then, in he comes, full of energy. You feel you should try to like him because he belongs here. It must be very intimidating, especially after your illness. He must make you feel you could never keep up with him."

Mandy thought about it, digesting what Ann had just said. It was, indeed, the way she felt.

"Just remember one thing, Mandy." Ann looked at her

fondly. "He's probably just as worried about you."

"Oh?" Mandy was astonished.

"Why, yes. He's wondering if you like him, and how he fits in here with you around. Particularly since he's been away at school." She leaned forward and stirred the dying embers of the fire with a poker.

"It will take time for you to learn to like each other. You mustn't worry if it doesn't happen. You may find you'd rather keep to yourself until you go back to the orphanage. It's not going to upset Bill or me."

Then she changed the subject.

"I wondered if you'd like to get up for a little while tomorrow. I thought maybe we could celebrate your getting better, and Jon's being home, too, and all have dinner together downstairs tomorrow evening. We could really bundle you up warmly, and Samson could light a big fire in the lounge. Just for an hour or so."

Though Mandy would rather have stayed in bed in her comfortable, safe room, she felt she couldn't hurt Ann by refusing the invitation. So she said politely, "Yes, thank you, that would be very nice." She hoped the evening wouldn't prove too much of an ordeal — with Jonathan there and everything.

6 ❧❧❧❧❧❧❧❧❧❧❧❧

AS IT TURNED out, the evening was a smashing success. Mandy hadn't realized how thrilling it would be to see the downstairs of the big house. There was so much to do and talk

146

about that she hadn't a chance to feel shy. Ann insisted she take a nap in the late afternoon. She bathed and tidied herself afterward, and, when Bill came to take her downstairs, she was feeling refreshed and, secretly, rather excited. He made a tremendous fuss, taking her arm, and leading her down the big staircase with so much ceremony that Mandy felt as though she were being escorted to a very special party.

As she descended the stairway, she looked about her in awe. The main hall was tremendous — three flights of wide, shallow stairs on three sides of a stairwell. The banister beneath her hand was solid and smooth, the wood polished to a high gloss.

On the fourth side of the stairwell a tremendous tapestry was hanging. Portraits lined the other walls, each one separately lit from above and glowing in the evening dusk.

A thick carpet lay beneath Mandy's slippered feet. At the bottom of the stairs Ann and Samson were waiting for her. She smiled nervously and clung to Bill's hand. She was trembling a little, though whether from excitement or the fact that it was her first time downstairs, she couldn't tell.

Samson pushed open two huge doors, and the small party moved into the lounge. It was a beautiful room, long and narrow. A big fire was burning in the grate. There were comfortable furnishings with deep, soft cushions, and fresh flowers in vases about the room.

Jonathan sprang up out of a chair as they entered.

"Well, Jon, here's the young lady," Bill said. "We can go into dinner now. Hungry, Amanda?"

Mandy smiled at Bill's correct use of her name. "Maybe just a tiny bit," she said, trying to sound enthusiastic.

"Well, I'm starving." Jonathan led the way to another series

147

of double doors and opened them wide. They opened on to a small dining room. There was a table set for four people. Dishes were steaming over hot plates on a long sideboard.

Beyond the table were more double doors and a smaller door set into the left wall. Jonathan explained, "That door leads to the hall again, Mandy — and look here." He pushed open the second set of double doors and stood back. Mandy gasped. She was looking into a vast, long room, obviously a larger, formal dining room. Marble pillars at either end rose to the exquisite plaster ceiling above. A huge refectory table in the center ran almost to the far wall. And the room had the same beautiful windows as the lounge.

"You know your way around already." Ann spoke to Jonathan as they seated themselves for dinner.

"I'm not surprised," Bill interrupted. "I haven't seen him all day. Have you been exploring?"

Jonathan grinned. "Yep. I found a secret passageway, too."
"Oh, where?"
"Between the second and third floors."
Bill smiled. "Oh, *that* one."
The boy's face registered total surprise.
"You mean there's another one?"
"Mm — I'm not going to tell you."
"Oh, Dad, where?"
"Wait and see."
The boy squirmed and howled in protest as his father teased him.

Ann laughed and Mandy joined in. She couldn't help it. Bill looked wickedly at them all, his eyes gleaming with merriment.

"I'll tell you tomorrow, Jon, then you can show Mandy."

"Oh, please tell us now," Mandy spoke up. She, too, was anxious to know where a secret passageway might be.

"In the back of the cupboard in our bedroom, there's a door that gives access to a passageway. It leads to another cupboard in the big guest bedroom. Long ago the lord of the manor could visit his lady without having anyone know about it. Clever, wasn't it?"

"Bill, I don't think even you know where all the nooks and crannies are in this house." Ann smiled across at him.

"I don't."

Dinner progressed. It was a joyous affair. Mandy found that she had a hundred questions to ask. She completely forgot her shyness and found herself laughing and giggling and chatting with great zest.

Ann looked lovingly at the group around the table. "It's really nice being together like this," she said.

"Here's a toast to Mandy." Bill suddenly lifted his glass. Jonathan and Ann paused to do the same. "We're glad that you're better and delighted to have you with us this evening."

"Oh, thank you." Mandy's face was rosy with happiness.

After dinner, Ann led the way through the main lounge to the library.

"Here, Mandy, you want to see another secret of the house? Look at this." She pressed a button in the molding on the wall and the entire panel slid back to reveal a small pipe organ nestling in an alcove. It was of the same wood as the library paneling — but painted with gold-leaf embellishments. Two pretty candle brackets were attached to the music stand. A small bench covered in soft, rose-colored silk straddled the pedals on the floor.

"How absolutely beautiful," Mandy breathed.

"This was put in the house by one of Bill's eccentric ancestors." Ann smiled across at him. "Bless the old gentleman!"

"Where are the pipes?"

"Up there, and there." Ann pointed to the wall high above the organ. "A lot of them are behind the paneling, but, see, just by the ceiling you can see the tops of them."

"Play it, Mother," Jonathan begged

"Oh, please." Mandy couldn't wait to hear it.

"Well, some of the stops are missing, but it does still function. We'll have it restored properly one day." Ann slid onto the stool and pulled at the knobs and touched some buttons. She let her hands run over the keys. Warm, golden sounds poured forth, with the wonderful, "breathless" quality that is so characteristic of a pipe organ.

"Here, Jon, you know this one." Ann began to sing and play an old English melody. Jonathan and Bill joined in, their voices blending with hers.

Mandy listened with delight. It was a lusty, country song, and it ended with them all collapsing in laughter. Jonathan tried to reach a high note and his voice cracked dismally, quite ruining the melodic effect.

"Do you know any songs, Mandy?" Ann asked.

"Only hymns, mostly."

"Like what?"

"Oh, gosh, I can't remember any right now." She was suddenly shy.

"Let's sing some carols," Jonathan suggested.

"That's right. It's nearly Christmas," Bill agreed. "Carols couldn't be more appropriate."

Ann played "Good King Wenceslaus," and "In the Bleak Midwinter," and "We Three Kings." Everyone sang loudly and, in spite of her shyness, Mandy found herself joining in. The acoustics carried her sweet, soprano voice and enhanced it. The others fell silent to listen to her. As she sang, Mandy thought that she had never been so happy in her life. And with the thought came a sadness, too. She knew she would have to return to the orphanage soon, and that this happiness would end. Her voice faded as the song finished.

Ann noticed the little girl's forlorn expression.

"That's enough for tonight," she said. "This poor thing will collapse if we play it too much." She touched a button and the organ rolled back into the alcove. The panel slid into place again, completely concealing it from view.

This procedure was enough to distract Mandy from her own thoughts and within seconds she had brightened.

"I think it's time for one young lady to get back into bed." Bill swept Mandy up in his arms. "Are you tired, Mandy?"

"No." She giggled as he held her.

"Tell you what," said Ann. "You go and get into bed, Mandy, and I'll bring you up some hot lemon and honey. How would you like that?"

"Lovely, thank you."

"Can I have some, Mother?" Jonathan wanted to know.

"Yes, you great lump — you may have some, too."

And so it was. Mandy climbed into her warm, comfortable bed. Bill and Ann sat by as she and Jonathan drank the steaming liquid from big, china mugs.

Later, when they had all gone and she was left alone in the darkness, she relived every moment of the wonderful evening.

It had been better than any other party could ever possibly be. She would remember it all her life. She purposely shut out all thoughts of the orphanage and her imminent return.

7

IT SNOWED the following day. Great white flakes drifted down, creating a new world outside the big house.

Inside the house, it was warm and cozy. Ann was triumphant. "I told you it would snow soon. We're going to have a white Christmas. I just know it." She insisted that Samson light big fires in all the main rooms. Drafts from the chimney caused the wood smoke to spiral slowly to the ceiling from time to time. It made the house smell wonderful.

By midafternoon the countryside was covered with two to three inches of virgin snow. Every tree was traced in white, and the branches of the fir trees bowed down with the weight. The banks of the stream became softly contoured. The formal garden all but disappeared. Black crows winged across the white fields, their voices cawing and harsh in the silence. It was a picture-postcard scene.

Jonathan was out all morning bundled up and ruddy-faced. He and Brendan, the groom, made a huge snowman in the stableyard. At lunchtime Jon bounced into the house, trailing snow behind him and leaving wet footprints in the main hallway. His mother reprimanded him in no uncertain terms.

Mandy slept late and remained in her room until after

lunch. Then she, too, dressed warmly and was allowed down-stairs. Jonathan approached her. He seemed in unusually good spirits.

"Mother says maybe you'd like to see the rest of the house."

Mandy's heart jumped. Did he really want to show her, or had Ann insisted? She couldn't tell from his expression. She hoped she need not stay with the boy for long. Seeing him in the company of his mother and father was one thing, but she knew she'd be miserably shy and nervous if she were with him alone.

Her spirits sank as Jonathan led her off down a corridor. He took her into a big, unused kitchen that in olden times had been the busiest place in the house. It had a huge fireplace and an iron pulley over it that must have held the sides of beef and pork for roasting. There were great black ovens and marble counters and wooden chopping blocks, and there was a big sky-light overhead. Jonathan's voice echoed through the room. "Dad says this'll be the the first room he'll restore when he can."

"Where is the kitchen that you use now?" Mandy felt lost and small.

"In the pantry. Well, it used to be the pantry. Come on, I'll show you the rest."

The boy went tearing off down the hall. Mandy breathlessly tried to keep up with him. She was too shy to ask him to slow down a little.

He took her to the top floor of the house. Here were the small rooms where the servants had once lived.

The only advantage to being up so high in the big house was the splendid view it afforded. Mandy pressed her nose to a windowpane and wondered if she could see the orphanage across the trees. But it was snowing so hard that any view was obliterated.

Jonathan showed her the secret passageway he had discovered between the second and third floors. It had a small, spiral staircase, no more than a foot and a half wide, and it was very dark. Jonathan plunged ahead, leaving Mandy to find her own way. Suddenly, in the darkness, she became very scared. Groping her way downward, step by step, she had the feeling she would never get out.

"Jonathan!" She screamed his name. She heard him running back to the foot of the stairs.

"What is it?"

"Help me, please. I'm frightened." She began to cry and stood where she was until she heard him in the darkness climbing back up to her. She felt his strong hand grasp hers.

"It's all right, Mandy. Just one more corner and there's light on the stairs. Come on now." Gently he led her safely down and she stumbled out into the hallway gasping for air.

Jonathan saw her white face and felt compassion for her.

"Are you all right?" he asked anxiously.

"Yes — I — thank you." She bravely tried to stop crying.

Jonathan looked at Mandy as if seeing her for the first time. To his surprise he became aware that she was a person with feelings and instincts and thoughts. Until now she had seemed to him to be just a silly girl who happened to be visiting for a while.

"Here, Mandy. I know what you'd like. Come and see something."

He took her downstairs, this time staying close by her side.

Mandy was beginning to feel really tired but she went along.

He took her to the doorway leading to the stableyard.

"Look." Jonathan pointed outside, and she saw the snowman he had built. It was a ridiculous snowman, straw hair sticking out under a riding hat, with a whip in his hand. Already he was half-covered with fresh snow. Mandy began to laugh. "He looks huffy, sort of angry."

"Well, so would you be, if you had to stand out there in the cold all the time." Jonathan smiled.

Ann came down the passageway. She called anxiously, "Mandy, come away from the door. It's much too drafty there." Her voice was sharp. "Really, Jon, you ought to know better."

Mandy was exhausted. Ann noticed the circles under her eyes and suggested she rest for a while. Mandy willingly complied and went upstairs. When Ann looked into her room seconds later she had already fallen into a deep sleep.

8

WHEN SHE awoke a couple of hours later, it was dusk. Mandy had been dreaming. She felt depressed and as tired as when she had gone to rest. She lay in bed listening to the sounds of the house. They were comforting sounds, soothing and peaceful: Ann speaking quietly to Samson; Bill's footsteps going to his study; a door closing; music coming faintly from the radio in the kitchen. Mandy wished she were truly a part of it all.

She got up slowly and wandered to the window. It was still

snowing and almost dark. An owl flew evenly across the garden and disappeared into the night.

Her thoughts turned to little Chip. She wondered if he were safe and tucked warmly away somewhere out there in the woods.

The familiar aching sadness suddenly gripped her as she gazed out at the silent world. It would be cold in the cottage. The garden would be white and desolate. There was no one to take care of it now. She shuddered. How long would it be before she was returned to the orphanage? What would she do with herself when she got back? School was probably over until after the holidays. Would she go to the cottage? Matron would surely forbid it. Did she truly want to see it again? She wasn't sure. It held so many unpleasant memories. But there had been pleasant ones, too — before the nightmare. She re-membered the lovely summer and the thrill of growing her beautiful flowers and the peaceful, quiet days that were all her own.

Yet, now, as she looked back on them they seemed to have been lonely days, too. She hadn't thought so at the time. Mandy supposed it was some sort of comparison with being in Cranton House. The warmth and comfort she had received from Bill and Ann was like nothing she had ever known before. She was going to miss them desperately.

Mandy turned away from the window.

She climbed into bed again and huddled beneath the covers. Her heart was throbbing with emotion and anxiety. It was an effort not to cry.

There was a light tap on the door.

"Mandy? Are you awake?" It was Bill. He came into the

room and quietly switched on her bedside light. "Ann wondered if you wanted supper downstairs or on a tray up here." He noticed her sad and tearstained face. He sat down on the bed beside her and put a hand on her brow. Mandy spoke quickly. "Oh, Bill, I think I'd rather stay up here. Do you mind?" She brushed her eyes.

"Fine. I'll tell Ann." But he made no move to go. Presently he said, "What've you been thinking about? Looks to me like you've been having a serious thought or two." His voice was light and easy.

"Not really. I was thinking about the orphanage. And last summer."

"What about last summer?"

"Oh, you know. The Shell Cottage and the garden . . ." Her voice wavered ". . . and everything."

"You did a marvelous job on the little garden, Mandy."

"Did you see it?" She was surprised.

"I certainly did." Bill smiled. "Didn't you get my notes?"

"Why . . ." Mandy's eyes opened wide. She held her breath for the longest moment. Her thoughts went tumbling and spinning in all directions. "You mean it was *you* who left . . ."

"Yes, Mandy. I'm afraid I'm the culprit. I left you the messages." Bill laughed as he saw her incredulous expression. "I left the chrysanthemum plant, too. Did you get that? Oh, and I had to clear the garden."

"And mend the gate," Mandy whispered.

"Yes, that as well. I've been meaning to tell you, Manders. But I wanted to wait 'til you were better."

"But how did you . . . *when* did you see me?"

"I was riding around the estate when we first moved in. I

saw you working in the garden. I knew you must be from the orphanage, so I didn't disturb you. You seemed to be so . . . occupied with it all . . . and busy. I didn't want to interrupt. Maybe you weren't supposed to be there. Perhaps you wouldn't have come back if I had surprised you. It would have spoiled your fun."

Mandy stared at Bill. She was so stunned she hardly understood what he was saying.

Bill continued, "I got the idea of leaving you a note from time to time. I had a thought that you might like the mystery of it. It was a silly game really. I realized that almost immediately. I was going to come to visit you and explain the next time I was near the cottage. But you beat me to it. You got sick and came to visit me instead!"

Mandy shook her head in bewilderment. She was trying to put her thoughts into some sort of order. It was a painful shock to realize that there was probably no such person as the handsome prince she had imagined. He was just a fantasy. AN ADMIRER was just this ordinary human being. This kind, big, somewhat frightening man. And he had sought to amuse her with a game. She grasped for some meaning.

"But . . . what made you clear the garden? Why did you do it?"

"Mandy, I had to. There are other cottages on the estate, you know. They were all in a bad way. I needed to see what I had, so I just sent a tractor in to clear everything. Of course, I paid a bit more attention to the Shell Cottage," he smiled. Mandy felt an emotion rising within her which she couldn't understand. She had a sudden desire to weep. She turned her head away from the light and looked toward the window. The white flakes were still falling through the black night, brushing gently on the glass. Tears rolled down her cheeks on to the pillow.

"What is it, Mandy?" Bill took her hand. "Can you tell me?"

She moved her head. And the sobs shook her small frame. Bill waited.

"Won't you try to tell me?"

There was a long pause as she silently fought to gain control. And then in a small, lost voice she whispered one word, "Snow."

9

MANDY HAD a fever the following morning. Her temperature went soaring up. Though she was not nearly as ill as she had been the night of the storm, she lay in bed feeling very sick indeed.

Dr. Matthews hurried over to Cranton House earlier than usual. Ann had telephoned him the minute she discovered Mandy's condition.

He teased Mandy gently. "Now, my dear young lady, don't tell me you're getting sick again. We can't have that." After a careful examination he announced that she was suffering a small relapse. "Nothing too serious," he told Ann. "We'll just have to retrace our steps a little, that's all."

He turned to Mandy. "I'm afraid it's back to bed with you for a while, Mandy. You've just been coming along a little too fast. Recovering from these illnesses takes time." He patted her hand. "I'll come by this evening. You do as this good lady tells you, and you'll be on your feet again in no time."

Mandy felt reassured. Truthfully, she was quite glad to be confined to bed again. She was still emotionally confused from her talk with Bill the night before, and bed seemed to be the safest and most peaceful place right now. She slept a great deal, and when she wasn't sleeping, she lay listlessly, staring out of the window at the snow-covered garden.

Jonathan visited her in the late afternoon. Seeing Mandy's wan face and knowing that she was ill again seemed to scare him a little. He didn't stay with her long. Having confirmed for himself that she was still alive, he left her in Ann's capable hands and went about his business.

When Dr. Matthews returned in the evening, he brought Matron Bridie with him. Mandy had no wish to see Matron or to be reminded of the orphanage. She would be returning there soon enough. She felt petulant at what she took to be Matron's interference.

Matron requested that she be left alone with Mandy to discuss something important. Was she going to deliver the long-awaited lecture? Or was she going to say it was time to pick up the threads of her old life again?

Mandy sank down into the warmth of the bedcovers and wished she didn't have to hear anything at all. She stared fixedly ahead as Matron drew up a chair and sat beside her.

"Mandy, I have an invitation for you from the Fitzgeralds. I wanted to speak to you alone to find out your thoughts on the matter before I got back to them. They'd very much like to have you spend Christmas here with them at Cranton House.

160

Do you think you might like to do that?"

Mandy couldn't believe her ears. She turned her head slowly and stared at Matron. Relief and happiness washed over her in a great wave. She was so thrilled that for a moment she couldn't think of anything to say.

Matron smiled as she looked at her joyous face. "Well, well, I see that you would like it very much indeed. I'm delighted. In that case, I'll tell Mr. and Mrs. Fitzgerald that you may stay and that I shall collect you the day after Christmas—say, around noon. How does that suit you?"

Mandy found her voice. She spoke with emotion. "Oh, that's fine, Matron. Just fine. Thank you so much. Oh golly — it's going to be *such* an exciting Christmas."

The days sped by quickly. Mandy's health improved rapidly though she stayed in bed most of the time. But she was busy, happily painting and drawing and cutting out cards as gifts for everyone in the house.

On Christmas Eve, Mandy and Jonathan made paper chains to hang in the library where the Christmas tree was going to be. And in the early evening, after dinner, Mandy was allowed downstairs to help the family with the rest of the decorations.

Bill and Brendan had brought in a huge fir tree that they had cut down on the estate. It nearly touched the ceiling. Bill stood on a ladder, and the children passed up to him the tinsel and lights and ornaments.

At the appropriate time Bill signaled for everyone to stand back and he turned off the overhead lights. Then he touched a separate switch and the Christmas tree suddenly burst into life. Glowing and twinkling in the darkened room, it shone like

a fairy-tale tree. The silver and gold ornaments reflected color from the lights, and toy soldiers and gingerbread men and dancing ladies spun lazily from the branches. The tinsel angel at the very top of the tree seemed to be smiling down on everyone.

They all applauded loudly. Samson served mulled wine for the grown-ups and hot chocolate for the children, and then they all sat by the fire in the darkened room and roasted marshmallows and told Christmas stories.

Mandy felt suffused with happiness. She wondered what all the children at the orphanage were doing and remembered her other Christmases there.

It was a surprise to discover that feeling this good was actually a painful experience. She shut out her memories and tried to concentrate on this most wonderful time.

Christmas morning was noisy and cheerful.

Mandy and Jonathan received stockings filled with all manner of goodies and nonsense and sweets and fruit. Jonathan had a toy bugle in his stocking which he insisted on blowing outside Mandy's room at a terribly early hour. He made so much noise that she laughingly hid beneath the bedcovers until he stopped.

The day swung joyously from one happy moment to another. Presents were distributed to everyone. Mandy had never received such lovely gifts. Bill and Ann gave her a beautiful red dress. It had an old-fashioned white lace collar and frilly lace cuffs and there was a pair of red shoes with silver buckles on them to go with the dress. They also gave her a tiny gold signet ring with her initials carved on it, and, miraculously, it fit her third finger perfectly. Mandy vowed to herself that she would never, ever take it off. Jonathan gave her a cuddly teddy bear made of something that was as soft as rabbit's fur. It was a dark brown bear with black ears and a black nose, and its eyes were a deep hazel color and seemed to be looking straight at Mandy. She received books to read and crayons to color with, and she thought that no other girl in the whole world could be so lucky.

At lunchtime, a light meal was served in the small dining room, and Bill told so many silly stories that Mandy and Jonathan practically slid under the table with laughter.

In the afternoon everyone slept. And later Jonathan and Bill left the ladies and went out for a walk by themselves.

In the early evening, everybody dressed up in his best clothes. Mandy wore her new red dress and shoes. When everyone was ready Ann led them all to the big, formal dining room. She flung open the double doors and everyone cried out with delight.

The room was completely illuminated by candlelight. Candles were everywhere—on the tables, on the mantelpiece, and on the small pedestal tables by the windows. It was a beautiful sight.

Bill looked at his lovely wife and murmured, "I think you must have used up this month's and next month's allowance."

Ann nodded happily. "I did, darling, but this is our first Christmas here, and I want us to remember it always."

He planted a kiss on her forehead.

"I somehow think we will."

The turkey dinner was delicious. Afterward, Ann played carols on the organ in the library and they all sang until they were hoarse.

Finally, at a very late hour the wonderful day came to an end and everyone retired to bed.

Long after Bill and Ann and Jonathan had said good night, Mandy lay in the darkness of her room, holding her new teddy bear close and reflecting how happy she had been the past few weeks. With a sudden shock she realized that it was all going to be over tomorrow. Matron was coming for her at noon, and she was going to be taken back to her old life at the orphanage. It was an unbearable thought.

Sadness overcame her, and, though Mandy fought it with all her strength, she submitted to the worst depression of her whole life.

She tried to tell herself that it was selfish to feel this way after having had such a wonderful Christmas. She was so much luckier than the other children at the orphanage. But it didn't help because, although she felt guilty, she wanted desperately for the happiness to go on. She wanted to hold on to it and keep it for always.

Mandy tried to console herself with thoughts of the beautiful gifts she had received that day. She would treasure them always. They would remind her of this best-ever Christmas. But *why* couldn't it go on? Why couldn't she stay here with Bill and Ann and Johnathan forever and ever? She remembered her conversation with Ann, and Ann telling her that they weren't sure they could afford to keep Cranton House. So, obviously, they couldn't afford to take care of one extra person as well. And even if they could, why would they want to?

It seemed to Mandy that all the good things in life had to come to an end. It had been that way with the cottage, too. She wept silent tears and her emotions spun around and around.

The night lengthened. Mandy heard the clock in the lounge chime twice. The minutes ticked away. She stared at the windows and a pinpoint of light that was the moon. And she came to a brave decision. No matter how sad she felt, she would not show her sadness to anyone. She would let Bill and Ann know that this had been the happiest time of her whole life. She would not let them see her greed and selfishness and would leave them with as good an impression of herself as possible. She would try to be strong. Having made the decision, Mandy wept all over again.

10

MATRON CALLED for Mandy at exactly twelve o'clock the following day. Mandy was packed and waiting for her and she kept to her resolve to be brave. It was the hardest thing she had ever tried to do. Jonathan and Bill and Ann walked outside with her to the car. Mandy felt as though she were carrying around a big floating bag of sadness inside her. It was so full that she thought it must surely burst at any moment.

Matron voiced for Mandy some of the things she wanted to say to Bill and Ann.

"Thank you so much for having her. I know it has just been the most wonderful time. Hasn't it, Mandy?"

Mandy nodded. She forced her eyes wide apart so that the tears would not show. The strain was nearly unbearable, and her throat was aching horribly. She gave Ann a brief, fierce hug and managed to whisper, "Thank you for everything."

166

She stared at the ground as she offered Jonathan her hand.

" 'Bye, Jonathan."

" 'Bye, Mandy. Hope to see you soon."

Bill looked lovingly at the girl standing in front of him in such obvious emotional pain. He placed his hands on her head and pulled her close to his side.

Mandy buried her face in his coat. They stood that way for a long moment.

"Come again soon, Mandy. Come and visit us often. We shall miss you a lot."

Mandy could only nod her head. She tried to summon a smile and gave a small hiccup of emotion. Bill quietly handed her his handkerchief and then moved to open the car door.

"Take care of her, Matron. She's very special to us."

Matron climbed into the car and Mandy followed. Her eyes were so full of tears that she could barely see. The car door slammed and the Fitzgerald family shouted their good-byes. The limousine pulled away from the house, its tires crunching noisily on the gravel.

Mandy did not look back. She sat stiffly on the edge of her seat and averted her head so that Matron could not see her. She gazed sadly out of the window.

Matron was saying, "The children are terribly excited about your coming home, Mandy. You've no idea how much you were missed at Christmas."

The car stopped at two big gates leading on to the main road. Mandy watched the gates swing wide to let the car through, and she felt a surge of bitter resentment toward Matron for taking her back to the orphanage. She felt as though she were a piece of baggage being shifted from one

place to another. She had a sudden desire to jump out of the car and run far away from everyone.

How wonderful it would be to live her own life, to be free to decide things for herself.

The orphanage seemed smaller than Mandy remembered. It looked bleak and gray as they arrived. The only cheerful thing about it was the welcome of the children who came rushing out, as the car pulled up to the front door. She was glad of the distraction. It momentarily took her mind away from the unhappiness she felt .

Mandy discovered that she was something of a celebrity. The children wanted to know every detail of her Christmas and her illness and her being away for so long. The attention was very flattering, but Mandy had no wish to talk about anything. She was achingly tired and there were dark shadows under her eyes. She found herself yawning, and Matron suggested that she go upstairs for an afternoon rest.

Sue carried Mandy's case up to the attic, and she chattered happily as Mandy undressed for bed.

"I'm so glad you're back, Mandy. It was terribly quiet here without you. Christmas was really lonely."

Mandy gazed around the familiar attic room. It was so different from the large, airy bedroom she had occupied at Cranton Hall. She wished she could be in that quiet, peaceful room at this very moment. She took from her case the brown teddy bear that Jonathan had given her and climbed into bed.

"I've got masses to tell you," Sue said. "Will you show me your Christmas presents when you get up?"

Mandy smiled and nodded wearily. She touched the signet

ring on her finger and gazed at it lovingly. A deep sadness overcame her and she pulled the bear close and held it tightly. She cuddled down beneath the covers, pulling the sheet up over her head. Sue, sensing Mandy's mood, wisely left the room and pulled the door to a close behind her.

Mandy wept until she fell into an exhausted sleep. To everyone's surprise she didn't wake at dinner time. She slept through the night.

11

MATRON PEEPED in just as Mandy was waking up the next morning. When she saw that Mandy was stirring, she came into the room.

"Good morning, Mandy. How do you feel today?"

For a moment Mandy couldn't remember where she was and then she realized that she was back at the orphanage. She sat up in bed and rubbed her eyes.

"Goodness, is it morning?" she said. Matron pulled open the curtains and came to sit on the edge of her bed.

"It is. And it's ten o'clock, believe it or not. Sue has been up and about for ages and is waiting for you to come downstairs."

Mandy thought about Bill and Ann and tried to imagine how she would get through the day without seeing them. Her insides ached from missing them so. Would she ever feel better? Would her sadness ever go away?

Matron noticed that Mandy's eyes were swollen from so

much crying, and she saw the tears that threatened to gather there again.

"Mandy, Mr. and Mrs. Fitzgerald telephoned early this morning to find out how you were."

"Oh, did they?" Mandy felt a warm feeling spreading through her. "What did they say?"

"They were most anxious about you. They were glad to know that you were still sleeping. They sent their love and wanted you to call them later if you felt like it. Otherwise, they said they'd phone again tonight."

Mandy thought about this and wondered if she should return their call. One part of her wanted to most desperately. But, on the other hand, she was reluctant to get in touch with the Fitzgeralds. It would make her feel so sad to speak with them again. She was sure she would cry, and Mandy was beginning to be angry at the chaotic emotions that seemed to turn her inside out and upside down.

"I — I don't think I'll call them just yet," she said, evasively. "I mean, I've only just come back, and I want to see everybody and catch up on things, you know."

Matron seemed to understand and she changed the subject.

"Mandy, I don't want you to be too active today. Dr. Matthews told me that you must get plenty of rest. You may get up and play for a while, but just don't overdo it." She leaned forward and gently brushed aside the hair on Mandy's forehead. "Everything will seem all right again in time, you'll see."

Mandy smiled bravely. Matron was kind. She told herself that soon she would feel glad to be back with her friends again. In the meantime, she would find an excuse to avoid speaking

171

to the Fitzgeralds when they called. It would be so much easier that way. She lay back on her pillows and prepared to face the long day ahead.

Later in the week Matron Bridie rang the Fitzgeralds at Cranton Hall. Ann picked up the receiver and spoke with some relief as she heard Matron's voice.

"Oh, Mrs. Bridie, we've been trying to talk to Mandy for the last couple of days. But we don't seem able to reach her."

"I know; that's why I'm calling." Matron sounded a little troubled. "She's deliberately avoiding getting in touch with you. I really believe it's so painful for her that she just can't face it."

"Oh, dear, that's so sad." Ann's voice echoed her feelings. "We miss her most terribly."

"Yes, and I know she misses you, too. She's really having a bad time of it," Matron said. "She doesn't seem to have an interest in anything right now. She is very controlled. I almost wish she would break down. I think it would help her. She was questioning me the other day about her parents and how they died. That's something she hasn't done for a long time. I think she's quite desperate to create the feeling of a family about her."

"How can we help?" Ann asked. "Should we come to visit her?"

"I don't think there is anything you can do at the moment," Matron replied, "except to keep trying to telephone Mandy. Even if she doesn't speak to you, it's important that she knows that you care. And she will settle down after a while."

Ann related her conversation with Matron to Bill. He looked

172

thoughtfully into the fire. It was a long time before he spoke. "It's too bad. It really is. Dammit — I miss that little girl."

Ann sat down beside him and he put an arm around her shoulders.

"Well, at least she had a wonderful Christmas, darling," Ann said, trying to sound more cheerful than she felt. "That'll be something good for her to remember always." She didn't sound very convinced.

"I'm not sure if she isn't in more trouble because of her Christmas here," Bill said. "Before she came to stay with us she knew nothing of our kind of warmth and love, and therefore she had no reason to miss it. But now . . . " He didn't complete the sentence, but Ann knew what he meant. She felt miserable. She wished there were a way of letting Mandy know how badly they missed her.

12

AT THE ORPHANAGE the New Year was ushered in quietly and with little ceremony. The children settled down after the festivities of Christmas and prepared themselves for the new school term ahead. Routines were established once more and things reverted to normal.

For Mandy, nothing was the same and it never would be again. She could not stop thinking, painful as it was, about Bill and Ann and Jonathan. She found herself reliving every moment of the time that she had spent with them. She wondered how they were and what they were all doing. Did Samson miss her? Had Jonathan found the other secret passageway? Had his snowman melted? She pictured the family getting up in the morning. And sitting down to dinner at night. Mandy couldn't know it, but, for the first time in her life, she was feeling home-sick.

The knowledge that she could not go back to the Fitzgeralds was so painful that it was almost unbearable. Mandy knew that she would certainly be allowed to visit them once in a while. At one time she would have welcomed the possibility. But now she was not prepared to settle for anything less than she had already experienced. If Bill and Ann could not take care of her and be her family, then she would go and find some-one who could.

Mandy was so miserable that she made a characteristic move. It wasn't in her nature to tolerate sadness, and so she became determined to do something to rid herself of her unhappiness. Somehow, somewhere she would find a way to show someone that she was worthy of love. But she would not find it by staying at the orphanage. Matron and Ellie and Jake and Sue were all good to her and very considerate. But they could not give her the kind of love that she craved. And besides, Mandy felt that she had had enough of people telling her how to con-duct her life. "Mandy, do this. Mandy, do that. Mandy, get to bed early. Mandy, don't go outside. Mandy, do as you're told."

Well, Mandy would show them all that she didn't need any-one, anymore.

She made a decision born of great desperation. She spoke to Sue about it.

"Sue, if you promise not to tell anyone, I'll let you in on a secret. I'm going to run away."

"Oooh, Mandy." Sue was immediately concerned. "Where will you go?"

"I don't know yet. But I just have to leave. I can't stay here anymore."

"But why not? It's not such a bad place and everybody likes you."

"I can't explain it, Sue. It's just something I feel inside. I can't spend the rest of my life here in the orphanage. I want to be somebody and prove I can do something. I'll probably go to a big town. I'd like to go miles and miles away," she said wistfully.

"But what will you do for money?" Sue was concerned with the practical side of things.

"I have a little that I've saved. And I'll probably find a job."

"When will you go?"

"I thought I'd try tomorrow morning — before anybody's up. I'll pack this evening and get a good night's sleep. But you're not to say anything, Sue. Do you promise?"

Sue was solemn and quiet for a moment. And then she nodded her head. "I'll help you pack," she said.

Later in the day, Sue came to Mandy, clutching a paper bag in her hand.

"Mandy, I want you to take this. It's some money that I was given for Christmas. It might help you a tiny bit. No, I really want you to have it," she said, as Mandy started to protest.

She helped Mandy put her few precious possessions into a

suitcase. Mandy packed her new red dress and shoes and her teddy bear and some trousers and sweaters and two pairs of pajamas. Then she pushed the case under her bed so that it would not be seen.

"Oh, Mandy, I do wish you wouldn't do this." Sue was becoming increasingly anxious. "I understand how badly you feel, I really do. But what'll I do when you're gone? Do you suppose I should come with you?"

Mandy thought how good it would be to have Sue's company when she traveled. Truthfully, she was quite nervous about going. But she shook her head and said, "No, this is something I've got to do myself. Besides, I'll need you to cover for me as long as possible after I'm gone."

"Will I ever see you again? Will you write to me or anything?"' Sue was tearful.

"Well, I couldn't write to you, silly, because everybody would know where I was. But we'll see each other one day, I promise."

The girls prepared for bed. They were both on edge and talked to each other in whispers long after the lights were out.

Mandy looked up at the skylight over her head. It was a cloudy night and she could see no stars. She hoped that the weather would be fine by the morning. She was anxious about waking up early enough. Mandy decided that she would just catnap all night and not really go to sleep after all.

Her mind drifted to thoughts of Shell Cottage. She hadn't thought about it for a long time. It was a pity that everyone knew of the place, because it would have been a perfect spot to hide for a while. But she wasn't sure that she ever wanted to see it again. Anyway, it was up to Bill and Ann to take care of it now.

Mandy felt sad. Tomorrow would be the last time she would see the orphanage. Maybe when she was much older she would come back to visit everyone. She wondered how she would feel without Matron and Ellie and all the friends she knew.

She thought of Bill and Ann and wondered if they'd be anxious about her after she'd gone. Perhaps she should go and say good-bye to them? It would be wonderful to see them just once more. But they would try to dissuade her from running away. And she was determined to go. There was no point in saying good-bye to anyone, except Sue.

In spite of her resolve to stay awake, Mandy drifted into a light sleep.

"Mandy — Mandy, wake up."

A voice was calling to her as if from a great distance.

Mandy cried out in her sleep and stirred.

"Mandy."

She awoke with a start and became aware that Sue was standing beside her bed and shaking her vigorously.

"Mandy, oh, Mandy, please wake up. You'll never guess what's happened."

"What? What is it?" Mandy sat up anxiously. Sue seemed very excited.

"I heard a car coming up the drive so I got out of bed to look. No one ever comes to visit at this hour. But, Mandy, I think it's Mr. and Mrs. Fitzgerald. I'm sure it's their car down there."

Mandy was out of bed so fast that for a moment she felt

quite dizzy. She ran to the window and peered out into the darkness. She could see the shape of a car parked in the drive-way below, but it was so dark that she could not tell if it belonged to Bill and Ann or not. She discovered that her heart was thumping loudly. Grabbing her dressing gown she ran to the door of her room and opened it.

"Come on," she whispered.

Sue eagerly followed her, and the girls tiptoed to the top of the main stairway. The house was very dark except for a small light in the hall. Mandy crept farther down the stairs and leaned over the banister. She could see a beam of light coming from under the door in Matron's study. And she could hear voices, soft and indistinct.

"Can you hear what they're saying?" Sue asked.

"No, I can't."

"Do you suppose it's them?"

"Sshh." Mandy was trembling.

Suddenly, before the girls could run away, the study door was flung wide open and Matron came out. She turned on the main hall light, and both girls were left standing in the bright glare.

Matron blinked in surprise at the sight of them both. Then, instead of being angry, she gave a slight smile and said in a very ordinary voice, "Oh, Mandy, I'm glad you're up. I was just coming to wake you. There's someone down here to see you." As she spoke a figure came to the door of the study and gazed up at her.

"Good evening, Manders," said Bill.

Mandy's heart did a huge somersault. Ann came to the door and stood beside him.

"Hello, darling," she said. Both the Fitzgeralds were smiling.

Mandy had such an urgent desire to run to them that she thought she would fall and tumble down the stairs in her excitement. But she contained herself and stayed where she was.

"Hello," she said and was surprised at how flat and noncommittal her voice sounded.

What were the Fitzgeralds doing here at this time of night? Had they come because she hadn't telephoned them? Were they angry with her? Were they hurt?

"Well, Mandy, aren't you coming down?" Matron moved to the staircase. "Why don't you come and visit for a while and I'll take Sue back to her room and keep her company."

Mandy walked slowly down the stairs gripping the banister tightly, feeling that her legs would buckle beneath her unless she did.

"How have you been, Mandy?" Bill asked warmly as she reached the bottom step.

"Oh, fine." Again, her voice sounded remote and disinterested. The three of them moved into the study.

"Mandy, you can't imagine how badly we've missed you," Ann was saying.

Mandy looked at Bill and Ann and a pain began in her tummy. She was so desperately glad to see them both. She sat down in a chair by the fire and folded her hands together tightly in an effort to stop them from trembling.

"Has everything been all right since you've been back?" Ann asked. Mandy nodded.

"Did you miss us?" Bill smiled his teasing smile.

Mandy wondered how she could ever explain just how much

179

she had ached to see them both. It was more than words could describe.

"Yes, I did," she said in a small voice, thinking, "What is the matter with me? Why am I behaving so strangely?"

Bill sat down and leaned toward her. "Manders, we came especially to see you tonight because we have something to tell you. It's very important and it concerns us all. Listen carefully now and try to let me finish before you speak." His voice was serious, and he glanced at Ann before he continued. "Ann was right just now, Mandy. After you left us, we discovered that we missed you terribly. It just wasn't the same in the house without you. Even poor old Jonathan seems lost and out of sorts. We discussed our feelings and since we all felt the same way, we decided that we would ask Matron if it would be possible for you to come and live with us." Mandy's eyes widened and she drew in a deep breath.

"We wanted to come and speak to you about it right away," Bill went on, "but first of all it was necessary to find out from the authorities whether they would let us adopt you. It didn't seem right to talk to you about it until we were sure. And, of course, the authorities took forever to find your records and check your history and so on. But, darling, just tonight, we finally got permission to come and speak to you. And that's why we're here. We were so excited, we couldn't wait until the morning, so we came over right away."

Mandy discovered that the palms of her hands were wringing wet. She blinked hard and looked at the clock on the mantelpiece in an effort to control her chaotic emotions. One remote part of her noticed that the hands of the clock were made of

180

golden filigree and that the time was ten minutes to eleven.

Ann moved forward and spoke in a warm and loving voice. "Darling, we do love you very much. We've always wanted to have a little girl and somehow you seemed so special to us from the very first night you came to the house. You don't have to make up your mind about this just yet. There's no hurry for an answer. But, do you think you could consider coming to live with us for always? I think we could make you very happy. How do you feel about taking us on as a family?"

There was a moment of silence. The only sound in the little study was the loud ticking of the clock.

Mandy found that she was completely and utterly speech-less. For a moment she wondered if she were in the middle of some terrible, yet wonderful, dream. It was hard to believe what she had just heard. But one look at Bill and Ann and the concerned expectation on their faces told her that this was a very real moment indeed.

Then why was she feeling so bewildered? Why couldn't she answer as her heart dictated? Why couldn't she say that this was the most fabulous, wonderful, marvelous thing that had ever happened to her in her whole life?

To be adopted. To live in Cranton Hall forever. To be with this family that she had come to adore so much. Not to have to live at the orphanage for the rest of her life, or run away as she had planned to do. To know that Bill and Ann really cared enough after all.

"We love you very much, Mandy." "We think we could make you very happy." "We've always wanted a little girl!"

Suddenly, Mandy was filled with the most enormous, brimming happiness. The delayed emotion surged up within her, reaching from her toes to the top of her head, and she experienced a wildly joyous feeling of release.

She rose unsteadily to her feet and looked first at Bill and then at Ann. "Oh, gosh," was all she could say. "Oh, *gosh*."

Bill began to laugh. Ann held out her arms and Mandy went into them and clung tightly. She had never been so happy in her whole life and she could not stop weeping. Ann bent to kiss the dark head and found herself weeping, too.

13

THINGS SEEMED to happen very fast after that. Matron came downstairs and was delighted to learn that everything had turned out so well. The Fitzgeralds were anxious to take Mandy back to Cranton Hall with them that very evening. But, strangely, Mandy decided she would prefer to wait until the following day. She couldn't help thinking of Sue, and she knew that she could not say good-bye to her friend so abruptly and leave her to spend the rest of the night alone.

So it was decided that Bill would call for Mandy in the morning.

The Fitzgeralds bid her a fond goodnight, and afterward Mandy broke the wonderful news to her friend. As she had anticipated, it was a difficult and ambivalent moment for Sue.

"Oh, Mandy, you are lucky. What a fabulous thing to happen. I know you'll be very happy." There was a pause and then quite suddenly Sue burst into tears. Mandy put her arms around her.

"Oh, Sue, don't cry. Please don't. Think how super it's going to be. We'll be able to see lots and lots of each other. You can come to the house and play and maybe spend the night sometimes."

Sue nodded and rubbed her eyes. "I'm really terribly thrilled. It's just that I'll miss you so badly." She blew her nose hard.

"I'll miss you too." The girls clung to each other for a moment. Sue looked up and said, "Golly, how lucky it was that they came to see you tonight. You'd have been gone by tomorrow."

Mandy nodded. It was a sobering thought.

The following morning Mandy was consumed with anxiety. She could hardly wait for Bill to come and pick her up and she had the terrible fear that he might forget all about it or change his mind completely. Her packing was done in no time at all since she had been prepared to leave the night before anyway. The entire orphanage knew about her departure, and when Bill finally drove up in his station wagon it seemed that every child was waiting to say good-bye.

It was almost more than Mandy could bear. She clambered into the front seat of the automobile and rolled down the window to wave to everyone.

Matron was smiling happily and waving. Sue was smiling also, but her eyes were filled with tears.

Mandy's last impression as the car pulled away was of the

young, eager faces of the orphanage children and their voices raised high in farewell.

"Good-bye, Mandy." "See you soon." "God bless, Mandy." "Please come back and visit."

Mandy waved until the orphanage was completely out of sight. When she turned back in her seat she discovered that she was crying.

Bill looked across at her and smiled fondly.

"A little sad?" he asked.

"Yes."

"And happy, too?"

"Oh, yes."

"A bit of both. Well, that's understandable."

"It's silly, but I wish they could all come, too. It's terrible somehow to leave them behind."

Bill nodded. "I know, Mandy. I know. But those children will find a life for themselves one day, just as you have. You'll see. It may not be right away, perhaps it will be when they grow up or when they marry. But it will happen. And in the meantime, Matron isn't going to let them be unhappy, now is she?"

"No." Mandy wiped her eyes. There was silence for a moment. The car sped through the country lanes and Mandy looked out of the window at the crisp winter morning. Traces of snow were everywhere. Clear sunshine bathed the country-side in a silvery light, like a watercolor. Mandy shook her head in bewilderment.

"I just don't understand why it was *me* that got to be so lucky," she said.

"Oh, gosh, Mandy. What shall I tell you?" Bill looked

thoughtful. "I suppose luck does have something to do with it. But you're a very special little girl. And I think you're strong and not afraid to go looking for your life. You know, I think you could be a good example to the orphanage children. Perhaps, one day when you're truly settled in with us and you know that we're not ever going to let you go, you might consider going back to visit them from time to time. I'm sure it would help them."

Mandy thought about it.

"I'd like that," she said simply.

14

BILL BRAKED the car to a halt just outside the big gates to Cranton Hall. Mandy remembered passing through them a couple of weeks earlier and how unhappy she had been. The long driveway stretched ahead. Mandy drew in a deep breath of the clear, fresh air coming in through the open window. She looked at the trees and the fields all around her and experienced a feeling she had never felt before. It was a warm contentment, something like the feeling one gets when hot tea and honey slide way down into one's stomach, only ten times better.

Bill said, "You've never really seen Cranton, have you, Mandy? C'mon. We've got time. I'll give you a quick guided tour."

He drove the car around the beautiful estate, pointing out the various places of interest.

"There's the dairy, Mandy, and the courtyard beyond used to be the old kennels."

There were hay barns, and places for grain storage and silage and tractors and equipment. Mandy saw cows in the cowshed and a huge bull in an outside stall. There were chickens and cockerels, pigs and horses. A large, silly dog ran around in happy circles trying to scare the fowl. There was a big kitchen garden and beyond were rows of empty wire pens.

"Those are for the baby pheasants when they're strong enough," Bill explained. "We'll be breeding them early in the year. You'll see."

Bill swung the wagon onto a wide rutted track. A ribbon of water ran under a small humpbacked bridge and beyond was the flat, smooth surface of a beautiful lake.

Bill stopped the car on the bridge and pointed.

"Mandy, see the trees on the island in the middle of the lake? Notice the ragged collection of twigs and mud and old leaves in the tops of them? They're herons' nests. We must have had at least three pairs this year. I bet they'll be back in the spring."

Mandy remembered the heron she had seen flying over the cottage one day. It must have been heading for the lake. She was struck by a thought.

"Bill, I suppose the little stream by the cottage runs into the lake, doesn't it?"

"Yes, darling, it does."

"Who used to live in Shell Cottage?" Mandy wanted to know.

"Well, at first, no one did, believe it or not. In the old days it was a sort of playhouse. My ancestors would have picnics there; it was a place to ride to, to shelter in when it rained, that sort

186

of thing. That's why the shell room was built — it was purely a fun house."

"But then . . . ?"

"Then, of course, when times became difficult and the family was so hard up, it was rented out to whoever could afford it." Bill turned to Mandy. "Incidentally, Manders, what would you like to do with the cottage? It's yours now, you know. I thought I'd make a sign to that effect and put it on the gate. And I can paint it up a bit. Would you like to plant the garden again this year?"

Mandy thought about it. She became suddenly serious. She remembered last summer and her passionate concern for the garden and the house. But, now, it didn't seem so important. Her new life promised such a wonderful future. Would she want to spend time at the cottage? She looked at Bill. And suddenly, she knew what it was she wanted to say.

"Bill, if I could do anything with Shell Cottage — if it's at all possible, that is — what I'd really like to do is to let the other children at the orphanage have it."

Bill looked surprised, but Mandy warmed to her subject.

"You know, like Sue and everybody. They could come to it and play and have a part of the garden to make pretty. I think it would be marvelous to have a special place like that. It would mean having something of their very own, don't you see?"

There was a pause. Bill's eyes narrowed in thought. Mandy waited for him to speak. He did so finally, quietly and deliberately.

"I think it's a wonderful idea, Manders." His voice was low with emotion. "It would be simple to grant a right-of-way

187

through the woods. We'd have to build a gate in the big wall. But it could be, indeed, a playhouse for the children." He turned and smiled. "Just as it used to be. That's a good thought, Manders. I'll speak to Matron about it this evening."

He turned the ignition key in the car and started it up again. "Now, darling, we'd better get back to the house. Ann'll be wondering what happened to us. I told her we'd be there for lunch."

Mandy felt a thrill as Cranton Hall came into view. The station wagon drove around a circular lawn and came to a stop in front of the big house. Bill paused a moment, his hands resting on the wheel. He grinned at Mandy.

"Well, Manders, here you are. You're home."

Mandy's feelings soared with happiness, and laughter bubbled up inside her. She gave Bill a brief hug and then stepped out of the car and raced up the steps to the front door where Jonathan and Ann were waiting for her.

"Hello." Mandy's voice was breathless with excitement.

"Hello, Mandy. Welcome." Ann folded her in her arms. Jonathan was grinning good-naturedly and he patted her on the back in an embarrassed sort of way.

Bill ran up the steps to join them and as the family turned and walked through the front door, Mandy experienced a great warm feeling of contentment. She realized that never again would she go through long nights of aching sadness. There would be no more depressions that she couldn't understand. At last she had a home and a family and people to love and be loved by.

She had found what she had been looking for all her life.

The Last of the Really Great Whangdoodles

The Last of the Really

Great Whangdoodles

BY JULIE EDWARDS

HARPER & ROW, PUBLISHERS

For
BLAKE
and
Emma, Geoff, Jenny, Kim, Tony, Frank, Herb, Dad . . . and all the other kids around our house . . . for their love, patience and help.

Contents

PART ONE

Challenge

ONE

It was a crisp, sunny October afternoon and Benjamin, Thomas and Melinda Potter were visiting the Bramblewood Zoo.

They hadn't particularly wanted to visit the zoo, but Mrs. Potter had been very firm about it.

"Daddy has been working extremely hard," she had said, "and I think he needs an afternoon of peace and quiet. Here's some money. I suggest you go to the zoo."

There was no arguing with Mrs. Potter in this mood. So the three children had dutifully taken the bus from the stop at the corner of their street and had ridden through the pretty university town of Bramblewood as far as the zoo.

Although it was the end of October and very cold, the sun was shining brightly from an unusually clear sky. Only a few clouds on the horizon gave a hint of possible rain. Late autumn leaves blew along the pavement and rolled in through the main gates of the zoo as if inviting the children to follow.

On this lovely Sunday the place was crowded with visitors and there were popcorn sellers, balloon vendors and a man pushing a yellow cart piled high with toys. Children yelled happily as they scampered to the rides and to the animal cages.

In spite of their early reluctance to venture out, Benjamin, Thomas and Lindy had to admit, now that they were there, that the zoo didn't seem a bad place to visit after all.

"I want to see the tigers," Tom announced.

"I want to see the donkeys and the ducks," countered Lindy.

"*Donkeys* and *ducks*," Tom scoffed. "*Anyone* can see a donkey or a duck, and you don't have to go to the zoo for it. That's just a waste of time."

"I know, I know," Lindy replied. "I just feel like seeing a donkey and a duck today. I don't know why."

"Oh, look—if we're going to spend the afternoon trailing around, looking at animals like that . . ."

"Well, we're not," Ben interrupted firmly. He was used to his younger brother and sister squabbling with each other. "We're going to see the elephants first. Because I'm the oldest and I'm in charge. C'mon."

The children visited the elephants and then the lions and the tigers. They slowly moved on to see llamas and leopards and rhinos and reindeer; crocodiles and hippopotamuses and brown bears and polar bears. They watched the performing seals and Lindy saw three ducks and twelve penguins, which made her very happy.

Tom suggested that they visit the aquarium. They wandered through the dim corridors whose only light came from the many illuminated tanks in which turtles, sharks, eels and other underwater creatures were to be seen. It was gloomy and damp inside. Lindy was very glad when Ben chose to go to the reptile house. But she clung tightly to his hand as she gazed at the cobras and rattlesnakes and a giant python.

"I'd love one of those for a pet," Tom said enthusiastically.

"Ugh! I think they're gross. Really *gross*," Lindy exclaimed.

"You just say that 'cause you're scared of them."

"No, I don't. They're not my favorite things. But I'm not scared."

"Then why are you sucking your thumb?"

"I like the taste."

"Cut it out, you two," said Ben. "What shall we do next?"

Lindy announced that she was tired, cold and extremely hungry.

The children bought a bag of delicious, sticky-looking doughnuts and three cups of hot, sugary chocolate. Carefully, they carried the steaming mugs to a bench that caught the late afternoon sunshine and which was close to a fenced yard containing two large, disdainful-looking giraffes.

Lindy had no sooner sat down than one of the giraffes spotted the doughnut she had in her hand and immediately undulated towards her on spindly legs, looking as though his knobby knees would buckle beneath him at any moment. The animal lifted his long neck over the wire netting and brought his face to within inches of Lindy's—just as she was about to take a large mouthful of her doughnut.

The giraffe and the child gazed at each other with serious concentration for a moment. Then Lindy solemnly said, "No," and moved herself and her doughnut farther along the bench out of the giraffe's way.

"That's really an extraordinary animal," mused Ben as he watched. "Imagine being born with a long neck like that. Imagine being able to reach the tops of trees quite easily."

"I'd like that," said Tom. "You could see the world from up there."

"I like giraffes a lot." Lindy spoke with her mouth full.

"If you could have any animal out of the zoo, which one

would you like to take home?" Ben suddenly asked.

"The python." Tom spoke without hesitation.

"Gross," said Lindy. "I'd have a penguin. What would you have, Ben?"

"Mm, I dunno." Ben thought about it as he sipped his hot chocolate. "I'd like something unusual. An orangutan, perhaps. Or an anteater. Maybe a gorilla."

"You'll excuse my butting in," said a voice immediately behind the children. "But if you're looking for something *really* unusual, have you ever considered a Whangdoodle?"

The children spun around.

Sitting on the grass behind them, knees drawn up almost to his chin, was a small man. He was holding a rolled umbrella made of clear plastic.

"I beg your pardon, sir," Ben said, "did you say something?"

"Yes, I did. I said, have you ever considered a Whangdoodle?"

The little man got up slowly. He had a round cheerful face with bright blue, sparkling eyes, and the few hairs still growing on his balding head were long and grey and flying in all directions. He wore an old brown sports jacket and a blue-checked shirt with a purple, yellow-spotted scarf tied in a casual bow. He had shabby brown trousers and old, but highly polished, shoes.

Ben said, "Excuse me, but I don't think I've ever heard of a Whangdoodle, sir."

The remarkable-looking gentleman smiled, leaned on his umbrella and crossed one small foot over the other.

"That's not surprising. It's an extremely rare creature. In fact, I believe there's only one left in the whole world."

"What does it look like?" Tom asked.

"Well now, I've not actually seen the Whangdoodle myself," countered the stranger. "Although I do hope to one day."

"Then how do you know about it?" Lindy wanted to know.

"Ah—that's a long, complicated story," he replied. "Here we are chatting away, and I don't even know your names."

Tom tugged at Ben's sleeve. He was suspicious of the stranger and wanted to warn Ben that they should be leaving immediately and heading for home.

But Lindy was already cheerfully giving out information. "My name is Melinda Potter. Everybody calls me Lindy."

"How old are you, Lindy?"

"I shall be eight on December third."

"Which means she's seven," growled Tom.

"Ah, but of course." The stranger turned to him. "And how old are you, young man?"

"Ten. My name is Thomas Potter."

"And I'm Benjamin Potter," Ben offered. "I'm thirteen."

"What about you? What's your name?" Tom wanted to know.

The stranger placed a hand on his forehead. "Goodness me, what *is* my name? It seems to have escaped me for the moment." Lindy giggled. Tom nudged Ben hard and jerked his head as though to say, "Let's get out of here."

"But it's really of no importance," continued the man. "What *is* important is that this is a most pleasant afternoon, and, if I'm not mistaken, it is only two days before Halloween, is it not?"

Lindy gave a little hop of excitement. "Do you know what I'm going to be when we go trick-or-treating?" she asked.

"Let me see if I can guess." He looked thoughtful. "Snow White? Or possibly Cinderella?"

"No. I'm going to be a lion," she said proudly.

"And very ferocious I'm sure you'll be. What about you, Thomas? What are you going to be?"

"I'm going to be the Hunchback of Notre Dame."

"And you, Benjamin?"

"I haven't quite decided yet. I don't know whether to be Dracula or Frankenstein."

"Well, I just hope I don't bump into any of you in the dark. I think I would be very scared."

"Maybe I'll change my mind and go as a Whangdoodle," Lindy said brightly.

The little man chuckled. "What a good idea."

"You know, I really don't think there is such an animal," Tom blurted out. Ben actually thought so too, though he was too polite to say so.

"I assure you that the Whangdoodle exists," said the man. "Look it up in your dictionary when you get home."

"What does it look like?" asked Lindy.

"That's sort of hard to describe. It's a little like a moose— or a horse, perhaps. But with fantastic horns. And I believe it has rather short legs."

"Where does it live?" inquired Tom.

"Oh, far, far away. Which is a good thing, for if it were here, it would be in a cage like all these other poor animals. I do so hate to see things in cages, don't you?"

"Then why do you come to the zoo if you don't like it?" asked Lindy with her usual candor.

"I come to study the animals. I'd prefer to study them in their natural environments, but I just haven't the time."

Ben suddenly remembered to look at his watch. "Gosh, we're late. You'll have to excuse us, sir, but we have to go now, or we'll miss our bus."

The little man took a large watch from his pocket. "Yes, it is late," he said. "And we'd better hurry, because it is going to rain."

He unfurled his umbrella with a flourish and opened it over his head. Large yellow butterflies were painted all over the clear plastic.

"Allow me to escort you," he said, and walked briskly towards the front gate of the zoo.

Lindy fell into step beside him. "I *love* your umbrella," she said admiringly.

"I bought it because it's cheery and it makes people look up. Have you noticed how nobody ever looks up?" The man's voice was suddenly irritable. "Nobody looks at chimneys, or trees against the sky, or the tops of buildings. Everybody just looks down at the pavement or their shoes. The whole world could pass them by and most people wouldn't notice."

Ben and Tom discovered that they were looking at the pavement as he spoke. Quickly, they lifted their heads to the sky, only to get wet faces, for it was beginning to rain. They also bumped straight into Lindy and her escort, who had come to a sudden halt.

"This is where the bus stops, isn't it?" asked the stranger. "Ah, here comes one now. Very good timing, that. I hate to waste time, don't you?"

Visitors from the zoo were running for the bus or for their cars. Umbrellas seemed to be popping up everywhere. People who didn't have umbrellas went scurrying by with newspapers on their heads or their coats buttoned up tight.

"You see what I mean," said the man. "None of them look up. Ever." He helped the children onto the bus. "It has been a great pleasure meeting you all. A most happy afternoon." He waved a red handkerchief as the bus pulled away from the curb.

"Goodbye. Goodbye," he called after them.

There was a sudden terrifying sound of rubber tires skidding to a stop and the blaring sound of a car horn. Tom, Ben and Lindy turned quickly in their seats and looked out of the back window of the bus. The little man was standing in the middle of the street, apologizing to a taxi driver who had nearly run him down.

"I'll bet he was looking up," grinned Ben.

The bus turned a corner and the scene disappeared from their view.

TWO

Tom turned to Lindy in annoyance. "Boy, Lindy, you are the end. You talked and talked to that man. I don't think we should have encouraged him. He seemed as nutty as a fruitcake."

"Oh, I liked him," Lindy said defensively. "Did you notice he was wearing blue and white striped socks?"

Ben laughed. "I wonder if he was joking when he said there was something called a Whangdoodle."

"I'll bet he wasn't," said Lindy.

"I'll bet he was," countered Tom. "Anyway, I'm going to look that word up in the dictionary when we get home."

Lindy peered out into the rain. The bus was passing a

large park and on the other side of it, half obscured by trees, she saw a tall, thin house with shuttered windows.

Pointing to it, she asked Tom, "Is that place really haunted?"

"Sure."

"Who lives in there?"

"A terrible ogre and a witch with yellow fangs."

"Well, nobody's sure about that," Ben said. "But most people stay away from there, Lindy. Especially on Halloween."

"Well, it wouldn't scare me," she declared. "I don't believe in ogres . . . just fairies."

"You mean you wouldn't be scared to go up and knock on the front door?" Tom asked.

"Not at all."

"I bet you would."

"I wouldn't." Lindy raised her chin defiantly.

"Well, I'll make you a bet. I'll bet you five cents that you won't go and knock on the front door of Stone House on Tuesday night," said Tom.

"Pooh, that's not a good bet," Lindy hedged.

"Then I'll make it twenty-five cents."

The little girl hesitated. She wanted more than anything to join her brothers this year for Halloween. But she wasn't at all sure that she'd have the courage to do what Tom had suggested. Besides which, twenty-five cents represented her week's allowance.

"You see, you *are* scared," Tom said triumphantly.

"No, I'm not," she declared loudly. "It's a bet."

"Stop it, you two. You're both being stupid," Ben said.

"Don't look at me. She's the one who started it. If she's too scared to do it, then why doesn't she say so?"

"I'm *not* too scared."

"Okay." Ben threw up his hands in disgust. "But remember, Mom will probably make the final decision about it all anyway."

The subject came up again that night at dinner.

"Lindy, what would you like to do about trick-or-treating this Halloween?" Mr. Potter asked.

Lindy looked at her brothers. Tom stopped eating and watched her intently across the table.

"I was wondering if I could go with Tom and Ben."

Mrs. Potter looked at her sons.

"What do you think, boys?"

"Well, I don't know. . . ." replied Ben. "It's fine for the other two. I mean, they just have to tag along and everything. But I'm always the one who has to be in charge. I mean, look at today. I was constantly watching out for Lindy and trying to stop her and Tom arguing."

Mr. Potter smiled. "Tough, being the eldest, isn't it? Accepting responsibility is quite a chore sometimes."

"It sure is," Ben agreed solemnly.

"But that's part of growing up, I'm afraid. Part of being thirteen years old."

Ben considered this. Lindy held her breath.

"I guess I don't really mind all that much," Ben said finally.

"I think that's very nice." Mrs. Potter seemed quite pleased. "Then it's fine with us, Lindy, if that's what you'd like. Now, I suggest that we all sit by the fire for the last half hour before bedtime. Will one of you get the Sunday paper for your father?"

Ben ran to fetch it.

The Sunday evening get-together had become a habit all of the Potters enjoyed. The children talked about any problems that may have arisen at school. Holiday plans were discussed and everyone was encouraged to exchange ideas.

The children arranged themselves comfortably. Mrs. Potter took up her knitting and Mr. Potter lit his pipe, settled back in his favorite chair and opened the Bramblewood *Sunday Courier*.

"My word, Freda, look at this."

"What, dear?"

"Professor Savant has been awarded the Nobel Prize."

"How nice."

"Who's Professor Savant?" Tom wanted to know.

"Head of the Biology Research Department at the University," Mr. Potter explained.

"What did he get the Nobel Prize for?" Ben asked.

"According to this, for his work in genetics," said Mr. Potter.

"I don't even know what the Nobel Prize is." Lindy sounded bewildered.

Mr. Potter looked over his glasses at his eldest son.

"Can you tell her, Ben?"

Ben thought for a moment. "I think," he said slowly, "that it's a prize given every year to people who have done something really great—like in chemistry, or in writing, or in medicine. Something like that."

"Very good," said Mr. Potter. "It's also given for achievement in physics and physiology. And, very importantly, for the promotion of peace."

Mrs. Potter interrupted her husband. "I really think you

should write to the professor, dear. Just a small letter of congratulations. It's really so wonderful for the University. Which reminds me . . ." She turned to the children. "Would you all start thinking about doing a card or a letter to Grandma? You know, she's not been at all well. It would mean so much to her to hear from you all. Lindy, perhaps you could make one of your special cards?"

"Okay."

"Tell us about the zoo today," said Mr. Potter.

"We met the funniest little man there," Lindy suddenly remembered. "He told us about an animal called a Whangdoodle. Have you ever heard of it, Daddy?"

"A Whangdoodle? No, I can't say I have. What is it?"

"I don't know. He said it looks a bit like a horse. It has horns. . . ."

"I don't think there is such an animal," said Tom. "I told him so. He said to look it up in the dictionary when we got home."

"Well, go ahead," said Mr. Potter.

Tom ran into his father's study and took from a shelf a large, heavy, black dictionary that had obviously seen a great deal of use. He carried it carefully back into the living room and placed it on the table.

The children gathered around him as he thumbed through the tissue-thin pages. "Watchband, waybill, webbing, Wessex, West Orange, whammy. Here we are," he suddenly cried excitedly. "Whangdoodle."

"Oooh, what does it say?" Lindy pushed in close.

"It says—'noun, slang: a fanciful creature of undefined nature.'" Tom looked up. "What the heck does that mean?"

Mr. Potter rose and knocked his pipe against the side of

the fireplace. "It probably means that a Whangdoodle is a made-up word for some kind of imaginary creature. Which, I would think, is why the dictionary uses the word 'fanciful' to describe it."

"So I was right," Tom said. "A Whangdoodle doesn't exist."

"Probably not," replied Mr. Potter.

"There you are." Tom turned to Ben and Lindy. "I told you so."

"But you're not sure about that," Lindy protested.

"Yes, I am. I knew that old man was a phony."

"Oh, he wasn't." Lindy turned to Ben. "You don't think he was, do you, Ben?"

"Oh, Lindy. Who knows?" Ben sighed. "But if he wasn't a phony or crazy or anything, then what do you suppose he meant by all his talk?"

"We shall probably never find out," Mrs. Potter summed up. "Come on, children, it's time to get ready for bed."

 THREE

The following day Lindy wished very much that she had not accepted Tom's dare. The more she thought about it, the more she became convinced that she would never be able to approach Stone House on Halloween, or at any other time, for that matter. She was inwardly terrified at the whole idea, but her courage and pride forbade her from mentioning this to anyone. So she spent a very miserable day worrying about it.

At bedtime, when Mrs. Potter came in to kiss her daughter

good night, she found her lying wide-eyed and clutching her teddy bear.

"Don't turn the light out, Mummy. I need to talk to you for a moment."

"What is it, darling?"

"I want to know something. Is it true you can die from fright?" she asked.

Mrs. Potter tried not to smile at the solemnity with which Lindy asked her question. "Why? Are you frightened about tomorrow night?"

Lindy nodded.

"In what way are you frightened? Because you're going with the boys for the first time? Or is it something else?"

"No, it's sort of that," Lindy said.

"Well, you know, it's very easy to change your mind and come with Daddy and me instead."

Lindy hesitated. "No, I really would like to go with the boys. I was just thinking about it."

Mrs. Potter tucked the blankets snugly around her daughter.

"Why don't you speak to Ben and tell him you're a bit worried? He's very understanding about things like that."

Lindy felt a wave of relief at her mother's suggestion. Ben would watch out for her and keep her safe. She hugged her mother and kissed her.

"Good night, Mummy."

"Good night, darling. Sleep well."

In spite of Mrs. Potter's comforting reassurance, Lindy had terrible nightmares that night. She spoke to Ben immediately after school the next day. "Ben, can you keep a secret?"

"Of course I can."

"Well . . ." Lindy took a deep breath. "You see, I'm a bit scared about tonight. I want to keep my dare and win the twenty-five cents. But I was wondering . . . would you please stay very near when I go up to Stone House? And if I scream or faint or anything will you come and save me?"

Ben was flattered that Lindy would turn to him in a time of crisis and he answered in a big-brotherly way. "Of course I will, Lindy. Don't you worry about anything. I'll be right beside you."

"Oh, Ben, that's super."

At six thirty P.M., after a very early dinner, the children assembled at the front door to say goodbye to their parents.

Lindy's lion costume was a great success. She wore a furry bonnet with two soft, pointed ears on top of it, and furry mittens. She had ruby lips and there were black whiskers painted on her cheeks and a large black spot on the tip of her nose. On the back of her costume, Mrs. Potter had pinned a long silken tail with a gold tassel at the end of it.

Tom looked incredibly mean and ugly. He had put on his oldest clothes and padded them into a grotesque shape. He wore a pair of his father's shoes, which were much too big for him. He had used a gluelike substance to pull his face into an agonized expression. It made Lindy shudder just to look at him and even Mrs. Potter remarked in a startled voice, "Good heavens, Tom. Is that really you?"

Ben looked rather dashing, considering he was meant to be Dracula. He wore a long black cloak with a high collar over a black turtleneck sweater and brown trousers. He had painted his face white and his lips a dark, purplish red. His wig was shiny black. The only really frightening touch was the two fangs he had attached to his teeth.

Mr. Potter gave last-minute instructions. "Now, Dracula,

you're in charge. Act in a responsible manner. No egg throwing, no vandalism."

"How about shaving cream?" Tom asked.

"Well, all right. In moderation. Off you go. Be home by nine thirty or ten. No later."

It was dusk already and the streetlamps were glowing. Lindy, Tom and Ben saw people in costumes of every shape, color and size. There were ghosts and hoboes, Frankensteins and monsters, princesses and ballet dancers, gypsies, chimney sweeps and all manner of other disguises. Ghostly music emanating from some of the houses mingled with the sounds of cackling laughter and shrieking vampires. Candlelit pumpkins flickered while the moonlight cast moving shadows on the lawns.

As the night grew darker Lindy pressed closer to Ben. Tom studied her.

"Now, Lindy, are you sure you want to go through with this? I mean, it's going to be spooky and dangerous."

She nodded her head bravely.

"Well, okay." Tom spoke with grudging admiration.

The three children pushed on towards the town, occasionally pausing to knock on the door of any house that looked appealing and cheerful.

They collected a sizable bag of candy, chewing gum and toffee apples—a good portion of which they happily ate. By the time they reached the park Lindy was feeling decidedly odd. She couldn't tell if it was from fear or from too many treats.

There were two magnificent bonfires on the grass. Children were piling sticks and dry branches onto the flames, and sparks rose high into the air.

But the nearer the Potter children got to Stone House the less activity they saw. The area was heavily wooded. The grass was higher and obviously uncared-for. Stone House loomed tall and ghostly grey in the moonlight.

Lindy pulled Ben to a halt outside a pair of large iron gates. "You've got to come in with me," she whispered. "I'll never make it alone." The gate creaked on rusty hinges. Lindy's heart was pounding.

There was not a sign of life anywhere as they tiptoed along the edge of the gravel drive. Dry leaves crackled under their feet. A loose shutter banged noisily in an upstairs window of the house and all three children jumped with fright.

The wind moaned through the branches of the trees. A dog howled and, as the children paused near the front door, an owl hooted mournfully in the darkness. Lindy's legs almost gave out beneath her and she was close to tears.

"I told you this'd be too much for her," Tom hissed nervously.

Ben motioned him to be quiet. A light swung and glowed on the porch, revealing grey paint, cracked and flaked from wind and rain. Another light shone high up in the house, and another at the back spilled a ghostly yellow beam onto the grass.

"Lindy, it's now or never," Ben said solemnly. He let go of his sister's hand. "Do you think you can make it?"

Her eyes were wide with fear and she swayed a little.

"Go on, go on," Tom said and he prodded her in the back.

"*Don't do that,*" she snapped.

She took a deep breath and began to walk. She fixed her eyes on the elaborate door knocker and looked neither right nor left. The few yards to the porch seemed endless. Her shoes made a hollow sound as she climbed the wooden steps.

The owl hooted again as she stood on tiptoe and raised a trembling hand to the door knocker. With a burst of courage she banged it hard three times. The sound rang out in the stillness of the night and echoed through the trees. For a brief moment nothing happened. Then, suddenly, the front door swung open and a very sweet and cheerful-looking lady stood smiling down at her.

Lindy let out a piercing scream.

Tom and Ben charged out of the darkness.

"I'm here, Lindy!" shouted Ben.

"You leave my sister alone!" Tom yelled.

The boys' sudden appearance scared the lady so badly that she screamed too. This had the interesting effect of completely silencing the children. There was a sound of running footsteps inside the house and a voice cried out, "What is it, Mrs. Primrose? I'm coming." A small, funny-looking gentleman raced out of the house and flung a protective arm around the lady's ample figure.

"What on earth have we here?" The man peered at the children. "A lion and a Dracula and some other weird fellow. No, it's the Hunchback of Notre Dame. But wait a minute. Wait a *minute*. Bless my soul. Haven't we all met before?"

Ben cleared his throat. "Yes, sir. We met you at the zoo last Sunday."

"Of course. But how *very* nice." He seemed genuinely pleased as he turned to his housekeeper. "Mrs. Primrose, these children are my friends. What on earth is all the fuss about?"

Everyone started talking at once. The man held up his hands. "I really think this should be explained inside, where

we will be out of the cold. Mrs. Primrose, we'll have some
hot chocolate and whipped cream for everyone, please.
Come in, come in," he said to the children, and he held the
door open invitingly.

 *FOUR*

The house was marvelously interesting. To the left of a wide
staircase stood a complete suit of armor. There were portraits
on the walls, and it was easy for the children to guess that
they were ancestors or relatives of their host since the resem-
blance to him was unmistakable.

There was a round table in the center of the hall, overflowing with books and magazines. The brass centerpiece
was bursting with orange and red and yellow chrysanthemums.

The man ushered the children into a small room. There
were so many books that there didn't seem to be space for
anything else. Yet there was also a desk with a swivel chair
behind it, and a large globe of the world standing in the
corner. Three complex and wonderful mobiles hung from
the ceiling.

The man motioned for them to sit down by the fire. "You'll
have to sit on the carpet, I'm afraid," he said. "You see, I
never have more than one armchair in here. It discourages
company. Though of course I'm very pleased to see you this
evening." He sat down in the chair. "Now, let me see if I can
remember your names. You're Melinda and you're Benjamin.
Right?"

Ben and Lindy nodded.

"And, oh dear." He paused as he looked at Tom. "Is it Teddy?"

"Thomas, sir."

"Thomas, of course. Silly of me. Allow me to introduce myself. I am Professor Samuel Savant."

Ben gasped. "Golly. Are you *the* Professor Savant? The one who works at the University?"

"I am."

"Dad was telling us about you the other day," Tom said.

"Was he, indeed?"

"Yes. Where's your prize?" Lindy asked.

"My prize?"

"She means the Nobel Prize, sir."

The professor chuckled. "I won't be receiving it for a while. But come now. I am most interested to know how you found me."

"We didn't know this was your house," said Tom.

"We were out trick-or-treating," explained Ben.

"Tom bet me twenty-five cents that I wouldn't knock on the door," added Lindy. "I thought an awful witch lived here."

"A witch? Mrs. Primrose, are you a witch?" the professor asked as the sweet-looking woman entered the room with a tray.

"I sometimes think I'd like to be one, sir," she said with a smile.

Mrs. Primrose gave a steaming mug of hot chocolate to each child, and placed a plate of cookies on the floor in front of them.

The professor sipped his hot chocolate. "Mm, that's good. So, you thought a witch lived here, eh?"

Ben felt embarrassed. "Everyone at school thinks this house is haunted."

Their host suddenly became serious.

"I'm afraid I'm responsible for that rumor. You see, I do hate to be bothered. I need a lot of peace and quiet when I'm working."

"What do you really do?" asked Tom.

"Well—I think a lot."

"That's not much," said Lindy.

"On the contrary. It's a great deal," replied the professor. "Right now I'm thinking about life. I ask myself questions about it—its origin and its meaning. Believe me, that takes a great deal of thought." He leaned forward in his chair. "Do you know that the secret of life has almost been captured? It's part of the alphabet now. Have you heard of DNA and RNA?"

"I think so, sir," Ben said, but he looked puzzled and Tom shook his head.

"DNA. That stands for deoxyribonucleic acid. Good word, huh?" The professor grinned.

"What does it mean?" Ben wanted to know.

"Well, let's see if I can explain it very simply." The professor touched the tips of his fingers together as he gave it some thought. "Try to imagine a human cell. A single, microscopically small unit of life. Inside the nucleus, the very center, is a sort of ladder, a ladder twisted into a spiral. On that spiral is all the information as to how life comes about."

"That's a bit too complicated for me," said Tom.

"It is indeed complicated," answered the professor. "Actually it's miraculous. And DNA and RNA are the codes to life itself."

"I always thought life had to do with G.O.D.," said Lindy in a clear voice.

"Oh, my dear." The professor laughed and touched her head gently. "I'm sure it does have a lot to do with G.O.D. Believe me, I think about Him a great deal too. But, however life began—and some scientists say it was by an incredible accident, and some say it was by God's design—we do have the unique privilege of being on this earth right now, and that's something we shouldn't take lightly."

"I like life very much," declared Lindy. She was a trifle confused by all the talk, though she was trying her best to understand it. "There's only one thing I really hate, and that's P.E."

"P.E.?"

"Physical education."

"Oh, I see."

"I'm absolutely no good at it," complained Lindy. "And I'm always being forced to do it."

Tom spoke in a disgusted tone. "Lindy, that has absolutely nothing to do with what we're talking about."

"I know, I know," she fibbed.

"I hope P.E. is the most serious problem you ever have to contend with," the professor said. He paused and then asked, "What do you suppose is the most serious problem that grown-ups have?"

The children gave it some thought.

Tom said, "Ecology."

"Daddy says it's too much starch in his shirts," said Lindy.

"I think it's the hydrogen bomb," said Ben after a moment.

"They're good answers. Ben is the closest, I think. But there is one thing more serious than that."

"More serious than the hydrogen bomb?" Ben was surprised.

"Oh, yes, indeed. You see, in a very short time the scientists who have discovered the secret of life will be able to *make* life. Then in a way we'll be playing G.O.D., as Lindy so aptly puts it. That's a huge responsibility. And we must hope that people won't be foolish. You know, the mind is a thing of extraordinary beauty. It has taken several million years for the human brain as we know it today to develop. Now all we have to do is to learn how to use it properly."

Nobody in the room spoke for a while. The fire crackled noisily. The professor seemed lost in thought.

Suddenly he came out of his reverie and addressed himself to Tom. "Did you look up 'Whangdoodle' in the dictionary as I suggested, young man?"

Tom smiled knowingly. "I did. And it doesn't make sense. Dad says a Whangdoodle probably doesn't exist."

"Of course it exists," the professor declared. "I *told* you it did."

"Well, where is the Whangdoodle? Where does it live?" challenged Tom.

Professor Savant looked at the children for a long moment, as though trying to make up his mind about something. Then he leaned back in his chair, closed his eyes and said quietly: "The Whangdoodle lives in Whangdoodleland, where he is king. He is the only animal left of his species, although there are other wonderful, fascinating creatures that live with him. There are Gazooks and Sidewinders, Tree Squeaks and Swamp Gaboons. There is an animal called an Oinck and another called a Prock. They have hardly ever been seen; in fact they would do anything possible to avoid mankind. So far, they have been remarkably successful."

The boys were enthralled. Lindy was so fascinated that she gazed at the professor with her mouth open as he continued. "Hundreds of years ago, things were very different. Man believed in magic and miracles and folklore and legend. Myths and witchcraft and the spirits and such were all quite real because people believed in them.

"There were many Whangdoodles. They were found mostly in China and Greece, Africa, England and the Scandinavian countries. Later, I believe, there were some Whangdoodles found in the islands of the Pacific."

The professor opened his eyes and stretched his legs towards the fire. "The popularity of the Whangdoodle was probably at its height in the Middle Ages, when people also believed in animals like the Unicorn and the Wyvern and the great Roc and the Hippogriff. The Whangdoodle was said to be the wisest, the most generous and the most endearing of all the creatures.

"As the years passed, man became involved in technology and agriculture and industry. Of course, it was natural for him to want to learn about his environment and the laws of nature, about the universe and how to get to the moon, and so on. But as he broadened the new part of his mind, so he closed down a beautiful and fascinating part of the old—the area of fantasy. The more knowledge man gained, the more self-conscious he became about believing in fanciful creatures. People began to think that such things as dragons, goblins and gremlins didn't exist. The terrible thing is that when man dismissed all the fanciful creatures from his mind, the Whangdoodles disappeared along with them."

"But where did the Whangdoodles go?" cried Lindy.

"By the time the Whangdoodles and the other animals realized what was happening to them, it was almost too late," said the professor. "There was a tremendous upheaval. The dragons and the monsters became fearfully anxious, and they made a great fuss and fought with each other and killed or destroyed themselves by the thousands. Which was no help at all, of course. Many of the wonderful creatures from the past just faded away from sadness and neglect. That is why only a few remain today.

"King of them all is the last of the really great Whangdoodles. Being very wise and very clever, he retreated to a realm where man could not see or harm him."

"But if no one can see him, how do you know he's there?" asked Lindy.

The professor took a moment to drink the last of his hot chocolate, then he carefully set the cup to one side. "I know he's there, because I have been to Whangdoodleland."

The children sat in stunned silence.

He continued, "I have not actually met the Whangdoodle. He's elusive, and of course, he's as anxious to avoid me as I am determined to try to meet him."

"Well, where is Whangdoodleland?" Lindy whispered. "How do you get there?"

The professor spoke slowly and distinctly.

"There is only one possible road you can take," he said, "and that is to go by way of your imagination."

"But that's ridiculous," Ben cried. "You couldn't use your imagination to go *anywhere*."

Tom said in a disbelieving voice, "That's just impossible."

"No it isn't. Nothing is impossible," replied the professor. "In fact, I have a saying in my office: 'Whatever man imagines *is* possible.' I've proved that hundreds of times in my work."

"Okay. Then how did you do it?" challenged Tom.

"I had to go into training. I had to stimulate and teach my mind to become aware and open to any possibility. I was like an astronaut preparing to go to the moon. Think how long they study before they begin their journey. That's a perfect example of what I'm talking about." The professor jabbed a finger at the children. "Two hundred years ago who would have believed it possible that man could get to the moon? It would have seemed just as fanciful as my saying today that I have been to Whangdoodleland. But man *imagined* going to the moon, and now it's a reality."

Lindy asked a vital question. "But do you suppose *we* could ever get to Whangdoodleland? Do you suppose ordinary people like us could ever see it?"

The professor smiled a secret smile. "Yes, I believe you could," he said casually. "It would mean a great deal of hard work. But you're young and you actually stand a better chance of getting there than most adults. Your imaginations are vivid and fresh and you haven't closed your minds to possibilities the way so many grown-ups have."

"What would we have to do?" Tom asked cautiously.

"You would study with me," said the professor. "We would have to meet each day and work hard. When I thought you were ready we would begin trying to find the Whangdoodle. But you would have to do exactly as I say. More importantly, you would not be able to mention this to another living soul."

"Couldn't I tell Mummy?" asked Lindy.

The professor shook his head. "No, Lindy, it would spoil everything. You see, most grown-ups would not—indeed, they *could* not—understand what we would be trying to do."

"Then how come you understand so much about the Whangdoodle?" demanded Tom.

"That's because I am different. Some people consider me an eccentric. I specialize in imagination. I imagine things most people wouldn't even dream of."

"Like DNA and RNA," said Ben.

"Precisely. And the Whangdoodle. I have made it my life's work to study this extraordinary creature."

"I'd sure love to see a Whangdoodle," Ben said thoughtfully. "Gosh, what a thrill that'd be. To be the only people to have seen it in all these years."

"I still don't really see how it's possible," said Tom. "But it would be fun. What about Lindy, though? Do you suppose she should go? She's too young, isn't she?"

"Of course I'm not," Lindy protested instantly. "I'm old enough to go. Aren't I, Professor?"

"I would think it important that you go, Lindy," he replied. "Being the youngest, your imagination is the most fertile. You could help where the rest of us might fail."

"See!" She turned in triumph to her two brothers.

"But wait a minute." The professor held up his hand. "I have not yet said that you could go."

The children all spoke at once. "Oh, please, Professor, do let us." "We'd love to go." "We'll do anything you say."

The professor deliberated a moment.

Finally he said, "All right. But there have to be conditions. First of all, I must be in complete charge. Secondly, you must tell your mother that we have met this evening and that I will be telephoning her to discuss your coming visits. I think that is correct and it will save your parents worry. The third condition is the one I have already mentioned. You must not talk of this to anyone. Is that quite clear?"

The children nodded.

"Then I see no reason why we should not try this experiment together. I should just add that, once committed, there can be no turning back for any of us." He turned to Tom and Ben. "Are you ready to take on that responsibility?"

Without a moment's hesitation, the boys nodded. The professor looked at Lindy.

"When can we get started?" she asked eagerly.

The professor walked to the study door and called for Mrs. Primrose. He said politely, "I'm afraid that I must leave you now. Ah, Mrs. Primrose, I would like you to jot down the telephone number of my friends here and then perhaps you'd show them out for me." He smiled at the children. "I shall expect you after school on Friday. Goodbye for the time being. Goodbye."

The children were left with the feeling that there were a thousand questions they would like to have asked. The evening had passed so rapidly. It was already late.

Professor Savant walked quickly up the wide staircase of his house until he came to the third landing. He passed through a draped archway and proceeded to climb a narrower flight of stairs until he reached a small white door. He took from his waistcoat pocket a key on a silver chain and, inserting it into the lock, he let himself into a most unusual room. At the far end, at the top of a spiral staircase, beneath a wide skylight, there stood a large telescope pointing to the heavens. Next to it was a large planetarium globe. A bench in the center of the room contained a most complicated series of beakers and flasks.

Against the right wall stood a pyramid of cages containing white mice, a hamster, a toad and one extraordinary, multi-colored rabbit.

Hanging from the ceiling above the bench was an amazing structure. It resembled a finely wrought stepladder and it was made of different-colored plastic segments, all brightly illuminated. A high-backed wing chair faced away from the door.

The professor closed the door behind him and approached the chair, speaking in a quiet voice. "So sorry to keep you waiting, Prock. I had some unexpected visitors."

"So I gathered," said a distinctly unusual voice. A unique figure rose from the chair in one sinuous movement.

The visitor was tall and exceedingly thin. He had a long, narrow face which accentuated his large black eyes and prominent nose. He had a long body and very long arms. His legs seemed permanently bent at the knees and his shoulders hunched forward. His hands were limp, the fingers thin and tapered.

The stranger wore baggy pants and a loose turtleneck sweater which did not sit comfortably on his narrow shoulders. On his head a battered grey trilby hat was pulled down at a rakish angle.

"So, you're thinking of taking those three to Whangdoodle-land, eh?" he said. His voice had a stretched, echoing quality —a rasping whisper that seemed to hang in the air long after he had spoken.

"I was considering it, yes," replied the professor easily.

"Well, you're a fool," said the Prock rudely. "Except for you, no one has ever reached Whangdoodleland, and no one ever will again. You're wasting your time, and you'll find yourself saddled with children who'll turn out to be a big nuisance."

"That's a possibility," said the professor. "But on the other hand, we could just make it, my friend."

"Hmph." The Prock looked bad-tempered. "It's a clever idea, I'll grant you that. One thing's for sure—you'd never reach the Whangdoodle on your own. And I'm going to do everything I can to stop you and the children. I'm not even going to mention this to His Majesty. He'd only fret."

"I wish you'd tell him that I mean no harm."

"I'll do no such thing." The Prock was highly indignant. "Can't see why you're so anxious to pursue this idea of yours anyway. Why don't you just leave us in peace?" he grumbled.

"But I've no intention of *disturbing* the peace. Can't you see that?" said the professor.

"It's not only you we're worried about," the Prock continued. "If you make it to Whangdoodleland with the children, what's to stop others from doing it? It's too big a risk to take and I won't allow it," he snapped.

"Nevertheless, I do intend to try this experiment." The professor was quietly adamant. "Right now, I don't think there's a thing you can do about it, Prock."

"Not now, no." The Prock was distinctly annoyed. "But I'll be waiting for you, and you won't get far." He wagged a spindly finger at the professor. "Those children won't be so easy to teach, although I'll enjoy watching you try. In fact, I'll be watching everything you do from now on."

He eased himself to the door with a slithering, sliding walk. "I'm going," he declared. "This whole conversation has given me a terrible headache."

Without even bothering to say goodbye, the Prock drew himself up to an immense height and then, as if being pulled by an invisible hand, he slid down to the floor in a single motion and disappeared through the crack under the door.

 *FIVE*

Mrs. Potter was thrilled when the professor telephoned to ask if the children could come to tea. She asked them again and again for details of their visit. "What is the professor like? What did he say? What kind of house does he live in?" They told her all they could without once mentioning the Whangdoodle. It was hard on Lindy, for she was very excited and she desperately wanted to tell someone about their plans. But her brothers reminded her of the professor's warning and she remained silent.

The following Friday after school, Ben, Tom and Lindy found themselves back at Stone House.

"The professor is out in the garden," Mrs. Primrose said cheerfully as she showed the children into the lounge. She opened the French windows and pointed to a small pavilion on the other side of the lawn. "He's over there."

"Hello, hello, hello." The professor's head popped up over the trellis. "Come and see what I've got."

The children ran across the grass. Professor Savant was kneeling on the floor of the summerhouse, playing with a large multicolored rabbit.

"Ohhh." Lindy dropped to her knees. "Isn't he beautiful."

"What's his name?" asked Tom.

"Sneezewort. He lives in my laboratory. I hate to see him in a cage all the time, so I bring him down for a walk as often as I can."

"Where did you get him?" Ben wanted to know.

"Sneezewort is the result of a study I did in crossbreeding," the professor said proudly. "His great-grandfather was a Belgian hare and his great-grandmother was a Himalayan black-and-white. I went on from there. You should have seen the combinations I produced." He chuckled.

Lindy held out a rolled piece of paper that she had been carrying. "Here, Professor. I did a drawing for you." She shyly handed it to him. "It's a Whangdoodle."

"Why, Lindy. How nice." The professor unrolled the paper. "But that's wonderful. That looks very much like a Whangdoodle. But you've left out his bedroom slippers."

"Bedroom slippers?" asked Tom.

"Yes. He always wears bedroom slippers. Actually he *grows* them, and each year he grows a different pair—a different color and a different style."

Lindy drew in her breath. "That's fantastic."

"It is, isn't it?" agreed the professor. "And what's more, the Whangdoodle never knows what the slippers will look like until he has shed the old pair and grown the new. It's a surprise even to him."

The children hardly had time to digest this piece of information when the professor continued. "There's one other remarkable thing about the Whangdoodle. He can change color whenever he feels like it. It's a safety device. He can blend in with anything so no one can see him."

Lindy whispered, "What color is he normally?"

"Oh, a sort of warm grey-brown. Rather ordinary, really," the professor replied. "But of course if he's feeling cheerful he can turn Scotch plaid if he wants to."

The children laughed delightedly. "He sounds like such

fun," said Lindy. "Does he have a beautiful palace?"

"Well, I've only seen it from a distance. But it is rather remarkable. Lots of turrets and things, you know."

"Does he live there alone?" Ben asked.

"Oh, yes. Totally."

Lindy was concerned. "Doesn't he get lonely?"

"I would think so."

"Why is the Whangdoodle a king?" asked Tom.

"Because he's the best of all the creatures. I told you about that, remember?"

"So he's very smart?"

"Smart? I should say so," the professor replied emphatically. "Could you grow bedroom slippers? Or change color? Could you preserve peace? Yes, indeed—he is quite remarkable, and if we are ever going to see him we must get to work."

The children seated themselves beside the professor and he pointed to the garden.

"First of all, take a look around," he said. "A very good look. Now, I want you to tell me all the colors that you can see. Benjamin, I think you should begin."

Ben had the feeling that he was not going to be very good at this kind of exercise. "Well," he began hesitantly, "I see the grey house. Brown trees and a blue sky. Oh, and green grass, of course."

"Is that all?"

"Well, I see a dark-brown roof and the curtains at that window."

"Tom, what about you?"

"This white summerhouse," Tom began, "and I see

Sneezewort. A green door. Er—that's all, except for what Ben said."

The professor turned to Lindy.

She took a deep breath. "There are little white clouds in the sky and those leaves are golden. There's a bird with a red-brown chest. Your logs over there are sort of yellow. Those flowers are orange and white."

"They're late chrysanthemums," said the professor. "We'll have a look at them in a moment. But first of all, look at the trees again. They're not just brown, are they? That one there is almost black. And the trunk of that one is copper and smooth, and that one is grey and rough. Those dead leaves are a russet color, aren't they? Now look under the hedge there. Do you see anything?"

The children looked. They saw nothing.

"Can't you see the cluster of red berries hanging up under the leaves?"

The children looked closer. Suddenly, as if the focus were being changed on a camera, the red berries came into their view.

"Why didn't I see them?" Tom was bewildered.

"Because you weren't looking," replied the professor. "There aren't many people in this world who really know how to look. Usually one glance is enough to register that grass is green and the sky is blue and so on. They can tell you if the sun is shining or if it looks like rain, but that's about all. It's such a pity, for there is texture to everything we see, and everything we do and hear. That's what I want today's lesson to be about. I want you to start *noticing* things. Once you get used to doing it you'll never be able to stop. It's the best game in the world."

The children found themselves beginning to share the professor's excitement; he spoke with such passion and enthusiasm.

"Every walk we take from now on, every place that we go," he continued, "I want you to tell me all that you see. Even this close to winter you'll be surprised how much color there is. In the town there'll be shops and rooftops, flags and curtains and bright lights, traffic signals, balloons, the colors of cars and the clothes people are wearing.

"In the country, there will be color in the leaves and flowers and trees, under the hedgerows, by the wayside, in the grass." He pointed to the ground. "Ben, look closely here. See the earth between the blades? See how rough and hard it is after the frost? Think of being as small as an ant down there. Look at it as if you were indeed a beetle or a worm. Wouldn't the earth be different to you then? Wouldn't it be a whole new countryside? The lumps of clay would be mountains and the blades of grass would be a forest."

Ben stared at the ground and to his amazement he saw what the professor meant. "I've never thought to look at it that way before," he said. He was completely fascinated.

The professor slapped his knee. "Well, that's just my point. Nobody thinks to look."

He turned to Lindy. "Tell me what you see in the hedgerow there, Lindy. Do you see anything beyond that opening in the branches? Can you see how the shadow on the grass makes it look as though there's a path in there and that it might lead somewhere exciting?"

Lindy looked at the hedge carefully and concentrated hard. The light and shade played strange tricks on her eyes. There was a shimmering quality to the afternoon, and her head felt a little fuzzy. It seemed to her as though the hedge began to move, to twist into a different shape, like a tunnel. She leaned forward, mesmerized. For one second she was convinced that if she could just go through the tunnel she would come out into a new and unknown land. She was so excited that she looked up at the professor to tell him about it, and as she did so the spell was broken.

"What is it, Lindy?" The professor watched her keenly.

Lindy turned to look at the hedge once again. She frowned because the illusion wasn't there anymore. All she could see was the green hedge in a perfectly plain winter garden.

"That's funny," she said, "I thought that . . ." She stopped, aware that the boys were staring at her. "Well—it's not important. I guess I let my imagination run away with me for a moment."

Professor Savant looked at her thoughtfully. Then he turned and walked onto the lawn.

"Come and look over here," he called. "I want to show you something." The children followed him. He moved to the small clump of chrysanthemums that Lindy had pointed out earlier. He picked a beautiful white one on a thick green stem. "Look at this. See how sturdy it is. A flower that blooms this close to winter has to be strong." He handed it to Lindy.

Ben shifted his weight from one foot to the other. "I think flowers are a bit sissy for a boy."

The professor moved to Sneezewort and picked him up. "Let's go inside and I'll show you something that just might change your mind, young man. Have you started science in school yet?"

"We began last semester, sir."

"Good. Bring that flower with you, Lindy," he commanded, and walked briskly into the warm house.

The children followed him as he climbed the three flights of stairs to the small white door.

"I'll have you know," he said as he unlocked it, "that I allow very few people in here. Very few, indeed." He stepped aside to let them through.

They gasped when they saw the room. Ben felt as if he had stepped into a small paradise.

"Look at that telescope," he said.

"What are all those lights?" Tom asked.

"That's a model of a problem I've been working on." The professor moved over to it. "It's made of special fiber-optic glass which allows the light to shine through in such an interesting way. It's good, isn't it?"

"It sure is." Tom sounded almost reverent.

The professor took the cover off a large microscope. "This is what I wanted to show you, Ben. This is called a binocular microscope because you look through it with both eyes. Give me that flower, Lindy."

She handed him the chrysanthemum. The professor carefully removed a single white petal and placed it under the lens.

"Look in here now," he said. "This should make flowers a little more interesting."

The children took turns and each saw something that resembled an aerial photograph of a river with many streams feeding into it, a latticework of tiny interconnecting tubes.

"Those veins, or tubes, carry energy to the cells in the petal," the professor explained. "See what happens if I put a drop of ink onto the stem of the petal? See how the blue circulates through every little vein? That's just how blood circulates through your bodies."

Lindy made a face. "I don't like blood. It's gross."

"Well, that's a silly remark. Blood carries nutrition and energy and food to every part of your body. So instead of saying 'gross' you should be saying 'How wonderful.' "

The professor turned to the boys. "I want to make a point and I want you to learn it well," he said. "I know there are times when things seem rather boring to you or not worth your interest. Like this flower today. Once you noticed its color and the fact that it was growing, you dismissed it; it was 'sissy.' A magnificent creation like a flower is definitely *not* 'sissy.' When I showed you the flower under the microscope, you learned that there was a whole new dimension to it."

"What's a dimension?" Lindy asked.

"In this case it means going one step beyond what you already see or know. Finding another world, one that has been there all along, just waiting for you to discover it."

"Like Whangdoodleland," she said. "Is that a dimension?"

"In a way, yes," said the professor. "My point is this: I don't want you ever again to take something at face value—to take things for granted. Let your curiosity run away with you. Know that beyond every ordinary explanation there is a deeper and more exciting discovery to be made."

There was a knock on the door and Mrs. Primrose entered. "Tea is ready, sir."

"Fine," said the professor. "Then that will end our lesson for today. Tomorrow we are going to go on a picnic, so bring your bicycles. Also, you should dress in weatherproof clothes because it is going to rain."

"How on earth do you know that?" Tom asked.

The professor rumpled the boy's hair.

"I'm a scientist, Thomas, and I also heard the weather forecast on the radio."

They all laughed and clattered downstairs to tea.

That evening the children were elated. Lindy, especially, was keyed up. Her powers of concentration had been put to good use that afternoon. By dinnertime she was so excited she was almost unable to eat.

Mrs. Potter tried not to show her concern. "Lindy dear, don't just stare at your plate. Eat your stew and dumplings."

"It's not stew and they're not dumplings," Lindy answered. "It's a brown land with mountains and the dumplings are sponges—white sponges that will suck you up if you go too near them."

"What's this? What are you talking about?" Mr. Potter gave his daughter a keen glance.

"No, not sponges." Lindy changed her mind. "They're giant boulders and I wish I were small enough to climb one."

Mrs. Potter said, "I think this afternoon has been a little too much for you. You're being very silly."

"It's not silly, Mom." Tom came to Lindy's defense. "Look at the peas on my plate. Don't they look like tiny green stones? Like when you're at the seaside and the beach is all pebbles?"

"They just look like peas to me," replied Mrs. Potter. "I think you all need an early night."

As Lindy was preparing for bed, Tom knocked on the door of her room.

"Lindy? Can I come in?"

"What do you want, Tom?"

"Here's the quarter that I owe you." He put it on her bedside table.

Lindy examined the twenty-five-cent piece. "Thanks. But you don't really need to give this to me. Do you want it back?"

Tom was surprised and he thought about it for a moment. "No," he said. "You won it fairly and besides, if you hadn't gone up to Stone House, we'd never have met the professor."

She smiled at him. "Tell you what, I won't ever spend it. I'll just keep it to remind me of Halloween. It'll be my lucky piece from now on."

In a rare show of affection for his sister, Tom patted her on the shoulder. "Okay. Okay. Well, good night."

"Good night, Tom."

Lindy slowly removed her slippers and bathrobe. She pulled her curtains and brushed her teeth and then climbed into her comfortable brass bed. She lay back against the pillows and thought about the afternoon and how wonderful it had been. She thought about the professor and Sneezewort and the incredible microscope.

Soon, she began to drift into sleep. Through half-closed eyes she gazed at the curtains pulled across her windows. They were pretty curtains, printed with flowers of the countryside: red and orange poppies, white and yellow daisies, blue cornflowers. Lindy thought, as she often did, how nice it would be to walk in a field filled with flowers like that. The curtains moved very slightly. She stretched out a hand to touch the flowers, which seemed almost within her grasp.

When Mrs. Potter came upstairs to say good night to her

daughter she found her already asleep, smiling peacefully, and with one hand open on the coverlet.

 *SIX*

It was raining hard when the children woke the following morning.

Ben was sure they would not be going on a picnic in such weather. He predicted that the professor would cancel the whole thing.

The professor phoned at midday, but only to confirm with Mrs. Potter that it was all right for the children to meet him at two thirty that afternoon.

By two o'clock Lindy, Ben and Tom looked as if they could attempt an expedition to the North Pole. They wore heavy sweaters and trousers tucked into thick rubber boots. Lindy had on a cape that she often wore when she walked to school. It was a very sensible covering because she could keep her hands dry inside, and her books too. She wore a large sou'wester that came down so low on her head that only her nose and chin were visible beneath it.

Tom wore a duffel coat with the hood pulled up and a scarf, and Ben had on an old raincoat and an oilskin hat that his father used when he went fishing.

Professor Savant was waiting for them on the porch when they arrived. He was wearing a most extraordinary outfit— long waterproof pants and a transparent plastic coat tied at the waist, which gave a balloonlike effect to the upper half of his body. He wore a peaked cap and sturdy, heavy brogues covered by plastic overshoes.

He greeted the children with his customary enthusiasm. "Hallo there!" he yelled. "Isn't this just a marvelous day? I love the rain, don't you?"

"How are we going to have a picnic?" asked Tom.

"You'll see. You'll see."

The professor disappeared behind the house, and a moment later reappeared pushing the oldest bicycle the children had ever seen. The handlebars were bent, spokes were missing, the seat was tilted at a ridiculous angle and the whole contraption made a terrible squeaking sound.

"I haven't ridden one of these things for quite a while," said the professor. "Now, let me see." He attempted to swing a leg over the saddle. "Ha-ha. This is going to be tricky." He tried again, this time successfully enough, at least to get his feet on the pedals. With fierce concentration he began to wobble around the drive.

"Just getting warmed up," he announced with a grin, at which point his trousers caught in the chain and he came to a shuddering stop. "Oh, fiddlesticks."

The children giggled.

"Mrs. Primrose," he yelled, "I need bicycle clips!" He yanked the bike into an upright position.

"Bicycle clips, sir? You don't have any."

"Bother. What am I going to do?"

"Tuck your trousers in your socks," Tom suggested.

"Good idea. But my socks are too short, my underwear's too long and it would all get wet in the rain."

The professor illustrated this by hitching up his trousers. The children had a glimpse of white long johns on his skinny legs and a pair of startling red socks.

"I do have these, sir, if you wouldn't mind wearing

them." Mrs. Primrose put a hand in her apron pocket and shyly produced a pair of lavender garters.

The professor raised his eyebrows in mock surprise. "*Well*," he said, "I haven't seen a pair of those in a long time. They'll do splendidly, Mrs. Primrose." He folded his trousers and put the garters over them. "I think they look very fetching." He hopped about in the rain to show them off.

Mrs. Primrose pointed to his bicycle. "I do wish you wouldn't ride that thing, sir. It's lethal, really it is."

"Nonsense, woman. I shall be perfectly all right. Well, come along, Potters. The afternoon will be over before we get started."

He climbed on the bicycle and began to wobble his way down the drive. The children hurriedly pedaled after him, calling goodbye to an anxious-looking Mrs. Primrose.

It soon became apparent that not only was the professor's bike dangerous to ride, but the professor was a definite road hazard. He had a strong tendency to aim his bike at an object—a tree, a car, a pedestrian—and only at the last second would he swerve to avoid it. He turned corners sharply without so much as a hand signal and the children were never certain what he would do next. They discovered that it was easier and safer if they rode a few yards behind. The professor seemed to need most of the road for himself.

Lindy was rather concerned. "Are you going to be all right?" she called.

"Yes, Lindy. No cause for alarm. I'll get the hang of this thing in a while."

They pedaled slowly through the outskirts of the town. The children liked the feel of the raindrops on their faces. Their bicycle tires made a pleasant hissing sound on the wet road and sent up small fountains of spray.

The professor led them into a delightful country area. Busy streets gave way to empty lanes where the wet trees dripped noisily onto the thick carpet of fallen leaves. The ride obviously began to have a soothing effect on the professor, for he soon became less erratic and the children were able to pull abreast of him.

The professor began to sing "She'll Be Comin' Round the Mountain." He had a terrible voice, but his enthusiasm was contagious. The children joined in.

"You're not singing nearly loud enough," cried the professor. "I can't hear you at all."

The children sang at the tops of their voices. Fortunately there was no traffic about, because now they were all bicycling in a haphazard way and laughing so much that half the time they weren't looking where they were going.

The professor suddenly swung his bike off the road and onto a small track.

"Where is this?" asked Tom as they bumped and jogged their way along.

"This is where we have our picnic," replied the professor. He turned into an open field and braked to a halt in front of a dilapidated stone building.

"What a funny house," said Lindy. "Who owns this place?"

"I do." The professor removed a picnic basket from his bicycle and led the way through the tall wet grass to a large door at the front of the building.

"Ben, put a shoulder to this with me. You too, Tom."

The professor pushed hard against the heavy door and the boys added their weight to his. The door began to move and, after a second push, it swung open. The boys stumbled through a cloud of dust into a long, high room.

"What a great place," Ben declared.

"I'm glad you like it." The professor smiled proudly. "This old barn is all that remains of a farmhouse. I might restore the place one day. In the meantime, it seemed like a good spot to come and have a picnic."

"Look, I've found a horseshoe!" Lindy cried excitedly.

"Well, that's a lucky beginning. Now, we'd better get started on a fire; otherwise it'll be too damp and cold in here. Boys, go to the back of the house. There should be plenty of dry kindling under the trees. Lindy, help me put this cloth down so that we can spread our picnic on it."

It didn't take long to get things organized. Quite soon, everyone was sitting in the middle of the stone floor around a crackling wood fire.

The children were starving. Mrs. Primrose had packed all manner of goodies for them: sausage rolls and peanut butter sandwiches, a sponge cake with jam, and oatmeal cookies and bananas. There were milk and ginger ale to drink.

"This is really terrific," said Tom, his cheeks rosy from the fire and his mouth full of cake.

The professor pushed his plate away and leaned back on one elbow. "Tell me your favorite word, somebody. Better still, tell me the three nicest words you can think of."

"Yellow. Sunshine. Mother-of-pearl," Lindy said quickly.

"Splendid. What about you, Ben?"

"Acetylsalicylic," the boy replied.

"What's that?" asked Tom.

"It's what aspirin is made of, isn't it, Professor?"

"Right, Ben. The chemical name for aspirin is acetylsalicylic acid. That is a good word. It rolls off the tongue nicely."

Tom said, "I've got the best word. Antidisestablishmentarianism."

"Oh, everybody knows that," Ben pointed out.

"Does everybody know what it means?" asked the professor. The children were silent. "It's no use using a word unless you know about it. Antidisestablishmentarianism. The word came out of nineteenth-century England. We'll look it up when we get home."

"What's *your* favorite word?" Lindy asked.

"Good heavens. There are thousands that I like."

"Choose one."

The professor thought for a moment. "Papilionaceous," he said. "From Latin, meaning resembling a butterfly, or shaped like a butterfly. The French word for butterfly is similar. It's *papillon*."

"Papilionaceous. That's lovely," said Lindy.

"Your name is French, isn't it, Professor?" Ben asked suddenly. "Isn't Savant a French name?"

"It is indeed. My father was French. My mother was an American."

"Do you have any children?"

"Yes, Lindy, I have two grown-up daughters. The eldest is married to a dentist in Boston, and the youngest is with the Peace Corps."

"What about your wife?" Ben asked.

"She passed away many years ago." The professor gazed into the fire. "She was very pretty. She loved to travel and to give parties. You might say she was papilionaceous. A very sweet butterfly."

He leaned forward and threw another log into the flames. "Speaking of butterflies, wait until you see the ones they have in Whangdoodleland. You won't believe your eyes."

"What's so special about them?" Tom asked eagerly.

"Well, they're about the size of a robin and brilliantly colored. They're called Flutterbyes."

"Wow. If butterflies are as big as robins, then how big are the birds?" Ben laughed.

"Well, one bird is quite big," replied the professor, "and I can't wait for you to meet her. She's the Whiffle Bird. She's quite wonderful and very, very beautiful. She'll be a good friend to us in Whangdoodleland, for she loves company, although she is shy and easily frightened. Now, we had better continue our lessons, or you'll never get to see her at all. Ben, throw me one of those ginger-ale bottles. This wood smoke is making me thirsty."

Ben took a bottle from the picnic basket and handed it to the professor who proceeded to shake it violently. "Watch out," he said with a grin and unscrewed the cap. A fountain of ginger ale shot into the air. The children screamed with delight.

"I haven't done that since I was a boy," said the professor wickedly. "My word, look at all those bubbles. Hold the bottle up to the light. It's like a waterfall, only falling up instead of down."

Lindy said, "The bubbles are like tiny crystal beads. How do they get in there?"

"That's the carbonation," replied the professor.

"What's carbonation?"

"Adding carbon dioxide to liquid. Since gas is lighter than liquid the bubbles rise, as you see." He held the bottle close to his ear. "Listen, they make a nice hissing sound."

Lindy took the bottle and listened. Her face registered surprise. "Ooh, it goes up. The noise goes up."

The professor said, "You must practice the art of listening. It will be most important when we get to Whangdoodle-land. Do you ever lie in bed and count all the things you can hear?"

"I do," said Tom. "I can hear Mom in the kitchen in the morning and Ethel using the vacuum cleaner, and cars and airplanes and birds. It's nice. Trouble is I never want to get up."

"Listen to the noises right now," said the professor. The children were silent. They heard the rain, a bird calling out in the wood, the fire crackling.

"I'd like to try an experiment," said the professor. "I want you all to close your eyes and keep them closed until I say you can open them. Now I want you to tell me what you can smell. For instance, can you smell the smoke from the fire?"

"Yes," chorused the children.

"Okay. Can you smell the dampness and the rain?"

After a moment's hesitation they nodded.

"Good. Anything else?"

Tom kept his eyes tightly closed and concentrated. "It smells dusty in here, like hay."

"Good boy," said the professor. "Ben, what am I holding under your nose? Keep your eyes closed."

Ben sniffed, then grinned triumphantly. "Plastic raincoat," he said.

"Lindy, what's this?"

Lindy smelled something vaguely familiar, yet she couldn't quite place it.

"Peanut butter?"

"Terrific," said the professor. "All right, Tom. Keep your eyes closed. What's this?"

"Banana."

"And this?"

Tom sniffed. "I'm not quite sure."

"Can't you smell toasted marshmallow?"

The boy hesitated.

"I'll hold it closer, Tom. Can you smell it now?"

"Yes. Yes, I can."

"Let me smell!" cried Lindy. "Mmm. That's good."

"What about you, Ben? Do you smell it?"

"That's funny. I don't."

"Quite sure?"

Ben tried again. "Yes, quite sure."

"Very well, you may open your eyes," said the professor. Ben looked around. "I don't see a marshmallow."

"That's because there wasn't one," replied the professor.

"But I smelled it," cried Tom. "I really did."

"I know. I'm delighted. It means you're beginning to make your imagination work for you."

"I wish I could have smelled it," said Ben wistfully.

"You will, Ben. Your turn will come." The professor began to pack what was left of the picnic into the basket. "I think we had better start heading for home. We've quite a ride in front of us, and I don't want to be out after dark without lights. Ben, pour this ginger ale on the fire, will you?"

The children reluctantly helped the professor to tidy up. They donned their raincoats and walked outside to their bicycles.

"I wish we weren't going," said Lindy with a backward glance at the barn.

"We will come again another day." The professor looked

up at the sky and drew in a deep breath of rain-fresh air. "I think it's going to clear up." He paused to watch a large bird flying silently across the field toward the wood. "Look. Look. It's probably going to roost for the night. How I'd love to be a bird."

"A Whiffle Bird?" asked Tom with a grin.

The professor chuckled. "No. I'd settle for being a sky-lark, or maybe a kestrel." He swung up onto his bike and began to pedal unsteadily toward the road.

"Do you know how homing pigeons home, Ben?" he called as the children followed after him.

"No, sir."

"It's probably vision. And it's thought that dolphins use vision above water and guide themselves by the stars?" He swerved to avoid a chuckhole. "Amazing, isn't it?"

Lindy brought her bike alongside the professor's.

"You know so much," she said. "Don't you sometimes feel bewildered when you think of the millions of things that put life together?"

The professor smiled. "I'm not bewildered. I'm filled with the deepest awe and wonder. The miracle is that in its complexity it all works." He bumped through a puddle and was drenched with water. "Oh, fiddlesticks, I'll never get the hang of this contraption."

For the rest of the journey he grumbled and swore at his bicycle. This kept the children in fits of laughter, which was his intention, since it took their minds off the long ride home.

PART TWO

Capture

 *ONE*

As each day passed, the children's ability to look, listen, feel, taste and smell improved immeasurably.

The professor taught them the wonders of music; not only instrumental music, but the music of running water and the sighing of the wind, the hum of a city and the song of the birds.

Lindy was by far the best pupil. Her imagination was so vivid and her senses so aware that she easily pulled ahead. The professor knew that she was already capable of making the journey to Whangdoodleland, but the decision to go had to be delayed because the boys were not ready. Tom was doing well, but Ben was having difficulties. For the first time in his life he discovered that being the eldest did not make him the most competent. Being thirteen years of age, he had more to question, more to doubt. He had to fight logic and his own stubborn opinion of things.

Mrs. Potter asked Lindy one day, "What on earth do you find to do over there all the time?"

"Oh, we play and have tea and the professor teaches us." Lindy's voice was deceptively casual.

"What does he teach?"

"He talks about life and stuff like that. We look through the microscope, and we go for walks and rides. It's great fun."

Mrs. Potter changed the subject. "You know, Daddy and I are going to see Grandma on Saturday. We'd love to take you with us, especially since it's your midterm holiday next week.

But Grandma just isn't well enough. We'll be back a week from Sunday. In the meantime I've arranged for Ethel to stay with you."

"What if the professor asks us out?" Lindy wanted to know.

"That's all right. I'll tell Ethel that you'll probably be spending a great deal of time with him. Then she won't worry about you."

When the children visited the professor the next day, Lindy told him about her parents' plans.

He looked thoughtful. Then he made a startling announcement.

"I think that the time has come to start a new phase of your lessons. I think you are ready to try the sympathetic hats."

"Sympathetic hats?" said Tom.

"Actually, I call them scrappy caps," said the professor with a smile. "A scrappy cap is a covering worn on the head, which is sympathetic to the brain's impulses and desires."

"Do they have some special power or something?" asked Ben.

"I would say that there is something very magical about scrappy caps," replied the professor. "Let me show them to you."

He left the children and a moment later returned carrying three brightly colored objects.

"These hats are your passports to success. In spite of all our hard work, I doubt that you'd come close to seeing the Whangdoodle unless you were wearing one of these. Once we begin the great adventure, you may not—indeed you *must* not

—ever remove them from your heads. Not only will they help us to get to Whangdoodleland, but more importantly, without them, we will not be able to find our way home."

The professor held up an exquisite bonnet made of white lace and linen and brilliant red chintz. "Lindy, this is your hat. It comes from the Netherlands. The underlining is made of the finest linen. See how the red topping is covered with meadow flowers and hens and roosters and rabbits?"

"It's lovely," said Lindy.

"Hold it carefully. But don't put it on your head," cautioned the professor.

"Tom, this is yours." He held out a bright blue felt cap that resembled a funnel with the cloth pipe pointing backwards. "It comes from Madeira. The purpose of this little pipe was to hold a sprig of rosemary which gave the wearer the benefit of its magical powers. Did you know that in ancient Greece students wore rosemary twined in their hair while studying for their examinations? It is supposed to strengthen memory, and is thought to bring success to any undertaking."

Tom took the hat and held it carefully.

The professor handed Ben an Indian headband with a small tassel hanging from it. "Ben, yours comes from Guatemala. It was made by the Mayas. They were highly skilled people who were able to record history by means of picture writing. You can see some on this band. Notice how it is actually one long piece which has been wound around thirteen times, and that the coils have been sewn together to keep the shape. Thirteen was considered a magic number."

The professor looked at the children and smiled. "You will discover that your sympathetic hats make all the difference.

Once they are upon your heads you will experience a great feeling of exhilaration. Tomorrow we will begin to practice wearing them."

Lindy walked eagerly home from school the next day, happily contemplating the midterm holiday and the time she and her brothers would spend with the professor. She was desperately eager to begin the new lessons with the scrappy caps. She had the feeling that something wonderful was going to happen. She began to sing:

> *I've got a pretty hat*
> *To wear upon my head,*
> *And it is filled with magic,*
> *Or so the professor said.*

She skipped around a lamppost and ran full tilt into someone who was leaning against it. Her books went flying in all directions.

"Oops, I'm so sorry." Lindy was very startled.

"Hello, little girl," said a distinctly unusual voice.

Lindy looked up.

The stranger smiled and lifted his hat in greeting. "You dropped your books. Allow me."

Lindy watched as the man bent from the waist and scooped up her books with his extraordinarily long arms.

"Clumsy of me," he said. "I wasn't looking where I was going."

The sound of his voice reminded her of wind whistling through a long tunnel.

"May I walk with you a little way and carry your books?" he asked.

Lindy remembered her parents' warning never to speak with strangers. "Well, I—"

"You're Melinda Potter, aren't you?"

She was completely taken by surprise.

"Yes, I am."

"The professor is a good friend of mine."

"You mean Professor Savant?" Lindy experienced a wave of relief.

"The very same. We have spent many pleasant evenings together. He talks of you so much."

The stranger pulled a golden Yo-Yo from his pocket and executed a quick trick with it.

Lindy fell into step beside him as he began to walk.

"How are things coming along with your trip to Whang-doodleland?" he asked casually.

Her jaw dropped. "You know about that?"

"Good heavens, yes. I've known about it for some time. The professor and I often chat about it."

"Oh." She was surprised that someone else knew of their plans. The golden Yo-Yo flashed in the sunlight and made a soft humming sound. She glanced up at the odd-looking stranger.

"I expect you'll be making a move before long?" he said.

"To Whangdoodleland?"

"Yes."

"Er . . . well, as a matter of fact we will. We're trying the scrappy caps this afternoon."

"Scrappy caps?" He looked startled.

"Oh, I should say sympathetic hats," Lindy said and smiled. "They're very pretty." She was fascinated by the whirling, bobbing Yo-Yo. "They're going to make all the difference. It'll be the most wonderful adventure in the whole world. We'll meet the Whiffle Bird and see the Flutterbyes and lots of other creatures."

"You really think you'll get there?"

"Of course we will. The professor says we're nearly ready. It'll be any day now."

"I'm beginning to believe it." The stranger spoke in a grim voice, but Lindy was too enthusiastic to notice. She pulled him to a halt at the gate of her house.

"This is where I live. I'm afraid I have to go now."

"Well, we'll be seeing each other again, I'm sure." He bowed and shook her hand.

Lindy had the impression that she was holding a piece of wet seaweed.

"Take care, little girl. I would hate to see anything happen to you."

"I will. Goodbye."

Lindy took her books and walked to the front door of her house. She turned around to wave politely, but to her surprise her escort had vanished. The street was completely empty.

 *TWO*

It was four o'clock when the children arrived at the professor's house.

"I met a friend of yours this afternoon," Lindy said.

"A friend of mine?" The professor seemed preoccupied and a trifle nervous as he ushered the children into the garden.

"You know, the funny thin man. He didn't tell me his name. But he said you were very good friends and that you spent many evenings together."

The professor stopped and looked sharply at Lindy. Then he said quietly, "Tell me exactly what he looked like."

"Oh, sort of long and wobbly-looking. Kind of sharp at the elbows. He has a funny voice too."

"You say you met him this afternoon?"

"Yes. He walked home from school with me. He knew all about Whangdoodleland and everything."

"Good Lord," said the professor. "Good Lord."

"What's the matter?" asked Lindy. "You do know him, don't you?"

"I certainly do." He seemed a little stunned and passed a hand across his brow. "Did you talk about the hats this afternoon? Did you tell him we were nearly ready?"

"Yes," she said, beginning to feel anxious. "Wasn't that all right? If he's a friend of yours . . ."

The professor put a reassuring arm around her shoulders. "Do you realize you were talking with the Prock?"

The boys looked startled and Lindy's heart gave a big jump.

"Who's the Prock?" she whispered.

"He's one of the most important creatures in Whangdoodleland. He's like a prime minister. Besides helping the Whangdoodle run the country, his job is to maintain the safety of the place. The 'oily' Prock, as he's sometimes called, does everything he can to stop anyone from gaining entry and getting close to the Whangdoodle."

"But why did he come and see me?" asked Lindy.

"To find out all he could about our trip. Since you are the

youngest, Lindy, he knew you'd be the most unsuspecting. Dear me, this puts a whole new complexion on things. We had better have a talk."

The professor led the way to the summerhouse and the children sat down and waited for him to speak. He paced up and down for a while. Finally, he turned to face them.

"Look, this is the situation. The Prock has found out that we are almost ready to leave for Whangdoodleland. He is a very clever fellow and I have no doubt that he will do everything he can to stop us. I had hoped we would be able to get a head start without his knowing about it, but I underestimated him. So, we have to make a decision. Knowing that he is waiting for us, are we going to attempt our journey or aren't we?"

"Let's go anyway," Ben said instantly.

"Me too," Tom agreed. "I'm not afraid of a dumb old Prock, even if he is a prime minister."

The professor looked at Lindy. "How do you feel, darling?"

She hesitated and then asked in a small voice, "Can he hurt us?"

The professor thought about it. "He can do a great deal to frighten us."

"He didn't seem frightening when I met him," Lindy reasoned.

"Then let's go," said Tom eagerly.

"Come on, Lindy," Ben said. "Look how brave you were on Halloween."

Lindy clenched her hands tightly. "Okay. It would be a shame to waste all our hard work."

The professor smiled approvingly. "Then we are unanimous. There remains only one thing to be said. Stay close to me and do as I say! No matter what happens, you must obey me. Is that understood?"

The children nodded.

"All right then. Put on the scrappy caps."

"How come you don't wear one?" asked Tom.

"I've been studying Whangdoodleland for a long time. After years of practice I am able to go without a hat."

The professor helped Lindy tie her bonnet under her chin. He placed the blue felt cap on Tom's head and straightened it. Ben put on his headband and the professor adjusted the tassel so that it hung correctly.

"Now," he said, "I want you to remain seated and be very still. Do not be surprised if you feel just a little dizzy or if there is a buzzing in your head. The caps are powerful, but they will not harm you."

The children did as they were told. Lindy felt lightheaded. It was the feeling she had experienced before. She was acutely aware of the garden and the summerhouse and the professor standing close by.

Tom was so excited that he gripped the sides of his chair until his knuckles showed white.

Ben tried to shut out the distracting thoughts that were threatening his concentration. He was trembling and hoped he would not let the others down at this crucial moment.

The professor spoke quietly. "Relax. Be calm. Allow the power of the magic hats to flow into you. Listen to the sounds. Feel the fresh air. Look at the garden and imprint the scene upon your memory. Very slowly close your eyes and remain aware of it all—just as we have always practiced."

The children had the odd sensation that the world was beginning to spin and tumble around them. The professor's voice continued. "Feel your minds opening, floating. Remember where we are going. Reach out for it. Reach. It's there. Right there. Open your eyes now, and look. Look, dear children, and you will see that it is time we were on our way."

Ben, Lindy and Tom became aware of the most incredible light. It surrounded them. It was dazzlingly bright and for a moment it was hard to see anything at all.

But as their eyes adjusted to the brilliance, they saw that the garden hedge in front of them was spinning around like a pinwheel on the Fourth of July. There was the sound of a rushing wind and they felt themselves being pulled forward as if by unseen hands.

The professor was smiling and nodding his head and beckoning. "Come along, come along."

Their vision gradually focused and then, quite suddenly, everything became crystal clear. In front of them the hedge had twisted into a long mossy tunnel. The children knew that at the other end of it lay the most wonderful of all surprises.

"Come on!" Lindy got up from her chair and raced towards the opening.

Tom yelled, "We did it! We did it!" He leaped into the air with excitement and ran after his sister.

Ben remained where he was for one uncertain moment. He was still dizzy, and blinked as he tried to see the tunnel. The professor moved to take his hand. "Come on, Ben," he said gently, "we mustn't keep the others waiting."

Lindy turned and cried out, "Oh, Ben, come and look! Just come and see what I see."

Ben took a hesitant step forward and then gradually began to walk, faster and faster until he broke into a run. He emerged from the tunnel a moment behind Tom and Lindy.

It seemed that the world was full of flowers, brilliant flowers that were orange and blue and yellow and white. They were waving slowly on long stalks like tall grass in the wind. There were shady trees and a river close by, making a soft, singing sound as it flowed. But, astonishingly, the trees were purple and the river was golden and the sky above was a bright translucent red.

There were pale pink mountains in the far distance, and high atop the tallest one was something that sparkled and shone like sunlight dancing on the water.

Lindy was tugging at the professor's sleeve. "Look. Oh look. Look. What is that? That thing up there? That shining, lovely thing?"

"That's where the Whangdoodle lives." The professor gazed at the mountain and for a moment he seemed overwhelmed.

"You mean that's the Whangdoodle's palace?" Tom's voice rose with excitement.

The professor nodded.

"Can we go there right now?" Lindy asked. "Can we go and find him?"

"Oh, it isn't as easy as that. We will have many, many things to learn and to overcome before we can reach the palace. Today is just a beginning."

"But we made it!" yelled Tom. "We're really here!"

Ben said, with some awe, "I did it. I never thought I could."

"I'm very proud of you," the professor said. "Shall we explore a little? Just remember my warning. Stay close and do as I say."

He set off along a small path that led to the melodious

Golden River. Lindy walked beside him and took his hand. The boys followed.

"The Whiffle Bird should be along fairly soon," declared the professor. "She's insatiably curious. She's bound to know we're here."

Lindy said, "It's awfully quiet, isn't it? I mean, there aren't any birds singing or anything. All I can hear is the river."

The professor looked anxiously around. "I'd noticed that too, Lindy. It is unusual."

Lindy sniffed the air. "I smell fresh-baked bread."

"It's the flowers," replied the professor.

"You're kidding. Can I pick one and see?"

"No, I wouldn't pick one, Lindy. It would only die and Whangdoodleland is a place for living things. But you can certainly smell the flowers."

Lindy bent and put her face close to a bright yellow bloom that was growing beside the path. "It does smell of baked bread," she said. "Do all the flowers smell like that?"

"You'll see."

"Look at the signpost!" Tom said. He pointed to a post standing at a fork in the path. Its four arms were decorated with elaborate signs.

"*Ploy. Gambit. The Stump. The River,*" Ben read aloud. "What does it mean?"

"They are some of the places we will have to pass in order to reach the Whangdoodle," replied the professor.

As they walked, the sound of the water grew louder. Soon the children were standing by the edge of the river.

"Where does it go?" asked Lindy.

"I think it flows through the Forest of the Tree Squeaks. But after that I don't know."

"Tree Squeaks?"

"Rather nasty little creatures, Ben. I hope we can avoid them."

"Are they dangerous?" Lindy quickly asked.

"I've never met them, Lindy. But I've heard they're terrible tattletales."

Tom said, "Why does the river make that sweet singing noise?"

"If you think that's unusual, put your hand in the water and stir it around," said the professor.

Tom knelt at the river's edge and splashed with his hand. The movement made the river change its gentle tune to a series of thrilling, rippling sounds.

The professor bent and picked up a stone. "Here, Lindy, throw this. See what happens."

She hurled the stone as far as she could. It landed in the water with a splash and chords of music rang in the air for several seconds.

Ben said, "That's incredible. I don't understand why that should happen."

"Why not?" replied the professor. "I told you not to expect anything ordinary in Whangdoodleland." He shielded his eyes. "Look, children," he cried excitedly. "The Whiffle Bird is coming."

In the distant sky something was rolling and tumbling and soaring and dipping in a most peculiar manner.

The professor chuckled. "She never could fly properly. I don't know how she manages at all. She has so many feathers, you see. She's totally uncoordinated."

The children watched as the Whiffle Bird approached. Her long, fluffy feathers were being blown about in all directions.

It was impossible to see a head or a tail or even feet in the feathery profusion.

The Whiffle Bird made a stumbling and very undignified landing onto the branch of a nearby tree and proceeded to shake and shuffle herself into some kind of order. It was not until she settled down that the children were able to see how truly beautiful she was. Her plumage was a brilliant rainbow of colors—red, pink, yellow, orange and purple. She was a silky bird, rustling and smooth, and she gave out a delicate perfume that reminded the children of orange blossoms on a summer evening.

"Greetings, my dear Whiffle Bird," said the professor. "It is a great pleasure to see you again. Won't you come down and join us? I would like to introduce you to my friends."

The bird jumped a foot into the air as he spoke, and every feather flew up and got tangled and had to be rearranged all over again. She retreated along the branch making odd little humming sounds.

The professor stepped forward. "You're looking very pretty," he said. "In fact, I don't think I've ever seen you look so lovely. Dear Whiffle Bird. Sweet Whiffle Bird. Won't you come down and say hello?"

The Whiffle Bird gave a few startled squeaks and turned around and around on the branch. It was impossible for the children to tell which end of her was which.

Quite suddenly she leaned forward, or perhaps it was backward, and somersaulted out of the tree and down to the ground, landing just in front of the professor.

"That's very gracious of you," the professor said, kneeling beside her. "The children and I are so glad you came by." He held out his hand to Lindy. "May I introduce Miss Melinda Potter."

Lindy knelt beside the professor. "Hello, Whiffle Bird. You are the prettiest thing I have ever seen."

The Whiffle Bird began her humming sounds again.

"These young gentlemen are Benjamin and Thomas Potter."

"How do you do," Ben said courteously.

Tom felt a trifle embarrassed and said in a gruff voice, "Hello, bird."

All of a sudden the children noticed two tiny birdlike hands coming through the beautiful feathers. As if holding a curtain to one side the hands parted the waving plumage and they saw two jet-black beady eyes peering out at them.

Lindy cried, "Oh, professor, how sweet she is. I wish there were something I could give her. What does she like to eat?"

"Just feed her compliments and she'll be perfectly happy."

Tom said dryly, "In that case she's probably full up already."

The Whiffle Bird suddenly flew into the air and landed on Tom's shoulder. He was taken completely by surprise.

"Here, get off!" he said in a startled voice.

The professor grinned. "She likes you, Tom. That's a great compliment."

Tom was embarrassed. "Listen, I like her too. But she's got to get down." He looked at the bird, now only inches away from his face. The tiny hands appeared again and the button eyes stared at him without blinking.

The professor and the children doubled up with laughter. "Once she takes a fancy to someone, Tom, she never changes her mind. You're stuck with her, I'm afraid."

Before Tom could protest further, a dreadful, dry rattling sound came from somewhere across the fields of waving flowers. The Whiffle Bird stiffened and then flew into the air.

"MAYDAY!" she shrieked in an incredibly shrill voice.

"What does she mean?" gasped Lindy.

" 'Mayday' is the recognized international call for help," said the professor grimly. "I fear we are in for a surprise."

The horrible sound came again, but closer this time.

"Tom, climb the tree and tell me if you can see anything," commanded the professor.

The boy did as he was told. "There's a big cloud of dust out there and it's moving!" he yelled. "It's coming our way!"

Lindy took hold of the professor's hand and held it tightly. "I think I'm going to be frightened," she said.

"Lindy, you must try hard not to be, because that is exactly what the Prock would want. This is his work, I know it."

"I can see something now," cried Tom. "Hundreds of strange-looking animals."

"What do they look like?"

"Weird. Like huge anteaters. No, more like cannons, but instead of wheels they have five legs in a circle on either side."

"Sidewinders," declared the professor. "That devil has sent the Sidewinders to drive us away."

"What are they?" asked Ben in consternation.

"They're the Whangdoodle's private guard. I've never seen them, but they have a nasty reputation."

Ben cried, "There they are, Professor! Look!"

In the distance a company of extraordinary creatures was marching towards them. They did look like cannons. Their long, funnel-like noses were held rigidly in the air at a forty-five-degree angle. They moved with a rolling, thrashing gait, their five legs churning at either side of their mud-brown bodies. The noise they made was constant now and terrifying.

Tom scurried down from the tree. The professor put his arms about the children.

The Whiffle Bird shrieked at the top of her voice, "STAND AND DELIVER!" Then she flapped away in a panic-stricken fashion up the river.

The Sidewinders were so close now that their staring eyes and slobbering mouths could be clearly seen. Above the roar, percussive music began. The moving sea of creatures shifted and bunched together. As their bodies touched, bright sparks flew in all directions and they began to glow, first green, then red, then green again, and blue.

Lindy could stand it no longer. "Professor," she cried, "I can't look at them. I want to go home." She began to weep and her thumb went into her mouth.

"We shall, Lindy. We shall. You don't have to look, but you must not move. It is imperative that we obey the Whiffle Bird and stand our ground."

The Sidewinders were almost on top of them. They could see the warts on the creatures' sandpaper skin. Their long trunks towered above their heads and their hot breath singed the leaves off the purple tree. The earth shook from the marching of so many hundreds of feet.

Lindy screamed.

Just as it seemed that the professor and the children must be trampled to death, there was a mighty crash of cymbals and the entire army turned and headed towards the river. Ben cried out with relief, "They turned. How come they turned?"

"They were only sent to frighten us," shouted the professor.

Lindy opened her eyes.

Tom suddenly grew very daring. He took a step forward and glared at a passing Sidewinder. "Boo!" he yelled.

The creature looked extremely startled and backed into a

Sidewinder behind it. This started a chain reaction and, all of a sudden, chaos reigned. Sidewinders went tumbling and falling all over each other in their efforts to get out of the way. The music ran down like an old record. The drums stopped and the creatures piled one on top of the other as they reached the river's edge. They fell with colossal splashes into the golden swirling water and there were terrible discordant sounds as they gurgled and gulped and gasped.

The professor said firmly, *"Now,* children, is the time to move. Run home as fast as you can."

The boys needed no second bidding. Grabbing Lindy by the hand, they raced with her along the path they had traveled earlier. The professor, showing surprising agility for one of his age, kept up with them all the way. In no time at all they burst through the hedge into his garden and safety.

 *THREE*

Lindy was tearful. "I hated those things. I don't like it when I get scared. Don't let's go there again."

Feeling decidedly shaky, the party limped across the lawn, and were completely unprepared for the surprise that was waiting for them in the summerhouse.

The Prock was sitting comfortably in one of the chairs.

The professor steadied himself against a post. "Prock, you are an annoying fellow. You turn up at the most inconvenient times." He sank into a chair, breathing heavily.

It was the first time the boys had ever seen the Prock and they gazed at him apprehensively.

Lindy stepped forward and said in an angry voice, "You

know, you're a very nasty man. You made us horribly frightened and that's not fair. You just apologize."

The Prock nonchalantly crossed one long leg over the other. "Don't blame me, little girl. The professor knew what to expect. It's his fault for getting you into a situation like that."

"It's not his fault. And stop calling me 'little girl.' My name is Lindy."

The Prock rose, eyes glittering with anger. "I came here to give you a warning. If you persist in this adventure, then the Sidewinders are just a beginning. Give up this foolish idea of seeing the Whangdoodle, or it will be the worse for you all."

The professor said quickly, "Prock, you have said enough. Anything else should be said to me personally and not in front of the children."

"No, I intend them to hear this. They are the only ones who can prevent you from continuing this mad scheme." The Prock pulled the golden Yo-Yo from his pocket. It bounced and danced violently in front of the boys.

"Put that thing away!" The professor spoke in such a sharp voice that the children jumped. "You have delivered your warning. Now please go."

The Prock moved to the doorway in a single sinuous movement.

"Mark my words well. Think on them. Think hard, or you'll be sorry." Taking hold of a post, he slid around it three times and was gone.

Lindy said in a small apologetic voice, "Professor, I'm not sure I want to do the adventure anymore. I know the Sidewinders didn't harm us, but they did frighten me so."

The Professor looked at her fondly. "I know. You were very brave about it."

"No I wasn't." She began to get tearful again. "I cried, and everything."

"Well, it's all right to cry. It helps a great deal sometimes, and just think what you accomplished today. *You made it to Whangdoodleland.* Apart from me, you are the first humans to have been there in hundreds of years. It's a fantastic accomplishment."

Lindy brightened a little. "We did do it, didn't we?"

"You bet we did," the professor replied enthusiastically. "And we learned a valuable lesson from our experience with the Sidewinders."

"What was that?" asked Ben.

"If you remain calm in the midst of great chaos, it is the surest guarantee that it will eventually subside."

"But those creatures were really gross," said Lindy, "and the Prock said they were just a beginning."

"Yeah, what else could he come up with?" demanded Tom.

"Well," the professor answered, "what weapons has he left? Powerful ones, you may be sure. When all else fails he will resort to using things that can do us most harm. Things like the weapon he used today, which was fear. The Prock banked on the fact that we would be afraid. Tomorrow he may use greed, envy, superstition, pride, lust or selfishness. Not only will he play on our vices, he will undoubtedly use our virtues as well."

"How could he do that?" asked Ben.

"Oh, by relying on your generosity, or sentimentality, or even your sense of humor."

"I don't understand any of this," said Lindy.

"Lindy, all you have to know is that *your* greatest weapons are reason and lack of fear."

"You've been through a lot of this before, haven't you, Professor?" Ben asked.

"Indeed I have. I have made many excursions into Whangdoodleland and I have faced many dangers, and you can see I'm none the worse for my adventures."

"Well, there you are, Lindy," said Ben comfortingly. "If the professor can do it, so can we. How about giving it another try?"

Lindy looked at the professor and the two boys. "Would we see the Whiffle Bird again?" she asked.

"Undoubtedly."

"When should we go to Whangdoodleland again?" Ben wanted to know.

"As soon as possible. I am sure the Prock is banking on the fact that we've been thoroughly scared. He won't be expecting us to try anything right away. That gives us a great advantage."

"Won't he know we're there?" said Lindy fearfully.

"I doubt it. Don't forget, he has a lot to do just being prime minister. I'm certain he only knows where we are when he has time to check."

"Like he did with me," said Lindy, remembering her walk home from school.

"Precisely. Now, the best remedy for a bad scare is to turn right around and face whatever frightened you. So are you game for another attempt tomorrow?"

"Yes," said Ben.

"Yes," said Tom.

"Okay," said Lindy.

"Bravo." The professor beamed. "I have three of the bravest friends in the world. I am tremendously proud of you. Give me your scrappy caps. I don't want you wandering around with those on your heads. Go home now. Sleep well. Don't be afraid. I will see you early tomorrow."

The children wondered how on earth they were going to face their parents. How would they stop themselves from talking about their fantastic adventure? To their surprise it turned out to be much easier than they anticipated.

When they arrived home they found their mother packing suitcases for the visit to Grandma. Mr. Potter was busy making last-minute phone calls. Ethel was preparing dinner. Nobody paid any particular attention to the children.

"I want you to start dinner without us," Mrs. Potter said. "Daddy and I still have lots to do."

"What time do you go, Mummy?" Lindy wanted to know.

"We're leaving tomorrow morning. We'll be back a week from Sunday."

"Did you tell Ethel we'd be visiting the professor?" Tom asked.

Mrs. Potter smiled. "You and your professor. That's all you talk about these days. Yes, I did speak to Ethel. It's perfectly all right."

The children went downstairs to dinner. They were not very hungry and they toyed with their food as they talked quietly together.

Mrs. Potter would have been very surprised had she been able to hear the conversation. The children went over every detail of their amazing visit to Whangdoodleland. They talked about the terrible Sidewinders, the "oily" Prock and the beautiful Whiffle Bird. They thought with pleasure of the beautiful flowers and trees, and the incredible singing river. Uppermost in their minds was the fact that tomorrow was the beginning of their school holiday and they were going to visit Whangdoodleland again. Each child wondered what fresh adventures the day would bring.

 *FOUR*

When the children arrived at his house, the professor wasted no time in getting down to essentials. He put them through a grueling set of warming-up exercises that demanded every ounce of concentration they had. Before giving them the scrappy caps again he spoke once more of the need for caution. "I know that I repeat myself. But please be alert and watchful and stay close to me."

The children were eager to begin. Forgotten were the terrors of yesterday's adventure. Whangdoodleland was a place of beauty and wonder and they longed to be there.

They felt no fear as they donned the scrappy caps, welcoming the tumbling sensation that told them they were once again on their way.

The brilliant light surrounded them and they found themselves standing at the edge of the Golden River.

"No Sidewinders," said Lindy with relief.

"None at all," said the professor happily. "Come along."

They walked by the river. It sang its joyous song and today the birds were singing too. The children saw bright flashes of color as wonderful feathered creatures flew among the purple and mauve foliage. There was a special feeling to this second day in Whangdoodleland.

"We will head towards Ploy," declared the professor. "But we will go by way of the river."

"What's Ploy?" Tom asked.

"It's a place—kind of rocky and interesting country. You'll see."

"What's this part of the country called, right here?" asked Ben.

"This region is called the Blandlands. Because it is so flat, you see."

Lindy's nose was twitching. "I smell baked apples," she said. She saw a tree covered with white blossoms. She looked up at the professor. "It's the tree, huh?" He nodded and she sighed, "I'll never get used to this place."

"Professor, the palace looks nearer today. It's bigger and sort of different," Ben said.

The children looked at the shining edifice on top of the distant mountains. "It's probably the angle of the sun," said the professor. "It's quite a long way away, believe me."

Lindy made an impatient sound. "Oooh, I can't *wait* to meet the Whangdoodle." She kicked at a brightly colored stone on the path and it bounced and rolled ahead of her. It hit a rock and cracked apart. A beautiful jewellike flower grew out of it.

Lindy was about to examine it when Tom said in a thunderstruck voice, "Look at *that!*" He pointed towards the river, and the children gasped.

At the river's edge, rocking gently in the water, was a beautiful red barge. It had a burnt-orange sail, a soaring mast, glowing teak decks and a magnificent ship's wheel. A polished brass handrail encircled the boat. Painted on the transom in bright letters were the words *The Jolly Boat*.

"Holy cow!" said Ben. "Do you suppose we could go aboard?"

"I don't see why not," said the professor.

The children raced up the gangplank.

"Look at the ship's bell!" yelled Tom, and he rang it loudly. It produced a wonderful melodious sound.

"But who does this belong to?" asked Ben.

"This is the royal barge. It belongs to the Whangdoodle," the professor explained.

It was easy to tell that the barge was a master shipbuilder's creation. It was exquisitely fitted together and varnished to perfection. The companionways were gleaming white. Silk line was coiled in neat circles fore and aft and amidships. The cleats and davits and winches were highly polished brass. The prow bore a beautiful carved figurehead: a lady with her head flung back and hair streaming in the wind. Beneath a striped canopy a table and chairs were laid out with a bright tablecloth and comfortable cushions.

The professor said with enthusiasm, "Well, shall we get under way?"

"You mean we can go for a ride?" asked Tom incredulously.

"Of course. Now, which of you knows a good joke?"

The children looked puzzled.

"Come on," cried the professor. "This is *The Jolly Boat*. We need a joke to get started."

"I know a joke," said Lindy. "It goes like this. How did the telephone propose to the lady?"

"How?" asked the professor.

"By giving her a ring."

"Boy, Lindy." Tom spoke in a disgusted voice. "That's pathetic."

"I was only trying to help," she said.

The Jolly Boat trembled.

"Well, that's a start," encouraged the professor. "Tom, what about you?"

"Er—what sings, has four legs, is yellow and weighs one thousand pounds?"

"What does?"

"Two five-hundred-pound canaries."

The Jolly Boat began to shake and rumble. The professor laughed.

"One more joke," he said, "and we'll be on our way."

"Why did the lobster blush?" yelled Ben.

"Because he saw the salad dressing!" everyone yelled back.

The barge heaved and very slowly began to move.

"Terrific," shouted the professor. He ran to the ship's wheel to steer the lovely craft away from the shore. "Keep it up, keep it up," he encouraged.

"I can't think of anything funny," said Ben desperately.

"What happens to ducks when they fly upside down?" Tom cried.

"Well?" The professor chuckled and spun the wheel.

"They quack up."

The Jolly Boat shook all over and began to sail erratically. The professor was laughing so hard that he had a difficult time steering her into the middle of the river.

"Go on, go on!" he called. "We need more power."

"I don't know any more," said Tom.

"Well, you're a fine crew, I must say," the professor said

cheerfully. He thought for a moment. "What do you have when a bird flies into a lawn mower?"

"What?" chimed the children.

"Shredded tweet!" He practically collapsed with laughter at his own joke.

The children began to giggle uncontrollably. *The Jolly Boat* was really shaking now and gaining speed.

"What happens when you cross a chicken and a poodle?"

"What does happen?" asked Ben in a strangled voice.

"The chicken lays pooched eggs."

They all roared with laughter. The professor peered ahead upriver. "Phew. I think that'll keep us going for a while." He sank gratefully into a deck chair, pulling out his spotted handkerchief to wipe his forehead.

Tom giggled. "Speaking of chickens, here comes the Whiffle Bird."

The children looked up as the Whiffle Bird flew in and attempted to settle on top of the mast. She crashed into it and spun around and around on one of the spars until she finally steadied herself. Swaying backwards and forwards, her feathers blowing violently in the wind, she looked like a tattered flag on top of the pole.

"Good afternoon, Whiffle Bird!" the professor shouted up at her.

She shrieked, "YOU'RE BEING TAKEN FOR A RIDE!" and then she tumbled off the mast and plummeted to the deck. She obviously winded herself on landing, for she let out an undignified squawk. Then she saw Tom. She moved towards him and began her humming sounds.

"Oh-oh," he said, backing away. "Here we go again."

She flew onto his head and perched there. He looked as

though he were wearing a ridiculous fluffy hat. The others folded with laughter once more.

"Professor, you have to do something about her," Tom implored. "I can't put up with this for the rest of the journey."

"Whiffle Bird, *dear* Whiffle Bird. You simply must come down." The professor spoke in a firm but soothing voice. "It's not fair if Tom has you all to himself, and he cannot possibly admire your beauty if you stay so close to him."

She turned around and around. Then, to Tom's great relief, she flew to the handrail and settled there.

"This might be a good time for you all to go below and have a look around," announced the professor. "Be sure to take a peek in the main salon."

Tom needed no second bidding. The others followed him down the companionway to the lower deck.

It was even more beautiful than topside, with white, softly carpeted corridors and a large master cabin, in the center of which was an ornate, lace-canopied bed. The portholes were ringed with gold and there was a captain's desk with a remarkable emblem engraved upon it: a golden shield decorated with a heart and a pair of clasped hands and the words *Pax amor et lepos in iocando.*

"I wonder what that means," said Lindy.

"I think it's Latin," replied Ben. "We'll ask the professor."

They walked along the corridor and into the main salon. It was paneled in various shades of glowing mahogany. There were bright curtains and deep leather armchairs, tables with antique lamps and a beautiful old piano with candle brackets. But what mainly attracted the children's attention was a large structure at the end of the room, so colorful as to make them draw in their breath.

It looked a little like a pipe organ. It had silver and gold decorations, shining levers, pistons and knobs. In the center was a many-faceted mirror surrounding a fountain which poured sparkling liquid into an exquisite porcelain bowl.

Lindy was awestruck. "What do you suppose it is?"

"I'm going to find out." Tom raced up the stairs with the others close behind him.

The professor was at the ship's wheel singing limericks in a very jaunty fashion.

"What is that thing down there?" Tom asked breathlessly.

"What thing?"

"That thing at the end of the big room."

"Mm? Oh, that. I thought you'd be interested. That's a soda fountain."

"A *what?*"

"Haven't you ever heard of a soda fountain? It's the Whangdoodle's favorite plaything. He has a very sweet tooth, you know. Why don't you all go and get an ice cream?"

"What do we have to do?" asked Ben.

"Stand in front of the mirror and tell the machine what you would like," said the professor. "While you're at it, would you get me a Sidewinder Surprise?"

The children stared at him. Then without a word they raced back downstairs.

"Who's going first?" asked Tom.

"You go," said Ben.

"No, you go."

"I'll go," said Lindy. She planted herself in front of the mirror.

"Er . . . is it possible . . . I mean, do you have something like . . ." Lindy cleared her throat and jumped violently as a bell rang from within the machine and a deep mechanical voice said, "I am here to serve. Speak clearly and place your order."

"Oh gosh. I think . . . well, I would like a raspberry ice cream with something like blackberry sauce and . . . and whipped cream . . . and could I have a cherry on top, please?"

"One or two scoops of ice cream?"

"Oh . . . two, please."

"One Whiffle Bird Delight," announced the machine.

The children stared in fascination as lights flashed and the levers and pumps began to work. There were ridiculous noises: splashes and gurgles, wheezes and sneezes, squeaks and squelches, burps and belches. More bells rang and the sparkling fountain changed color three times. Suddenly, high, sweet voices sang in harmony. A door opened and a tray slid forward. Lindy found herself holding a silver platter upon which was a lace doily, a napkin, a silver spoon, and a china bowl filled with the most delicious-looking raspberry ice cream and all the trimmings she had asked for.

"Oh, thank you," she managed to whisper.

"Next, please," said the machine.

Tom moved to stand in front of the mirror.

"Do you, by any chance, have a banana split?" he asked, then added, "I'd like chocolate and vanilla ice cream, please."

"One Prock's Passion."

The machine began all over again. The voices finished singing, and Tom was presented with the most fantastic banana split he had ever seen.

It was Ben's turn. He asked politely for a vanilla ripple with some kind of hot sauce.

"One Flutterby Fudge, coming up," the voice declared and Ben was given a mouth-watering concoction.

"Don't forget the professor," Lindy reminded the boys.

Ben turned back to the mirror. "We have a friend who would like a Sidewinder Surprise."

The machine outdid itself. It chattered and chimed furiously. When the order arrived, the children couldn't help smiling. The professor's choice was three scoops of chocolate ice cream, chocolate sauce, toffee crumbles, chopped nuts, peppermint pieces, whipped cream and six luscious marshmallows.

"That looks *gorgeous*," said Lindy. She turned to the machine and said politely, "Thank you so much."

"Not at all," answered the voice. The lights went out and the noise subsided.

The children made their way to the main deck carrying their dishes carefully.

The professor greeted them. "Aha . . . I see you have lots of goodies. Let us sit at the table under the canopy. I think the barge will keep a straight course for a while."

"That machine is just unbelievable," said Tom.

"This is the most wonderful afternoon of my whole life," declared Lindy, leaning back in the cushions. She looked around her. The countryside was bursting with color. The fields, the flowers, the trees, the rocks and mountains had a radiant quality. Golden weeping willows trailed their long branches into the water. The river sang its rippling song; shining, shimmering fish, bright as silver dollars, leaped and played as the stately barge sailed calmly and slowly along.

"I don't ever remember seeing Whangdoodleland as beautiful as it is today," said the professor. "Perhaps it is because you are all with me." He blinked fondly at the children.

The Whiffle Bird, who had been sleeping, shook herself and muttered, *"You're being taken for a ride."*

"You keep saying that, my friend. I wish you would explain yourself."

"Professor, why does the Whangdoodle have a lady carved on the front of the boat?" asked Ben.

"My guess is that the Whangdoodle uses the figurehead to remind him of the world he used to know—the world of human beings."

"What's that writing on the desk in the cabin?" Tom inquired.

"It is the Whangdoodle's motto. *Pax amor et lepos in iocando.* Latin for Peace, love and a sense of fun."

Lindy said idly, "How come there aren't any cows by the river? At home you always see cows by a river."

"Here you'd be more likely to see an Oinck or a Tree Squeak or something like that," said the professor with a smile.

Lindy suddenly jumped up and ran to the railing. "Look!" she cried excitedly and pointed to the shore. "Flutterbyes."

There were hundreds of them—beautiful, multicolored winged creatures, flying and clustering around a dark-blue tree that was bursting with pale-blue flowers.

"They're swarming to the ambrosia tree," said the professor. "It produces a delicious nectar, which Flutterbyes love."

"They hang on the leaves like jewels on a necklace," Lindy marveled.

"We're getting pretty close to Ploy. See how rocky the terrain is becoming." The professor took over the wheel once more. "Children, I'm not going much farther today. There's a Gyascutus that lives somewhere in this region. I met him once and I wouldn't want to bump into him again."

"What's a Gyascutus?" Tom wanted to know.

"A very large, bad-tempered bird with a huge wingspan."

"How huge?" asked Ben.

"About fifteen feet."

"Wow!" Ben looked duly impressed.

The barge was sailing through a high, narrow gorge. Sheer, smooth rocks rose up on either side and the Golden River appeared darker from the shadows and sang a deeper song.

The Whiffle Bird seemed anxious and began to strut up and down.

The professor looked for a point upriver where it was wide enough to turn and when he found it he put the wheel hard over. The lovely barge came around slowly. Her burnt-orange sail flapped noisily, startling the children and sending the Whiffle Bird into a panic.

"YOU'RE BEING TAKEN FOR A RIDE!" she screamed for the third time. She circled once around the barge and then flapped away upriver.

"Dash it. Dash it. Fiddlesticks," the professor muttered to himself.

"What is it, Professor?" Ben asked.

"Something peculiar is definitely going on today. The Whiffle Bird only speaks when there is an emergency, yet nothing has happened to us. I don't understand it."

The beautiful *Jolly Boat* moved out of the shadow and into the sunlight and sailed majestically past a large out-jutting rock.

The professor's suspicion of danger was well founded.

The "oily" Prock was only inches away, hidden from their view behind the big rock, smiling and watching the barge as it moved on downriver.

A large, incredible-looking animal appeared beside the Prock and brushed against his legs. Absentmindedly the Prock stretched out a hand to stroke the silky creature, and then he let out a low and evil chuckle.

 *FIVE*

The journey home was uneventful. The professor kept looking around as if expecting an attack, but nothing happened. He remained very puzzled. All too soon, the children found themselves back on the path by the river.

"Can we come here tomorrow, Professor?" asked Tom. "Can we go on *The Jolly Boat* again?"

"No, Tom. The purpose of each visit is to get closer to the Whangdoodle. We must press on to other things tomorrow. But we'll come back to *The Jolly Boat* another day, I promise you."

As they came out of the tunnel and into the garden, **Lindy** tugged at the professor's sleeve.

"It was the best afternoon in the whole world," she said.

The professor looked pleased. "I'm glad you liked it. I enjoyed it, too. My instincts must have been correct. Our second trip came sooner than the Prock expected. Though I still can't understand why the Whiffle Bird kept saying the same thing over and over again. Well, I will say goodbye now and see you all tomorrow after breakfast, if that is convenient."

The children were very happy and relaxed as they walked home.

Ethel cooked them a good dinner and they discovered that, in spite of all the ice cream they had eaten, they were still hungry.

Later, even the boys were willing to retire early. They wanted to be in the quiet of their own rooms to reflect on the wonders they had seen in Whangdoodleland that afternoon.

Lindy changed into her pajamas, brushed her teeth, pulled her curtains, and was just about to turn down her coverlet when to her surprise she saw, neatly folded on her pillow, a bright and cheerful-looking piece of material. Her heart leaped as she recognized her scrappy cap.

She ran to find the boys. "Look," she said. "Look what was in my room."

"But I thought you gave it back to the professor," said Tom.

"I thought I did, too," replied Lindy.

"Well, don't worry about it. Just keep it safe and give it back to him tomorrow."

Long after the lights went out and the house became quiet, Lindy lay in bed clutching the hat and trying to recall why she had not remembered to give it back to the professor. She hoped he would not miss it. He might be upset.

She took the scrappy cap from beneath the blankets and gazed at it in the moonlight. It certainly was pretty.

On an impulse she put it on her head and tied the ribbons beneath her chin.

Lindy's curtains seemed to be moving slightly in the breeze coming through the open window. The flowers on them looked just like the flowers in Whangdoodleland. Lindy wished that the curtains would stop moving, because she felt a little dizzy. She blinked several times, and looking more closely at them, saw with growing excitement that it was *only* the flowers that were moving and not the curtains at all. She watched them swaying on their long stalks. Far out in the field, something like a plume was moving slowly backwards and forwards and coming towards her. Fascinated, Lindy watched as it came nearer and nearer. Suddenly she realized it was not a plume at all but a tail.

The flowers at the edge of the field parted and into her room stepped the most wonderful creature that Lindy had ever seen.

It was a cat. But no ordinary cat. This one was as soft as a Persian kitten, yet as big and powerful as a mountain lion. He was silver grey with large velvetlike ears and glowing amber eyes. His paws were enormous, with great pads that pushed into Lindy's rug, kneading it gently. His back legs were much higher than his front legs and all four of them were so profusely covered with shining, silky fur that he looked as if he were wearing soft, voluminous pantaloons.

The extraordinary creature looked slowly around the room, and seeing Lindy sitting up in bed, blinked and twitched his long tail in surprise.

"Oh, goodnessss," he hissed, his voice both deep and sibilant. "I'm sssso sorry to interrupt. I sssseem to have lossst my way."

"That's all right," said Lindy faintly. "Won't you please tell me who you are?"

"I'm the High-Behind Sssplintercat." He moved around Lindy's bed, his tail trailing over the brass railing. "No need to tell me who you are. I can tell at a glance that you're Missss Lindy."

"How do you know?" she asked in surprise.

"I've heard the Prrrrock sssspeak of you." The animal bunched himself and sprang very gently onto her coverlet. "He was talking about you jusssst the other day." He stretched languorously. "That fellow'ssss a bully, I mussst say. I sssaid to mysssself, if ever I meet that charming girrrl, I'm going to apologizzze for his rrrrude behavior."

The High-Behind Splintercat suddenly rolled over on his back like a playful kitten. Lindy found his head in her lap and the amber eyes gazing up at her.

"I wonder if you'd do me a trrrremendous favor?"

"Why, of course." Her hands stroked the silky fur.

"Would you—ah—could you, jussst scrrrratch beneath the chin a little? Mm . . . oohhhh, that'ssss the spot." A dreamy look came over his face. He pushed his nose against Lindy's hand and then rolled over again. "Now, jussst on my back, by the tail. Thank you sssso much. You don't know how long it'sss been sssssince anyone did that for me."

Lindy rubbed and scratched and the creature responded by arching his back sharply, so that Lindy had to stand up in bed in order to continue. This gave the Splintercat the opportunity to wind himself around Lindy's legs, and his tail passed under her chin and over her shoulder. Then, quite suddenly, he sprang lightly down from the bed.

"Do you mind if I look arrrround?" he asked cheerfully, stretching once again. "I love sssseeing people's pads. This is purrfectly delightful."

Lindy quickly got out of bed. She didn't want to miss one second of her visit with this interesting creature.

"Is there something I should call you?" she asked. "I mean, do you have a name?"

"Oh, you can call me Kitty if you like, or Fluffy. How about Rrrrover?"

"But Rover's a dog's name." Lindy giggled.

The cat's tail whisked across her face to stifle the sound. "Shhhh. We musssstn't wake anyone. They'd be bound to ssspoil the fun." The cat suddenly tensed. "Wait a minute. Look out."

He crouched low and then gave a mighty leap forward. Lindy wasn't sure what was happening until she saw that the silky creature had hold of a little toy mouse.

"Be careful!" she cried. "That's my favorite toy."

"I thought it was a rrreal one. Oooohh, *look* what I've found." He produced a large ball of wool from beneath Lindy's bed and proceeded to play with it. He patted the ball and ran after it, then tossed it in the air and rolled on his back to catch it.

Lindy sat on the floor enchanted as the High-Behind Splintercat executed a dazzling display of tricks.

"Oh, this is ssssuch fun." The cat threw the ball again. It bounced off his high behind. "I ssssimply adore sssstring." He caught the ball with his tail and lobbed it the length of the room.

"Exxxxcuse me . . ." He skidded across the floor. ". . . *Got* it. Just give me a ball of wool to play with and I'm an absssolute sssssucker."

After several moments of play the cat stretched out beside Lindy on the floor. His tail switched from side to side and he purred loudly.

"This has been sssssenssssational. How glad I am that I

passed this way. You're a ssssweet girl." He nuzzled close to her and then yawned, revealing a startling row of sharp teeth. "I ssssuppose I should be getting along now. It'ssss quite late."

"Oh, must you go so soon?" Lindy was dismayed. "You've hardly been here any time."

"I'm afraid I musssst. I don't want to go, but the beastly Prrrrock might discover that I'm missssing. How I wishhh that I could take you home with me and shhhhow you *my* pad."

"Do you have a lovely pad?" asked Lindy, hoping that if she kept the conversation going she might keep him a little longer.

"Well, it'sss a rather sssspecial pad, in that it's made of ssssilk and ssssatin—with tassels, of course." The cat got to his feet.

"That sounds fabulous," Lindy breathed. "I would love to see it. Do you suppose I ever could?"

His fluffy tail stroked her cheek. "Well, I'm not ssssure if the Prrrock would allow it, but you could take a peek now if you rrrreally wanted to, because I know he's sssssleeping."

"Gosh, I . . . I don't know." Lindy was hesitant. "It's . . . very nice of you. But I don't think the professor would want me to do anything like that."

"Of coursssse. I'm a ssssilly ssssap to ssssuggest it."

He padded slowly to the curtains. "Well, sssso long, Missss Lindy. It'ssss been sssssmashing."

"Oh, wait!" Lindy cried desperately. "Will I ever see you again?"

"I doubt it." The cat seemed dejected. Lindy saw that the

beautiful eyes were moist. There was a long pause. "You know—it occurssss to me that if you did come with me, we'd only be gone for an hour, maybe lessss. The rrrrisk would be ssssmall because everrrryone is assssleep."

Lindy had a sudden idea. "Do you think I could wake my brothers? Do you think they could come too? I'd feel a little better about it."

"Gracioussss, no." The cat's eyes flew wide open and his hair stood on end. "No boys, pleasssse. They're always thrrrrowing things and pulling tailssss. Besides, we get on sssso well and they'd ssssspoil our fun."

"That's true," conceded Lindy. "You're quite sure we could be back in an hour?"

"By my eight lives, I sssswear it."

"I thought a cat had nine lives," Lindy giggled. She ran to the closet to get some warm clothes.

The High-Behind Splintercat examined one long, razor-sharp claw. "Well, I'll be truthful. I had a little scrrrape a few yearssss ago and I ssssuffered rather a ssssetback."

"You mean you lost a whole life?" asked Lindy.

"It was ssssilly of me, but I got carried away for a moment. The rrrresult was rather messy."

"Messy?" Lindy's voice rose.

"I'd rather not talk about it, if you don't mind. It'ssss bad enough losing a life, but then, to have to dissssscuss the ssssordid details . . ." He shuddered.

"That must have been really gross. I can understand why you'd rather forget it."

"You're a ssssweet, ssssympathetic, ssssustaining soul."

Lindy came out of the closet and the cat straightened expectantly.

"Here I am," she said a trifle nervously.

"How prrrretty you look," said the Splintercat admiringly. He spun around in sudden pleasure. "Hot dog! Thissss is going to be ssssuch fun."

Placing his soft tail protectively around her back and chatting all the while, the High-Behind Splintercat escorted Lindy carefully into the field of waving flowers and, without a backward glance, they disappeared into the night.

 *SIX*

The next morning, Ben woke early and ambled into Tom's room. He found his brother sitting on the side of his bed looking somewhat groggy.

"Did you just wake up?" asked Ben.

"Yeah. I had a terrible night. I couldn't sleep."

"Neither could I. I guess we were excited about today and being with the professor. Let's see if Lindy is awake."

They went to Lindy's room and cautiously opened the door. Her bed was empty and the covers were in disarray.

"I guess she couldn't sleep either," said Tom with a yawn.

Ben walked to the open closet and picked up Lindy's pajamas from the floor. His eyes scanned the rack of clothes. "Do you know her blue slacks aren't here? Neither is her cloak. Her shoes are gone too."

"What did she get dressed for?" Tom scratched his head. "She never dresses till after breakfast."

After a thorough search of the house the boys were more puzzled than ever. Ben said, "You know, I've got a feeling something's wrong."

"Maybe she went over to the professor's house," suggested Tom.

"At seven in the morning?"

The boys looked at each other. Suddenly, Ben said, "I think we should call him."

"What if we wake him up?"

"Then it means that Lindy isn't with him or she hasn't reached him. Either way, we ought to check."

As Ben dialed the number, Tom said, "Boy, if she's there, I'm really going to tell her off. What a stupid thing to do."

The professor's voice came over the phone and Ben spoke hurriedly.

"Hello, Professor? This is Ben. I'm sorry to bother you. I hope I didn't wake you. Er . . . have you seen Lindy? I mean, is she with you? We can't find her and we thought that . . ."

The professor interrupted. "I know, Ben, I know. I was just about to phone you."

Ben detected an anxious quality in the professor's voice.

"Lindy isn't with me, but I know where she is. Don't ask questions now. I'll explain when I see you. It's imperative that you come over right away."

"What about Ethel? What shall I tell her?"

"Say that I invited you over for a very early breakfast. Be careful and get out of the house before she realizes Lindy isn't with you. Don't panic now, but *hurry*."

A half hour later, the boys jumped off their bicycles and ran up the steps to the professor's front door. He was waiting for them, his face pale and angry-looking.

"You got here quickly. Come with me."

"Where is Lindy?" Ben asked as they followed him into the house.

"She's in Whangdoodleland."

"What!"

"You're kidding!"

"I'm afraid I am not kidding," the professor said bitterly. He strode up and down the room. "That miserable Prock. That cunning, devious demon. Apparently, late last night, Lindy received a visit from a creature called the High-Behind Splintercat, a devastating animal; seductive and as smooth-talking as you please. She must have had her sympathetic hat with her. . . ."

"She did," interrupted Tom. "She showed it to us last night."

"Yes, well, I only discovered it was missing this morning. She must have forgotten to give it to me, or maybe the Prock stole it."

"How do you know all this?" asked Ben.

"I had a visit from the Prock just before you telephoned. That smug devil was so pleased with himself, I could cheerfully have punched him in the nose. The thing that makes me angriest of all is that if I'd had an ounce of sense yesterday, I'd have realized what the Prock was up to."

"What do you mean?" Tom was puzzled.

"Well, the whole journey in *The Jolly Boat*—the wonderful afternoon and the fun we had—was all designed to lull us into a false sense of security. Lindy had such a good time that she completely forgot her fears. By the time the Splintercat finished his charming act, Lindy was more than willing to go with him. Now I understand what the Whiffle Bird was trying to tell us. We *were* being taken for a ride, and I was just too stupid to see that it was all part of the Prock's evil plan."

Ben was furious. "You know, kidnapping is a crime."

"What are they going to do with Lindy?" Tom asked with concern. "She must be really scared."

"I don't think so," said the professor. "The Prock informed me that she is happy and will be well taken care of. He will release her when I promise on my honor to give up trying to reach the Whangdoodle. I have until tomorrow morning to give him my decision. Of course, I'll agree to his terms."

"You mean, we have to give up the whole adventure?" Ben said in a horrified voice.

"I'm afraid so."

"But why?" cried Tom. "Why not just call the Prock's bluff? I'm sure he wouldn't do anything to hurt Lindy. You said yourself that all the creatures in Whangdoodleland are peace-loving."

"Yes, Tom. But I sense that the Prock's getting desperate. Remember he feels that Whangdoodleland is in great danger. With so much at stake, he might not harm Lindy, but he could keep her there indefinitely."

"But there must be something we can do," said Tom desperately. "It just turns me inside out to think that the Prock has won—and we'll never get to see the Whangdoodle."

"Wait a minute." Ben looked up suddenly. "You don't have to give the Prock an answer before tomorrow. Right, Professor?"

"That's right."

"Then why don't we just go and try to rescue Lindy now, while we've still got time?"

"What a great idea!" Tom said excitedly. "We could sneak in and get her out of Whangdoodleland before the Prock knew anything about it. He'd never expect us to do something like that."

"Hold on, hold on," the professor said. "I'm not sure that's wise. The Prock could capture us, too. Then where would we be?"

"It is a risk," agreed Ben. "But we could be extra careful. I'll bet the Whiffle Bird would help us."

"Oh, go on, Professor. Say we can do it," urged Tom. "This is the one chance we have to put things right. Then we could still try to see the Whangdoodle if we wanted to."

"Well, I must say, I do hate to give up the experiment. . . ." The professor wavered.

"We can't give up now, after all our hard work. You know Whangdoodleland better than anyone. You could take us to find Lindy, I know you could. *Please* say yes," Ben pleaded.

The professor walked to the French windows and gazed out across the lawn. After what seemed like an eternity, he said quietly, "Very well. We will try it. Perhaps we will be lucky and find Lindy before anyone finds us."

He turned to the boys. "I shall phone your house and speak to Ethel. I will tell her that we've planned an excursion."

Tom said, "She won't mind that. Mom told her that we'd be spending a lot of time with you."

"Good. But on second thought, it might be better to tell her we'll be gone for a few days. That way, if something unexpected happens and we're delayed, she won't worry."

"If she thinks we'll be gone a few days, she'll expect us to take some clean clothes," Ben pointed out.

"That's using your head," replied the Professor. "You'd better go back home and pick up some things. Get something for Lindy, too. I'll have Mrs. Primrose prepare us a good hot breakfast before we leave. It could be the last meal we'll get for a while. Now let's hurry. Whangdoodleland is a large country and we don't know where Lindy is. We haven't a moment to lose."

Lindy was beginning to feel anxious. It seemed as if she had been walking for hours.

"Dear frrrriend, are you getting weary?" the Splintercat asked. "Would you like a ride?"

Before Lindy could answer, the cat's tail encircled her waist, lifted her high into the air, and deposited her gently on his back.

"There, now issssn't that nicccce? Much more fun, too."

Lindy had to admit that sitting on the Splintercat's back was much better than walking, even though she had a tendency to slide forward since the cat's behind was so much higher than his front. But she soon made herself comfortable by hooking one arm around the cat's tail and tucking one leg under herself.

A brilliant sun came up over the horizon, bathing everything in a soft pink glow. The springlike air carried tantalizing aromas of popcorn and cinnamon toast that wafted past Lindy's nostrils, reminding her that she was rather hungry. She knew instinctively the smells were coming from the unusual shrubs and bushes so abundant in this area. She made a mental note to tell the professor about it when she saw him.

They came to the bottom of a big mountain. "Hold on tight now," said the Splintercat and he began to climb. Surefootedly he moved up the almost vertical face of the rock.

"This is where my long back legssss become very usssse-
ful," he said. "They make going up mountains sssso easy."

Lindy shuddered to think of what would happen if she
fell off the Splintercat's back. She took a firmer grip on his
tail and told herself not to be afraid.

They reached a wide plateau. There were boulders and
rocks lying as if a giant hand had scattered them about the
landscape. There were trees, too: short scrubby ones that were
shiny black like patent leather, and larger ones with generous
branches and bright melon-yellow leaves in clusters.

"Now, are you rrrready for a ssssurprise?" said the Splintercat, lowering Lindy gently to the ground. She followed
the cat into a small grove where he pointed and said proudly,
"There it is. Home ssssweet home."

Lindy saw a big lollipop-shaped structure, which looked
as if it were made of something soft and furry. At a second
glance she saw that it was a tree which was completely
covered with colored yarn, laced and interlaced in such a
way that the structure was strong and durable.

"Come and ssssee inssside," purred the Splintercat. He
sprang across the clearing and leaped into the tree, disappearing from view.

"Don't leave me. Please don't leave me," cried Lindy.

"Jusssst a minute. Jusssst a minute." The cat's head appeared through the skeins of wool and grinned at her. Then
he withdrew and reappeared higher up, eyes shining mis-
chievously. "I'm ssssending down some ssssstairs."

A rope ladder tumbled out of the tree. It swung invitingly
beside her.

"Come on up," called the cat. Lindy placed a foot carefully on the first rung and climbed until she found herself in an amazing and ingeniously built room.

It was like the inside of a cocoon. The floor, walls and ceiling were a continuous curve of geometrically woven yarn in rainbow colors. Yellow leaves in the tree pushed through the weaving and the room looked as if it were sprigged with flowers. The bottom of the cocoon was low-slung, like a hammock, and it held a large, luxurious pillow. It was easily as big as a bed and it was made of silk and satin patchwork squares. It had a beautiful orange tassel at each corner.

"Come and ssssit by me." The Splintercat padded into the middle of the bed and settled down. "Mm. It'ssss good to be home."

He held out a large box of delicious-looking candies. "Have some wodge."

Lindy was very hungry. She gratefully took one of the candies. It tasted of marzipan and honey and sweet caraway seeds. "What are these? They're terrific," she said, taking another one.

"They are the Whangdoodle's favorite food," grinned the Splintercat. "He has a very sssssweet tooth, you know."

Lindy ate six more pieces of candy and felt a lot better.

"Well, how do you like my pad?" The cat gazed at her and his tail brushed softly across her forehead.

She blinked sleepily. Her eyelids felt heavy. "I think," she said, yawning, "that it's the loveliest . . . and the most beautiful place . . . that I have ever seen."

A great drowsiness overcame her. She lay back and gazed up at the domed ceiling where patches of persimmon-colored sky showed through the latticework of wool. The sun shone onto the yellow leaves and they caught the light and sent reflections dancing around the room. A breeze stirred the tree. Lindy felt herself being rocked. She slipped down, down, down, into the warmth and luxury of welcome sleep.

 SEVEN

The professor and the boys were standing in the middle of the Blandlands plain. The waving sea of brightly colored flowers stretched ahead for miles and miles. In the distance the Whangdoodle's palace sparkled in the early-morning sunlight.

The professor leaned on his umbrella and said, "Now this is the way I see it. The Prock said the High-Behind Splintercat took Lindy away. What would he do with her? Where would he put her for safety? He wouldn't take her to the palace because the whole point is to keep us *away* from the palace. My hunch is—Lindy is still with the Splintercat."

"But how do we find the Splintercat?" asked Ben.

"I only know he lives in the mountains," replied the professor, "but it could be those mountains, or those mountains, or those." He pointed north, east and west.

Ben's heart sank. "Oh, gosh. She could be anywhere. It's going to take *ages* to find her."

"Perhaps not. Let's use our heads and work this out. The Splintercat is probably just like any other mountain cat. He would need a rocky terrain, with trees—perhaps a cave or two. Those mountains to the west have a forest, but it looks a bit dense. Too dark and gloomy for a Splintercat."

"Those mountains are open and grassy," said Ben, pointing north.

"Right. So I'll bet that the Splintercat's lair is in the east, somewhere beyond Ploy. Probably in the Gambit region. That's perfect cat territory. Come on, boys. We've got a long way to go!"

They walked for what seemed like hours. They grew hot and thirsty and it was a relief to hear a soft singing sound that told them they were near a stretch of the Golden River. The boys ran to it and drank their fill of the cool refreshing water.

"Can you two swim?" the professor asked suddenly. "It occurs to me that we could reach the mountains faster if we crossed the river."

"Let's do it," said Ben enthusiastically.

They took off their clothes and rolled them with their shoes into tight bundles. They waded into the water and swam slowly across the river, holding the bundles above their heads. It was a fascinating swim. At every stroke, the water changed its tune, making sweet music.

Once on the other side, they dressed hurriedly.

Tom looked around. "You know, it's odd that the Whiffle Bird hasn't turned up."

"It is odd," agreed the professor. "Of course, she may be watching out for Lindy."

"She may not know we're here yet," suggested Ben.

"Well, I sort of miss her company," declared Tom. "Even though she's a nuisance sometimes, it's nice having her around."

Ben noticed a movement off to his left. He pointed and whispered, "I thought I saw something."

They crouched on the ground and remained absolutely still. A group of fierce-looking creatures emerged from a break in the rocks and moved slowly in a line towards the Golden River. They were at least six or seven feet high at the shoulder, with shaggy, caramel-colored fur and enormous, curling, sharp-pointed horns.

"What are they?" gasped Thomas.

"That's a herd of Flummox." The professor's face was alight with excitement. "They're distant relatives of the great aurochs that roamed Europe thousands of years ago. We'd better give them a wide berth. They could be dangerous."

When they finally reached the foot of the mountains, they were travel-stained and weary.

Tom, trailing a few paces behind the others, noticed something small and shiny lying against a stone. "Professor!" he cried excitedly.

The professor whirled in alarm. "Hush, Tom."

"Look. Look what I found."

The professor examined the shining object. "Why, it's a twenty-five-cent piece."

"It's the one I gave Lindy. I know it is. She said she would keep it in her pocket as a lucky piece. She must have dropped it, don't you see?"

The professor was excited, too. "This proves we're on the right track. Lindy passed this way. What a stroke of luck."

"Professor, look at *this*!" cried Ben and he knelt down to look closely at the ground. "It's a paw print. A really large one."

"It's the Splintercat's, all right," confirmed the professor. He looked up and scanned the mountain towering above them. "See that plateau? I'll bet you anything that's where he went."

"How are we going to get up there?" asked Ben.

"There must be a way up somehow. Come on."

At that moment a great shriek rent the air. It was so loud and so close that the professor and the boys practically jumped out of their skins. Terrified, they flung themselves to the ground.

Tom found his voice. "What do you suppose it is?"

"Whatever it is, it's pretty big," whispered the professor. "Let's be careful."

They crawled forward. A faint mist hung just above their heads and there was a damp feeling to the air. They became aware of a heavy panting sound. Cautiously they peered around a high wall of rock, and there standing at the foot of the mountain, enveloped in clouds of steam, was the most remarkable train they had ever seen.

It was pure white and gave the impression of being made from thick, fluffy cotton wool. Yet, the rods and wheels and couplings and the great engine itself looked strong and shone like polished steel. Written on the side of it in bold letters were the words THE BRAINSTRAIN.

The professor was staggered. "I expected wonders in this incredible land, but I never thought I'd see anything as wonderful as that." He looked at the mountain. Silver rails went straight up the sheer rock face and disappeared into the clouds.

"If I'm not mistaken," he said, "that train goes right to the top. That, my friends, is how we're going to reach Lindy and the Splintercat."

"But what makes the train go?" queried Ben. "I don't see an engineer. I don't see anybody."

The professor scrutinized the train intently. He mumbled

to himself, "Steam—hot air—brainstrain." His face suddenly brightened. "Got it!" he said triumphantly. "That thing is full of hot air. Hot air rises. That's how it goes up the mountain. That's why it doesn't need an engineer."

"How does it get down the mountain again?" asked Tom.

"I have absolutely no idea. But come on. We've got to board that train."

They started around the wall but the professor suddenly grabbed the boys and pulled them back. "Look out," he whispered tensely. "Sidewinders."

Three of the horrifying creatures were emerging from the trees. They were deep in conversation. Their trunks waved in the air and their feet crunched the gravel path as they made for the train.

The Brainstrain gave another shriek and began to puff and blow mightily. Clouds of steam belched out of the engine and rolled towards the professor and the boys.

"Let's go," said the professor urgently and he began to run.

Under the protective cover of billowing steam the boys made a dash for it. The train was beginning to move. Ben was the fastest and he was the first to gain a foothold on the steps of the moving caboose. He turned in time to see the professor reach out and hook his umbrella onto the railing to pull himself aboard.

Tom was in the rear and to everyone's horror he suddenly stumbled and fell. The train was gathering speed and the boy's face took on a look of panic as he saw it pulling away from him.

"Come on, Tom! Come on!" the professor cried.

Tom scrambled to his feet and ran as hard as he had ever

run in his whole life. His legs began to ache and a desperate sob caught in his throat.

The professor leaned out as far as he could. He handed one end of his umbrella to Tom. The boy grasped it tightly. The professor yanked hard and Tom, stumbling and lurching, was hauled aboard the train, where he lay panting and gasping with relief.

The professor pulled him to his feet. "Hold on, Tom. We're climbing fast." The boy gripped the railings and gave the professor a weak grin of thanks.

The Brainstrain heaved and puffed its way up the face of the mountain. Higher and higher it climbed. They were nearing the plateau. Over the noise of the engine the professor shouted, "It isn't going to stop. We'll have to jump."

Suddenly, the train leveled off and began to gather speed at an alarming rate.

"Now!" yelled the professor and the three of them leaped from the speeding train.

They hit the earth hard, rolling over and over, tumbling and bouncing. Tom was flung into a bush and the professor disappeared.

Ben staggered to his feet, weaving unsteadily towards his brother. "You okay?" he gasped.

Tom nodded. "Where's the professor?"

"Here," came a faint reply. "Over the edge."

They rushed to the precipice. The professor's umbrella had caught on a root and he was hanging on to it for dear life and swaying gently out over the void.

The boys leaned over and grabbed him. Ben clasped his wrist and Tom caught hold of his collar. With a mighty heave they pulled him to safety.

He was deathly white and lay for several moments face

down in the grass. Presently, he rolled over and gazed up at the sky. Then he looked at the boys. "Thank you both," he said simply. "That was a close call."

He sat up and looked at the mountain where, high above, *The Brainstrain* came to a halt. The Sidewinders got out. Then a remarkable thing happened. The train slowly vanished before their eyes.

"Good Lord!" The professor shook his head in disbelief. "That answers your question, Tom. *The Brainstrain* doesn't have to get down the mountain. It dissipates at the top."

"How could it do that?" asked Ben.

"Like any hot air that rises—it just dissipates. That accounts for all the clouds up there. I presume the train reassembles itself at the bottom of the mountain and when it has gathered enough hot air, it moves up once again. Fantastic."

Tom and Ben helped him to his feet. They could see that the adventure had been quite a strain for their friend. He looked pale and not very steady. But he gazed around with interest and said, brightly enough, "Well, I wonder where we go from here."

EIGHT

When Lindy woke up, she found the Splintercat sitting beside her, washing himself.

"Goodness," she said. "Did I sleep for very long?"

"Not too long," replied the cat, licking his paw. "How do you feel, Missss Lindy?"

"I feel fine. But I think I ought to be getting home. My brothers might find out that I'm gone and be worried."

The cat sprang up. "Ah. Missss Lindy. I have a trrrremendous favor to asssssk you. I wonder if you would help me with thissss." He produced a large ball of wool. "Everrrry friend that comes to visit makes a cat's crrrradle with me. I add it to my house. It'ssss like ssssigning my guesssst book."

Lindy frowned. "All right. But *please* let's hurry." She was beginning to feel a little annoyed. "What do I have to do?"

The Splintercat worked the wool quickly between his paws until it made a pattern of crossed threads.

"Now, Missss Lindy, use the finger and thumb of each hand and pick up the wool in the middle."

Lindy did as she was told and the cat transferred the threads to her hands.

"Purrfect," breathed the Splintercat. He lifted a paw to take up the wool again. Somehow, the threads slipped and Lindy found her hands bound by the brightly colored strands.

"Oh dear." The cat blinked in alarm. "It sssslipped out of my grassssp. Hold on, dear frrrriend, let me unwind you."

He turned Lindy around. "I think the wool goessss under here, and thrrrrough here."

Lindy began to feel dizzy, for the cat passed the ball of wool under her arms and round her waist and then over her hands so quickly that she hadn't time to follow his movements.

The results were disastrous, for by the time the cat had finished she was so tangled up in the wool that she couldn't move.

"What have you done?" she said in an angry voice. "I told you I wanted to go home. It's terribly late and you promised we would be back in an hour."

"Well, well, well. How goes it?" said a familiar voice and Lindy felt a chill run up her spine.

The Prock's tall frame filled the doorway.

The Splintercat cast a quick look towards Lindy.

"Good heavens, Splintercat, what have you been up to?" The Prock began to laugh.

The cat chuckled.

Lindy had seen and heard enough to know that she was in terrible trouble.

She glared at the Prock. "I know what you're doing," she said, trying desperately not to cry. "You just stop all this and let me go home. The professor is going to be furious with you when he finds out."

"He already knows, my dear," the Prock replied casually. "And I've told him that if he wants you back, then he must stop trying to reach the Whangdoodle. If he agrees, you may go home at once."

"What if he doesn't agree?"

"Well, that's a problem we'll just have to face when the time comes." He turned to the Splintercat. "Keep her here. I'll be in touch. I've got to push on to the palace."

"Is the Whangdoodle very upsssset?" the Splintercat asked.

"He's beside himself," replied the Prock. "He believes this is all my fault and he's keeping me twice as busy just because he's cross."

The cat shook his head sympathetically. "Don't worry, Prrrrock. It'll be over ssssoon."

"Yes. Thank goodness." The Prock raised a hand in farewell. "Goodbye, Miss Lindy. I apologize for the inconvenience, but I have no alternative."

Lindy turned her head away and didn't answer. When she looked back again, the Prock had gone.

The Splintercat stretched and yawned. "Oh, my! It'ssss

going to be a long day. How about some wodge, Missss
Lindy?"

"Don't you talk to me," she snapped. "You false friend.
If I had my way, you'd lose all the rest of your eight lives—
right now."

The Splintercat winced, but he said simply, "Jusst as you
pleasssse."

He stretched back on the pillow and idly stroked the
geometric pieces of wool above his head. Rippling notes of
music came from the taut strings, and Lindy watched with
surprise as the Splintercat played on the wall of his house
as though it were a harp.

Her thoughts turned to the professor and Thomas and
Benjamin. She knew how worried they must be. What
would the professor do in a situation like this? Would he
give in to the Prock? Or would he try to rescue her? Lindy
thought that the boys would encourage such a move. But
if they did try to find her, how would they know where
she was?

Suddenly she had an idea. It wasn't a very good one, but
it was the best she could come up with.

She began to sing a song to the Splintercat's music. The
creature looked startled. But he smiled happily and, to
Lindy's great relief, continued to play.

Ben, Tom and the professor had been searching for hours
but there was still no sign of Lindy. Suddenly Tom noticed
something on the horizon. He studied it for a moment, then
he shouted, "Professor, look! It's the Whiffle Bird."

They watched as the Whiffle Bird flew straight to them

and settled on Tom's shoulder. He patted the beautiful feathers and said, "I knew you'd turn up sooner or later. We're in a terrible fix, Whiffle Bird. We can't find Lindy and we simply must reach her somehow."

The bird made sympathetic noises and preened herself. At that moment an eerie sound echoed across the plateau.

It was a dreadful noise; mournful and lonely, a wailing, sobbing cry that moved up and down the scale and went echoing around the mountains.

"What on earth was that?" Ben spoke in a hushed voice.

The professor held up a hand. "Listen. There it goes again."

Tom frowned, then he said tentatively, "I may be imagining things, but I think I hear something else. Another sound underneath. Do you know what I mean, Professor?"

The professor looked at the boy sharply. "Are you sure, Tom?"

Tom listened carefully. "Yes, yes. Do you know what it is?" he cried. "It's Lindy. I can hear Lindy singing."

"Where, Tom? Where is it coming from?"

The boy strained to pick out the tiny, fragile sound from among the shifting echoes. Then, for a moment, the wailing stopped and in the silence Lindy's voice came through clearly.

"That way," Tom yelled, pointing. "That's where she is."

No one was prepared for what happened next.

The Whiffle Bird suddenly shot up into the air. "MAYDAY!" she shrieked, and then again: "MAYDAY!"

The professor looked up and saw a huge shadow coming towards them. "Look out!" he cried. Grabbing both boys, he shoved them to safety under the nearest tree. Seconds later a whirling wind, like a hurricane, flattened them all to the ground.

"What is it? What is it?" gasped Ben in panic.

"Gyascutus," coughed the professor as the dust swirled about them.

The huge shadow passed overhead again and the boys caught a glimpse of a colossal wing with large ragged feathers. Black talons scraped the earth as the monster above them banked to avoid the tree, and the swirling air engulfed them again.

"Where's the Whiffle Bird?" Tom looked for her anxiously. She squawked indignantly from the branches above his head.

The professor and the boys waited a full five minutes before coming out from under the tree. To their relief the giant bird was nowhere in sight.

The professor wiped his brow with his spotted handkerchief. "Good Lord, that was close. We were lucky. Very lucky indeed."

Ben was badly shaken. "Do you think the Gyascutus saw us?"

"I doubt it. It would surely have attacked us, for it's a dumb creature that acts first and thinks later. You know, had it wanted to, it could easily have picked up that whole tree."

Tom said fervently, "Well, I sure hope we don't run into it again."

The professor scrutinized the sky and the mountains. "I think we're safe now. Let's hurry and get Lindy and ourselves out of this mess."

He set off in a westerly direction, the boys falling into step beside him. The Whiffle Bird shook herself, then flew ahead as if leading the way.

The Splintercat had been howling ever since Lindy completed her first song.

In the beginning he had played the accompaniment for her, overjoyed at the sweet music they were making together. But as the song progressed and Lindy's clear voice sang the melody to perfection, the cat's amber eyes filled with tears. He continued to play, and every once in a while drew a paw across his face and sighed deeply.

When the song was over he said, with feeling, "Oh, Missss Lindy, you ssssing sssso ssssweetly."

"Thank you. It's because you play so well," replied Lindy. Seeing that the cat was flattered, she added, "Let's do some more. This is fun."

The cat took up the accompaniment once again and Lindy put all the expression she could into her voice. The Splintercat began to blink furiously, and suddenly he could control his feelings no longer. He rolled back his head and howled. Lindy quickly realized that the howling was much louder than her voice and would carry twice as far. If the professor and the boys were anywhere in the vicinity, they would certainly hear it. She continued to sing.

"Oooooooooh, Missss Lindy," the cat bawled. "Ssssstop. I can't ssssstand it. That'ssss so pretty." His back leg drummed the floor in ecstasy and his fluffy tail waved rhythmically back and forth.

"Please play something else," coaxed Lindy. "I'm having such a good time."

The Splintercat hiccoughed and wiped his nose. He began

to strum another melody, but when Lindy joined in, the strain became too great and he broke down completely.

"Sssstop. Sssstop. Sssstop. Sssstop," he sobbed, and rolled on the floor, covering his head with his paws.

Lindy took a deep breath and wondered how much longer she could keep this up. She almost choked with surprise as the professor's head came into view over the threshold. He cautiously peered into the room, saw her and put a finger to his lips, then ducked out of sight.

The professor ran back to the bushes where the boys were hiding.

"She's in there, all right," he puffed excitedly. "Now the question is, how are we going to get her out?"

He had no sooner uttered the words than the Whiffle Bird, who had been sitting quietly in a nearby tree, flew to the ground, landing a foot or so from the Splintercat's pad. She squawked horribly and lay very still.

"What's the matter with her?" Tom asked anxiously.

"Hush," said the professor sharply.

The howling of the Splintercat had stopped. In the silence, the Whiffle Bird squawked again, as if in great pain.

The Splintercat's startled head popped through the strands of wool, his amber eyes red with emotion and tears. The cat looked around quickly and saw the apparently helpless Whiffle Bird lying on the ground. His ears pricked up, his eyes opened wide and then became gleaming, calculating slits. He disappeared.

"Professor," whispered Tom, "we've got to do something. The Whiffle Bird's in trouble."

"Wait, Tom. Wait." The professor laid a restraining hand on Tom's arm.

The Splintercat came out of his house, his belly pressed flat to the tree. The Whiffle Bird fluttered in panic and rolled a few feet away. She began to emit a series of agonized squeaks and gasps.

The Splintercat eased his way down the tree, ears flattened, a wicked grin on his face. Then, he pulled himself forward, one paw at a time, until he was within a few feet of the Whiffle Bird.

Ben held his breath. Tom, horror-stricken, tugged at the professor's sleeve, but the professor again signaled for the boy to wait.

The Splintercat's body tensed and his high behind began to move from side to side. With a mighty leap he sprang for the Whiffle Bird.

She rocketed into the air, evading the grasping claws by mere inches. Beautiful feathers flew in all directions. She landed a little way from the cat and dragged herself along the ground.

The cat looked surprised and pounced again. Once more the Whiffle Bird took to the air. She flapped around and around in low circles and the cat's head twisted wildly, his neck a veritable corkscrew.

The professor took a small penknife out of his pocket. "I'm going to get Lindy. Wait for me here and *don't move.*"

The Splintercat had been lured a considerable distance from the tree. The professor waited until the cat had his back to him and then, quickly and silently, he ran to the ladder and climbed up.

Lindy was overwhelmed with relief when she saw him. The professor quickly cut her loose. "Stay close to me and when I tell you, run as fast as you can."

As the professor and Lindy climbed down the ladder, they

glimpsed the Splintercat thrashing wildly in the air and the Whiffle Bird spinning and rolling and tumbling in all directions.

While the cat struggled to recover both balance and senses, Lindy and the professor ran to the bushes where the boys were hiding. The children embraced each other silently.

"Now what do we do?" whispered Ben.

"We wait to see if the Whiffle Bird is going to be all right and then we get out of here."

By some miracle the Whiffle Bird had evaded all attempts at capture. The cat, obsessed with the desire to catch this annoying and elusive bird, made a last flying leap, jaws snapping, teeth tearing, yowling, snarling, and slashing the air with his claws.

The Whiffle Bird shot up into the air and shrieked, "GET TO THE POINT!"

The Splintercat crashed to the ground.

"Get to the point . . . the point . . . the point." The professor looked around in desperation. "That's where she means! That point up there!" He indicated a needle-sharp rock at the top of the hill. "Run, children, run for your lives!"

He grabbed Lindy's hand and began the steep ascent, scrambling over rocks and stones. The boys followed. The Whiffle Bird flew above them and shrieked again, "GET TO THE POINT!"

Dazed and completely frustrated, the Splintercat picked himself up and looked around. As his vision cleared, he saw the children and the professor. With a demented howl he streaked towards them, legs churning, his powerful high behind propelling him up the hill in giant leaps and bounds.

"He's gaining on us!" gasped Tom.

"Don't look back!" the professor yelled. He put on a burst of speed and Lindy, who still clung to his hand, felt herself momentarily lifted off the ground.

They were almost at the top of the hill, but the Splintercat was horribly close. Ben felt the ground shaking and he heard the cat panting behind him with murderous fury.

With a last mighty effort the creature sprang.

"Got you! Got you! Got you!" he roared triumphantly, his huge paws spread wide, the wicked-looking claws flashing like steel knives in the sun.

The professor grasped the narrow rock and swung around it, pressing himself and Lindy flat against the rough stone. The boys flung themselves to the ground, and the cat sailed over their heads, a crazed, fearful look on his face.

"Whoa . . . oh . . . ow . . . eeeow!" he shrieked, his back legs trying desperately to brake his tremendous speed. But it was too late.

On the other side of the rock the hill fell away sharply and the Splintercat sailed over the edge, and landed on the steep incline. His long back legs pushed him forwards and upwards and over and he rolled and bumped and crashed from side to side, trying desperately to gain a foothold. Great furrows of earth appeared as he dug in his heels. Billowing clouds of dust rose behind him as he plunged, howling at the top of his lungs, all the way down. At the bottom of the hill, he tumbled into a field of bright mustard-yellow flowers, and completely disappeared.

The professor began to chuckle. Relief and exhaustion flooded over him.

"It's a well-known fact," he explained, "that Splintercats, with their high behinds, are very good at climbing up hills, but they're very bad at going down. Good old Whiffle Bird. She knew what she was doing when she told us to get to the point."

"I can't help feeling sorry for the Splintercat," said Lindy.

"Don't, my dear. If I'm not mistaken, our furry friend just landed in a field of catnip. He should be ecstatic for quite some time."

"What's ecstatic?" she asked.

Suddenly, with a squeal of happiness, the Splintercat exploded out of the flowers. He did a double somersault, and landed in the blossoms again. His head popped up with one of the blooms clamped idiotically between his teeth. There was an intoxicated, happy grin on his face and he began to leap about as if dizzy and delirious.

"Oooo . . . wheeee!"

The children and the professor watched as he yelped and bounced.

"Sssstop. Sssstop it, I *like* it!" He rolled on his back, kicking his legs in the air.

"Oh . . . ha . . . ha! Ssssweet, ssssibilant Ssssplintercats!" He howled with laughter as though he were being tickled unmercifully.

The children began to giggle as well.

"Help! Help! I *love* it. I love it. I love it," they heard the cat mumble passionately, and he went tearing off around the field, tumbling and turning, sniffling and sneezing, twittering and fluttering in an absolute dither of delight.

"That, Lindy," said the professor, "is a perfect example of the word 'ecstatic.' "

PART THREE

Conquest

ONE

The professor and the children discovered that the other side of the mountain descended in a series of gentle, rolling hills. Streams and waterfalls poured forth, splashing, leaping, and gurgling down the slopes to join the Golden River. The grass was lush and thick, of a sparkling aquamarine blue.

Ben noticed a mass of plum-colored trees in the distance. "What are they?" He pointed.

"I'm not sure," replied the professor. "But if my sense of direction is right, that's the Forest of the Tree Squeaks. I would say that right now, we are in the heart of Whang-doodleland."

The Whiffle Bird flew around them and landed in a tree. She fluffed out her beautiful feathers. "EASY DOES IT," she said.

The professor looked around. "Let's take the Whiffle Bird's advice. This seems a good place to rest for a while. There's lots of shade and I don't think we'll be spotted here."

"You know, I'm hungry," said Lindy. "I haven't had anything to eat for ages."

"Yeah, I'm starved," said Tom.

The professor reached into the low branches of a strange-looking tree. "That's easily put right." He pulled down a soft fruit that resembled a large maroon pineapple.

Lindy bit into it. "That's fabulous. What kind of tree is that?"

"It's a Fruit-of-the-Month Tree," replied the professor.

"You mean each month it grows a different kind of fruit?" asked Tom.

"My first trip to Whangdoodleland the trees were growing Tangerangos. A few months ago it was Passionanas." The professor plucked one for himself and took a bite. "Mm. This month it's Razzapple. Have some," he said to the boys. "It'll do you good."

They ate their fill of the delicious fruit, then relaxed in the shade of the tree.

The professor said, "You know, I've been thinking. It might be wise to stay here for the night. It's getting dark, and it will be difficult finding our way back."

The children loved the idea of camping out in Whangdoodleland. The boys rolled up their jackets and used them for pillows. Lindy covered herself with her cape and rested her head in the professor's lap.

They watched a pale, translucent moon rise in an emerald green sky, while brilliant stars sparkled overhead. The Whangdoodle's palace gleamed in the night like a huge chandelier.

Lindy said wistfully, "I wish we were up there looking down here, instead of the other way around."

"So do I, Lindy. Oh, so do I." The professor's voice was full of longing.

Ben pushed himself up on an elbow. "Professor, how close have you come to seeing the Whangdoodle? I mean before you met us?"

The professor reflected for a moment. "I only came close enough to know that he was there, Ben. Of course, I talked to the Prock a lot and I met our good friend the Whiffle Bird." He looked at her perched in the tree close to Tom. She appeared to be fast asleep, although it was hard to tell.

"I never really got much beyond the Gambit region," he continued. "I discovered that it wasn't possible for me to reach the Whangdoodle by myself. I needed youthful minds to help me." He smiled. "That's why I was so thrilled when you came to my door at Halloween, for I had almost given up hope."

"It was kind of a miracle, wasn't it?" said Lindy sleepily.

"Well, I'd call it more of an opportunity," said the professor. "Miracles, contrary to popular belief, do not just happen. A miracle is the achievement of the impossible, and it is only when we put aside our greed, anger, pride and prejudices so that our minds are open and ready to accept it, that a miracle can occur. The Whangdoodle managed to think and do the right things, and look at the miracle he brought about for himself and his friends."

"He surely must have tried hard," said Tom thoughtfully. "Do you suppose we will ever get to meet him?"

"If you want to badly enough, the chances are it will happen. Actually, I've been doing some thinking. Since we've come this far, how would you feel about making one last all-out attempt to reach the Whangdoodle? If we are careful and lucky we might reach the palace before the Prock has any idea we are in the vicinity."

"How do you know the Whangdoodle will let us in even if we do reach the palace?" asked Ben.

"I don't. But I have a feeling the closer we are able to get, the more regard he will have for our determination."

"Let's do it," said Tom enthusiastically. "We haven't got that much farther to go, have we?"

"I don't believe so."

"Please, Professor," said Ben, "let's give it one more try."

Lindy was nearly asleep, but she managed to murmur, "Yes, please."

The professor smiled and opened his plastic umbrella with the yellow butterflies. "I guess it's settled then. Tomorrow we'll make an early start. I suggest we get some rest now." He pushed the umbrella handle into the soft earth and it made a perfect shelter from the gentle night breeze that was blowing across the hills.

He stroked Lindy's hair and talked quietly in the darkness, about the stars and constellations. He told them about the furry little creatures called Flukes, and how, when the Whangdoodle first left the human world, they had hidden away in a pair of his old slippers. When they were finally discovered, it was too late to send them back.

Lulled by his soft voice, the children pulled their scrappy caps down over their eyes and fell into an easy and comfortable sleep.

The professor woke them early. It was barely light and the sun had yet to show itself. Pockets of mist lay among the vivid blue hills.

He said quietly, "It is imperative that we get through the Forest of the Tree Squeaks before they wake up. If they see us they'll warn the Prock. Let's go, keep very quiet."

He led the way down the hill and the Whiffle Bird flew onto Tom's shoulder.

"Professor," whispered Ben. "There's a road just over there."

The professor nodded. "Probably the main highway. What a bit of luck!"

The sky was beginning to redden. The professor quickened his pace. They reached the road and discovered that it was made of shell-pink flowers, clustered so tightly together that they were like a carpet. A signpost stood on a grassy bank. One arm pointed to the trees and read, *To the Forest of the Tree Squeaks*. Another arm below it pointed in the same direction. It read, *To the Palace*.

"Not long now," the professor murmured happily. "Let's take off our shoes. We'll make less noise."

The road was cool and springy beneath their feet. Tom noticed some white star-shaped blossoms growing in a hedge with huge berries hanging beneath them. He tugged the professor's sleeve and asked if he could eat some.

The professor picked a berry and tasted it. "Delicious," he pronounced.

"*Shut your mouth*," muttered the Whiffle Bird.

"Why did she say that?" asked Lindy.

"She's saying we really must be quiet," whispered the professor and he handed Tom a fistful of berries.

"Yes. But does she have to be so rude about it?" Lindy picked one of the berries and popped it into her mouth.

By the time they reached the entrance to the forest everyone had eaten a scrumptious breakfast.

Their first impression of the forest was that it was dark and gloomy. But as their eyes adjusted to the light, they saw that it was unusually colorful.

The plum-colored trees had brown, gnarled trunks. Most of them were embraced by a vivid pink ivy, growing and twining around the tall columns and twisted limbs. Garlands of honey-cream flowers hung from the branches, linking one tree to another. The floor was mossy and bedded with ferns the color of amethyst. Huge pearl-white and crimson orchids grew at the side of the road, which pointed straight as an arrow into the dark interior.

Then they saw the eyes. There were thousands of them—large, unblinking, tortoiseshell-yellow orbs staring down through the leaves from every part of the forest.

It was such a chilling sight that the professor and the children came to a complete halt. Gradually, they were able to discern the bodies of the Tree Squeaks, which were hanging upside-down by their tails from every tree. They were like little russet-colored monkeys, with wings folded at their sides.

Lindy took the professor's hand. "Are they awake or asleep?" she whispered.

"Asleep, I think. They have a strange characteristic of being able to sleep with their eyes open. Come on."

They moved forward again, clutching their shoes in their hands. The forest was full of soft rustling sounds and an occasional tiny squeak. The professor and Lindy led the way, with Ben and Tom and the Whiffle Bird bringing up the rear.

Suddenly Ben startled everyone by giving a clear, loud hiccough. He dropped his shoes and clapped a hand across his mouth.

The professor spun around. Ben's eyes were wide with horror. His shoulders heaved as he hiccoughed again.

The Whiffle Bird nervously fluffed out her feathers. "*Shut your mouth,*" she mumbled.

"Sssh," hissed the professor.

Everyone looked up at the Tree Squeaks. They had not moved. The professor picked up Ben's shoes and motioned to the children to follow him.

They had only gone a few more paces when Lindy made a high, squeaky sound, like a mouse with a bad attack of the sneezes. She looked panic-stricken and started to apologize, but all that came out was another squeaking hiccough. "Oh . . . *heec* . . . oh! Professor . . . *heec* . . . what shall I . . . *heec* . . . do?"

She could not stop. The professor hurriedly pulled out his big spotted handkerchief. Lindy grabbed it and promptly dropped one of her shoes.

Everyone tried to do something at once. Lindy stuffed the handkerchief into her mouth. Ben bent to pick up Lindy's shoe, still keeping one hand across his mouth. The professor caught his umbrella handle in his pocket, and Tom suddenly gave such a loud *hic* that the surprised Whiffle Bird took off. The professor dived for her and caught her just as she was flying past him. His umbrella and the shoes scattered in all directions.

"Dear Whiffle Bird," he breathed fervently, "*please* don't make a sound."

By now all three children were hiccoughing violently.

The professor signaled for everyone to stand still. He stroked the Whiffle Bird and looked up at the Tree Squeaks. In spite of the noise, they remained undisturbed.

"I'm going to tie your shoes together so that you can hang them around your necks," he whispered. "That will leave your hands free to cover your mouths." He gathered up the shoes and gave a pair to each child.

"Now then, we will start again. Follow me, and please *try* to keep quiet," at which point he gave the loudest hiccough the children had ever heard.

The professor looked so startled, it was all they could do to keep from laughing. The professor lifted up the collar of his jacket and pulled the coat above his head. Muffled sounds came from beneath it as he struggled to stem the attack.

The children waited, twitching and shaking, trying desperately to rid themselves of their own fearful spasms.

Presently, the professor emerged from beneath his coat, his face beet-red. He gasped, "We should never have eaten—*hic* —those berries. Take a deep breath and—*hic*—hold it as long as you—*hic*—can."

The children did as they were told until they thought their lungs would burst, then they carefully exhaled. To their surprise the hiccoughs seemed to have gone.

They all looked at each other. Everything was silent again. Not a sound, not a single peep came from any of them. They smiled with relief.

"Everybody okay now?" the professor whispered. They nodded.

"Right. Let's get out of here."

They moved off. Without warning, each one of them let forth an explosive, unguarded *hic* at exactly the same moment.

The noise was so loud that it seemed to split the forest wide open. The result was disastrous. Every Tree Squeak rose up into the air, squealing, squawking and screeching, and the entire place rang and throbbed with the terrible sound.

Lindy screamed. Tom covered his ears. The Whiffle Bird cried, "MAYDAY!" and the professor grumbled, "Fiddlesticks. *Hic.* Fiddlesticks."

Ben watched the black cloud of Tree Squeaks swirling above him. To his amazement, he realized they were screaming "PEOPLE, PEOPLE, PEOPLE, PEOPLE!" as loud as they could. The Prock and every other creature in the land could not fail to hear such a warning.

The Whiffle Bird's voice cut through the frightful din. "CHEER UP!" she squawked.

"Well, that's a stupid thing to say," shouted Ben angrily.

The professor hugged Lindy close because she was sobbing with fright. "Cheer . . . up. Up. Up. *Cheer.* That's it," he cried. "Let's cheer. Let's drown out the noise. I refuse to be intimidated by this racket."

"What's intim-*hic*-idated?" asked Lindy.

"Oh never mind, darling. Just sing. Sing as loud as you can. All of you. Remember when we went on our picnic and sang in the rain? Sing louder than that."

The professor started to sing a rousing march. The children joined in, stomping and banging their shoes together, making so much noise that the Whiffle Bird got quite excited and flew around shrieking ferociously, "SHOOT THE WORKS!" The terrible clamor above them diminished and their hiccoughs grew less as the professor, waving his umbrella like a baton, led the way through the forest. Quite suddenly, they emerged from the trees and into the daylight. The morning sun was so bright that it took a moment or two to get used to it. They continued singing until they were well away from the forest. The sound of the Tree Squeaks subsided and gradually faded away altogether.

The professor sank onto the grass. "My great godfathers!" he said with feeling. "I have never been through such a frightful experience. Those miserable Tree Squeaks and those *ghastly* hiccoughs." He clasped a hand to his stomach.

"Was it the berries that made us hiccough?" asked Tom.

"Of course," replied the professor. "That's what the Whiffle Bird was going on about when we were eating. When she said 'Shut your mouth' she meant 'Don't eat.'"

Ben stroked the Whiffle Bird's beautiful feathers. "You always know the right thing to tell us, don't you, Whiffle Bird?"

The Whiffle Bird made her humming sounds and strutted around proudly.

The professor said, "I really must pay more attention to her. That's the second time I have missed the sense of what she was saying, and both times we got into trouble." He prodded Tom. "There's a lesson in that, young man. Learn to listen well when people are talking. First, it's a great art, and second, it's quite possible that when people say one thing, they mean another." He rubbed his forehead wearily and looked at the children. "You know, we haven't a hope now of reaching the palace without trouble of some kind. I am quite sure the Prock heard the Tree Squeaks and is already making plans to stop us."

"But we are going on, aren't we?" asked Ben hopefully.

"I'd like to—that is, if you all agree," said the professor. "We're really so close . . ."

"I say it's the Prock or us," Tom declared.

"How do you feel about it, Lindy?"

"Oh, I feel fine," she said in a small voice. "I just wish we could stop being surprised all the time."

The professor nodded understandingly and looked around. The region was very different from anything they had seen before: a white desert with cherry-red cactus plants growing out of the sandy ground. There were small foothills in the immediate area and beyond them, the giant mountains and the Whangdoodle's palace.

The professor got to his feet. "Well, if we're going to continue we'd best be on our way." He strode off at a good pace and the children followed.

 *TWO*

It was a warm sultry morning. The pink road wound through the desertlike country, and quite suddenly, in the middle of nowhere, it divided. One way went northwest, the other northeast. Signposts at the junction pointed both ways and each sign read *To the Palace.*

"Here's a dilemma," said the professor. "Which way shall we go?"

"WATCH YOUR STEP," squawked the Whiffle Bird.

The professor looked at her closely. "You couldn't possibly explain that remark, could you?" he asked.

She remained silent.

"There's only one thing to do," the professor declared. "We must take a gamble. Come along."

They took the road heading northwest. Having traveled for some time, they turned a corner and there, sitting in the middle of the road, was a creature. He was staring at his very tiny toes and singing a sad mournful song.

He had a small head and a large body; in fact he was completely pear-shaped. He was the color of early-morning mist and had two soulful brown eyes with extremely long, silky eyelashes and a topknot of hair that stuck out of his head like the bristles of a scrubbing brush.

The professor pulled the children to a halt. The creature obviously had not seen them, for he continued to sing and stare at the ground.

> *Oh . . . woe . . . woe is me.*
> *I'm fat, and my toes are so ti . . . neee.*
> *Hi diddley, dum de din,*
> *I wish I knew what place I'm in.*
> *Ho . . . alas . . . alack . . . hooray,*
> *I'm here tomorrow, gone today.*

The professor cleared his throat and tapped the whatever-it-was on the shoulder. The creature looked up quite unsurprised and stared for a long time. Then he simply said, "Oh. Hello."

"Good morning," said the professor brightly. "We were wondering if you could give us some help."

"Help? Oh yes, it would be nice," the creature replied absently.

"My name is Savant. May I know yours?"

"Know my what?"

"Your name."

"Ah. Yes. I have a name. Somewhere." He looked around vaguely. "I think I'm a Grick. Or is it a Dunk? I'm sure I'm somebody. It's on a piece of paper. I don't know where I put it."

"Would it be that paper in your hand?"

"What hand?" The creature looked startled. "Oh yes, here we are." He peered at a piece of faded parchment which he had been clutching. "Yes. This is definitely what I am. I'm an Oinck."

The professor was excited. "I thought you probably were, but I wasn't sure. It's a great pleasure to meet you."

"Is it?" said the creature. "I've never met me, so I wouldn't know."

"Could you tell me if this is the correct way to the palace?"

"What palace?"

"That one up there." The professor pointed.

"Gracious. What *is* that?" The Oinck peered at the mountain. "I don't see very much, you know. Only my toes." He looked back at the ground and began singing again.

> *If I had eleven toes*
> *I would use one for a nose,*
> *Which I haven't got*
> *Because it's much too hot.*

He looked at the professor and said, "It is too hot for a nose, isn't it?"

"Well, it certainly is warm," agreed the professor.

"Yes, indeed." The Oinck rolled his eyes up to the sky and rocked slowly backwards and forwards. "No doubt about it. A nose would be miserable in this heat."

The children burst out laughing.

The professor decided to try again. "Is this the road to the palace?"

The Oinck jumped. "You startled me. Who are you?"

The professor sighed. "I'm just trying to find out if this road leads anywhere."

"Ah. Well, I'll tell you nothing for something," said the Oinck solemnly. "If you follow this road long enough, you're definitely going to get somewhere. You haven't seen an Oinck by any chance, have you?"

The professor grinned. "Funny you should ask. I was just talking to one."

"*Were* you?" The Oinck seemed very impressed. "I haven't been in touch since I left the Whangdoodle."

"When did you last see the Whangdoodle?"

"Ooh. Perhaps it was yesterday."

"Which direction did you come from?"

"I came from where I was," said the Oinck.

"Did you take *this* road, or the other road back there?" pressed the professor.

"Yes, definitely," nodded the Oinck, and he began to sing again.

> *It's left or right to any place,*
> *Depending on the way you face.*
> *And when you're left and looking 'round,*
> *Then right seems much the better ground.*
> *But just when right is Paradise,*
> *The left appears to be as nice.*

"That fellow isn't as absentminded as he makes himself out to be," the professor confided to the children. "He can't remember anything, yet he suddenly spoke of the Whangdoodle. I'm sure that last song was meant to confuse us."

"I'll bet the Prock sent him," said Ben.

"My guess, exactly. Come on."

The professor led the way around the Oinck, who continued singing to himself, apparently oblivious of everything but his toes. However, after they had gone a short distance, the professor and the children turned for a last look and the Oinck was nowhere in sight.

"Ha," said the professor. "I thought as much. He's probably gone straight to the Prock."

"Oh, dear." Lindy suddenly felt anxious.

"Don't worry, Lindy. Look how content the Whiffle Bird is. I'm sure we're doing the right thing."

"Could I take off my scrappy cap?" she asked. "I'm feeling awfully hot."

"I should say not," the professor replied. "You must all keep your hats on. I told you how important they are." Then he cried excitedly, "Well, look at that. No wonder you're feeling hot."

The pink road ahead wound its way among a number of steaming, bubbling pools. Surrounded by the white desert, they heaved and swirled like cream in a mixer, making the most wonderful bubbly, squelchy sounds. Suddenly, one of the pools began to rise like a cake in an oven, swelling and expanding, and finally exploding in a shower of white foam. Another pool exploded and then another.

"We must be in a kind of geyser basin," declared the professor.

"What's a geyser?" asked Lindy.

"Just what you see—a series of fountainlike jets coming from boiling water underground that has turned to steam."

Lindy moved around to the far side of a pool just as a plume of water rose into the air.

"Ooooh, Professor," she cried. "I can see you through the water. You look all wavy. Can you see me?"

"I can indeed." The professor peered at her through the

fountain. "It's like looking through the mirrors at a fun house, isn't it?"

Ben and Tom walked on down the road. The Whiffle Bird gave a squawk and flapped around the professor's head.

"WATCH IT," she called. She flew to the top of the fountain and balanced on the crest, tumbling over and over on it, looking like a multicolored spinning ball.

"I am watching, my friend," the professor called out to her, "and very pretty you look, too."

The boys were a considerable way down the road. Ben said, "Look. There's another signpost. Let's see what it says."

The sign read: *To the Stump.*

"I've heard of that," said Tom.

"Yes, of course," cried Ben excitedly. "Don't you remember the first signpost we ever saw . . . back in the Blandlands? The professor said then that we would have to pass 'The Stump.' Now this really proves we're on the right road."

"That must be it over there." Tom pointed to a large rock, shaped like an anvil with a flat smooth top. Beyond it was a grove of stringy-looking trees, ash-grey and without foliage, standing like ghostly sentinels guarding the foothills.

Ben said, "Let's run and tell the professor."

"No, wait." There was a quality in Tom's voice that Ben had seldom heard. He followed his brother's gaze. His mouth fell open and his legs felt as though they were turning to jelly.

Standing a little way from "The Stump," glittering and gleaming in the sunlight, were two of the most beautiful mini-motorcycles the boys had ever seen. They had thick, deeply grooved tires and bold, upswept handlebars. The powerful engines were slung beneath a backbone of gleaming silver tubing, and the jet-black gas tanks had orange and red and acid-pink flames painted on them.

A large sign near the bikes proclaimed:

TRY THE GAZOOK 200.

WORLD'S MOST POWERFUL MINICYCLE.

NO BETTER WAY TO GET WHERE YOU'RE GOING.

FREE RIDES FOR ALL.

Ben forgot all about being the oldest and the fact that he ought to be responsible and set a good example for the other children. "Come on . . ." he said ecstatically.

The professor, who had been hurrying to catch up with the boys, saw them running towards the minicycles. It took only seconds for him to grasp the situation.

"No, boys! No!" he yelled at the top of his voice. But one of the geysers erupted behind him and his warning was drowned by the noise.

Ben and Tom swung into the thick leather saddles and kicked the starters. The Gazooks sprang to life with a roar—crackling, growling, snarling, quivering with suppressed power.

With sure instinct the two boys opened the throttles and let out the clutches. The bikes leaped forward, spitting flames and belching clouds of exhaust that hung like an ominous black snake over the white sand.

The professor came to a halt, with Lindy beside him.

"Oh, fiddlesticks," he said angrily.

"What great minibikes," said Lindy. "Ben has been wanting one for ages."

"Unfortunately, Lindy, those are not what they seem; they are Gazooks."

"What are Gazooks?"

"Some of the most diabolical creatures in Whangdoodle-land. I warned you all that the Prock would stop at nothing

. . . that when all else failed he would use our weaknesses for weapons. The boys' desire completely overcame their sense of caution and they walked right into his trap."

Lindy was stunned. "You mean that they aren't motorbikes? They're actually creatures?"

"I mean just that."

"Wow."

The boys careered past her in wide, sliding turns, the tires gouging out deep furrows of flying sand.

"What's so terrible about Gazooks, anyway? The boys are just taking a ride."

"No they're not. What they don't know is that once you get on a Gazook you can never get off."

The noise was deafening. Lindy put her hands over her ears.

The boys raced back and forth across the desert, laughing and joking, mowing down the little red cactus plants and generally causing havoc.

When they finally tired of their high-speed maneuvers, they tried to slow down and discovered, to their horror, that they could not. The brakes would not respond at all.

Ben's Gazook turned sharply and raced towards "The Stump." As it came abreast of the professor, the Gazook reared up, giving Ben a split second in which to yell, "I can't stop this thing!"

The creature crashed down and roared off across the sand with Ben bouncing hard in the saddle. He saw Tom heading directly towards him and swerved to avoid a collision.

Tom was shouting, "What do I do, Ben? What do I do?"

The Whiffle Bird flew into the air and screamed, "UP A GUM TREE!"

"What does she mean?" asked Lindy.

"It's an expression meaning there's no place to go," said the professor, looking very bewildered.

"Is that *all* it means?"

"Don't bother me, Lindy. I'm trying to figure it out."

"UP A GUM TREE!" shrieked the Whiffle Bird again. She flew around and around frantically.

The professor covered his face with his hands. Lindy tugged at his sleeve, but he seemed not to notice her. She tugged again.

"What is it?" His voice was sharp with annoyance.

"I'm sorry, Professor, but I just want to say one thing." She waited until the Gazooks had roared past. "Are you sure that the Whiffle Bird doesn't mean something else? Perhaps it's like you told us . . . you know, she's saying one thing and meaning another."

The professor looked at Lindy. Then he looked around and spotted the grove of weird-looking trees behind "The Stump."

"My gosh, Lindy!" He clapped a hand to his head. "You're an angel. An absolute angel."

He ran across the sand, waving his arms and yelling to the boys as loudly as he could, "Head for the trees! Head for the trees!"

Ben heard him and nodded in understanding. He could feel the creature beneath him straining to pull in a different direction. It took all his strength to keep the Gazook pointing towards the trees. They crashed headlong into the grove and a remarkable thing happened.

The Gazook sank into a thick, sticky-looking substance that covered the ground. Long bands of rubbery pulp became enmeshed in the spokes of the wheels, clogging and slowing them down until the bike was forced to a halt.

The professor ran to the edge of the grove. "Get off, Ben, get off now!" he yelled, and jumped neatly to one side as the Gazook carrying Tom shot past him and also plunged into the mire. The boys leaped from the thrashing, churning creatures.

"Try to climb the trees!" the professor cried.

Stumbling, plunging, dragging themselves along through the thick gum, muscles trembling with fatigue, the boys managed to pull themselves into a tree.

The Gazooks roared with frustration and lay on the ground in paroxysms of rage. Their wheels were jammed, their fenders dented and buckled from the crash. They lunged and struggled until they were upright once more, then shook themselves and spat and choked on the cloying gum.

Slowly, laboriously, they heaved themselves out of the grove and onto dry land. With a howl of rage they raced away towards the foothills, snarling, snapping and belching black exhaust until they became mere specks on the horizon and finally disappeared.

The professor stood gazing up at the boys.

Ben saw the anger written on his face. "I'm sorry, Professor. I'm really sorry."

"I should hope so. You could have been killed . . . or you could have broken something. Any one of us could have been run over."

The professor was shaking with mingled relief and rage. "Seldom have I seen such a brilliant display of enthusiasm and daring. What a pity that you wasted it on a mere self-indulgence. How much better it would have been had you channeled all that energy and directed it towards something constructive." He sat down and put his chin on his hands and gazed moodily across the desert.

Ben discovered that however he tried he could not get down from the tree. The more he moved, the more he was trapped by the horrible sticky substance.

After a few moments, he cleared his throat and called tentatively, "Professor, I . . . er . . . I'm having a bit of a problem. I'm stuck."

"I'm not surprised," the professor replied. "You're up a gum tree."

"I am?"

"You both are."

Tom asked, "How are we going to get out of this mess?"

The professor did not look at them. "I can only think of one way right now, and that is to chew your way out. It'll take a while. You'd better get started."

There was a pause. "You mean we have to chew this stuff? The whole tree?" Tom was appalled.

"Well, it's gum, isn't it? I thought all boys liked gum. If you can think of a better way down, then by all means try it."

Benjamin reluctantly picked a piece of the bark and chewed on it. His eyes widened with surprise. "This tastes like bubble gum. It really does. Try some, Tom."

Tom took a bite. "It *is* bubble gum. It's delicious. This is going to be easy." He took a whole sticky fistful.

Lindy sat down beside the professor. Seeing him so upset made her quite tearful. She slipped her hand into his. "I've never seen you so angry before," she said quietly.

"I've never been so angry before."

Lindy thought about it for a while. Then, with her usual candor, she said, "I don't mean to be rude or anything, but I think you're being a bit unfair." She struggled to find the right words. "I don't think Ben and Tom did anything so really terrible. I mean . . . they are boys, and boys just love machines and powerful things like motorbikes. Didn't you feel that way when you were a boy?"

The professor looked at her for a long moment. He slipped an arm around her shoulders. "Yes, Lindy, I felt exactly that way when I was a boy, and I did many things that were foolish. But occasionally an angry, sensible adult showed me the error of my ways. Tom and Ben were foolish and irresponsible. Their actions put us all in great danger and, as a sensible adult, I think I had a perfect right to get angry and, thereby, teach them an important lesson."

At that moment there was a very loud report behind them, and they turned in alarm to look at the boys, whose cheeks were bulging with gum.

"What was that noise?" inquired the professor sharply.

Ben pointed to his brother and, with his mouth full, he mumbled, "He just blew the biggest bubble you ever saw." He was beginning to look green. "I don't think I can chew much more," he said. "I like bubble gum and this stuff is great, but it's awfully sweet."

Lindy, astonished, said, "Look at Tom."

He was blowing another bubble. They all watched in amazement as it grew and grew. Tom was going cross-eyed in his effort to expand the bubble, which was already the size of his head and still growing.

The Whiffle Bird flew into the air and flapped past the boys. "KEEP A STIFF UPPER LIP!" she squawked.

The professor looked startled. Then he said, "Do exactly as she says, Tom. Keep a stiff upper lip and don't let that bubble burst, whatever you do."

Tom could only wave a hand to show that he understood. He had to concentrate very hard, for the huge bubble was now bigger than he was. He felt a tugging sensation and realized that the bubble was pulling him, lifting him out of the tree. He kicked his legs as hard as he could. There was a loud squelchy *pop* and Tom suddenly floated up into the sky.

Lindy, the professor and Ben witnessed the amazing spectacle of a boy soaring through the air at the end of a giant balloon.

"Keep it up, Tom! Keep it up!" cried the professor.

Ben stopped his chewing for a moment and observed his brother with considerable respect and awe.

A little way out of the grove, Tom floated gently down to earth, landing near the professor. The tremendous bubble collapsed in a sticky heap on top of him. Lindy and the professor quickly cleared it away and the boy sat up, greatly relieved to be on firm ground once again.

The professor called out, "All right, Ben. You know what you have to do. Let's see if you can blow a bigger bubble than Tom."

Ben chewed hard and tried a number of times before he produced a bubble with any promise of success. He blew it up very, very carefully, and everyone sent up a terrific cheer as he rose out of the ground and high into the sky, up and up, until he was eventually just a dot among the clouds.

Then a terrible thing happened. The huge bubble exploded and Ben tumbled towards the earth.

Lindy screamed, Tom gasped and the professor shouted, *"Blow another bubble!"*

Ben worked frantically at the wad of gum in his mouth. It was difficult because he was rolling over and over as he fell.

It was only a matter of seconds, but it seemed like an eternity before he was able to blow another bubble large enough to break his fall.

He made a very bumpy landing. He looked pale and uttered strange, garbled sounds. It was apparent that he had swallowed his gum.

The professor gave him a tremendous thump on the back and Ben coughed the gum up. He drew in deep breaths of fresh air and it was not long before his color returned to normal.

"We have wasted valuable time," said the professor. "The Gazooks will certainly have used this delay to go to the Prock, and that means more trouble." He tipped his head and said, with gentle scorn, "It would be such a help if we could stay together from now on and work as a team. Do you think we might manage that?"

The children nodded fervently.

"Right. Then let's get out of this miserable spot."

 THREE

They were glad to be on the move once more. Ben said, "Professor, I meant to tell you something. When I was up in the air I had quite a good view of the palace."

The professor was intrigued. "What did you see?"

"There's a long bridge over a deep chasm."

"Ha. That's good to know. Did you see a path going up the mountain?"

"Yes, it's the same pink trail that we're on now."

Tom sniffed the air. "I smell something good."

Lindy's nose twitched. "It's like honeysuckle."

A wonderful smile appeared on the professor's face. "It *is* honeysuckle—it's coming on the breeze," he said. "I've heard that the Whangdoodle's palace has the perfume of honeysuckle around it all the time. We *are* getting close."

They were almost at the base of the Whangdoodle's mountain. Through a natural rock arch, the pink road wound its way to the summit. They could see the gleaming turrets of the palace above the scudding clouds.

"Not long now, Professor," said Ben encouragingly.

He had no sooner spoken the words than they were echoed by a chorus of soft voices in the surrounding hills. "Not long now. Not long now."

The professor said distractedly, "Fiddlesticks. What is that? What's going on?"

"What's going on? What's going on?" said the voices, and they grew a little louder.

The children moved close to the professor. They could see nothing to account for the voices and there was no clue as to where they were coming from. The echoes chased themselves around and around.

The professor rubbed his head irritably. "This is too much. I mean, a fight is a fight, but the Prock goes too far." He raised his voice. "Come on out. Come on, whoever you are. Let's see you."

"Let's see you. Let's see you," mocked the voices, laughing shrilly.

Lindy took the professor's hand, her face white with fear.

Ben felt the anger welling up within him. "Now stop that," he cried.

"Stop that. Stop that. Nyaa! Nyaa! Nyaa!" The voices grew louder yet.

Then, quite suddenly and with tremendous energy, a large

furry creature hurtled out of nowhere and landed on the path in front of the professor, who gasped and recoiled with shock.

The creature was a bright bilious green, with shaggy fur and apelike features. It had a hideous grin and displayed a startling array of sharp pointed teeth. It was screaming and dancing up and down, hurling abuse at the professor and the children.

"Get out of here. Get out. Yaaa! Miserable people. *Miserable!*"

The Whiffle Bird panicked and screamed her traditional "MAYDAY!" as a horde of identical creatures swarmed over the hilltops towards them. They were shrieking and skulking and leaping and lurking and saying the most appalling things.

Horrid people! Go away—
Don't come back another day.

Ugly busybody!

Sticking your nose in where it doesn't belong.

Beastly human, leave this place;
We can't stand your silly face.

This last remark was directed at the professor. He spoke calmly over the noise of the jeering mob. "Children, try not to be frightened. Stand perfectly still and do not answer back."

"What are these awful things?" Ben gasped as one green monster poked his arm with a sharp finger.

"Awful things! Awful! Awful!" yelled the furry horde.

"They're called Swamp Gaboons, I think," said the professor. His head was beginning to pound from the noise.

Swamp Gaboons. Swamp Gaboons.
Handsome, happy, crazy loons.

The creatures linked arms, completely blocking the archway. They executed a series of precision high kicks, and the sight of them bobbing up and down like a chorus line with their shaggy green fur shaking and shimmying was almost funny.

But the abuse was hard to take. One Gaboon skipped forward and pushed its face close to Tom. "Blaaah . . . silly boy," it said, sticking out its tongue and waving its arms.

Tom couldn't help himself. He stuck out his own tongue and yelled back, "Blaaah to you too."

The Swamp Gaboon was delighted. "Oooo . . . isn't he rude!" he screamed, and danced away to join his laughing companions.

The professor spoke sternly. "Thomas, that is *not* the way to behave. I warned you not to answer back. It only encourages them."

The Gaboons bunched together and chanted in hideous harmony:

We don't care, we don't care.
Sleek of fur and green of hair.
Tough of tooth and sharp of nail.
Legs that kick and arms that flail.
Even if you scream and fuss
We've no feelings. Can't hurt us.

They began hurling twigs and small stones at the professor and the children.

Lindy said through clenched teeth, "I hate them. I absolutely, positively hate those bullies. They're gross!"

"Gross. Gross. Gross. Gross. Oh . . . isn't she cute?" The creatures simpered and sneered.

The Whiffle Bird flew onto Tom's shoulder. She too was disturbed by the shrieking mob and she screamed, "MIND YOUR MANNERS!" in an angry voice.

The Swamp Gaboons rolled on the ground in delight. "Mind your manners. Listen to Mommy. Listen to Mommy."

Lindy could contain herself no longer. She took a step forward. "You know what I think?" she shouted. "I think you're all very, *very* rude. You have no right to speak to people like that."

One Gaboon blew her a loud raspberry. Another stood on its head and wiggled its ears.

"Lindy, that's enough!" said the professor sharply.

But Lindy had been pushed too far. "If *my* mummy were here right now, do you know what she'd say to you?"

"What would she say? What would your mummy say?" A Gaboon raced up to her and sat down with crossed legs and a hand under its chin.

Lindy scolded, "She'd say, it's perfectly all right to think bad things . . ."

"To think bad things," echoed the Gaboon.

". . . But you don't have the right to say them. It's *not* polite. Mummy wouldn't like you at all . . . and I wish she were here now." Lindy's thumb went into her mouth and she began to cry.

The Gaboon pulled a sad face. "Aaah . . . the little girl

is all upset. See what you've done, fellers . . . you've made her cry."

"Aaaah." All the Gaboons pretended to be sad. They mocked Lindy and each put a thumb in its mouth. One raced up to her and screamed nastily, "Serves you right," then it jumped in the air and ran away.

Benjamin was furious. Until now, he had been able to control himself. But seeing how cruelly the Gaboons were teasing Lindy made him lose all reason. The professor caught him just as he was about to hurl himself upon the offending creatures.

"Benjamin. Control yourself. Lindy, stop that crying. Now listen to me, all of you."

The Swamp Gaboons, feigning interest, crowded around. But as soon as the professor began to speak, they made such a racket it was hard for the children to understand what he was saying.

"The Whiffle Bird said 'Mind your manners' and that's what we're going to do. The more you respond to these miserable creatures"—the Professor ducked as one of them tried to pull his hair—"the more ammunition you give them. Unless we ignore them, we'll never get through."

"You'll never get through. You'll never get through. You stupid, sloppy, no-good human." The Gaboons shrieked and formed a line across the archway again.

"The madder you get," continued the professor, "the more they love it!"

"We love it. We love it," roared the furry mob.

"So we are going to ignore them. I believe that if we do this and concentrate on the important issue, which is *why* we are here and *whom* we came to find," said the professor, speaking the words with great emphasis, "then I do not think they can stop us. Come on now. Stare the creatures down if you have to, but do not respond to them."

The children and the professor began to walk slowly towards the arch.

The Swamp Gaboons went berserk. "Hateful boys, silly girl, monster man!" they yelled. They tugged at the professor's clothing and pulled Lindy's hair and pinched Ben and Tom.

The professor raised his voice again. "I do believe it's going to be fine weather at the top of the mountain, don't you?"

Ben took the cue. "I think you're right, sir. Lindy, can you see the palace up there? Don't you wonder what it's going to be like?"

"I . . . I . . . oh, yes I do," Lindy replied bravely. She was still close to tears, but she put an arm around Ben and said fiercely, "Ask me something else, quick."

"Well now, Professor, Lindy wants me to ask her something. Tom, do you have anything to say?"

Ben had no idea what he was talking about, but just saying things made it easier to ignore the tormenting crowd.

They reached the arch and the Gaboons were in a frenzy. "Don't you dare go through! Don't you dare!" they bawled.

One Gaboon with foul breath thrust its face close to Tom. "Do you know you have a silly nose?" it hissed.

Tom swallowed hard. The professor said lightly, "Steady, Tom."

"You have cauliflower ears, too," mocked the Gaboon, "and crossed eyes and yellow teeth!"

"Thank you *so* much," Tom managed to say politely, and to his surprise he felt rather good.

The professor tapped a large Swamp Gaboon on the shoulder with his umbrella. "Excuse me, my good fellow, we'd like to get through, if you don't mind. Now, Ben, you were saying . . . ?"

He walked past the creature slowly and calmly. It bellowed with anger. "Don't touch me, you measly wart. I hate you."

It belched loudly in Ben's ear. The boy jumped, but he kept his arm around Lindy and continued to walk beside the professor.

"Not long now, I think," said the professor encouragingly. "See, we're under the arch and there is the road ahead. Keep your eyes on it, children."

"Look out! Look out! There's a monster behind you!" screamed the Gaboons.

"Don't look back," urged the professor.

"Your shirt's hanging out, you ridiculous boy."

Tom felt something tugging at his pants. He put his hand behind him, and a Swamp Gaboon grasped his fingers and held them tightly. Tom looked imploringly at the professor.

"Keep walking, Tom, even if you drag the creature with you. Just keep moving."

The Swamp Gaboon hung on and dug in its heels. It sat down on the road like a sulky child refusing to walk. "I'll bite you," it said cunningly. "I'll bite your hand off, you nasty boy."

Tom felt sharp teeth nibbling at his fingers. It took all his self-control to overcome his panic. Then he had an idea. He turned quickly and whacked the Gaboon sharply on the top of its head. At the same time, he pumped the hand that was holding his and said politely, "It was such a pleasure meeting you, old boy. Goodbye." The Gaboon was so surprised that it released Tom's fingers and the boy instantly put both hands in his pockets.

Now the Swamp Gaboons changed their tactics. As the professor and the children walked farther and farther away from them they sobbed and howled and tried all manner of last-minute tricks to gain their attention.

"Come back, come back. I was only joking."

"Take me with you. *Please.*"

"Ouch. I've hurt myself badly."

"*Help.* I've broken my finger."

"I've broken my back."

"I'll eat worms if you don't turn around."

"I'll hold my breath until I explode."

"You'll be sorry when the Whangdoodle hears of this."

Their voices began to fade. The professor smiled in weary triumph. He looked at the children.

"Well done, my friends. Listen to how truly silly they are. I think they will not bother us any more. We shall walk a few more yards, until we are around the next corner. Then we will relax, for if we don't, I think I shall collapse. I don't recall ever being so exhausted."

 *FOUR*

They rested for a half hour. The professor was weary, though he tried hard not to show it. He talked about the Swamp Gaboons.

"I hope you realize what a valuable lesson you all learned just now."

Tom said, "You mean about turning the other cheek?"

"Yes, that's part of it. There will be many times in your lives—at school, and more particularly when you are grown up—when people will distract or divert you from what needs to be done. You may even welcome the distraction. But if you use it as an excuse for not doing what you're supposed to do, you can blame no one but yourself. If you truly wish to accomplish something, you should allow nothing to stop you, and chances are you'll succeed."

The professor leaned back against the mountain and took a deep breath. "You see, the Gaboons' words didn't hurt you, once you resolved not to let them."

"They did hurt a bit," Lindy confessed in a small voice.

"Yes. But when you remembered your main purpose, you were able to put aside your feelings and concentrate on the important issues."

He mopped his brow. "I think we should try to push on."

They followed him as he slowly and laboriously climbed the steep and narrow path. The children shuddered as they looked down at the ground hundreds of feet below.

The professor began to act in a way that was very unlike him. He paused frequently, sometimes shielding his eyes and gazing into the distance. Occasionally he mumbled to himself. Once, he said quite clearly, "I must remember to pack my red socks."

The children could only think that the whole incredible search for the Whangdoodle had become too great a strain on their good friend. They clustered around him lovingly, in an attempt to encourage him.

Ben said, "Look, Professor, how near we are to the castle."

They could see now that the pure, transparent crystal was

buttressed by huge pillars of milk-white glass. The turrets were like the creamy frosting on top of a birthday cake and seemed to be reaching to touch the red sky.

Higher and higher they climbed. The altitude made them all short of breath and the professor gasped and moved more slowly with every step. Suddenly he stopped and leaned against a rock. He shut his eyes.

"My dears," he said in a tired voice, "I do not think I can go any farther. You must go on without me."

They all spoke at once.

"But that's impossible, Professor."

"We'll never make it without you."

"We're so close. If you could try just one step at a time."

He raised a hand wearily. "No, no. You don't understand. . . ."

But they wouldn't listen.

"We'll help you, Professor."

"We'll wait for you."

Tom said, "Lean on me, sir—put your whole weight on me. I can take it."

Ben ran ahead to a bend in the road. When he turned the corner, he was so staggered by what he saw that for a moment he could not move. Then he raced back to the professor.

"Sir, you just *have* to go on," he cried. "We're there. We're actually there. I've found the bridge. It's around the corner. All we have to do is cross over it to reach the palace. Come and see for yourself. Come on, Professor. You can do it. You *can*."

The children were wild with excitement. Their sheer enthusiasm carried the professor forward.

With triumph in his voice, Ben said, "There. You see? See the bridge? We've made it."

The children gazed with awe at the sight before them, and they were all close to tears.

Ahead, the ground fell away into a tremendous chasm, thousands of feet deep, and far below was a thundering waterfall, so huge that the sound of it echoed back to the top of the mountain.

Spanning the abyss was the bridge. It was incredibly beautiful, like an inverted silken rainbow swaying gently in the cool breeze. At the far end of it, two bronze doors were set into a colossal archway. They were open, and beyond them was the Whangdoodle's palace.

Ben turned to the professor.

"We've done it, Professor. Aren't you proud? Aren't you thrilled?"

The professor did not answer. He was staring at the palace with intense concentration. He sat down on a nearby rock and put his head in his hands. In all the weeks the children had known him, they had never seen him so dispirited.

They gathered around him. He raised his head and looked at them for a long moment. Then he said, "You are going to have to do something for me which I know you will not want to do. But there must be no argument about it. I want you to go on to the palace by yourselves. Listen to me," he said firmly as they started to protest.

"When I first conceived the idea of trying to reach the Whangdoodle, I realized only too well that I might fail. I was too old, too set in my thought patterns. Then the three of you came along. I hoped that, through you, I might re-awaken the younger part of my mind, the imagination that has been shut down for so many years. In other words, if your eyes could see it, perhaps mine could see it too."

The professor's voice broke. "I must tell you," he continued, "that the closer we have come to the Whangdoodle, the harder it has been for me to keep up with you. This last part of our journey has been almost impossible for me."

"But we wouldn't be here if it weren't for you," Tom burst out. "We didn't help *you,* it was the other way around. You helped *us.* You made it all possible."

Ben said, "Only a little while ago, you said that if you really try, then the chances are you'll succeed."

The professor shut his eyes again. "I said the chances for success were good. I didn't say they were a hundred per cent certain. One must always take into account the possibility of failure."

Ben spoke desperately. "But how can you say that, Professor? All you have to do is cross the bridge."

The professor smiled sadly. "I must tell you. I cannot see the bridge."

"What do you mean?" Tom was aghast. "Of course you can see it. You can see the palace, can't you?"

"Yes, I have always been able to see it. But seeing how to *get* to the palace is another matter. For me, the bridge just isn't there. Only the chasm."

The boys fell silent.

Lindy said in a choked voice, "You should've had a scrappy cap." She burst into tears and rushed into his arms. "I didn't think that all this would happen," she sobbed. "I just can't bear to think of you not going with us. It's too sad."

"Are you sure you've tried hard enough?" asked Tom.

"You must believe me, Tom. I've tried as hard as I can. You know how much I want to see the Whangdoodle. This is simply one of those times in life when in spite of every effort, one fails. But you mustn't feel sad, because I don't. Without you I wouldn't have been able to get this far."

Ben said determinedly, "Professor, I don't care what you say. If you can't go, then I won't either."

Tom and Lindy agreed instantly.

"No, that's right."

"We won't go without you."

The professor blinked hard and said, "That's very dear, and just like you. But you will go on, and I will tell you why: because, for me, it will be the next best thing to being there. I will wait here for you. I shall be perfectly all right. When you have seen the Whangdoodle, you will come back and tell me all about him—every single wonderful detail. Now, be off with you. I don't want to see your faces again until you bring me news of the Whangdoodle. By the way, send him my fondest regards."

Tom said sharply, "Look at the Whiffle Bird. What's the matter with her?"

She had been sitting quietly on the silk supporting rope of the bridge. Now she was strutting up and down stiffly, as if hypnotized.

"What on earth . . ." The professor rose frantically, looked up, and recoiled in horror. "*Look out!*" he shouted. The sky became suddenly dark.

The children had a glimpse of a monstrous head with a huge sharp-pointed beak coming straight towards them. It was the Gyascutus.

Too late, the Whiffle Bird flew into the air. Startled out of her trance, she screamed, "MAYDAY!"

The children flung themselves clear of the slashing talons.

The professor bellowed in dismay. "No," he cried. "No, no, no. You shall not do this!"

In desperation he found strength. As the Gyascutus banked

around for another attack he took a firm grip on his umbrella. When the huge bird flew past him he swiped at it with all his might, giving it a resounding *thwack* that sent it careering off course.

He yelled to the children, "Run! Run to the palace!"

"What about you?" Ben cried, horrified.

"I shall be all right. I promise you. *Now go on.*"

The children ran towards the bridge.

The professor jumped up and down and waved his arms wildly. "Come on, you devil," he called out to the giant bird. "Let's see what you're made of. You big, dumb, pea-brained bully!"

The Gyascutus was diverted by the noisy, dancing figure. It swooped down for another attack. As the children clattered onto the slats of the bridge, the professor put his back to the rock and, using his umbrella as a sword, he fought the monster with the last ounce of his strength.

The Gyascutus screamed with outrage. One giant claw reached out for the tired and desperate man. It picked him up as though he were a rag doll and dashed him against the rock. The professor fell to the ground in an unconscious heap.

The children were running so hard for the palace they did not see what was happening behind them. Ben was in front with Lindy. Tom was close behind and the Whiffle Bird just above his head.

They had not realized that the bridge was so long. Their frantic chase made it sway dreadfully and Lindy gasped as she glimpsed the boiling, foaming river thousands of feet below.

"Ben, Ben, don't go so fast!" she cried.

Her foot slipped between the slats and she crashed to her

knees, crying out in pain. Ben turned to help her and suddenly screamed with fear. "Look out, Tom!"

The Gyascutus was only inches away from Tom.

There was a rushing wind that moved the bridge violently from side to side. Ben and Lindy clung desperately to the guide ropes. Tom felt two sharp claws hook into the shoulders of his jacket and he was lifted high out over the chasm.

The Whiffle Bird went berserk. With a shriek, she rocketed towards the Gyascutus, aiming straight for its eyes. Her brilliant feathers momentarily blinded the monster and it flapped desperately back over the bridge.

Ben scrambled to his feet and flung his arms around Tom's legs just as he passed overhead.

The Gyascutus pulled and pulled and Ben hung on with all his might. The Whiffle Bird attacked again and again.

Sick with fear, Lindy managed to cry, "Undo your jacket, Tom! Get out of it!"

Tom heard her. He plucked at the buttons of his coat and raised his arms. He slid out of the sleeves and crashed onto the bridge just as the Whiffle Bird screamed, "RUN FOR YOUR LIFE!" She flew at the Gyascutus again. The children picked themselves up and raced the last hundred yards to the huge burnished gates.

Then a terrible thing happened. The confused Gyascutus was trying to rid itself of Tom's jacket. The giant wings were thrashing, and the Whiffle Bird was helplessly caught up in the whirlwind. She received a mighty blow that knocked her to the bridge, where she lay horribly still.

Tom gave an agonized cry and raced back to her side. "It's all right, Whiffle Bird. I'm here. I've got you. It's all right." He picked her up gently.

Ben was yelling, "Tom! *Come on!*"

Tom looked up and saw that the Gyascutus was coming at him once again. He began to run.

It was a desperate race. The three children stumbled off the swaying bridge and under the tall archway, with the Gyascutus only a few feet behind them.

"The doors. Close the doors!" Ben flung himself against one side and Lindy and Tom pushed hard against the other. With a mighty clang the great bronze portals closed and the enraged Gyascutus slammed into them. The earth trembled. But the doors held.

The children leaned against the cool metal, fighting to regain their breath. When they had recovered sufficiently to turn around and see where they were, they received yet another shock.

Standing in front of them was the Prock.

 *FIVE*

"You surprise me," he said. "I didn't think you'd make it." He noticed the Whiffle Bird in Tom's arms. "What's the matter with her?"

Ben said, "She's hurt. She tried to save us and the Gyascutus knocked her down."

The Prock looked dreadfully concerned and took a step forward. Tom clutched the bird protectively.

"Come along, boy," the Prock snapped. "Give the Whiffle Bird to me."

"Not on your life, you big bully," Tom whispered fiercely.

"Oh! This is really too much!" The Prock stamped a long,

thin foot in annoyance. "Do you realize the trouble you have caused? This is all your fault—the first accident we've had in the kingdom for a century. If you hadn't been here, none of this would have happened. You're an absolute menace."

Tom was so angry that he yelled at the towering Prock, "Our fault, is it? Well, that's a stupid remark. Who sent that . . . that monster out there to attack us? Who tipped off the Gazooks and the Sidewinders and the Swamp Gaboons? Who arranged to have Lindy captured by the Splintercat? It was all *your* fault."

The boy choked with emotion as he looked down at the feathered bundle lying so still in his arms. "If she doesn't get better, if she dies, I'll never forgive you. Never."

The Prock looked at Tom intently. Then he said in a quieter voice, "I suggest you give the bird to me. We know how to take care of her. She will be all right, I promise you."

Tom hesitated.

Ben said, "Do as he says, Tom."

The Prock clapped his hands together. "Guard," he called.

A large Sidewinder came trundling around the corner. It looked very startled at the sight of the children. Lindy gave a squeal of fear.

"You will not be harmed," the Prock reassured her. He took the Whiffle Bird from Tom. She was whimpering with genuine pain and sounded very different from the brave bird who had pretended such agony in front of the Splintercat.

"You're sure she'll be all right?" the boy asked anxiously. "You know, she was trying to save me when she got hurt." He touched her gently in farewell.

"We will do our best," the Prock replied gravely. He handed the bird to the Sidewinder, who walked quickly away.

"Now, tell me about your friend, the professor," the Prock said. "Why is he not with you?"

"He just couldn't get here," Lindy answered. "He was so tired and he couldn't see the bridge."

"It was too much for him," explained Ben. "He would've been all right if it hadn't been for all the things you put in our way."

"He hasn't really been feeling well since we jumped off *The Brainstrain*," growled Tom. "That's when it started."

"He told us to come on by ourselves," said Lindy. "He said he was sure the Whangdoodle would understand and would see us."

"I see." The Prock looked thoughtful and there seemed to be a trace of disappointment in his voice. Then his expression changed and he said briskly, "Well, I'm sorry, but this is the end of your journey. I can tell you now that the Whangdoodle will not receive you. You might just as well turn around, find your professor and go home."

"Oh, don't say that!" Ben cried desperately.

Tom said, "We promised the professor that we would speak to the Whangdoodle."

"I've got to give him his regards," added Lindy tearfully.

"There's nothing I can do," said the Prock firmly and he began to usher them towards the gates.

The children hung back.

Tom had never felt so depressed. "I want to wait and see if the Whiffle Bird is going to be all right."

Huge tears rolled down Lindy's face. "We've worked so hard. It just can't end like this. Isn't there something you can do?"

The Prock was shaking his head. "I'm afraid not. . . .

You see . . ." But he didn't finish, for with a sob Lindy rushed to his side and flung her arms around him.

"Oh, please, *please*," she begged, and buried her face in his thick, baggy sweater. She wept as if her heart would break.

The Prock knelt beside her. He was distinctly uncomfortable. "Now, Miss Lindy. You mustn't cry. I can't stand to see people cry."

Lindy's hands stole up around his neck and she clung to him tightly. He was red in the face and covered with confusion.

Ben and Tom looked at each other.

"It's okay, Lindy," Ben said gently. "I guess it'll have to be like the professor says. Every once in a while people fail in spite of trying. He'll understand."

"But I don't understand," she wailed. "At home, if somebody tried hard and really, really wanted to see the President, then they could."

She gazed imploringly at the Prock. "Dear Prock, couldn't you just this once forget about being in charge and that sort of thing? Couldn't you speak to the Whangdoodle for us? I want to see him more than anything in the whole world."

The Prock hesitated. He looked at the boys and looked back at Lindy. He touched her tearstained face.

"Oh, you human beings," he said with feeling. "When will I ever learn?" He rubbed Lindy's cheek with the sleeve of his sweater. "Come along. I can see there's only one way to get any peace around here, and that's to let you meet the Whangdoodle."

Lindy hugged him with all her strength.

Tom and Ben could not believe the sudden turn of events.

"All right, all right." The Prock waved away their thanks.

Taking Lindy's hand, he said, "Come along, Miss Lindy, but for pity's sake try not to cry any more. It gets me all emotional and I start to itch."

He led them across the courtyard and under another archway, past two sentry Sidewinders standing rigidly at attention. The children gave them a wide berth.

The palace was more beautiful than they had ever imagined. There were crystal courtyards with bright mosaic floors; others were grassy, with wildflower borders, and contained sparkling fountains or tranquil pools with ambrosia blossoms floating on the milk-white water. The trees were magnificent and there were flowers such as the children had never seen before. Flutterbyes were everywhere.

There was a cool breeze and the scent of honeysuckle was strong and heady. Wind chimes made sweet music.

The Prock walked quickly down a long, vaulted passageway, and paused in front of a wrought-silver door. "Wait for me here," he said and went inside.

Ben, Tom and Lindy looked at each other, their hearts pounding with excitement. The boys straightened their hair and Lindy smoothed the wrinkles out of her clothes.

She said longingly, "I *wish* the professor were here."

"We must remember every detail for him," Ben declared solemnly.

The silver door opened and the Prock emerged. "You may come in now," he said quietly. "When you meet the Whangdoodle, you must address him as 'Your Majesty.' Don't talk too much and don't get bouncy with excitement, because the Whangdoodle seldom has company and is not used to it. Remove your hats and give them to me. Always go bareheaded in front of royalty. It shows respect."

The children took off their scrappy caps and gave them to the Prock. He held open the door and as they walked past him he announced in a clear voice, "The Potter children, Your Majesty. Benjamin, Thomas and Melinda." He closed the door behind them.

They were in a cool, high-ceilinged room. It was white, with tall windows through which the sunlight fell onto a polished marble floor. The room was sparsely furnished. There was a long table bearing some choice pieces of silver, and a large, richly covered chair which was framed by a beautiful tapestry that hung on the wall behind it.

There was no one in the room. The children waited. The silence lengthened. Tom coughed and a hollow echo came from the high ceiling.

Quite suddenly a cheerful voice said, "Well, I must say, you humans have changed a bit since the old days."

The children jumped with alarm and found themselves witnessing an amazing sight. Two eyes and a very large pair of antlers began to materialize from the tapestry, followed by the mooselike head that bore them. Next came four rather short legs attached to a round, barrellike body. The children watched in wonder as the Whangdoodle crossed to his throne and sat down, nonchalantly folding his front legs across his chest, and crossing one back leg over the other.

"Don't look so surprised." His voice was deep and he spoke with an engaging lisp. "I was playing it safe. Didn't want you to see me before I'd had a peek at you, so I changed myself into the colors of the tapestry."

The Whangdoodle was truly an extraordinary creature.

He was the size of a small pony. His face was big and friendly with large brown eyes and long, fair eyelashes. His eyebrows were arched, giving him a constant look of surprise. His muzzle looked soft as velvet and when he grinned he displayed strong horselike teeth which protruded over his lips. His antlers were amazingly large and very handsome. He held his head proudly, in keeping with his generally regal air. His body was a warm, grey-brown color and his small, rather thin tail was fashioned into a love knot. On his hind feet he wore a pair of old pink knitted bedroom slippers with floppy tassels.

Ben remembered the Prock's instructions. "Your Majesty, thank you for allowing us to see you."

"Hmm. The Prock tells me you've given him a lot of trouble. I didn't want to see you. Not at first. Then, I confess that I did feel some slight desire to make contact again after all these years. I do get lonely. Not that I mind, and I wouldn't go back. Not ever. Even if you begged and pleaded. Humans can't be trusted. Have a piece of wodge." He held out a large box of candy.

The children hesitated.

"Come on, you must be starving. I'm sure you haven't eaten for ages."

They hungrily accepted the delicious sweets.

"Aren't they good?" The Whangdoodle munched one happily. "This is my favorite kind. I have a very sweet tooth, you know. Would you like to see it?" he asked Lindy.

"Oh. Yes, thank you, Your Majesty."

The Whangdoodle grinned. "It's this one here," he said, indicating it with his tongue. "See the little daisy on it?"

"Why, that *is* a sweet tooth," Lindy said in surprise.

"Thought you'd like it. All Whangdoodles are born with

one, you know." A shadow passed over his brow. "At least they used to be," he added sadly. He helped himself to another piece of wodge.

"As I was saying. You look different from the children I used to know. Cleaner, neater, taller. Are you an exception, or do all children look like you?"

Tom answered, "I don't think we're different from other children, Your Majesty."

"How is your world these days? The Prock never tells me anything because he doesn't want to upset me. Do you still use that barbaric rack and boiling oil on your enemies? Do you still fight over territory and so on?"

"We still have wars, Your Majesty, if that's what you mean," Ben replied.

The Whangdoodle look depressed. "Thought so. It didn't seem as though things were going to change much when I left." He began to turn blue.

Lindy said, "Your Majesty, you're changing color."

"Am I?" He looked at his stomach. "So I am. I do it without thinking, you know."

"Can you really turn any color you want?" asked Ben.

"Yes, I can turn plaid if I want to. But that's a hard one."

"What's the hardest color of all to do?" Lindy inquired.

"Oh . . . I would say Flange."

"What's Flange?" Tom chuckled.

"It's nothing to laugh about, young man. It's every color of the rainbow, all at once. I seldom manage that one. Mind you, Omnipresent Blue is pretty tough as well. And Crash Pink."

"Is that pretty?" asked Lindy.

"It's stunning, absolutely stunning," replied the Whang-doodle.

"Harder than plaid?"

"Oh . . . ten times harder. Or is it eleven?"

"Lilac is my favorite color," Lindy told him.

"Is it, now. Well, allow me the honor." The Whang-doodle slowly turned the most beautiful shade of lilac that Lindy had ever seen.

"That's lovely. Thank you, Your Majesty."

"Not at all. Have some more wodge."

The Whangdoodle suddenly winced. "Oh dear, my poor feet. I know it's rather informal, but would you mind if I put them up for a while? I'm due for a new pair of slippers, you see, and right now my feet are *killing* me."

Ben said, "Oh, don't worry about us, Your Majesty. Is there anything we can do for you?"

"You could pass me that footstool over there."

Ben fetched it and placed it in front of the throne.

"Ahh. That's better." The Whangdoodle stretched his legs and smiled with relief. "Now, explain something to me. I was told that there were four of you in the expeditionary party, that your guide was Professor somebody-or-other. He's been seen poking about the country a lot. Why isn't he here?"

Taking turns, the children told the Whangdoodle all about the professor, from the day they had met him at the zoo to their sad parting at the bridge.

The Whangdoodle looked thoughtful. "Well, I must say, it's a pity your friend couldn't make it. I hoped I might get a moment to chat with him. I fancy we'd have a lot in common, and good conversation is hard to come by these days. It's very quiet here, you know, and I don't have a wife. Sad, that. I don't have anyone to carry on the family name. Makes me very blue sometimes. Pale blue." He changed back to the appropriate color.

Lindy said, "You'd like the professor, Your Majesty. He's the nicest person in the whole world next to Mummy and Daddy. Is there any way you could help him get here? He wants to meet you so very badly."

"I'm sorry, but there is nothing I can do. He had exactly the same chance as you. You saw the bridge. He didn't. I can't provide him with a new imagination, can I?"

"I'm not sure he did have the same chance," Tom said. "Remember, he had to outguess and outsmart every creature in the land to help us. He gave so much of himself—it's no wonder he couldn't concentrate at the end."

"Yes, I understand that and I admire the fellow." The Whangdoodle nodded solemnly.

Ben had a sudden inspiration. "How about if you came back with us across the bridge? You could meet the professor that way."

The Whangdoodle shook his head. "Impossible. If your friend can't see the bridge, then I doubt that he'd be able to see me. That's a simple, undeniable fact."

There was a moment's silence in the beautiful white room, then Lindy said in her clear, practical voice, "You know, the really sad thing about all this is that if the professor *could* have come here, he probably would have made you another Whangdoodle."

The Whangdoodle looked at her with wide, unblinking eyes. Then he carefully said, "Would you mind explaining that last statement, young lady?"

"Well, you see, he's a professor of genetics. You know, he

can make life. He told us he could." She gave a matter-of-fact wave of her hand. "If he can make life, he can make a Whangdoodle, wouldn't you say?"

The Whangdoodle looked at the boys. "Is she talking sense?"

"He did tell us that the secret of life had been discovered, Your Majesty," said Ben.

"He told us that we had a great responsibility on our hands," added Tom.

"I would say so," replied the Whangdoodle, raising his eyebrows. He looked stunned. "Well, well, well. What an incredible fellow your professor must be. It is indeed a shame that we could not meet."

Lindy said, "He could be rested, by now. If we helped him he might just make it across the bridge."

"It really doesn't seem right to be here without him," remarked Tom.

The Whangdoodle suddenly straightened in his chair. "PROCK!" he yelled and clapped his front hooves together.

The Prock entered the room. "Your Majesty?"

"Come here, old fellow. Something rather interesting has come up. Excuse me, Potters. Just for a moment."

The Whangdoodle got up and limped with the Prock to one of the tall windows, where they stood in quiet, close conversation.

Lindy tugged at Ben's sleeve. "What do you suppose is going to happen?" she whispered.

"I don't know. Wouldn't it be great if the professor could somehow get here after all?"

"Oh, gosh. My stomach just went all funny."

"Mine too," said Tom.

The Whangdoodle clapped the Prock on the back and turned to the children. "We have decided that it would be good if you tried to help your friend across the bridge. But only one may go."

The Prock said, "I advised His Majesty that it would be safer if only one was allowed out of the palace gates. If all three of you went, there would be no guarantee that you would bring the professor back."

"But of course we'd try to bring him back. That's the whole point, isn't it?" said Ben.

"I'm not sure," the Prock replied. "What if he does not make it, in spite of your help? What if he chooses not to come? It is possible. No, I think he'd be more inclined to try to reach the palace if he knew that two of you were here and being held hostage."

"Hostage!" Ben was horrified. "You can't hold us hostage. You can't keep us here against our will."

"Well, I'm hoping it won't come to that. I rather thought you'd see the sense of this," replied the Prock.

Tom said, "We can leave any time we want. All we have to do is turn around and go home."

The Prock smiled. "I'm afraid you're wrong there. You see, I have your hats. There's no going home without them."

The children gasped and remembered, too late, the professor's warning about taking off their scrappy caps. There was a moment's silence.

Tom growled. "I might have guessed you'd be up to some double-crossing trick."

The Whangdoodle interrupted brightly. "Oh, now let's not get in a tizzy. There hasn't been a tizzy around here in years. Have some more wodge and let's discuss this in a civilized manner. Prock, you silly old thing, you do lay it on a bit thick sometimes. This all seems very simple." He looked at the children. "You want your professor to meet me—I am most anxious to meet him. The surest way to get him here is for two of you to remain and one of you to go, and that's all there is to it. Now, which one of you will it be?"

Lindy turned to Ben. Ben glanced quickly at Tom.

The Prock leaned across the throne and whispered, "Might I suggest the little girl, Sire?"

"Really?" The Whangdoodle looked surprised.

"She seems to have the brightest imagination, Your Majesty."

"Ahh, of course." He nodded in comprehension.

Ben stepped forward. "We think Lindy should go, Your Majesty."

"Very sensible." The Whangdoodle was pleased. "Prock, escort the young lady to the bridge, will you?"

"Hey, wait a minute," Lindy protested. "I can't cross that big bridge all by myself. What if that awful bird comes back to get me?"

The Whangdoodle reassured her. "I give you my solemn promise that the Gyascutus will not bother you."

She turned to the boys. "Do I have to do this? Must it be me?"

"Lindy, if anyone can convince the professor to cross that bridge, it's you. He'll listen to you." Ben placed his hands on her shoulders and looked at her solemnly. "Think how important this is to the professor. Remember all that he has done for us. Can you be very brave and do this for him?"

Tom said, "Remember Halloween, Lindy. You were terrific then."

"Crossing a bridge is nothing compared to all the things we've been through lately," added Ben.

Lindy thought about it. "Oh, rats," she said in a resigned tone. "But I'll need my scrappy cap. I can't go without my scrappy cap."

The Whangdoodle nudged the Prock. "Get her scrappy cap."

"Your Majesty, is that wise? The professor might just send her on home. The hats are the secret, you see. That's what helped them to get here."

"Yes, and if they hadn't come here we'd never have heard of his remarkable discovery. It's a risk and we have to take it. Give her the scrappy cap, silly."

The Prock reached into his pocket and produced Lindy's bonnet. She put it on.

The Whangdoodle rose from his chair. "Miss Potter, I cannot begin to impress on you the importance of this mission. If you can help your friend to cross the bridge and return to the palace, you will be doing both me and my country a vital service. His coming here could be the most significant thing to happen to us in a long, long time."

He produced a beautiful gold ring. "Take this ring with you and show it to your professor. It may help."

Lindy gulped. "Goodbye, everyone." She reached for the Prock's hand.

They walked together through the courtyards and the gardens back to the bronze gates. The Prock swung them open wide.

Lindy's heart sank as she gazed out at the long silk span that stretched in front of her. It seemed a tremendous distance to the other side.

"I wish I didn't have to do this," she said in a small voice.

The Prock was surprisingly gentle. "I will stand right here and wait for you. There is no need to be afraid."

"You couldn't come with me?"

"I'm afraid not. I don't think the professor would be able to concentrate if I were around."

"Okay. Well, here I go." Lindy took a deep breath, grasped the silk handrails firmly and began to walk.

 *SIX*

The moment she was out on the bridge she wanted to turn around and run back to the Prock. There was a cool breeze blowing and the bridge was swaying. She could see between the wooden slats to the foaming, rushing river thousands of feet below. The noise of the waterfall was terrifying. She looked back.

The Prock raised his arm. "Go on, Miss Lindy. Once you get started, it doesn't seem so bad. Just make it halfway. From there it's easy."

Lindy walked on and tried to keep her head up. It was better if she did not look down. She thought of her brothers and wondered what they would do while she was gone. She remembered how sad the Whangdoodle had looked when he talked about being lonely, and how important he had made her feel when he asked her to try to bring the professor back. She clutched the gold ring he had given her and quickened her pace.

She looked for the professor but he was nowhere in sight. "Professor! Professor!" Her voice echoed from the chasm.

"*Professor!*" she cried louder, but there was no reply. Lindy ran the remaining length of the bridge. Looking around, she remembered the dreadful Gyascutus and hoped fervently that the Whangdoodle would keep his promise.

"Professor! Where are you?"

She noticed a bright clump of yellow flowers on the ground ahead of her. As she watched they moved slightly. With a jolt of happiness Lindy realized that they were not flowers at all, but the yellow butterflies on the professor's open umbrella.

"Hello. Hello." His head appeared over the rim. He looked startled. "Lindy, good gracious! What are you doing here all by yourself?"

"Oh, Professor." She ran to him and flung her arms around his neck. "I thought maybe you'd gone back without us or something."

"But I told you I'd wait for you."

"Why were you under the umbrella?"

"Ah. Well, if you recall, I was fighting with the Gyascutus when you left. The wretched creature knocked me out. When I came to, the monster had disappeared. I didn't want to take the chance of his coming back and finding me, so I camouflaged myself with the umbrella. Thought he'd mistake it for a bunch of flowers."

"That's what I thought it was," Lindy said with a smile.

"Now, what's been happening and where are the boys? Did you see the Whangdoodle?"

"Oh, golly." She sprang to her feet and began to pull at his sleeve. "Come on, Professor. You've got to come with me. It's terribly important. The Whangdoodle wants to see you."

"What!"

"He sent me to get you. The boys are still in the palace. We can't get home because the Prock has their scrappy caps. So you've got to come and tell him to let us go." She urged him towards the bridge.

"Wait, wait a minute, Lindy. I can't cross the bridge. I told you I couldn't."

"But you've *got* to. I came all this way to find you and bring you back. You just have to get across. The Whangdoodle is waiting to talk to you."

"Why would he want to see me?" The professor was puzzled.

"I don't know. He seemed really serious about it. Look. He sent you this ring."

The professor turned the ring over and over in his hand. "Amazing, just amazing." He looked with desperate longing across the chasm to the glittering palace.

Lindy suddenly knew that she had to be very firm. "Take my hand, Professor, and come with me."

"I can't, Lindy. I would give my soul to come with you, but if I can't see the bridge what can I do?"

"You can see the Whangdoodle's ring, can't you?" she cried.

"Yes."

"Well, that proves that the Whangdoodle is waiting for you. It proves that there really is a bridge too, because how could I bring the ring to you otherwise? All you have to do is trust me. The bridge is there, I promise. You only have to walk across."

"But I don't *see* it."

"Then don't look. Keep your eyes on me. Hold my hand and don't look down, whatever you do."

He hesitated and she gave a small cry of frustration. She pulled him towards the edge of the chasm, and began talking, saying the first things that came into her head.

"It's such a little way across, really it is. Just make it halfway and the rest is easy. Oh, Professor, wait until you see the inside of the palace. You won't believe how beautiful it is. It's shining and cool and peaceful. There's room for everybody in the whole world, but it isn't at all a lonely place. Keep looking at me, Professor. Hold my hand tighter."

She walked slowly onto the silk bridge and the professor took a deep breath and followed, never taking his eyes from Lindy's face.

"You'll see the most beautiful gardens, with such flowers and fountains. . . . The trees are mostly bright, bright blue, but the undersides of all the leaves have a different color. Some are emerald green, some are white and some are pale yellow. You'll see. There's music about the place all the time, a lovely sound that makes you feel calm and happy. There are Flutterbyes and pretty flags flying in the breeze."

Lindy gave a quick glance behind her. They were halfway across the bridge.

"You're going to love the Whangdoodle. You were absolutely right about him. He's the best creature you could ever meet. He's funny and nice. But he's lonely. I think he misses our world and would like to come back. Only he says he never would. He has the dearest, sweetest tooth. He says you must be a very clever man and I told him that you were and that you knew all about life and everything."

"Lindy . . ." The professor hesitated.

"Don't stop now," she said in a clear voice, "we're almost

there. Only a few steps more and you'll be off the bridge. Count them . . . one, two, three, four. There you are, Professor. You've made it. I told you it could be done. Here's the Prock. He'll lead the way from now on."

Lindy let go of the professor's hands and stepped back. She was trembling from head to foot.

The professor looked around, dazed and bewildered. He looked at the Prock, looked at Lindy, looked up at the shining turrets of the palace etched against the clear red sky.

When he spoke his voice was husky and his eyes were brimming. "It is every bit as wonderful as you said. Oh, dear. Oh, dear."

Lindy was as happy and proud as she had ever been in her life.

The Prock led the way into the palace.

"So, you're the one who's been causing all the fuss." The Whangdoodle stared at the professor. "In all my years, I don't think I have ever come across such a persistent, persevering man. You've been a nuisance, but you are welcome."

The professor gazed rapturously at the Whangdoodle and then he sank to his knees. "Your Majesty. This is a tremendous pleasure."

"Yes. Yes. Well, get up. Get up. There is much to talk about. You want some wodge?"

"No thank you, Sire."

"You have three staunch supporters, I must say." The Whangdoodle waved a hoof towards Ben and Tom and Lindy. "You trained them well. Very well. But for them, you might not be here."

"And vice versa," Tom interrupted loyally.

The professor smiled. "I consider myself a lucky man in every respect."

The Whangdoodle bounced in his chair. "Yes. Yes. I am glad you crossed the bridge. I look forward to some splendid talks. I cannot tell you how much I have missed the stimulus of human company. Later we will celebrate. But now, I have a favor to ask of you. A great favor."

"I will do anything, Your Majesty," the professor said, smiling.

"Splendid. Splendid. The children have been telling me about your wonderful discovery concerning the secret of life."

"Oh . . . have they?" The professor looked at them in bewilderment. "They know very little about it, Sire."

"Well, no matter. The point is, I want you to make me another Whangdoodle."

"I . . . beg your pardon?"

"That's the favor I want. I want you to make a Whangdoodle for me. Now, I know you're saying to yourself what *kind* of Whangdoodle. . . . Well, obviously I want a female Whangdoodle."

The Whangdoodle jumped up and paced about the room, changing color rapidly. "You see, it's been so quiet and lonely here all these years. Then, four human beings arrive on my doorstep, which is sensational enough, and then I learn that you are a professor with an incredible discovery and . . . and . . . I suddenly realize that all my dreams might possibly come true."

He paused in front of the professor. "I would have a family and I wouldn't be extinct. I would never be lonely again. You do understand how desperately important this is to me, don't you?"

"Oh, Sire . . ." The professor lifted a hand to his brow. "I . . . I'm afraid there has been a terrible misunderstanding. I would give anything to be able to grant your wish and make you a Whangdoodle. But . . . it is impossible. I would not know how to begin."

Tom said, "But you told us the secret of life had been discovered, Professor."

"Yes. You *did,*" lisped the Whangdoodle emphatically.

"But discovering the secret of life and being able to make it work are two entirely different things. It will be a long time before man is ready to take the next tremendous step."

"Well, be the first. Start a fashion." The Whangdoodle waved his arms excitedly.

Lindy ran to the professor. "I remember you said that in a *very* little while people like you would be able to make life."

"There you are!" cried the Whangdoodle triumphantly. "If you said that, you must have a great deal of knowledge."

"Go on, Professor. I bet you could do it," encouraged Ben.

"No, no. Listen to me. . . ." the professor pleaded.

They all started to speak to him at once. The noise was deafening.

"Just a minute! Just a minute!" shouted the Whangdoodle. He stamped his foot and winced with pain. He turned to the professor and said, "I want some questions answered. A simple yes or no will suffice. You admit that the secret of life has been discovered?"

"Yes, Your Majesty."

"If it has been discovered, I assume you know what makes life."

"Yes, Your Majesty. But . . ."

"If you know *what* makes it, you know *how* to make it?"

"Well . . ."

"Listen to me. There must have been a number of experiments?"

"Yes, Sire. There are many things being tried. There is something called 'cloning' and then there's micro-dissection and implantation. . . ."

"Have you been present at these experiments?"

"Most of them, Your Majesty. We've had some amazing success with frogs."

The Whangdoodle glowed pink with delight. "Well, then. This is all very clear to me. I don't see what all the fuss is about. If you have been smart enough to find the secret of life and it works on a frog, for heaven's sake, why not a Whangdoodle? I am a willing subject for research. All you have to do is get your thinking organized and I am certain that you will come up with the solution."

The professor gave an exasperated sigh. "Your Majesty, how can I convince you that you are asking for the impossible? I hate to disappoint you, but the work in genetics is really just beginning. I've devoted most of my life to research and yet I only have a few answers. How could I possibly know enough to create a Whangdoodle?"

The Whangdoodle stared at the professor and slowly turned a very pale blue. He looked terribly dejected and slumped back on his throne. After a moment he said, "Bother. That's very sad. I had such high hopes. I was so certain that your presence here meant that something special was going to happen. I must have been wrong. It's too disappointing for words."

The Prock said gently, "Your Majesty . . ."

"No, no." The Whangdoodle held up a hoof. "I'd rather

not discuss it any more. I think I'd like to be by myself for a while."

He got up and walked towards the tapestry. As he did so, he began to disappear until only his eyes and antlers remained. Eventually they also vanished. His voice was the last thing to go. "It's really depressing. I never wanted anything so much in my whole life. Silly of me to suppose it might be possible."

A large, shiny tear rolled down the tapestry.

There was a long silence in the room after he had gone. Lindy said, "That's awful, Professor. He was crying."

"What a shame," Tom said with feeling. "I wish we could have done something."

"I cannot make a Whangdoodle," the professor stated.

The Prock cleared his throat. He spoke slowly and was obviously having difficulty in saying what he felt. "Couldn't you just try? His Majesty wants another Whangdoodle more than anything else in the world. You know how he feels. You wanted to get to Whangdoodleland more than anything in the world. The King was gracious enough to meet with you. Won't you return the favor and try this for him?"

The children had never heard the Prock speak with such feeling.

The professor shut his eyes. "I would *love* to help. I don't *like* to see the Whangdoodle upset any more than you do. But I can't see how it's possible. . . ."

Lindy interrupted. "You know what, Professor? Ever since we met, you've been saying to us *you can, you can, you can* . . . but lately, all I've heard is *I can't, I can't, I can't!*"

Ben said quickly, "You once said that whatever man can imagine, he can do."

Lindy clapped her hands. "You said that you couldn't cross the bridge. But you did."

"Oh, Professor," cried Tom, "give it a chance. How do you know you can't make a Whangdoodle until you've tried?"

The children clustered around him. The Prock said, "Professor, I know you are a man of great strength. When you choose to believe in something, you are unshakable. Won't you believe now that this experiment is possible?"

The professor looked at the four of them. Four pairs of eyes, staring at him, unblinking . . . waiting for his reply. He mumbled, "I would need equipment. It's liable to take a long time."

"Tell me what you need," said the Prock. "I will see that you get it."

The professor held his forehead in concentration. "I would need a dissecting microscope, possibly a laser beam, ultrafine dissecting equipment. Saline solution, flasks, culture tubes . . ."

His words were drowned by the cheer that came from the children. They danced around the professor, hugging him, patting him, kissing him, laughing with happiness. Even the Prock smiled broadly.

 SEVEN

The Great Hall of the palace had been turned into a laboratory.

By some incredible means the Prock had managed to obtain all the things the professor asked for. The professor was stunned when he entered the hall for the first time.

The vast, normally empty room was now filled with the most modern scientific equipment, plus benches, chairs, blackboards, bottles and tubes of every description.

"But where did you get all this? How could you possibly manage it?"

The Prock looked a little smug. "I borrowed it."

"You *borrowed* it?"

"From your laboratory at the University."

"*What!*"

"Don't worry, don't worry. I'll put it all back. You do your job. I'll do mine."

The palace was bustling with excitement. Everyone had been advised of the remarkable experiment that was being conducted. As a result the professor was given the utmost respect and attention.

He began to work.

The children wisely left him alone, but towards the end of the first day, they did peek in on him just to make sure that he was all right.

They found him seated on a high stool, his head in his hands. Sheets of paper were scattered all over the floor. A wastepaper bin was full to overflowing. The blackboard was covered with formulas.

Lindy touched the professor's arm. "Everything all right?" she whispered.

"Mm? Oh, my dears. I'd quite forgotten about you." He seemed very distracted and rubbed his eyes wearily. "I just don't seem to be able to get anywhere," he sighed. "It will take a miracle."

"It's a miracle that we're here," Tom reminded him.

"Yes. Remember what you said about that," added Ben.

"You said that miracles only happen after a lot of endeavor. A mind has to be ready and open before a miracle can happen."

"But that's just it," the professor replied desperately. "That's the problem. Right now my mind isn't open. I've been sitting here, thinking so hard. I realize now why I was unable to cross the bridge—why I couldn't see it. I was torn between two worlds. I was preoccupied with my forthcoming journey to Washington, and I was worried about finishing my paper. I always worry if my work is not completed. So the real world was fighting with the world of my imagination. My concentration was hopelessly ruined."

"Well, if you realize all that, can't you make it right?" Ben said simply.

The professor was annoyed. "Do you have *any* idea of the magnitude of this miracle you're asking for? I couldn't see the bridge, yet you're asking me to make a Whangdoodle."

"I know what you need," Lindy said in her practical voice. "You need a scrappy cap."

"That's it!" cried Tom. "It would help you to concentrate."

"Great idea. Come on . . . we'll go and ask the Prock about it," said Ben.

They rushed towards the door. "No, children, wait . . ." the professor called after them. But they had gone.

A short time later the Prock arrived. He placed Lindy's bonnet on the workbench. "Having a few problems?"

"A few! That's a masterpiece of understatement."

"Well, try the bonnet. It might work."

"Oh, come on, my good fellow." The professor looked impatient. "You know as well as I do that those hats mean nothing. They're not magic at all."

"They're not?"

"Of course not. They are just a device . . . something for the children to believe in . . . to help them bridge the gap."

The Prock gave a small smile. "Well, they obviously work very well for them. I wouldn't underestimate those hats if I were you."

"I don't follow."

"It's quite simple. You say the hats are not magic, yet the fact is that without them the children would never have believed enough to get to Whangdoodleland. As you pointed out, by wearing the hats they were able to bridge the gap. Obviously you're having a lot of problems right now. You're trying to bridge a gap too. It would seem to me that Miss Lindy has a sensible idea. Try the hat. What have you got to lose?"

The professor banged his fist on the table. "But I'm telling you, the hats are just a contrivance. There's nothing special about them."

"If you say so." The Prock was irritatingly calm. He eased himself to the door with his long, gliding walk. "See you later."

"Prock! What if this experiment is a failure? Supposing I don't succeed?"

The Prock opened the door. "I suggest we wait and see how you get on."

"If I don't make another Whangdoodle, you're not going to give us the hats, are you? You intend to keep us here. You're not going to let us go at all."

"But how can I possibly keep you here?" the Prock replied, innocently. "You just said that the hats mean nothing. I couldn't stop you from leaving."

"Yes, but . . . you know the children believe . . ."

"Right now, the children are having a grand time and couldn't care less about going home. I suggest you stop worrying about them and concentrate on making a Whangdoodle for His Majesty. Plenty of time later to talk of going home." He quietly left the room.

The professor stared after him and thought for the umpteenth time that the Prock was a maddening fellow. He sighed deeply and looked at Lindy's hat on the workbench.

He picked it up and turned it over in his hands. In the olden days, people really believed that magic emanated from the hat. They believed in the hat just as much as they believed in the Whangdoodle. Ben and Tom and Lindy certainly believed that the hats were the reason for their success. Was it possible? Could he have underestimated the scrappy caps? Were they magic, after all?

The professor considered the possibility and, very slowly, put the bonnet on his head and tied the ribbons beneath his chin. He sat still and waited.

There was an uncanny light in the Great Hall, but he was used to that. His years of practice had taught him that any period of sustained concentration brought with it a feeling of bright strong light. The children had discovered that also.

He looked around the laboratory at the familiar equipment and at his notes and equations. He rested his chin on his hands and thought about the Whangdoodle.

Quite suddenly, it happened. A strange sensation crept over him. There was a feeling of lightness, as if a great weight were being lifted from his shoulders. He forgot about the children and the Prock.

Thoughts and ideas flooded into his mind like the water that raced down the hillsides to join the Golden River. The professor reached for a pad and pencil and began to write as fast as he could.

Hours later, the big double doors to the Great Hall opened. The Whangdoodle peeped into the room.

"Hi there," he said with a shy grin. "I just couldn't keep away any longer. How's it all going?"

The professor was wildly busy. Clouds of steam billowed from a pan at one end of the room. Several flasks containing colored liquids were bubbling noisily. The professor's spectacles were on the very tip of his nose. He was scribbling furiously on the blackboard.

The Whangdoodle crept forward and peered over his shoulder. He made noises of appreciation. "My word. You humans have come a long way since I was around. I confess, I haven't the slightest idea what you're doing."

The professor grabbed a towel and rubbed the board frantically. "I sometimes wonder myself, Your Majesty. Now, if you'll excuse me . . ."

"Oh, this is all so exciting," the Whangdoodle lisped happily. "I can't tell you how I appreciate this effort. So much seems to be happening. Have you seen my slippers?"

He lifted a foot to show the professor. "I lost the pink ones just a while ago, and look what's growing already. Aren't they sensational? Silver and gold, with bells on. I've never grown bells before. I can only surmise that it is due to the anticipation."

The professor put both hands to his head. "Your Majesty, I really do have to concentrate. . . ."

"Yes, yes, of course you do. Oh, goodness. I hope you will succeed. I can't eat, you know. I just can't. I must confess that even in the old days, when there were more of us, I seldom had the company of a lady Whangdoodle. The humans kept us so busy, you see. At one time they loved us very much and we loved them. I'll tell you a secret. I miss them a great deal. It's been very lonely these past five hundred years. You can understand my anxiety about the experiment?"

"I can, Your Majesty. But there won't be an experiment if I don't have a little peace and quiet."

"Ah. Yes. I was just going. Is there anything I can do?"

"Just try to keep everyone away from the Great Hall for a while."

"I will. I will."

"Sire . . . please don't get too excited. This may not work. I'm on to something. But it could fail," the professor cautioned.

"Come, come. A little perseverance." The Whangdoodle slapped the professor on the back. "Keep up the good work. I just know you can do it. You're a splendid fellow. Splendid."

He bounced to the door. "You will send for me the moment something happens?"

"Yes, Your Majesty."

"You're really on to something?"

"Yes, Your Majesty."

"Oooh. I can't stand it. I may suffocate with excitement. I will leave you now. *Pax amor et lepos in iocando.* Goodbye."

"Goodbye." The professor turned away.

The Whangdoodle popped his head around the door again. "Oh, one more thing . . ."

The professor sighed with exasperation.

"That silly hat looks simply stunning on you." The Whangdoodle grinned and disappeared.

The entire palace became a place of hushed expectation. The inhabitants crept around, speaking in whispers, not daring to make a sound in case it disturbed the professor.

The children spent a lot of time exploring. The Prock showed them the Whangdoodle's private apartments and the fabulous royal kitchens. There was a special pantry for wodge making.

"Is wodge the only thing the Whangdoodle eats?" Lindy asked.

"Good heavens, no," replied the Prock. "He adores olives. He'll eat them by the ton. Once in a while he'll take a piece of broccoli as well."

"Broccoli! How gross." Lindy grimaced.

The children discovered that the head chef in the kitchen was none other than the Oinck. They watched him making a fresh batch of wodge. He looked very efficient in his tall chef's hat, but he sang mournfully:

> Sweets for a sweet tooth,
> Confections for the royal.
> Put it in a saucepan
> And leave it there to boil.

The Prock patted the Oinck on the shoulder. "Keep up the good work. His Majesty is delighted with the cooking." He winked at the children and whispered, "He is awfully vague at times, but there's not a better wodge maker in the country."

The Oinck said solemnly, "Watch out for yesterday. It'll catch up with you every time."

The children learned how the palace was organized. The household chores were carried out by hundreds of penguin-like creatures called "Jiffies." They were always running frantically about the place and seemed terribly busy. The Prock explained that it was not in a Jiffy's nature to walk, which was why they made such efficient help. "You see, they get things done in half the time and that leaves them plenty of time to play, which is something they love to do."

The other important members of the palace staff were the little furry Flukes. They were couriers for the Whangdoodle, ran errands and generally made themselves useful.

Tom asked if he could visit the Whiffle Bird. He found her curled up on a pillow in a small cheerful room. She looked tiny and fragile, and her colors were dull, as she lay listless and alone. But the moment she saw Tom she brightened considerably.

"Hello, Whiffle Bird. We've all been so worried about you. How are you feeling?"

She fluffed out her feathers and began to make small crooning noises. Tom knelt down and stroked her fondly. He saw the tiny hands come through the waving plumes and the black button eyes staring out at him.

"I do hope you'll be well enough to get out and about soon. It's lonely without you, you know."

His words seemed to work wonders, for she began to strut up and down and behave much like her old self.

"I'll come back and visit again, if you promise to get well soon. In that a deal?"

At this she seemed very content and settled back in a

corner to rest. Tom left the room feeling much happier; after worrying so much about the Whiffle Bird, it was good to know that she was on the road to recovery.

The Whangdoodle sent for the children often and they spent long hours with him. They were wonderful hours, for he was the most gracious and fun-loving host. He was thrilled and stimulated by their visits, yet at times his mind was obviously elsewhere. Under the circumstances it wasn't hard to guess that His Majesty was most anxiously waiting to hear from the professor.

The weather became very cloudy and still. Late one afternoon it began to rain, slowly at first—large drops splashing against the crystal walls and running down in shimmering rivulets. The wind rose and the rain came down harder.

The Prock hurried into the salon where the Whangdoodle was having tea and wodge with the children. There was a rumble of thunder overhead. The Prock spoke with restrained excitement.

"Your Majesty, it hasn't rained in years. Not like this. You know what that could mean?"

"I know, I know, my good fellow. I was thinking the same thing myself." The Whangdoodle began to tremble and rose unsteadily to his feet. "Oh, my goodness, do you suppose that . . ." He gulped and was unable to finish the sentence.

The Prock seemed to be listening for something. "In olden days we believed that a storm such as this was an omen. Something out of the ordinary is going to happen. I'm quite sure of it."

The thunder rumbled once more and the wind chimes in the courtyards sang an eerie song. Over the sound came another sound—a faint chattering noise that brought the children to their feet as it grew louder and louder.

The Prock strode to the big double doors and flung them open.

The noise was almost deafening. Running towards him down the corridor were all the members of the royal household. They were chattering and tripping, and falling over each other in their haste and excitement.

The Jiffies were screaming, "It's done, Your Majesty! It's done! It's done!"

"Come and see! Come and see!" cried the little Flukes. They tugged at the Whangdoodle's slippers. "Hurry, Your Majesty!"

Sidewinders thrashed through the crowd, waving their trunks in the air and yelling, "The professor says to come straightaway!"

"Yes, yes! Straightaway!" everybody shouted at once.

Ben cried in triumph, "He's done it! He's done it!"

The Whangdoodle turned bright red and leaned momentarily against the Prock. He clutched his stomach. Then, regaining control, he began to gallop towards the Great Hall.

The Jiffies and the Sidewinders and the Flukes fell back to allow him room, but the moment he had passed, the vast throng closed ranks and followed after him.

Tom, Ben and Lindy found themselves being swept along. In their excitement they unashamedly pushed and shoved until they were at the head of the crowd and close behind the Whangdoodle. He skidded to a halt just inside the doors of the Great Hall. As abruptly as the noise had begun, it died away.

In the hushed, expectant silence, a weary and exhausted Professor Savant walked forward to greet the Whangdoodle,

"Your Majesty—" he said, and the children knew that it was hard for him to control his excitement. "There is someone I would like you to meet."

He stepped to one side. A gasp of astonishment rose from the crowd.

Seated on a white silk cushion in the center of the room, looking at everyone with much curiosity, was a smaller, daintier, and undeniably feminine replica of the Whangdoodle. She was the color of a fawn; her eyes were large and soft with long, curling lashes. On her head were small antlers which she wore like a crown. Her front hooves were crossed delicately on the pillow and her back hooves were covered by a pair of tiny satin slippers. She was breathtakingly beautiful.

She caught sight of the King and blinked with surprise, and then smiled to reveal one sweet tooth with a daisy on it.

In a voice that suggested the softest murmurings of a harp, she whispered, "Umbledumbledum."

The Whangdoodle stood absolutely still, momentarily stunned. He turned every color of the rainbow. Then his legs buckled beneath him and he fainted.

 *EIGHT*

The Great Hall was cleared in readiness for a celebration. As miraculously as it had been turned into a laboratory, it now turned into a banquet hall.

Lanterns and banners and silk canopies and ribbons were brought in. Tables and chairs were set for a tremendous feast. The royal gold and silver was polished until it shone brighter than ever before. Flowers were gathered. Great and exotic dishes were prepared.

The Whangdoodle had ordered the greatest party in the history of Whangdoodleland, and the palace staff intended to see that he got it. The King was beside himself with happiness, and the entire country rejoiced with him.

Lindy was concerned about a dress when the subject of a party was first suggested. "I don't have anything to wear," she cried in dismay. "I can't go to a party in these old clothes."

The Whangdoodle put her at ease. He commissioned a dress of ambrosia flowers for her, with a band of Flutterbye silk for her hair. New clothes were fashioned for the professor and the boys, and each was given a handsome cape for the occasion.

By sunset everything was ready and the excitement in the palace was intense.

The Splintercat was the first to arrive. He bounded into the Great Hall with tremendous enthusiasm and seemed genuinely pleased to see Lindy. He had brushed his silky fur until it shone. He wore a diamond bracelet around his tail.

The Whiffle Bird was well enough to join the party, and for most of the evening stayed close to Tom.

The Oinck came from the kitchens and, for a change, he looked quite cheerful. He wore a smart frilly hat which kept falling over his eyes.

The Sidewinders wore their dress uniforms with bright-red shoes and golden stockings on their ten legs.

The Prock surprised everyone. He arrived at the party looking resplendent in an embroidered frock coat and a silver trilby hat, and carrying a long, jeweled staff.

"You really do look like a prime minister," Ben said.

The Prock actually blushed. "Oh, this old thing. I haven't taken it out of the cupboard for at least two hundred years."

Lindy's flower dress was a triumph. Tom said candidly that she had never smelled so nice.

The boys were handsome in their new capes, and the professor looked particularly dashing. The Whangdoodle had presented him with a gold laurel wreath, which sat with distinction on his venerable head. He had tucked his new crimson corduroy trousers into his purple socks, and, of course, he wore the cape and the special ring that the Whangdoodle had given him.

By the time every Jiffy and Fluke had been packed into the hall, the place was filled to capacity.

At the appropriate moment, the Prock moved to a velvet covered platform at the far end of the room, where there were two golden chairs. Above them hung a silken canopy and a burnished shield with the words *Pax amor et lepos in iocando*.

The Prock banged his staff for attention and his voice rang through the hall.

"Citizens of Whangdoodleland. Honored guests. Your attention, please. It is with greatest pleasure that I present to you His Majesty the King . . . and his lovely Queen."

The entire congregation sank to their knees, and there was a sigh of delight, as the royal couple entered.

The Whangdoodle's antlers were adorned with the royal jewels and he glittered and sparkled like a Christmas tree. His shy and enchanting bride wore a simple diamond coronet.

Everyone cheered. Love and happiness filled the beautiful room.

The Prock danced with Lindy. Ben was an instant success with the female Jiffies. They thought him most handsome and plied him with sweets and paid him so much attention that he became quite embarrassed.

Lindy was asked to sing and she happily complied. Her sweet voice pleased everyone, and the Splintercat obligingly put his head in the punch bowl to keep from howling.

The Whangdoodle spent every second with his bride. He was unashamedly in love and very keen to impress her. At one point his exuberance got the better of him and he turned every color of the rainbow while dancing cabrioles and banging his new slippers together.

Lindy said, "Your Majesty, you're changing color. Is that Flange?"

"Yes! Yes! Flange! Flange! Flange!" the King yelled at the top of his voice. "It's surprisingly simple this evening. Can't think why."

The grand ball continued long into the night. Everyone agreed that there had never been such a party. The doors of the palace were opened and dancing couples spilled out into the crystal courtyards and waltzed beneath a sparkling, starry sky.

The professor sat quietly beside the royal couple and watched them proudly. The Whangdoodle moved over to speak with him.

"My good friend, my dear, dear Professor," he lisped affectionately. "How can I ever thank you for what you have done? You have given me all that my heart desired."

"I'm glad, Your Majesty. That makes me very happy. Remember that your wife will need a lot of care. She is still fragile and needs to gain strength. Have you decided on a name for her yet?"

"I thought that I'd leave the choice to you. Will you do me the honor and think of something pretty? We intend to have a quiet christening in a couple of days."

The professor thought about it. "I think that I would like the Queen to be named something simple. She is the very essence of what my work is all about, and I am most proud of the achievement. How about Clarity?"

"Splendid. Splendid. A lovely name. Claire for short."

The Whangdoodle turned to his wife and said, "My dear, the professor has thought of a perfect name for you. You are to be christened Clarity."

The little Whangdoodle looked at the King and murmured, "Umbledumbledum."

The Whangdoodle immediately turned Crash Pink.

The professor smiled. "What does that word mean, Your Majesty?"

"It is a special term of endearment known to all Whangdoodles."

The professor smiled. "Sire, there is one very important thing that I would like to discuss with you, and that is the children and the matter of their hats—the scrappy caps. It is imperative that you give them back to me."

The Whangdoodle looked uncomfortable. "Couldn't we talk about that tomorrow?"

"I'm afraid not. You see, tomorrow, we simply must be on our way."

"Bother." The Whangdoodle fell silent for a moment. He looked up. "I don't want you to go, you know."

"Oh, Your Majesty. We don't want to go either."

"I know that it will somehow get out that you came to see

me. That will be the beginning of the end. Life is so wonderful now. There's more reason than ever for me to protect it." The King looked worried and dispirited. "I don't see how I can possibly let you go."

"But, Sire . . . think of the children and their family. It would be unfair and not at all like you if you refused to allow them to go home. It is important that they continue to live their lives as they were meant to live them. Consider how you would feel if you were separated from your wife and were unable to see her again."

"Oh, my goodness." The King turned white. "I do see what you mean. But humans aren't to be trusted, are they?"

"Might I suggest you start learning to trust again, Your Majesty? You used to, in the old days. Why would any of us want to spoil life for you? We'd be destroying the very thing we've come to appreciate and love."

"I shall miss you." The Whangdoodle's eyes grew moist and he blinked several times.

"We will miss you too."

"Will you come back and visit?"

The professor spoke sincerely. "You have only to send word."

"Yes. Good." The Whangdoodle beckoned to the Prock. "Prock, old boy. Fetch the hats—the scrappy caps. The professor and the children will be leaving in the morning. Also, have *The Jolly Boat* brought up. I want to escort them home."

Everyone turned out to see them off.

It was a sparkling fresh morning. *The Jolly Boat* moved down the Golden River with the professor and the children and the Prock and the Whangdoodle aboard. Clarity stayed behind at the palace in order to rest for her royal christening.

The children felt mixed emotions of happiness and sadness. It was good to be going home, but sad to be saying goodbye. They brightened, however, when the professor revealed that the Whangdoodle had extended an invitation to come and visit again another day.

As they sailed along they made good use of the royal soda fountain. Having eaten their fill, the children reflected on all the exciting things they had done and the wonders they had seen.

Lindy looked at the mountains and remembered the Gyascutus and wondered how she had ever managed to pluck up enough courage to cross the bridge for the professor.

Ben saw the needle rock and thought how narrowly they had missed being caught by the Splintercat.

Tom recalled his valiant dash to catch up with *The Brainstrain*. Each child concluded that every danger, every challenge, had finally been worthwhile.

The Whangdoodle was deep in conversation with the professor. "I'm going to tell you a secret," he confided. "The Prock said never to tell anyone, but I want to tell you. When all the other Whangdoodles disappeared so many hundreds of years ago, it was because humanity chose to forget them. The only reason I was able to stay alive in those dreadful times was because I was certain that somebody, somewhere, still believed in me. I thought you might like to know how good it feels to have my faith justified after all these years."

The professor was so touched, he was unable to reply. The Whangdoodle continued. "I don't suppose *you* could stay on, could you? I understand about the children having to go. But couldn't you stay?"

"I'm afraid not, Your Majesty. There is a lot of work for me to finish."

"Mmm. I was just thinking that I could use your advice. I mean, I've never been married before. I hope I'll be able to look after Claire properly—you know, be a wise husband and everything."

"I don't think you'll have any problems, Your Majesty. Just love her very much, as she so obviously loves you, and you'll find the answers, never fear."

The Jolly Boat pulled into its mooring on the Blandlands plain. The children and the professor said their goodbyes. It was a sad moment.

There was a sudden flurry of feathers and the Whiffle Bird appeared out of nowhere and flew straight onto Tom's shoulder. She screamed "MAYDAY!" right in his ear.

"What is it, Whiffle Bird? What is it?" he gasped. She made frantic little sounds and hung on to his jacket.

The Prock stepped forward and said wisely, "It is because you are leaving. Come along, Whiffle Bird. Thomas will be back another day."

"Of course I will," said Tom bravely. He lifted her off his shoulder and handed her gently to the Prock. "Now, you take care of yourself, dear Whiffle Bird. I'll see you soon." He turned away so that she could not see his distress.

The professor glanced at the children, then looked at the Whangdoodle. He gave a meaningful nod of farewell. The children suddenly felt the world beginning to spin, and the familiar dazzling light surrounded them. Almost immediately they found themselves back in the professor's garden.

The professor said quietly, "You'd better hurry on home. Ethel will be waiting for you."

Lindy flung her arms about him. "Oh, Professor, thank

you for the best time ever. It was wonderful. Will we see you soon?"

"Yes, I'll be here from time to time, though Washington will be my base."

"It's not going to be the same without you," said Ben.

"Good heavens, you can't have life handed to you on a platter every day," said the professor. "That would be very boring and there'd be no satisfaction in it. You shouldn't be needing me at all for a while. You've learned your lessons well. Look around you. Don't you see things differently now?"

The children gazed at the garden and the familiar house and the sky above and realized that they were aware of every detail, every color, every texture. It was hard to believe there had ever been a time when they had not seen the world with the same clarity.

The professor put his arms around them and said firmly, "Listen to me. You have all the tools, all the equipment necessary to make your own world as wonderful as Whangdoodleland. So how about trying? If you set a good enough example you could start a fashion. Think of the favor you'd be doing the Whangdoodle. He might be persuaded to visit one day; he might just stay around if we all tried hard enough. It's up to each and every one of us. Now be off with you. I love you, and I'll write you a long letter from Washington."

Epilogue

It felt good to be home.

Mr. and Mrs. Potter returned on Sunday and Mrs. Potter cooked a delicious evening meal.

Mr. Potter said, "Well, how was your vacation? Did you miss us?"

"The professor gave us a lovely time, but yes, we did miss you," said Ben.

"How's Grandma?" asked Lindy.

"She's much better, darling. She knitted you these pretty slippers." Mrs. Potter handed Lindy a pair of pink woolen slippers with floppy tassels on them.

Lindy gasped in surprise. "Why, they're almost exactly like the Whangdoodle's!" she blurted out.

"The what?" Mrs. Potter looked puzzled.

The telephone rang and Mr. Potter got up to answer it.

Ben nudged Lindy fiercely under the table. He said evenly, "The professor was telling us about a funny creature in olden times that was supposed to grow slippers."

"Is that the creature you were looking up in the dictionary a few weeks ago?"

"Yes." Ben glanced at Tom. The conversation was getting out of hand.

Mrs. Potter began to clear the dishes from the table. "Did you ever find out if it existed or not?"

There was a long pause. Ben stammered, "The—the professor said it was up to us to decide."

Fortunately, it ended there, because Mr. Potter walked excitedly into the room.

"Freda, that was the University on the phone. The most amazing thing has happened. You know all that equipment that was stolen from the laboratory? Well, it has been returned. Every single piece."

"It must have been a student hoax, dear."

"It must have been." Mr. Potter sat down by the fire and opened the Sunday paper. "Fetch my pipe, will you, Tom? Did the professor say anything to you, Ben, about the theft? It was his stuff that was stolen, you know."

"No, sir."

"Hmm. It's very odd. Ah . . . here's a photograph of your friend in the paper. I see he's going to Washington as Special Scientific Adviser to the President. Well, let's hope he does some good."

"Oh, I'm certain he will, Dad," Ben said with a smile.

Mr. Potter frowned. "This work he's doing, this genetics thing. I'm not sure I like the idea. In the final analysis, I wonder if it'll be good for mankind."

Ben felt a sudden tremendous need to communicate with his father.

"Well, whether we like it or not, I think genetics is here to stay, Dad, and it could be the answer to a lot of things." He spoke slowly, choosing his words carefully. "We will have a tremendous responsibility on our hands. If we're going to play God we must try to do it with honor and decency."

Edwin Potter stared at his son. Then he said quietly, "Ben, you're growing up. Those are very wise remarks and you're absolutely right."

Ben felt a warm glow of happiness at his father's praise. "I . . . I think the professor helped me think it out," he explained.

Mrs. Potter took up her knitting. "Professor. Professor. That's the only word I ever hear," she admonished gently. "Will you ever stop talking about that man, I wonder?"

The children looked at each other.

"Oh, I don't think so," they all answered at exactly the same moment.